Beyond the Shining Water

'Now give over,' he told her firmly. 'I'll be home in three or four weeks time …'

'But three or four weeks is *forever*, Liam,' she wailed.

'No, it isn't. Now just get this date in your head, May the fourteenth, got it, an' every day after that you come down here an' see if I've arrived. About the same time. Now cheer up and give us a smile …'

She put her arms about his waist and buried her face in the middle buttons of his shirt, hugging herself close to him and without thought he stroked her silky hair and murmured some soft endearment before turning away and striding off down the beach.

She watched him go, her childish face wet with tears for it was like those days when Pa had left them, her and her Ma, both of them bereft without him.

About the author

Audrey Howard was born in Liverpool in 1929 and it is from that once great seaport that many of the ideas for her books come. Before she began to write she had a variety of jobs, among them hairdresser, model, shop assistant, cleaner and civil servant. In 1981, out of work and living in Australia, she wrote the first of her twenty-one published novels. She was fifty-two. Her fourth novel, *The Juniper Bush*, won the Boots Romantic Novel of the Year Award in 1988. She now lives in her childhood home, St Anne's on Sea, Lancashire.

Beyond the Shining Water

Audrey Howard

CORONET BOOKS
Hodder & Stoughton

First published in Great Britain in 1999 by Hodder and Stoughton
First published in paperback in 1999 by Hodder and Stoughton
A division of Hodder Headline

A Coronet Paperback

10 9 8 7 6 5 4 3 2 1

A CIP catalogue record for this title is available
from the British Library

ISBN 0340 71808 0

Printed and bound in Great Britain by
Clays Ltd, St Ives plc.

Hodder and Stoughton
A division of Hodder Headline
338 Euston Road
London NW1 3BH

Part 1

1

Lily Elliott narrowed her eyes and squinted into the low flaring of the evening sun which lay across the waters of the river. The sky to the east had gone quite mad with brilliant colours, blood red and apricot fighting with gold and lemon, blush pink and the palest green all merging into a delicate shade of lavender above her head where a solitary star kept company with a sliver of moon. Before this glory stood a tall forest of gently swaying masts towering above sheds and warehouses, a great multitude seemingly linked together with miles of rigging, halyards and reefed sails, dark and graceful against the sunset. For as long as Lily could remember the waterfront had been a magical mixture of spices and coffee, tobacco and turpentine, tar and soot, ropes and rigging, sails and smokestacks, horses and carriers, kegs, casks and barrels and ships flying the flags and colours of every nation. Even the new and ugly steamships had a place in her heart, for they were, after all, things of the sea, but, naturally, her true and everlasting devotion was given to the beautiful sailing ships that lined the dock, one of which belonged to her father.

Her ma and pa had walked on a little way and for a moment she was alone in the dusky subdued murmur of the dockland as it settled down for the night. The sound of gulls crying plaintively as they perched along yardarms and the roofs of warehouses. The gentle suck and slap of the moving water as it lifted and fell against the wall of the dock and swirled about the pilings that supported the piers. The sound of men's voices murmuring from decks and galleys as Lily moved along the cobbled roadway of the dock, gazing up in total enchantment at the dozens of bowsprits that jutted out proudly, sharply spearing the falling dusk from each ship's bow over her head. Voices in many languages, for these lovely vessels came from the four corners of the world, bringing grain from North America, nitrates and guano from South America, bales of raw cotton from the southern states of America, beef and mutton from the meat-exporting countries of the world, raw wool from Australia, timber from America and Canada and Newfoundland, tea and spices from the Orient.

She sniffed enthusiastically, inhaling the pungent aroma of cowhides and jute, the sweetness of molasses and sugar and all the sea-fresh tanginess of the river which was part of the lives of those who lived beside the great crossroads of the city that was second only to London in the British Empire. Lily loved it, its great vigour and swaggering life, its bubbling dynamism, its proud boast that there was no place on earth like Liverpool; every seaman who sailed the seven seas said so and Lily believed it implicitly.

Someone was whistling "The Bonny Sailor Boy", a song about a pretty Liverpool lass who fell in love with a handsome young seaman. Lily knew it well since it was a favourite of her father who sang it in a loud, rich baritone whenever he took a bath. Not that Lily had ever seen her pa in the bath, for that was a private affair that took place before a good fire in her parents' bedroom. Pa would hump the hip bath up the narrow stairs and then he and ma, going up and down a dozen times with cans of hot water, would fill it, close the door and after a good deal of splashing and singing, accompanied by much laughter, there would be silence, a silence that Lily would not dream of interrupting. Ma and Pa loved one another deeply, a love that spilled out and wrapped itself about her but there were times, especially when Pa was home, when Lily knew she was excluded from this special time they spent together. Pa said that he and Ma had taken one look at each other eleven years ago and had fallen instantly and permanently in love.

Her ma and pa were beautiful. Yes, that was how she would describe them, even her pa who was as tall and dark and handsome as her ma was tall and silvery and exquisite. A striking couple, she had heard them called and it was true, for wherever the three of them went she noticed that heads turned to gaze after them. She took after her ma in colouring and was already tall for her age, but whereas ma was serene, calm, tranquil as a swan gliding on unruffled waters, her pa was what Ma called a firebrand, hot-tempered, vigorous, noisy and ready to argue with anyone whose opinion he did not agree with – except Ma, who never really argued anyway – and she, Lily, was the same, determined to have her own way but reluctant to hurt Ma while she got it!

A waggon drawn by two gigantic Shire horses pulled away in the growing gloom bound for the transit sheds where the cargo would be sorted and weighed, the load of barrels on it the last to be discharged from a merchantmen, for it was almost dark.

There were neatly stacked piles of boxes and bales lying close to the water's edge waiting to be taken aboard a clipper ship bound for Lily knew not where, though wherever it might be she would dearly have loved to be aboard it. Lily loved the river, the sea and the ships that sailed them with the same passionate intensity as her pa, and when she was old enough and had finished the schooling her ma insisted upon, then she meant to sign her indenture to serve aboard the *Lily-Jane*, her pa's schooner, for however many years her pa would allow, taking over as master when the time came. That wouldn't be for a long time yet, of course, for Pa was only a young man, in his prime, he said, at forty-one, though it seemed very old to Lily. She would be taught the art, trade and business of a mariner or seaman, as it was quoted in the Certificate of Indenture, as her pa had done as a lad. She had not yet disclosed her plans to Pa since she was only ten years old and there was plenty of time yet, and she was not quite sure how all this would come about, or even how Pa would take it; but she had wanted only one thing in her life ever since she had first been taken aboard the *Lily-Jane* as a toddler, and that was to be a seaman like her pa.

A mongrel suddenly darted out from behind a bollard which it had been sniffing and then, as though it were satisfied with what it found, cocked its leg, urinating in a long stream against it. It turned to give her an enquiring look, stopping for a moment and she held out her hand to it, making the sort of encouraging noises one makes to an animal, wondering where it had come from. If it was a stray perhaps she could persuade it to come with her. It was a nice-looking little thing, a bit scruffy with one ear hanging down and the other pricked and she thought Ma might just take to it, for she was fair game for anything lost or helpless. Lily had always wanted a dog but this one was wary, regarding her suspiciously before walking off briskly in the other direction, evidently on some important business of its own.

Lily straightened up. She lifted her neatly bonneted head and again sniffed the salt-laden, spice-laden, tar-laden air, drawing great draughts of it greedily into her lungs, forgetting the dog that had temporarily diverted her, staring into the future with unfocused, dreaming eyes, almost tripping over a thick length of tarred rope that lay in her path. Unconcerned, she dawdled on over the narrow wooden bridge which linked George's Dock and Canning Dock. Each dock had a master all of its own and the master had a gateman under him whose job it was to attend to the hauling in and out of the vessels and to regulate the height of the water according to the tides. The dock entrance was fitted with massive lock gates fashioned from long-lasting tropical timbers such as greenheart. The gates penned the water inside the dock basins as the tide fell in order to keep the level high enough to float the ships. There was a walkway over these gates which parted to allow the entrance and exit of the ships, a narrow path of sturdy wooden planks with iron posts on either side linked with steel chains. She rattled the chains as she went, longing to swing on them over the water as she had seen daring lads do but she knew her parents might look round at any moment and Ma would be horrified, and upset, a state neither Lily nor her pa could bear to see her in.

Decorously she followed them. Ma and Pa had their heads together. Ma laughed, a lovely soft laugh that Pa said was like the tinkling of bells, and Pa, not caring whether anyone was watching or not, kissed Ma on the lips and she laughed again, holding Pa's arm close to her side. Lily was not surprised, for she was used to her parents' show of affection for one another, even in public.

There were high, many-windowed buildings on either side of them now as they passed between two enormous warehouses, then they were out in the dying sunlight again and on the approach to Canning Dock Basin where Pa's ship was tied up. Lily could see it, lamps shining along its length and, excitement suddenly bubbling up inside her, she began to hurry to catch up with Ma and Pa who had stopped to wait for her at the bottom of the short gangway.

"Come on, slowcoach." Pa smiled, holding out his arm and,

when she reached him, cradling her against him. "It's time we had our meal and got you into your bunk or you'll still be in the land of nod when we set sail in the morning. We have to catch the tide, you know."

"Oh, Pa, I'm sorry but there's always something new to see and even the old things are wonderful. Did you notice that four-masted barque from Buenos Aires? She must have just docked on the last tide. The *Santa Maria*, she was called and I could smell her cargo as I went past."

"You would, sweetheart. It was guano." Pa pulled a wry face, wrinkling his nose.

"It really is awful," her mother offered, but Lily, loyal to the sea and ships and indeed anything at all to do with either, frowned.

"Oh, no, Ma, I thought it was quite . . . interesting."

"Interesting! Lily, you'll have nothing said against even a cargo of guano will you, my darling? Thank heavens you don't have to carry it, Richard." Jane Elliott turned to smile at her husband and for a moment Lily was irritated by Ma's lack of understanding, then she sighed and smiled lovingly as though her mother were some small child who could not be expected to grasp what the adults were discussing. Ma would be happy if all cargoes were of silk or spices, China tea or Brazilian coffee, lovely things to look at and delightful things to smell, and the world of cargoes such as cattle or cement, brimstone or pepper, coal or salt which was where the money lay, her pa would agree with that, was beyond her sweet understanding.

"Well, it's time we were getting aboard, dearest, if we're to prepare for the morning tide. I can see Mr Porter looking at us with great misgivings as though already he believes we are doomed to fetch up at the bottom of the Irish Sea by taking women on board. You'd think he'd be used to it by now, wouldn't you?"

The disapproving face of Pa's second-in-command peered over the side of the ship. He was a lanky Yorkshireman with a craggy face which thirty years at sea had turned to the colour of mahogany. He wore the usual seaman's attire of navy blue gansey, a kind of heavy knitted jersey, and sturdy drill trousers tucked into his boots. In bad weather he would don waterproofs. His peaked cap was a badge of his status on board – the others wore woollen headgear which pulled

down over their ears – and Lily had heard Pa say that if he had
to leave his ship in the charge of one man that man would be
Jethro Porter. This was quite amazing really, for Mr Porter's
family had been in the woollen trade far from the sea for many
generations, and where young Jethro had acquired his love
of ships, never having seen one until he arrived in Liverpool,
was a mystery. His piercing blue eyes, surrounded by a web
of wrinkles, surveyed the two females, for that was how he
thought of all women, with great suspicion, but he had to
accept that on this trip they were to be passengers aboard
the *Lily-Jane*.

"Well, come along, Lily, let's go and see if the luggage is
aboard and whether Johnno's made up your bunk. See, the
hatches are battened down and we'll be ready to sail on the
morning tide. Up you go. Mind your step, Jane," handing his
wife solicitously up the short gangway, "and you, Lily, don't
stir from your mother's side while I go and get changed."

"I won't, Pa."

He smiled at this child of his who was in his eyes quite
perfect except for her gender. Her vivid face was aglow with
excitement and her eyes were a brilliant silvery grey. The
thick fan of her eyelashes constantly shadowed her rounded,
childish cheek as she blinked in what seemed to be a transport
of delight, trying to look at everything at once, determined not
to miss one moment of this memorable journey. She loved all
this as much as he did, as much as his own father had done
and he supposed the sea must be in her blood, for they came
from a long line of seamen. For over a century Elliotts had
been carrying small cargoes to and from all the ports around
the Irish Sea and there was even talk of one of them who
had involved himself in the most profitable trade of all: the
triangle of manufactured parts to Africa, slaves from Africa to
the West Indies and southern states of America and sugar and
tobacco from there to Liverpool. Richard could believe it, for
how had his ancestor been able to accumulate enough money
to purchase the schooner in which his great-grandfather had
finally settled to coastal trading? The *Lily-Jane* was the third
ship from that first one called *Seamaid* and his only concern
was what was to happen when he was gone. Jane should have
no more children, the doctor had told him that after Lily's birth.
No son then, just this one child, but still, he was not a man for
worrying about the future when the present was so hopeful

and filled with promise. He was a happy man who loved his family and his chosen trade and he wouldn't change his life with any man. There were many fabulously wealthy men in Liverpool, merchant princes, shipbuilders, men of vision who were making a fortune out of the sea but he, Richard Elliott, was the luckiest of them all, for wasn't he loved by Jane Elliott which none of the others could claim.

Her ma had shoe-horned herself into the tiny cabin she and Pa shared, laughing as she did her best to stow away – is that the expression, Richard? she asked – the small wardrobe she had brought with her. They had eaten a splendid meal of fresh plaice, bought only that morning from one of the boats of the small fishing fleet that operated from Liverpool, tiny new potatoes and newly picked green peas from the market, all prepared by Johnno who could have got a job in the kitchens at the Adelphi, Mrs Elliott told him in that gracious way she had, making him squirm with pleasure. The ladies had then retired for the night. Not that Lily considered herself a lady. When she was on the *Lily-Jane* she was a seaman, pure and simple, longing to do all the things Johnno and Mick, the fourth member of the crew, did. It was most mortifying to be put to bed like a small child, tucked up in the hammock which hung just outside the cabin in which her parents slept. Of course, to sleep in the hammock almost made up for the indignity of being told to go to sleep like a good girl. It swung most delightfully and was really very comfortable and she thought she might ask Pa if she could have one at home in her bedroom but she didn't think Ma would agree so she'd best make the most of this. The *Lily-Jane*, though she was tied up at the dockside by bow and stern, moved up and down with the rise and fall of the water and though Lily had made up her mind that she would not sleep for a moment, wasting precious time that could be spent in other more exciting ways, she was lulled by the lovely swaying movement of the schooner and was quite put out when Pa woke her to say that they were to cast off in ten minutes and was she to lie there all day!

There were dozens of vessels like themselves all racing to catch the tide, many of them with pilot boats to guide them over the treacherous sand bars: small, strongly built sloops painted white with a green stripe round their sides and a number displayed on their flag. Packet ships, built for speed, carrying the Royal Mail and going to New York, the journey there and back an incredible seventeen days. A beautiful clipper ship under full sail, off to China, Pa told Lily, to bring back tea and spices and opium. There were frigates and brigantines and all making for the estuary to catch the tide so that Lily wondered how her pa could possibly steer through so much traffic. Naturally, she knew he would, for he was the best seaman in the world and one day, when she stood beside him at the helm, she would be just as adroit.

She leaned against her pa, looking back to the hazed morning skyline of Liverpool. By now the docks were a seething mass of men and waggons, cargoes of every sort from timber to tea, the gentle patience of Shire horses, cranes and derricks, women and children selling something or other, and all backed by the cliffs of the warehouses, block after block, and the soaring elegance of St Nicholas Church.

She sighed with deep satisfaction, watching Pa's lean brown hands on the wheel, so strong and sure as he moved into the flow of traffic. They were sailing outward so their course lay to the north beyond the influence of the Gulf Stream and did she notice, Pa asked, that the homeward vessels were sailing south so as to avail themselves of the current? Pa was full of wonderful information like that, all the things he himself had learned and which he was passing on to her, which surely meant he intended her to follow in his footsteps. Ma stayed in the tiny cabin, not at all concerned with the steamships in tow of steam tugs, nor the brig *Henrietta* which passed them to starboard, preferring to read Charlotte Brontë's novel, *Villette*, which was incomprehensible to Lily. Not the novel, which she herself had read and enjoyed, but the fact that Ma could calmly sit below with her nose in a book when she might be up here with her and Pa. The wind sang in the rigging and the gulls wheeled and dived and made their usual cries which sounded just like a baby in distress. The slap of the wind made the sails crack menacingly but Lily wasn't afraid, for her pa had them all safe in his hands, with Mr Porter, who stood just to the right of Pa, snapping out orders to Johnno and Mick, ready to take over if he was needed. Lily had on what her ma called her "adventuring" clothes, a warm woollen skirt, quite short so as not to impede her movements on the deck, stout boots and woollen stockings and a gansey just like the ones the crew wore, knitted for her by her mother. On her head was a cabin boy's peaked cap into which the plait her ma had done for her, thick and heavy, was tucked up. She had a line on her, for Pa was most careful about safety, at least with her, though the men, in bare feet, ran and climbed without the least heed of danger, though the decks, as they raced for the estuary, were steep and slippery with spray. Lily felt the line was not needed, for she was as sure-footed as a cat, especially if she had been allowed to remove her boots and stockings like Johnno and Mick, but Ma said it was not ladylike and so that was that as far as Pa was concerned. Ma's word was law! She, Lily, had even offered to climb aloft to help Mick with the mainsail which had proved awkward but Pa had smiled at Mr Porter as though to say what could you do with a girl like her, but Mr Porter merely "hummphed" in his throat and exchanged a look with Mick as though he knew exactly what he would do. Mr Porter did not approve of her and Ma being aboard, for like many sailors he believed a woman on a ship was bad luck and they had enough to contend with, with storms and winds, or the lack of them, with the hazardous journey out of the river where the tide shifted the silt and sand from day to day, without adding to it by sailing with females!

At last they passed the rocks on which the New Brighton Lighthouse was built, moving out into Liverpool Bay and steering north. It was a glorious day, sunny and warm with the clear sea reflecting the blue of the sky. They sailed quite close to the shore, the lovely long golden beach of what was known as North Shore, backed by rippling sand-dunes which disappeared around the northern horizon at Formby Point and lined the coast of Lancashire for twenty miles.

A windmill stood close to the beach, a tall brick mill called the Wishing Gate Mill and it was at this point that Ma came out on deck to watch the bathers who were trundled down to the water in bathing machines. It was August and high water and the shore and the sea were crowded with visitors from the manufacturing districts "coom fur t'ha dip in't watter". The "dowkers" or "dippers", whose job it was to attend the machines and help the bathers, kept a watchful eye on the segregated sexes, for some gentlemen had been known to swim among the ladies which was strictly forbidden though for the life of her Lily didn't know why.

Mr Porter was mortified when Captain Elliott casually suggested that his daughter, ten years old for God's sake, might like to take a turn at the wheel and Mrs Elliott looked none too pleased, neither.

"Oh, Pa, can I?" Lily gave her father a look of radiant gratitude as she placed her small hands on the wheel with the reverence one reserved for holy occasions. It warmed his heart and yet at the same time squeezed it with anguish, for he was beginning to recognise what was in his child. This was perhaps the eighth or was it the ninth occasion when his wife and daughter had sailed with him on a coastal voyage. The truth of the matter was that he could barely bear to be apart from his lovely wife and every time he was forced to leave her, though it was not for more than a week or ten days, some part of him felt as though it were being cut out of him with a rusty knife. He knew it was ridiculous and he would not have admitted it to anyone, even to her who knew how much he loved her. If he could arrange for her to go with him, perhaps three or four times a year, he made the excuse that it made a little holiday for her and the child, but in reality it was for his own sake. He had been thirty years old and already a ship-owner when he met the eighteen-year-old delicately lovely daughter of a ship's chandler in Water Street, Liverpool, and, as he had told Lily a dozen times, fell instantly and enduringly in love with her. And she with him which was even more wonderful. They were married within the month and for the first year of their marriage she had gone everywhere with him, much to the disgust of Jethro Porter who had loved no woman and never would. Then Lily was born and the event put an end to the voyages, at least until she was old enough to accompany her mother and father. At five years old she had gone to school, a select private school for young ladies in Walton on the Hill where Richard rented a smart, semi-detached little villa, a school chosen by Jane where the pupils were taught by an enlightened staff of teachers. Not just embroidery and music and painting, which Lily thought to be a complete waste of time, for what use would they be to a seaman, but mathematics, geometry, a little algebra, arithmetic, of course, history and geography. Lily lapped all that up like a cat at a saucer of cream, along with current affairs which she knew would be helpful when she became a sea captain like her father. She would have to know what was going on in government, wouldn't she, and indeed everywhere else if she was to be a success in the world of trade and so she applied herself to the lessons which would not have been wasted on a son, if Richard Elliott had had one.

But when the school was closed for the summer holidays, when there was no threat of winter storms or icy squalls, he took his wife and daughter on one of his coastal trips, or sometimes further. They had been to Ireland for a cargo of grain, Cornwall for china clay and to North Wales for stone, but today they were making for Barrow-in-Furness just beyond Morecambe Bay, only a short run this time which, with *them* aboard, suited Mr Porter down to the ground, to deliver machinery for the ironworks and to fetch back a cargo of pig-iron.

The *Lily-Jane* had been built at Runcorn especially for trading to small ports about the Irish Sea. She had little change in her draught fore and aft and had flat floors to take ground and to remain upright at low tide. She responded with great readiness when sailing in narrow waters. She was a wooden sailing ship, a fast schooner of 298 tons, ninety-nine feet in length and twenty-five feet wide. She was rigged as a two-masted vessel with square sails on both masts plus an additional small mast behind the mainmast to carry a large fore and aft sail called a spanker. She was strongly built with a pointed stern with the rudder hung outboard. In fact she was the perfect vessel for Richard Elliott's trade and even his Lily could have handled her with perfect ease, which he was aware she was longing to do.

Together, his strong seaman's hands on top of her small, still childish ones, they steered the *Lily-Jane* through the relatively calm waters that ran up the coast of Lancashire. The wind blew into their faces, both of them rapt with their shared love of this sailing ship, this joyous union of ship and water, the sunlight creating a diamond path ahead of them into which they fearlessly sailed, and for a moment the mother, the wife, was startled, for their expressions were identical. Her daughter was a beautiful child, even she admitted that, like a white rose, a white rosebud, flushed at the edge of its petals with pink, new and fresh, delicate and fragile. But Lily was not fragile at all: Jane Elliott knew that, for she was like her father with a core of steel in her which, when she was older, would allow

her to submit to no one, man or woman. Even now she was
trying to edge her father's hands away from hers, longing to
have full control of the schooner. Mr Porter was beginning
to mutter, not quite loud enough for his employer to hear
what he said, but loud enough to make it known that he
was complaining about something.

"What are you thinking, sweetheart?" Richard bent his head
to Lily, for the moment ignoring his second-in-command's
muttering, his own words only just audible to Jane.

"That it's just like flying, Pa, or what I think flying would be
like. We seem to be gliding above the water just as that gannet
is doing, d'you see?" taking her hand momentarily from the
wheel and pointing to the long and slender bird just ahead
of the *Lily-Jane*.

Mr Porter "tcch-tcched" angrily. He'd never seen the like,
letting a small child, and a girl at that, take the wheel of a
ship this size, or indeed any size, and to top it all she'd
taken her hand *off* the wheel to point at something that had
no bearing on the matter at all, which could have caused
the *Lily-Jane* to veer most dangerously. Really, what was his
master thinking of?

Richard heard the sound of disapproval and knew reluctantly that he had gone too far in allowing Lily to steer the
schooner, even for a few minutes.

"You'd best let me have her now, sweetheart," he whispered, putting her gently to the side of him, hearing her
vast sigh.

"Can I do it again, Pa, can I? Perhaps tomorrow?" she
pleaded.

"We'll see, sweetheart, we'll see."

She put her arms about her pa's waist and buried her face
in the sea-smelling wool of his gansey. Her heart was filled
with the magic and delight of the last five minutes and with
anticipation, too, for surely her pa would see now what a
good sailor she would make and would let her sail with him
on all his voyages? She loved him so, her pa. Her ma was
lovely, special, kind, but Lily had something inside her that
belonged to no one but Pa. She loved her pa so much it hurt
her at times but she wouldn't have it any other way. There
was no girl in the world who had such a wonderful pa as
Lily Elliott.

2

"I've decided that I'm going be a sea captain when I grow up," Lily remarked experimentally at breakfast several days later.

She had made up her mind in bed last night that as she would have to tell her parents of her plans one day, that day might as well be now then they would have time to get used to the idea and her pa might even begin to take her on more frequent trips. As his . . . his apprentice, kind of.

"Have you, sweetheart?" her pa answered, his eyes on her mother, smiling in that certain way grown-ups have when they are not really listening. Ma was at the side table where Mrs Quinn had just brought in the toast and she stood in a shaft of hazed sunlight shining through the dining-room window. The sun turned her already silver pale hair, which hung down her back in a profusion of tumbled curls, to a radiant halo of light. Her flawless skin which was usually the colour of buttermilk had a creamy texture, almost honey-coloured and was touched at her cheekbones with a flush of carnation. Her eyes, as she turned to smile that smile she kept solely for Pa, though they were a dove grey in colour, had in them a hint of lavender. She had not yet changed from her morning robe, a drifting garment made from several layers of pearl grey chiffon tied modestly at the neck and waist with peach-coloured satin ribbons. She looked quite glorious; it was evident that Pa thought so, though Mrs Quinn was inclined to look the other way as though even now, after years of seeing to the Elliotts as a general cook, housekeeper, cleaner, laundry maid and dogsbody, she could not quite become used to the way her mistress dressed. She did it to please Captain Elliott, that much Mrs Quinn knew, and it worked, for the master could not keep his eyes, or his hands sometimes, off his wife. Even he was not properly dressed, decently dressed as Mrs Quinn saw it, but had on some sort of floor-length quilted robe. She shook her head as she left them to it and returned to the kitchen.

Lily made a shallow hole in the centre of the bowl of porridge Mrs Quinn had put in front of her five minutes ago. The sides of the hole kept caving in and with infinite patience she scooped them out again with her spoon. With Ma and Pa behaving in that dreamy way they had sometimes, which meant they were aware of nobody but each other, she had high hopes that she might be able to get away with not eating the gooey mess. Pa said, though she was not always sure he meant it, that she should clean her plate at every meal, for there were thousands of poor, starving children in the city who would be glad of it, and as far as she was concerned they were welcome to it.

She sighed gustily. It was very evident that neither had heard her remark about her future and she dithered about whether she should repeat what she had said. Perhaps not. She'd told them and if there was any argument later she would say, indignantly, that she had already told them and if they didn't agree why hadn't they said so at the time?

Pa was tucking into a vast plate of bacon, sausage and tomatoes, having already eaten his porridge, and Ma was nibbling on a sliver of lightly buttered toast. They were chatting now about the ballet at the Theatre Royal which Ma wanted Pa to take her to see before he set sail again.

"Agnes Mitchell tells me it's absolutely wonderful and I really would love to see it, darling." It seemed some famous dancer whose name Lily could not pronounce, let alone spell, was to perform and it was Ma's dearest wish to see her before the ballet company returned to London.

Pa reached tenderly for Ma's hand. "Then you shall, my angel, and this very night. Will Mrs Quinn stay over for a couple of hours, d'you think?"

"Oh, I'm sure she will, Richard. She's always glad of the extra money."

"I don't need Mrs Quinn, Ma," Lily ventured, but with little hope. "I can stay by myself. I *am* ten after all. Besides, I'd rather like to see the ballet myself."

They both turned to look at her then, smiling with great tolerance.

"You wouldn't like it, sweetheart," her pa told her.

"How d'you know I won't, Pa? How d'you know if I've never been? I might absolutely adore it. I've seen a picture in the art gallery of ballet dancers in perfectly sweet little dresses and Mary wants to be a ballerina when she grows up. She takes it at school," in way of explanation.

"Does she, sweetheart? But I still don't believe it's suitable."

"Why, Pa?"

"It's for grown-ups, Lily, not children. Perhaps when I come home next Ma and I will take you to the . . . the . . ." He looked to his wife for inspiration and Lily knew they would suggest some childish thing like the zoo which she'd already been to a million times.

She stirred her porridge slowly, quite pleased with the swirls and circles this made, then reached for the syrup. Sometimes, if Pa was adamant that she eat it, she was allowed to pour in a spoonful of syrup which made it marginally more edible, but not much.

"How about the Polytechnic Exhibition at the Mechanics Institute, then? It's in Mount Street," she went on artlessly.

"I know where it is, my love, but I don't think that would be suitable, either. It's really for gentlemen, you see."

"I know, that's why I'd like to see it. And why is it that everything that's of the faintest interest to anybody is only for gentlemen?"

"Eat your porridge, darling, or you'll be late for school."

Ignoring her mother, Lily tried again. "Well, will you take me to see the whale?"

"The whale?"

"Yes, the one caught in the Mersey the other day. It's twenty-four feet long and twelve feet across and weighs three tons. If I can't go to the ballet or the exhibition can I go and see the whale?"

Her pa sighed and glanced at his wife for help but she was absorbed with her toast, her eyes lowered, her long, curving lashes forming a fan on her slightly flushed cheek. They had made love no more than half an hour ago and the look about her, languid and sensual, told him that she would not be averse to starting again as soon as breakfast was over.

Lily sighed tragically but they took no notice of her and not for the first time she pondered on how this grand passion her

ma and pa had for one another could be a definite disadvant-
age. Sometimes she felt as though she were invisible. Totally
excluded from their life, though she knew they did not mean
to be like this. She supposed it was because Pa was away such
a lot that Ma felt she had to make up for his absences by being
. . . being more attentive when he was home. Mary and Grace
Watson's pa, who had several stalls at St John's Market and
who came home every evening to his wife and children, did
not act like her pa did, and neither did Mrs Watson. They put
their cheeks together and kissed the air between them when
Mr Watson came home, and she supposed they did the same
in the morning, though Mr Watson went out so early Lily had
never actually seen him go. The Watsons lived next door.

The Elliotts and the Watsons lived on Walton Lane in
Walton on the Hill. It was what was known as a "nice"
area of Liverpool. In fact it was almost in the country. Decent.
Respectable. Not that it was by any means peopled by the
wealthy but the families who rented the small, semi-detached
villas which stretched along the tree-lined lane from Everton
Valley to the vast acreage of the Walton Nurseries were in
regular work, tradesmen, craftsmen who had served their time
to many of the trades allied to shipbuilding. Bert Meadows
who lived several doors down from the Elliotts was a wheelwright with his own small business at the back of Strand
Street opposite Canning Dock, and Andrew Hale had his
own cooperage in Water Street. Sean Flanagan, come out
from Ireland twenty years earlier, was in house construction
with an endless supply of Irish labourers from the old country
to whom he paid starvation wages but who had helped him
to become what was known in Lancashire as a "warm" man.
Liverpool was growing fast, spreading out into the rural areas
so that any man who could lay a brick or fashion a window
frame was guaranteed employment.

Those living in Walton Lane were of the working classes,
Lily's pa said so, for didn't they all, including himself, work
for a living, but they were poles apart from the "poor" underprivileged working class who lived in the centre of the city and
about the dock area. Among them were the dispossessed Irish,
the itinerant Welsh, families from Scandinavia and Europe
who, unable to raise the money for the fare, had got no further
than Liverpool in their search for the "new world". These
men were unskilled and without a regular trade, working as

porters, lightermen, dung collectors, cess-pool cleaners and rubbish collectors, street sellers, pedlars and street labourers. The worst off poor were, of course, the Irish immigrants who took jobs even the most destitute Englishman would draw the line at if he had the choice. It was accepted that the proper thing to do was to save not only for your old age but for a rainy day, everyone knew that, but even the wages of a skilled man in full work allowed little margin for saving. So what chance had they in Netherfield Road which was in the centre of the northern dock system, in Park Lane, St James Street, Windsor Street, Northumberland Street and the southern dock area which, it was acknowledged, was where the worst of the slums were situated and in whose back-to-back courts the residents lived as close as maggots in cheese. They wallowed, there could be no other word to describe it, in three-storey houses the structures of which rose from a sea of stench and were so rotten they were ready to tumble to the ground with the weight of people they housed. A pitiful mass of humanity which sweated in the tottering tenements and wretched rat-infested cellars, a vast army of indigent poor who lacked all means of a comfortable existence and who had no prospect of ever getting one. Drunkenness, depravity and crime flourished in the festering warrens where it was said there were more people living, if you could call it that, to the square mile than there were fish in the sea.

Not so in Walton Lane. In fact it is doubtful that the children of the families who lived there were even aware that such people and places existed. Certainly not Lily Elliott or Grace and Mary Watson, Evie and Maggie Meadows, although the Flanagans, whose pa had come a long way from the sod cottage in Ireland where he was born, might have had an inkling, for Sean was proud of his success and was never tired of telling his children about it. There were fields, green and sweet and starred with poppy, buttercup and clover, spread out on the other side of the hawthorn hedge that bordered Walton Lane. There were cows standing knee-deep in pasturage, their placid heads turning to look at the children who sometimes stood on the bottom rung of the gate set in the hedge and called to them. There were farms where they were often sent by their mothers to fetch a can of foaming milk or a dozen eggs or a pound of best butter, and the foetid stink of the alleys off Netherfield Road and

Northumberland Street never reached their noses. They were children of the great seaport of Liverpool which gave their fathers a decent living, born and bred in it, used to the noise and vigour of their city through which poured the peoples of the world, the cosmopolitan population bringing its own cultures and language. They were at home in the bustle of the busy pavements where their mothers shopped at Lewis's, Owen Owen's and T.J. Hughes. The singing excitement of the River Mersey, the landing stage and the long esplanade which stretched from Princes Dock northwards and where their families took their Sunday afternoon walk. The teeming dockland and its fragrances, some heady and delightful, others rank and insidious from the cargoes that came from every part of the world.

But they were also children of the countryside, for they played in its fields and meadows and small woodlands where their mothers knew they were as safe as though they were in their own back gardens. They had been born in Liverpool and spoke with the adenoidal accent which was a mixture of Dublin and Cardiff and Glasgow, and the careful articulation of their teachers, since they all attended decent schools, did nothing to eliminate it.

The neat homes they lived in were well built and well kept. They were each set in a short walled garden to the front and a long stretch at the rear which backed on to a bit of spare ground. They all had a bow window each side of the front door and two flat sash windows above and in the roof a tiny dormer window which allowed light into a slip of an attic. The front door opened into a square, white and black tiled hallway off which were three doors, one to the parlour, one to the dining-room and the third to a modern kitchen which in turn led to a scullery. Upstairs were three good-sized bedrooms. Spacious and airy, or so it would be deemed by those who lived in their own filth down by the docks and who hadn't, in the eyes of the residents of Walton Lane, the gumption to get themselves out of it as they had done. Bloody hard work and perseverance, which they'd all shown, was needed, along with a bit of good old Liverpool common sense, for good fortune didn't come to those who sat about on their arses bemoaning their lot, as Sean Flanagan often said to his wife, in private, of course. He and many others had risen above it by gritting their teeth and getting on with it, working by day and spending their evenings at the Mechanics Institute learning to read and write and add up. They had found that it was possible in this growing and increasingly prosperous city, where shipbuilding trades and house construction opened doors to those willing to labour at it, or took a chance on a small business, working all the hours God sends, to make a success of it, which those in Walton Lane had done.

Having eaten enough of her porridge to please her pa, who told her she was a good girl, and her ma, who said it was time she got ready for school, Lily got down from the table and went upstairs to change from her dressing-gown, in which Ma allowed her to eat breakfast, into her school clothes. Her bedroom was at the back, looking out over the bit of rough ground that lay between Walton Lane and Walton Road. She could see Jack and Charlie Meadows with Finn Flanagan, who should by now have been on their way to the school their parents paid good money for, bending over something in the long grass. There was a sort of pathetic whining coming through her open bedroom window and she leaned out in an effort to see what they were up to. Suddenly they stepped back, their hands held up, almost tripping over their own boots in their effort to get away from whatever it was they had been fiddling with. At once what seemed to be a confused bundle of fur began to roll and writhe, going over and over in the rough and stony ground. Lily stared, leaning out even further as she tried to make out what it was and when she did she let out such a scream Mrs Quinn dropped her frying pan which she was just about to put into steep. It was a dog and a cat which the boys had tied tail to tail. The animals were much the same size and at first attempted to fight one another, but in a moment or two they had had enough and wanted to part company. The dog pulled and then the cat, dragging each other in terror backwards and forwards across the ground while the three boys slapped their thighs and howled with laughter.

It took her no more than twenty seconds to fling herself out of her room, down the stairs, through the kitchen past the startled Mrs Quinn, down the length of the garden and over the high wall like a monkey going up a stick. Her ma and pa had come to the door of the dining-room, ready to run upstairs, and as she flew past them they began to follow her, both begging her to tell them what was wrong and why had she screamed. There didn't seem to be much wrong with her by the vigour of her flight, for which they breathed a sigh of relief. Her scream had frightened them both.

"Lily"? her pa queried, but she was on the other side of the wall by then and when he reached it he was just in time to see her throw herself at the dog and cat, her hands scrabbling to untie the knotted twine that fastened the two animals firmly together.

"It's all right, it's all right," she was muttering to them as they bit and scratched at her, and at each other. In a moment she was dripping with blood, her own or the terrified animals' Richard could not tell. He leaped the wall with the same force as his daughter, unconcerned with the rich satin of his quilted bed-robe and as he held the demented animals apart and away from her, Lily managed to separate the tails of the two animals. The cat streaked away, a black, spitting bundle of fury, disappearing over the wall of a garden on Walton Road but the dog, no more than a puppy really, quivered and whimpered and pressed itself against Lily's chest where she held it, as though seeking human comfort.

"Give the dog to me, Lily," her pa said gently, taking the animal from her arms, wanting to get her inside where the extent of her wounds might be ascertained. It might be that Doctor Draper was needed, for his daughter was in a bit of a mess. "I'll deal with you later," he told the three boys savagely, but later was not good enough for Lily.

With a cry of fury she sprang towards Finn Flanagan, who was the biggest and the oldest at twelve and, completely unprepared for the ferocity of her attack, he was forced back, almost measuring his length as he tripped clumsily on the tussocky grass. Her hands reached as though by instinct for his most vulnerable part, his eyes, raking down his forehead and eyebrows and continuing across both cheeks. Blood flowed and when he put up his fists as though she were another boy and he would fight her she clenched hers and landed one just below his belly where his manhood lay.

He howled in agony, bending double, and so great was Lily's anger she even managed another kick at his shins before her father, hastily dropping the puppy, took her by the arms and dragged her off.

"Let me go, Pa," she shrieked. "Did you see what those buggers had done to those animals?" Her pa was shocked and startled by her language, for her mother was bringing her up to be a lady. "That poor cat . . . is it all right, d'you think? And the puppy? Let me go, please let me go. They deserve a thrashing, all of them. Please, why don't you fetch your whip and I'll see they get it."

"Lily, calm down, sweetheart, they'll all be punished, I swear. Anyway, Finn looks as though you've pretty much finished him off so come home, there's a good girl, and let your mother have a look at you. You've blood all over the place and—"

"No, Pa," struggling to be free of her pa's arms. Her hair, which she could sit on when it was free, was free now, hanging about her in a shroud of silvery gold where the sun caught it and her face was as red as a poppy. She glared about her and even though she was firmly held by her pa, Jack and Charlie Meadows put another few feet of space between them and her.

By now there was a row of fascinated heads peering over every wall within hearing distance, including that of Lena Flanagan who, on seeing her son reduced to a blubbering heap by Lily Elliott, God knows why, yelled for her husband to come and sort this bloody lot out, forgetting for a moment her Walton on the Hill manners and reverting to Scotland Road where Sean had married her.

Though Sean could not for the life of him see what all the fuss was about, since they were only a couple of strays, after all, Richard Elliott was probably the most prosperous and well educated among the residents of Walton Lane. He was a perfectly nice chap who always stopped for a chat and certainly put on no airs and graces, knowing where Sean himself came from, but Sean was a little bit in awe of him and if he said the lads had gone too far, which, in the captain's eyes, it seemed they had, then he was perfectly willing to administer the appropriate punishment to his son, and Bert Meadows was the same. The little lass was a bit of a mess, what with scratches across her hands and even a bite on her lip which had swelled up alarmingly, and the doctor had been sent for, so the captain said, and would he like him to come and see to Sean's lad who, he said with a twinkle in his eye, had got a bit of a pasting from the captain's lass.

Lily lay in a state of interesting suffering on the sofa in the parlour. The doctor had applied some stuff that stung like the devil and had deliberated on whether the bite on her lip might need a stitch. She quite liked the idea of that, for it would be something to show off when she went to school the next day.

"Keep her off today, Mrs Elliott," the doctor had told Ma, after deciding against the stitch. Doctor Draper was a believer in the new and radical "germ theory" and he went on to say that the wounds must be kept scrupulously clean to keep out the germs, and the patient should not touch that animal, referring to the puppy which was tied to the back door handle outside, where it could be heard howling dolefully, since Mrs Quinn would not allow it into her clean kitchen until it was properly bathed in a good carbolic soap.

"But it's not our dog, Doctor Draper," Ma said, horrified that the doctor should believe they would own such a filthy-looking animal.

"Well, your daughter seems to think it is, Mrs Elliott, but that is up to you."

Lily cried and howled and even considered fainting a bit when Pa said he'd take the mongrel off to the . . . well, wherever stray animals were taken, which, he knew very well, though he wasn't going to say so in front of Lily, meant it would be destroyed.

"Please, Pa, I can't bear it," she sobbed against her pa's chest. "Poor little beggar. First it's tied by the tail to a cat and now you mean to take it away and probably someone will wring its neck and make it into stew and it's only a baby. How would you like it if—"

"Now then, darling, you must not say such things to your pa. He's only trying to help. The dog is . . . is verminous and couldn't possibly be let into the house in its condition."

"Oh, Ma, I know that, but if Pa was to give it a bath in the washhouse with . . . with carbolic soap like Doctor Draper said, it'd be clean then and could come in here with me. Please, Ma, please. I can't bear it if you take it away." She had turned china white and her eyes, great brilliant pools overflowing with tears and too big for her face, rent her parent's hearts. They loved her. They knew they sometimes excluded their daughter from their own totally selfish love for one another, though they didn't mean to. It was just that whenever they were apart they missed one another so much and when they were together they felt the need to make every day, hour, minute full of loveliness to make up for the loneliness. Really, would it do any harm to let the child have what she wanted, which was a companion for herself alone? They could not give her a sister or brother which would have eased their own sometimes guilty hearts so what harm could come of letting her have a pet? At least have a look at the thing after it was cleaned up?

Lily could see them weakening and, knowing exactly when to strike, the iron being hot, so to speak, began to babble of never letting the puppy be a nuisance. She would feed it and keep it clean and brushed and take it for walks and never let it interfere with her homework and it could sleep in the washhouse – which she knew it wouldn't do and so did they – and it would never get under Mrs Quinn's feet and if she went back on any of these promises she herself would personally take the dog to . . . to . . . wherever it was Pa had intended taking it. She was not sorry she had given Finn Flanagan a good hiding, not seeing her parents' amusement at the very idea of a ten-year-old girl giving a hiding to a big, twelve-year-old lad, though it was true she had, and she'd not apologise to him, though they had not asked her. She did not tell them that when she was up and about she meant to have a go at Jack and Charlie Meadows, since they were equally as bad as that lout Finn Flanagan.

The puppy, a female, as it happened, which Mrs Quinn happily seemed to think made it more acceptable, was quite a nice little thing when she was washed and brushed. They did their best, her parents, but they couldn't keep Lily out of the washhouse while the ablutions took place. She was heaps better, she told them, dragging her old cloak about her nightgown, and she felt the pup would behave better if she were there to supervise. She didn't. She would keep leaping up and trying to lick Pa's face, then turning her attentions on her, her rough tongue everywhere at once in her canine delight. When Pa got her out of the sink she shook herself so vigorously both she and Pa had to get changed. Her coat was a mottled indeterminate brown and her ears seemed too large for her pointed face. The length of her tail was quite ridiculous, Pa said, which was why it had been so easy to tie it to the cat, which upset Lily all over again but when, at last, she was once more ensconsed on the parlour sofa, a mug of creamy cocoa in one hand, the other arm about the wriggling body of her new friend, Lily Elliott thought she had never, except when she was on the deck of her father's schooner, been so happy in her life.

"Villette," she said sleepily, stroking Villette's rough fur.

"What was that, sweetheart?" Pa asked, putting down the *Liverpool Mercury* which he was reading out loud to her mother. Ma paused in her sewing, and looked up smilingly since she knew what her daughter meant.

"I shall call her Villette. Villy for short."

3

Jane Elliott was the only housewife on Walton Lane to have a servant. Her new husband had told her that she needed one, for he could not bear to see her at the sink with her hands in water, on her knees with a bucket at her side, slaving over an oven or doing any of the hundred and one tasks the wives of working men did every day of the week without a thought. Of course, he could afford one, for when he married her he was already in a fair way of business in the coastal shipping trade and so it was that Molly Quinn, who was ten years older than her mistress, and who, despite her name, was not Irish, came to "do" for her.

Though she was married to a comfortably off sea skipper with his own small schooner Jane Elliott was not a lady in the true sense of the word. She was not allied to the gentry, for her father had been a self-made man with his own ship's chandlery business in Liverpool. He and her mother, overwhelmed by the beauty and seeming fragility of their only child, had not allowed her to work in the business though she had been perfectly willing to do so, being a good-natured lass with no conception of her own loveliness. It might have been that with the awed worship of her parents shaping her life she would become spoiled and selfish but she was a simple girl, not simple meaning a bit backward, but simple with an outlook on life that asked for no more than the content and peace she found in her home and the love with which her parents surrounded her.

When she was seven years old she was sent to a small, select school in Breckfield Road where, at a cost of £5 per annum, she was taught English reading, spelling, grammar, arithmetic, drawing, natural philosophy and chemistry, needlework and vocal music. She also learned to speak correctly, though she never lost her Liverpool accent, to walk properly, to sit gracefully and to use the correct cutlery at table.

Her parents were devastated when she fell in love with Captain Richard Elliott though they could not fault him as a husband. They felt he was exactly the right age for their unworldly eighteen-year-old daughter and was well able to support her, but to lose her, even though she was to go from the comfortable rooms above the shop where they lived no further than Walton on the Hill, was a great blow to them. Still, as she told them on her wedding day, they were welcome to come and visit her and Richard any time they pleased, particularly as he would be gone for days on end when he sailed away on his schooner, then called the *Seamaid*, after the first ship owned by the Elliotts.

There were sea captains, sailors, ship's mates, seamen of all kinds in and out of John Mellor's busy ship's chandlers and it was one of these who killed John and Frances Mellor. Not intentionally, of course, but somewhere on a voyage one of them had picked up one of the diseases that were rife in the tropics and it had swept through the small area about John Mellor's shop, taking fifteen people with it. John and Frances were among them.

Richard deliberated on whether to keep on their thriving little business, putting in a manager to run it, but, making one of the mistakes that seemed to dog him at times, he sold it instead, giving the small profit to his wife to spend as she pleased. Which she did, buying silk fans and gauze scarves, silk dresses and stunning little Zouave jackets, cashmere shawls, velvet gilets, dashing bonnets and morning robes that were nothing but a froth of gauze like sea foam.

Her husband was enchanted with her.

Molly Quinn watched it all with a jaundiced eye, for the pair of them were like children at play, she thought, with no conception of the real world, for they had never had to deal with it. Even the captain, though he worked hard when he was at sea and was what Molly called a real man, a real gent, had inherited what he had from his father. He had never had to struggle and neither had his young wife and yet could you condemn them, for they were the loveliest couple, not just in looks but in their dispositions as well. The same could not be said about herself, not that she was unattractive or had a mean nature but that her life had been one long fight to survive. Molly Quinn had had a hard time of it but she often thought if she'd looked like Mrs Elliott and been as sweet-natured and trusting and lucky she would probably have turned out just like her mistress and done just what she did. But she hadn't!

She and Seamus had been married for no more than four years with four babies to bring up when he had fallen from a crane and broken his neck. They had lived in Brooke Alley off Vauxhall Road with a fine view of the coal yards to one side, the Vitriol Works to the other and a stone's throw from the Borough Gaol where the young prostitutes hung about. Not to find customers from the gaol, though several of the gaolers made use of them, but because it was close to the docks. It was an appalling place to bring up children, with a gin-shop every two or three steps and the gutters awash with those who frequented them. Seamus, who had a steady job, and Molly had a basement cellar all to themselves, which was a luxury in an environment where it was quite normal for not one family but two or three to share a room. The alley was a narrow, flagged passage down the middle of which was an open drain in which floated sewage and all manner of nasty debris. The alley led to a close, a square around which tall, back-to-back houses stood and in which well over a hundred people, along with those who lived in the alley, shared one water supply and a couple of privies.

Molly worked hard to keep her growing family clean and decent, making sure every morning that she had enough water for the day, for sometimes the Communal Water Supply was turned off and there was none to be had until the next morning. She was lucky. She had three decent buckets in which to collect her water but it didn't seem to matter to many of the other tenants who, having no utensil in which to boil a potato let alone collect water, didn't bother overmuch with washing or scouring or anything that might take a little effort. In between pregnancies Molly went out to work, putting a bit by for when she was unable to carry on because of her condition. She went scrubbing or worked over a dolly tub in the laundry at the back of the Vitriol Works and they managed, she and Seamus, proud of themselves and their labours which kept them what Molly liked to think of as respectable. She squared her strong shoulders and worked beside Seamus despite the filth, the derelict people with whom she lived cheek by jowl, the men haggard, drunken, careworn, hopeless, the women weighed down by the yearly pregnancies they could not avoid, nursing their babies at dirty breasts as they sat on the steps that led up to the floors above her own basement. They reminded her strangely of the scurrying earwigs and other creeping insects that one finds when a log that has lain a long time on the ground is lifted, and she had no sympathy with them when they gave up. So many just sank into apathy, too overcome to make any further effort, but Molly was an intelligent young woman, bright and cheerful and optimistic. Until Seamus died.

For a while she sank into the same state of muck and muddle they all lived in, for without Seamus's wage how was she to manage? Her home became as dirty, as verminous, as cold and cheerless as all the others in the alley and it was not until her youngest, a sweet little boy of only seven months, died one night in her arms, because of her neglect, she knew that, that she began to haul herself little by little out of the cesspool her life had become since Seamus's death.

With three young children at her skirts, good little children, all girls, who obeyed her orders to stay where they were put, sometimes tied to a table leg for their own safety, she began a long, tortuous grind of scrubbing and scouring, holystoning the steps of better-off housewives in Everton and West Derby, laundry work at the local washhouse and in her own home at nights; of working in soap factories and pickle factories and indeed anywhere they would pay her for her labour. She was sometimes so exhausted she wished she had died with Seamus, despairing that she would ever get herself up out of the mire of poverty-stricken degradation. It would have been so easy to sell her body down at the docks – she was still a young and attractive woman – to get bread to put in her children's mouths and a rag or two on their backs but she savagely refused to consider that since she had loved Seamus and the children he had left in her trust.

It was not until she discovered, or was discovered by, the Society for Bettering the Condition and Increasing the Comfort of the Poor, that she began to get a proper toehold on a new life. As the children grew it became more and more difficult to keep them safe and quiet while she worked. Victoria, Mary and Alice – Molly was a fervent royalist and had called her children after those of the dear Queen – were obedient and well mannered, for she would have them no other way, but they were children, well fed after that first dreadful fall into despair after Seamus's death, healthy and lively and she began to fear that the fine tight rope she trod between managing, just, and not managing at all, was not going to hold her up for much longer.

The Ladies Benevolent Society, which visited distressed women in their homes and whom many of the inhabitants of Brooke Alley called "bloody interfering cows" were the ones to give her fresh hope. They directed her, through the Society for Bettering the Condition and Increasing the Comfort of the Poor, to a small school established twenty years ago and supported by the Anglican Church where her children would be looked after while she was at work, and indeed would be taught to read and write.

Though Molly Quinn had been brought up as a Catholic she let all the Church's teaching fly out of the window, for a fat lot of good it, or the Church, had done her in her desperate struggle to survive. If her children were to be taught by Protestants what did it matter? She was sure that Seamus up in his Catholic heaven wouldn't mind as long as his girls were safe, healthy and happy and the burden he had left on Molly's shoulders was lifted a little. She begged his forgiveness every night for letting his little son die, for he had loved the child, but perhaps the baby was with his daddy and Seamus happy to have him. She comforted herself with this thought and got on with cherishing the rest of his children which was all she could do, after all.

An added bonus was that the three girls went to Sunday School which meant she had extra hours free to do other jobs and by the time her eldest was ten years old and ready to go as scullery maid to a good and respectable family with a promise of promotion if she "shaped", which Molly knew she would, she was firmly in control of her life. It had taken her six years but she had done it.

But the hardships she had endured and overcome had made her intolerant, impatient with those who could not do, through sheer hard work and determination, what she had done. If she could keep herself respectable with three young children to fetch up then why couldn't others, those who lolled about on doorsteps in the alley where she still lived. Not that her room was anything like theirs. She kept it whitewashed: even the bricks on the outside wall above her cellar window and door and about the basement steps that led down to them were got at every six months. Her small home was scrubbed, polished and scoured every night when she got home from work, for it was constant war to keep down the lice, the fleas, the rats and other vermin that lived beside those all about her. Her stove was blackleaded, her brasses polished and her two remaining children set off each day to school with clean aprons and stout boots and a decent meal for their dinner wrapped in a clean checked napkin. She had a handsome clock under a glass dome, bought second-hand from Paddy's Market so that she was never late for any of her jobs. She had four matched glasses with a cut-out design on them. She had a dresser on which she kept her *full* set of English stoneware, cups, saucers, plates, dinner plates and tureens, second-hand, naturally, and in a drawer a well-polished set of cutlery. She had a good kettle, several saucepans, a round frying pan and a round egg roaster. There was a rug on her scrubbed floor and on her mantelshelf several small figurines of what looked like Chinamen, one or two chipped, certainly, but very pretty and proving that she was able to spend money not just on the necessities of life. She had a big double bed modestly hidden behind a shawl hung over a piece of rope in which she and the girls slept, three armchairs and a pine table scrubbed to the colour of rich cream with four chairs about it. She had snowy nets at her window and curtains she had made herself to keep out the rude curiosity of her neighbours who thought she had got above herself. And most important she had a good strong lock on her door and a shutter on her window for when she was not at home.

This, of course, was not until later in her life, after she had begun to work for Captain and Mrs Elliott.

It was at the church where she took her children every Sunday that she was asked if she would ever consider taking a full-time job as a housekeeper, cook, cleaner.

"It's a nice home where you'd be going, Mrs Quinn. Mrs Mellor, who is a member of our congregation, has a daughter who is getting married and her husband-to-be is keen to get a decent, hardworking woman to look after their home. He's a sea captain and will be away at times."

"I couldn't live in, Mrs Cooper. Me kids're still young as yer know, and I couldn't leave 'em alone."

"I don't think they need anyone to live in, Mrs Quinn. The captain, or so I was told by Mrs Mellor, intends taking his bride with him on his boat, for a time at least," meaning until the babies start putting in an appearance. "He is not away for very long," she went on vaguely, not being in any way familiar with the life of a seaman, even if she did live in Liverpool. "And then, when he's home they will need looking after. I believe the future Mrs Elliott has been . . . she's not very domesticated. She has been well educated and can sew but that seems to be her only accomplishment. Can you cook, Mrs Quinn?"

"A plain cook, Mrs Cooper, when I've summat to cook with," remembering those days when it had been nothing but potatoes and oatmeal mixed with water.

"I shouldn't think they will need more than that, my dear," not meaning the potatoes and oatmeal, of course. "They are ordinary people, not of the gentry or anything like that, if you know what I mean. Mrs Mellor is the wife of a ship's chandler but . . . well, think it over and if you're interested let me know. Don't be too long, though, for it will make a very nice job for someone."

They had just come back from their honeymoon a little over three weeks later when Molly Quinn knocked at the newly painted front door of the grand little house in Walton Lane. She'd walked up from Brooke Alley, along Portland Street and into New Scotland Road which led to Everton Valley and Walton Lane. A walk of no more than twenty minutes which was very convenient and would be an added bonus, for once you got the length of New Scotland Road you were in the prettiest countryside Molly had ever seen. That's if she got the job which, the more she saw of Walton Lane, the smart little semi-detached villa and the handsome couple who lived in it, became more and more desirable. God almighty, she could clean through this place in a morning and if they wanted a bit of cooking done, even the better kind, she'd soon learn.

They'd been to Southport, they told her, sitting on the sofa in the pretty parlour, holding hands and smiling at one another in such a way she began to feel somewhat embarrassed. It was very obvious they were made up with each other and were not really very concerned with how a house should be run or what she was to put in their mouths or whether or not she polished the brass every day. When could she start? the captain asked, not his wife who was mistress of this house, which was strange but then they were not what you'd call an ordinary couple at all, despite what Mrs Cooper had told her. They begged her to have another cup of tea, leaving her to pour it out for herself and would she like an almond tart, shop bought, she supposed, not being able to picture the elegant Mrs Elliott with a mixing bowl in her long-fingered white hands. The captain was to be off in a day or two, he didn't say where, and wanted to know that his wife would be looked after while he was away. He would have taken her with him, he explained, as he meant to do whenever it was possible but his cargo was not one he would like his wife to be close to and when he told her what it was, manufactured goods for Ireland which was quite reasonable but bringing back cattle, she understood what he meant. Over the rim of her china cup she considered the slender loveliness of Mrs Elliott, who looked as though she'd never been in close contact with anything other than flowers and butterflies, blue skies and golden sunshine, pretty dresses and fragrant perfume, kittens and satin ribbons, in fact all the beautiful things in life that Molly Quinn had never encountered. She and Seamus had once taken the ferry to New Brighton, walking on the golden sands, looking in wonder at the pretty houses along the esplanade, the lovely municipal gardens, the sparkling jewels scattered on the sun-kissed river. That had been *their* honeymoon and she would never forget that day as long as she lived. They had held hands as these two were doing, for they were eighteen and had been wed only a week and so she understood, for she had known love.

"Well, Mrs Quinn, I think that's about all," the captain said, "unless you've anything else you'd like to ask, my darling."

His darling proved to be not quite as oblivious to sensible matters as her looks seemed to imply.

"There is the question of Mrs Quinn's wage, Richard. And I'm not even sure she has agreed to come to us." She smiled so devastatingly it was then that Molly Quinn began on the long and enduring role of loving protector she was to play for the remainder of their lives, though no one ever knew of her feelings.

"Oh, dear, Mrs Quinn, forgive me? Of course, Mrs Elliott is right." They turned and stared at one another in wonder, momentarily speechless at the sound of her new name on his lips and Molly felt the smile begin inside her, for there was nothing more certain in this life than that these two needed someone sensible to look after them. How in the name of heaven did the captain manage to run a business if he was as feather-brained as it seemed he was, but she was to learn that Richard Elliott the seaman and Richard Elliott the husband were two totally different men.

Molly sat with her back straight as a pencil, as Mrs Elliott was doing, with a look so stern and disapproving they both leaned back a little, then stared at one another in dismay but, again, it was something they were to learn about her as she was to learn many things about them. Whoever Mrs Quinn cherished she chastised. Ask her daughters! Whatever she was asked to do she did it with such grudging reluctance one could be forgiven for thinking she was not at all pleased and it was only against her own better judgement that she would allow it, whatever it happened to be.

"I've two children, girls," she told them firmly, "an' another in service up near Toxteth Park. Nay, don't bother tha' selves, they're well looked after durin't day burr I've ter gerr'ome to 'em at night so I can't sleep in." She did not apologise, for that was not her way. She told the truth and that was that.

"How old are your children, Mrs Quinn?"

"Victoria's eleven now, Mary's ten an'll be goin' inter service 'erself shortly, and our Alice is nine."

"What pretty names, Mrs Quinn." Molly was to discover that whatever the situation or the topic of conversation, Jane Elliott always had something nice to say. "But what a shame they have to go into service."

"Well, ma'am, the devil drives where't needs must, an' bein' a widder all these years I 'ad no choice, but they're decent lasses an' I'm proud of 'em," and that's the end of that, her firm jaw and truculent expression told them. She wanted no sympathy. She was not prepared to tell them of the hardships she had endured nor the sacrifices she had made to keep them all decent. She did not even brag that they could read and write which was not an accomplishment many slum children could boast.

They loved her, they told one another in that extravagant way they had after she had gone, promising to be at Walton Lane at seven o'clock next Monday morning.

"Oh, there's no need to come quite so early, Mrs Quinn," the captain had demurred.

"Oh, yes, sir, there is. I don't like ter waste time lollin' in me bed an' I can see there's a few things what want putting right round 'ere," turning her gaze disapprovingly on what was evidently something that gave her great offence.

"Well, if that's the case you had better have a key, for I'm not sure . . . we'll be up."

"Right you are, sir." She stood up. Her wages had been agreed and her hours, which were to be somewhat loose, for there might be things, said somewhat vaguely, that Mrs Elliott might need her for. She was to come every day except Sunday, even when the Elliotts were at sea and would, of course, be paid her full wage, which, to Molly Quinn who had scraped along on so little for so long, was absolutely magnificent.

That had been eleven years ago and from that day she had bullied and loved and cherished them through thick and thin, though to be honest there was not much thin. The captain came home every ten days or so, staying perhaps three while he discharged his cargo and picked up another and their lives went on serenely. The time while Mrs Elliott was pregnant and then was forced to stayed at home with her new baby had been a tricky one, for she had pined for her husband.

"I don't know what I would do without you, Mrs Quinn; probably kill myself," she would say, drifting to the window as though it might bring her husband home that much quicker if she watched for him.

"Don't talk daft. I've never 'eard such damn nonsense in me life. You need summat ter *reely* bother yer then yer could talk about killin' yerself, my lass. D'yer not think I don't miss my man, even after all this time, so think on—"

She would get no further, for with a soft rustle of lace and chiffon and a waft of lovely perfume Mrs Elliott would be rushing to put her arms about her and hug her in that endearingly childlike way she had and though Molly loved it, and her, she could not allow it.

"Now give over an' let me gerron wi' this apple turnover or there'll be nowt fer yer dinner."

Molly's culinary efforts had come on apace since she had begun work at the Elliotts. On the quiet she practised all sorts of recipes from the *Ladies Journal* Mrs Elliott bought and was hugely gratified when the captain told her he had never tasted anything as good as her pastry and what had she put in the steak and kidney to make it so mouthwateringly delicious?

When the baby, Lily, was about eighteen months old, Mrs Elliott began to go again on the sea journeys her husband took. Sometimes the child went with them, though Molly often had nightmares about her safety on board that dipping, slippery deck which she herself had been persuaded to visit, and that was only tied up to the dock! She could so easily fall overboard, what with them two for ever canoodling, but she had underrated her employer's sense of responsibility when he was aboard his ship and the little mite had a line on her, apparently, and came to no harm. At other times they left her behind in Molly's care, begging her to bring her own two to stay with her in Walton Lane, which she did until they both went into service. They were good like that, the Elliotts. On Victoria's, Mary's or Alice's day off, her daughters would come to visit her there, despite the fact that she had kept on their home in Brooke Alley. They knew that though she was well set up here, in the pink, so to speak, she would never forget that time after their daddy died and Brooke Alley was a sort of bolt-hole, something to fall back on if anything were to go wrong with this grand job she now had. Not that anything would, for the Elliotts were a lovely couple. The girls had been shy at first but the Elliotts made a great fuss of them and really, life was so bloody wonderful she often shed tears of happiness as she whispered in the night of it to Seamus and it was all thanks to the Elliotts and their kindness to her.

And so the years passed and the child grew and was so different to her ma, not in looks but in her resolute determination to submit to no one. She was not disobedient or rude, in fact she was a well-mannered child but you could see that glint in her eye and that thrust of her small chin which said she didn't agree with you and though she might not say so out loud, she damn well would do what she thought best. Swift to anger she was, like him, but never bore a grudge, again like him, but with a will of iron which was a bit worrying in a child of her age. She had courage, too, which Molly admired. Look at the way she was over them big lads and that dratted dog which was for ever under her feet. Villette! Did you ever hear such a name for a dog? What was wrong with Gyp or Scrap or Rover, tell her that? she'd said to Lily.

"She's a lady dog, Mrs Quinn," the child had told her loftily, "that's why I didn't call her Rover." Her tone was scathing. "Besides, I don't like Scrap or Rover, even if she'd been a boy."

Villette, or Villy as she was called more often than not, ate what seemed to be her own weight in food every day, all the scraps from the family's meals and whatever else she could beg or steal from anyone who took pity on her. The child was very attached to her and often sneaked her into her bedroom to sleep at the foot of her bed and though Molly knew about it she never said owt to her ma and pa.

Molly loved her almost as much as she loved her ma. She scolded her and told her she was a handful and she didn't know what she was going to do with her and she would never grow up to be the lady her ma was, which had not the slightest effect on Lily who didn't want to be like her ma but like her pa! She allowed Mrs Quinn to take her to school each day because she had no option, and then bring her home at the end of it, talking nineteen to the dozen, and Molly listened to her going on about China and Australia and Newfoundland and Peru and her determination to visit all these places, wherever they were, and many more besides. Molly was the only one to listen to Lily's plans for the future which seemed to include becoming a sea captain and sailing away on her pa's schooner and though neither of *them* took any notice, that's if they heard her, Molly Quinn often felt a small sense of unease prick her, for if there was ever a child who would have her own way it was her. Tell her how it was possible and Molly wouldn't be able to say but if there was a way, Lily Elliott would find it.

4

Lily was playing hopscotch with Evie Meadows and Grace Watson when the hansom cab came slowly along Walton Lane, the cabbie leaning across his seat as though looking for the number of a house. With a great deal of "whoa-ing" and pulling of reins it stopped outside hers. The cab door swung open somewhat hesitantly and two men got out. She was surprised to see that one of them was Mr Porter. What on earth was he doing here? was her first thought, naturally, especially as the *Lily-Jane* was to dock today and her pa would need all hands to the pump, as he always joked. She didn't know who the other chap was.

It was the beginning of December and the weather had turned cold. It was not really the right time of the year for hopscotch, which usually took place in the summer months, but they had decided, she and Grace and Evie, that it was silly only to do something you really enjoyed doing when someone else told you to, like Easter for whip and top, July for marbles or "ollies" as they were called in Liverpool, and Cherry Wob which was played mostly by the boys in the autumn. The funny thing was that no one seemed to know who started it. Cherry Wob was understandable, for you needed cherry stones which you could obviously only get in season. They were flicked up the side of a house wall and when they came down if they hit a stone already on the pavement the owner claimed the lot. At least that was their version. But whip and top, wooden bowling hoops and skipping games seemed just to start of their own volition. One day it was whip and top, the next skipping ropes without a word being said and they all fell in with it unquestioningly.

Skipping had its own chanted rhythms.

Dip, dip, dip, my blue ship,
Floating on the water
Like a cup and saucer,
Dip, dip, dip, you're not in!

At this, whoever was skipping was then sent out. That was magical and complicated, the rope whirling with a girl at each end and, depending on the length of the rope, two or three, or sometimes four girls leaping in and out, plaits bobbing, skirts flying, cheeks flushed, eyes shining with the exertion.

But hopscotch was the three girls' particular favourite and this morning, a Saturday, they had carefully marked out their squares on the pavement with chalk and had intoned "Eeny, meeny, miny, mo, catch a nigger by the toe," which was their way of choosing who was to go first. Lily, who had won, had done four and had just slid her stone across the squares with the flair and dexterity for which, as a hopscotch player, she was famous among her peers. It landed as neat as you please on number five.

With a triumphant look at Grace and Evie she was about to hop on to the number one square, then place one foot on each of the squares marked two and three, and so on, avoiding the one with the five on it, and, of course, all the chalked lines, which if she had stepped on would have meant she was "out", when she became aware that neither of her friends was watching her. They had turned, along with every other child who was "playing out", to look curiously at the cab and the two men who had alighted. Both were dressed in sombre suits, just as though they were going to church. Dark jackets, neat black neckties, stand-up collars with turned-down points, narrow-legged trousers. The gentleman who was a stranger wore a top hat and Mr Porter, whom Lily scarcely recognised without his gansey and peaked cap, had a bowler. They both removed these as they moved up the short path to Lily's front door and knocked with restraint on the highly polished brass doorknocker which was in the shape of a mermaid. In unison and almost as though they had practised it, they each lifted their right hand and nervously smoothed down their hair, before turning to gaze for a moment into the lane.

The children stood as one, clutching ollies and hoops, staring, open-mouthed, wide-eyed, as though, already, they knew that something unparalleled was about to happen.

Grace nudged Lily. "They're knocking at your door, Lil," she remarked unnecessarily, putting her hand on Lily's arm.

"I can see that, you daft beggar."

"Wonder what they want."

"How the heck do I know?" Watching as Mrs Quinn opened the door which she had just wiped down with a clean cloth as was her habit when she "did" her windows. She even scrubbed the stone window sills along with the front step, the wrought-iron gate and its posts, the step into the lane, finishing with the pail of soapy water being chucked along the path then brushed vigorously into the gutter. The spilled water had caused considerable inconvenience to the three girls, for it had meant they could not get a decent chalk mark outside Lily's gate and had to move further up the pavement.

The men spoke to Mrs Quinn and after a moment of suspicious scrutiny she stepped back inside the house, holding open the door for Mr Porter and the other chap to follow her in.

"What d'you think's wrong, Lil?" Grace speculated anxiously. "I've never seen them before, have you? You don't think it's anything to do with those apples we scrumped at the back end, do you?" Grace was of a nervous disposition and often wondered why bold and fearless Lily Elliott ever bothered with her. "That chap who chased us might've recognised us, you never know. I didn't want to do it in the first place but you and Charlie made me and Charlie's hair would be recognised by a blind man, it's such an awful ginger."

"Don't be daft, Grace Watson, we never made you and besides, if he had they'd have been here long ago and going to Charlie's house, not mine."

"And who are you, calling our Charlie's hair an awful ginger, anyroad?" a furious Evie spluttered. Evie was Charlie's sister and had the same shock of almost orange curls.

"Oh, do stop it, you two. I know one of them, he's Pa's first mate."

She began to walk slowly towards her own gate, watched by her two friends. The other children had lost interest, since it was not really the men who had caught their attention but the hansom cab, something not often seen in Walton Lane, which had driven away. She began to shiver as an inexplicable fear slithered through her. The sun which had shone weakly from the pale wintry sky had been covered by a wisp of gauze-like cloud and the day seemed suddenly dark and ominous. It's going to snow, she told herself, trying to explain the sudden icy greyness that overwhelmed her and when Mrs Quinn opened the door, her face set like the one on the bronze statue of Her Majesty's husband that stood before St George's Hall, she wanted to turn and run and run to escape the awful something that waited for her in her home.

"Come inside, lamb," Mrs Quinn said, which further frightened her, for Mrs Quinn had never called her "lamb" in all the years she had known her, which was since Lily was born.

There was absolute silence in the house. Through the open doorway of the parlour she could see her mother sitting in the most unusual attitude, unusual for her since she was always so graceful. She was stiff, awkward, her head held at a strange angle as though she were listening for something as she perched on the edge of the seat of a coffee-coloured velvet button-back chair. Mr Porter and the other gentleman were standing awkwardly just inside the door as if reluctant to step on Ma's richly swirled carpet, both still clinging to their hats and their composure by the skin of their teeth, though why she should have such an odd thought Lily couldn't imagine. Nobody spoke and but for the awful, awful feeling of terror, of stark and unbelieving terror, that filled the room from wall to wall and ceiling to floor, it might have been the picture of two gentlemen calling on a lady who was just about to invite them to sit down and take tea with her. Mrs Quinn held Lily's hand and she could feel it tremble and when she looked up at her, her face was as white as the apron she wore and it was moving, twitching even, as though she were afflicted by some strange nervous condition.

Her ma's voice, when she spoke, was so normal Lily almost laughed out loud in her relief.

"I'm afraid you've made some dreadful mistake, gentlemen. You see my husband is due home today. His ship docks on the evening tide and he will be home shortly after that. Mrs Quinn is just preparing his favourite meal, aren't you, Mrs Quinn?" turning a bright smile in Mrs Quinn's direction and Mrs Quinn made some indeterminate sound in the back of her throat. She put her free hand to her mouth as though to keep the sound in and Lily's ma watched her, then began to shake her head, denying something, though what it could be Lily didn't know, or perhaps she did and was terrified to acknowledge it.

Why was Ma so frightened? Her face was expressionless, set in a mould of porcelain perfection with no hint of colour anywhere in it, even her eyes seemed to be blank and empty of their normal smoky grey which was so beautiful. They reminded Lily of rain on a window, or the fog that drifted across from the river, without substance, without tone or depth.

"I'm so sorry, Mrs Elliott, I'm so sorry . . ." Mr Porter began, and to Lily's amazement she could hear the break of tears in his voice. Again she was seriously alarmed, for in her childhood world grown-ups didn't cry so it must be something bad to have upset him like this. She held at bay with a stubborn hardening of her will whatever that something might be. "It happened so sudden, like. You know what a good seaman he was but the storm . . . it were blowin' a force eight and when Johnno slipped and was dashed agin the rail the captain . . ."

Again Mr Porter swallowed something that seemed to fill his throat and all the while her ma stared steadily at him, her face totally blank but in her eyes was a glimmer of something, like a tiny light that had come to illuminate her mind and was shining against her will out on the world. Her back was absolutely rigid, her head still cocked in that strange way, but she appeared to be waiting politely for Mr Porter to finish what he was saying and leave her alone. She was not listening, not really listening to his words but Lily was and inside her something tore in agony, spreading throughout her slender childish body which was not really strong enough or mature enough to cope with it.

"Can I offer you some tea, gentlemen?" her ma said defensively, determined to make this just an unexpected social visit. "Mrs Quinn . . ." She turned blindly to the woman to whose hand Lily's seemed glued and it was then that she broke open. Broke open as though her body had been attacked by some monster child, falling apart like a doll whose stuffing is leaking out. Her mouth opened wide so that every tooth was on display and from it came a scream, then another and another, her lips stretched cruelly. The two gentlemen were appalled, for they had never seen in the space of two or three seconds such a transformation from total disbelieving calmness to a mad and uncontrollable frenzy of emotion. Tears poured down her face in a torrent, falling as steadily as rain and still from her mouth, which the tears kept flowing into, came a wail of such despair they both moved instinctively towards her, for she was like an animal that is being tormented beyond endurance.

Mrs Quinn let go of Lily's hand, leaving her stranded in her own unbelieving nightmare and moved hastily to her ma, lifting her to her feet with great tenderness, clucking something incomprehensible as she began to lead her from the pitying gaze of Mr Porter and the other gentleman. Lily still had the stone in her hand that she had thrown on to the number five then picked up on her way back to Evie and Grace. She was holding it so tightly she felt the sharp edge of it break the skin of her palm and the blood flow between her fingers. She could hear Villy whining and scratching in the scullery where Mrs Quinn must have shut her when she went to answer the door and she dwelled on the thought that Mrs Quinn would be hopping mad if Villy scratched the paintwork.

Mrs Quinn took her mother away and Mr Porter told Lily how sorry he was, how terribly sorry, her pa was a brave man to give his life for another; if there was anything he could do, and . . . well, he supposed they had better be off. They'd come in on the morning tide, making good headway to get her pa back. Well, they couldn't . . . they were all so sorry . . .

Not knowing what else to do with the silent child who stood like a dead-eyed statue where the housekeeper had left her, they told her again how sorry they were and having no one to let them out they did it themselves, hurrying in great relief up the path and along Walton Lane towards the city as though pursued by a pack of wolves. It had been worse than they had thought it would be, they told one another, and what would the poor widow do now? It was known she had been devoted to the captain and as for the child, poor little bugger, who was going to see to her now, for it was plain her ma couldn't.

Lily moved through the next few days with little recollection of what went on, though the sight of a coffin coming through the front door with, she supposed, Pa's poor dead body in it, sent her into such a crescendo of screaming Mrs Quinn had to send for the doctor. He had given her something that made her eyes heavy and she could not remember much after that. There were faces which bent over her, mouths opening and closing, saying something to her, she supposed, though she couldn't decipher what it was. She stared at each one in turn as though they were speaking some foreign language, which, if she listened carefully enough, would make sense, but it didn't. Ma was shut in her bedroom from which no sound came, Mrs Quinn in attendance, and had it not been for Rosa Meadows, Evie's ma, Lily might have fared badly.

"I'll take the child," was one remark Lily did make out, though she was not sure who said it, but after finding herself in the same bed as Evie who slept soundly beside her, she decided it must have been Evie's ma.

"She's in shock," another hollow voice said sympathetically, "and can you blame the poor mite. Her ma's gone out of her mind, so Mrs Quinn says, and she's enough to do looking after her, so the child's best out of the house until after the funeral."

"When's it to be, then?"

"There's to be some sort of enquiry, or an inquest or something, but probably the beginning of next week."

"Poor soul."

It was strange really. She was totally numb, feeling nothing at all. She was convinced that if they stuck pins in her she would feel no pain. It was as though she were not there any more, visible, but at the same time invisible to those who moved around her, talked above her head, stared at her with great curiosity, especially the children who had never been close to anyone whose pa had died before. They didn't speak *to* her. They didn't ask her questions, like, "Would you like a piece of cake, Lily?" but said to one another, "D'you think she'd eat a piece of cake if I offered it to her?"

"Eeh, I don't know," would come the answer until she felt like standing up and shrieking, "I'm here! Ask me!" but it was all too much trouble. She simply didn't care enough, though she couldn't fathom why. The very worst thing she could ever imagine happening to her, had happened. Her pa was dead. Mrs Quinn had taken her on her lap and told her so, though if she was honest she had known that the minute she had seen Mr Porter get out of the cab.

And so she sat at Mrs Meadows's table with Mr Meadows, Mrs Meadows, Evie and Jack and Maggie and Charlie, considering nothing at all really except what an amazement it was that they all had exactly the same-coloured hair, bright ginger, bar Mrs Meadows who was dark and handsome, like a gypsy. It was funny, the odd thoughts that wandered so casually into her head, just out of the blue like that, and she wondered why, not realising that she was in deep shock, that nature was shielding her, for the moment, from the agony of her loss. She was washed and dressed with Evie, who was the same age as her and her best friend and when it was discussed whether to send her to school or not with Evie, for perhaps it might be best for her to continue with her normal routine, she docilely allowed herself to be put on Mrs Meadows's parlour sofa with a book in her hand when it was decided it might be best to keep her at home.

"Look at her, poor little thing," she heard Mrs Meadows say to Mrs Watson who had, apparently, popped in to see if there was anything she could do to help.

"She's not a scrap of trouble," Mrs Meadows continued from the parlour doorway where she and Mrs Watson studied her pityingly. "She's not even shed a tear. Poor little thing."

"What'll her ma do without the captain? I've never known a woman who relied on her husband as she did."

"Mmm, I said as much to Bert last night but she'll just have to get on with it like we all would."

"I know, but she's . . . well . . ." They were not quite sure how to describe Jane Elliott, who was as lovely as the day, always smiling serenely and with a kind word for everyone but about as useful in the house as a toddling infant. Good job she had that Mrs Quinn of hers to see to her. She'd no relatives, so it was said, and neither had he but he must have left her comfortable which was something, they supposed.

Lily managed quite nicely in the cocoon of insensibil-ity she had fallen into, going to bed with Evie when she was told, getting up, getting washed and dressed, eating what was put in front of her and spending her day on Mrs Meadows's sofa. She was so quiet and obedient it was quite eerie, Mrs Meadows said, knowing what a wilful little thing she normally was. She sat there like a little ghost but soon they got quite used to it, so much so that the usual domestic upheaval in which the Meadows family lived swirled about her as though she were nothing more than a chair or the piano that stood in the parlour. After the first fascinated awe with which they treated her and her loss, they found themselves quarrelling and singing and carrying on as they always did, her still little figure causing them little discomfort.

The next outburst was when, having been washed and brushed and put into the best dress Mrs Meadows had fetched from Mrs Quinn, she was led by the hand by Mrs Meadows to her own home. She went, compliant as dove and it was not until she was pushed gently towards the parlour door that it became clear to her confused mind that she was not only expected to enter the room and look at her pa in his coffin but to kiss him goodbye. She could see the magnificence of its gleaming woodwork as it lay on a draped table, the handles of what looked like gold, a sort of white frill all around its edge and just showing over the edge of the frill her pa's face on a pillow. Well, not all his face, just his forehead and his nose, and the curl of long, dark lashes of one eye. He looked as though he were asleep and for a moment joy raced through her but then it went again, for what would her pa be doing lying in a box on the parlour table if he was alive.

"Go and kiss your pa goodbye, sweetheart," Mrs Meadows said to her kindly, ready to sniffle, for it was all so sad. A lovely chap like him being cut down in his prime and his wife quite out of her mind, Mrs Quinn, who dared not take her eyes off her, had told her. The neighbours were taking turns to sit with her to give poor Mrs Quinn a chance to rest, but how long was it going to be before she could see to her own daughter? And there was the funeral to be got through yet! She gave Lily a gentle push.

Lily began to struggle, digging her heels into the carpet and pushing backwards against Mrs Meadows's skirt. Her hands flailed like the sails of a windmill and she began to scream, a thin scream like a rabbit in a trap.

"No, no . . . no, I won't. I won't. Pa, please, Pa, don't let them make me. No . . . no." Her body jerked and Mrs Meadows turned to whoever it was who stood supportively in the hall, her face uncertain and working with compassion. Poor little mite, they couldn't make her, could they? it asked. It was the custom for all friends, relatives and indeed anyone who knew the deceased to come and view the body, say goodbye, so to speak, but the child was ready to throw a fit.

"Go and fetch Mrs Quinn," she hissed, since it seemed she was losing control and perhaps the woman who had practically brought up Lily Elliott might be able to calm her.

From that moment it was as though she had re-entered the world, finding it full of such pain and sorrow she could hardly function but knowing she must. She sobbed for hours on Mrs Quinn's knee while one of the neighbours sat with the comatose widow and Mrs Quinn shushed her and petted her and kissed her until she fell asleep when she was undressed and put into her own bed. The easiest part was over now, at least for Lily, Molly Quinn knew that, for hadn't she suffered it when Seamus died. At first there is the numb, senseless lack of anything that could be called grief, then, when the realisation comes that you would never, in this world, see the person you loved again, a despairing pain that tore at you until it was unbearable. That stayed. That moved about with you wherever you went. That slept with you in your bed at night and was there waiting for you when you woke in the morning and this child would feel it, for she had loved her pa more than anyone in the world. But Lily Elliott was stubborn, strong, courageous and she would make it to the other side, as Molly Quinn had done. She was not so sure about Jane Elliott.

The funeral was lovely, they all agreed, since the whole neighbourhood turned out to follow the magnificent hearse to St Mary's Church where the service was to take place. Four black horses pulled it, plumes nodding, their coats with such a polish on them Lily wondered if Mrs Quinn had been out to them with her duster. On the coffin was a wreath of white flowers; Lily didn't know what they were or who had chosen them, for it was certain it had not been her mother. The doctor had been again that morning and Jane Elliott, under the influence of whatever it was he had given her, was as pale and calm as a lily. Mrs Quinn had dressed her in the appropriate black and draped her in a veil that covered her from the crown of her bonnet to her knees. She sat when told, stood when told, walked when told and, when told, climbed serenely into the carriage that followed the hearse. Mrs Quinn sat beside her, holding her hand lest the draught the doctor had given her wore off and God alone knew what she would do if she came to herself. Lily sat on Mrs Quinn's other side and stared numbly at the hearse within which her pa lay in his coffin and wished someone would hold her hand lest she slip away into some black place where no one would ever reach her again.

The Reverend Campbell met the hearse at the tiny arched gateway, watching gravely as the coffin was lifted out on to the shoulders of four men who turned out to be Mr Flanagan, Mr Porter, Johnno, and Mick, the last three crew of the *Lily-Jane*, and for a blessed moment Lily felt a tiny spasm of gladness, for her pa would have liked to think that he was to go to his last resting place carried by the seamen with whom he had sailed the waters. Johnno's face was awash with tears, for it was for him that Captain Elliott had died.

Inside the church Lily heard words spoken and her pa's name but she seemed to exist for the moment in a bubble of merciful silence which allowed her to keep a good grip on the realisation that her pa would soon be gone for ever. She huddled up to Mrs Quinn and though her heart felt as though it had a spear in it she took comfort from the closeness of the woman who had been, she knew it now, her one sure support all her life. Ma and Pa had always loved her, she knew that, but they had loved one another more and it had been only the scraps and crumbs of that love and caring that had been given to her. But Mrs Quinn, though she was not demonstrative and was downright blunt at times, had simply been there whenever some small crisis had turned up that Lily couldn't resolve on her own. She had never let Lily down, it was as simple as that and even now she was paying Lily the compliment of believing that she was strong enough to bear her loss with dignity. And so she would.

Her mother sat on Mrs Quinn's other side, her eyes on her husband's coffin but it was evident she was not really aware of where she was, or who she was, or even who was in the coffin. She rose obediently when Mrs Quinn told her and went with her out into the cold December drizzle that had begun to fall and it was not until she stood beside the open black grave in which her husband's coffin had just been lowered that she began to tremble. A handful of soil had been pressed into her black-gloved palm and Mrs Quinn was doing her best to persuade her to drop it on the coffin and it was then that she began to struggle. Not to get away but to fling herself into the grave. She began to weep loudly, throwing herself about in a frenzy and it was all Mrs Quinn and Bert Meadows, who stood nearby and had been pushed forward by his wife, could do to stop her downward spiral on to the coffin. Her voice pierced the reverent hush as she cursed fluently, loudly, harshly, furiously on the whim of fate that had taken from her the one complete, unchangeable love of her life.

It was over in thirty seconds, then she lapsed into the quiet hushed world where she was to stay for the rest of her life.

Lily watched her dispassionately, knowing with awful certainty that her mother would never be a woman again and that she would never be a child.

5

"Mrs Quinn."

"Yes?"

"D'you happen to know what happened to my pa's schooner?"

Molly Quinn turned to look at the child at the breakfast table, her hands stilled at their task of slicing bread, and for a moment she was startled by the intense expression on Lily's face. Poor little beggar. What in heaven's name was going through her head now? She'd been like a small ghost creeping round the house, saying little to anyone, grieving in silence for her pa who had been dead these six weeks now. Her ma was of no use to her at all, for her grief had sent her into another world where Molly was certain she searched for her husband who, if she couldn't have with her in hers she was eager to join in his. That was why Molly had to keep her under her eye all the time, even at night when she slept in a little truckle bed beside that of Jane Elliott. She hadn't been home to her place in Brooke Alley in all this time except to check that everything was all right but that had been for no more than a hurried hour while Mrs Meadows or Mrs Watson sat with Mrs Elliott. The trouble was, they didn't care for it, and they told her straight. She was no trouble, really, but she was so totally silent, not just speechless but as though she weren't there at all, her breast scarcely rising as she breathed. In fact Mrs Meadows said she gave her a terrible scare since she'd thought she'd stopped altogether. A house of mourning, but not the usual kind of mourning that afflicts a family where the shock wears off and life returns to normal. This was odd, creepy almost and it was the child she felt sorry for. She wondered what she was on about now.

She answered in what she thought was a comforting tone. "Nay, lass, I couldn't say burr I'm sure someone's lookin' after it."

"She."

"Yer what?"

"You always call boats 'she', Mrs Quinn, not 'it'."

"Yer don't say. Well, I still don't know, lass, an' that's a fact."

"Who d'you think could tell me, Mrs Quinn? You see, I'm worried about her."

"Her?"

Lily sighed and tried not to look too exasperated by Mrs Quinn's total lack of understanding of the jargon of the sea. She couldn't be blamed, poor thing, for though she was Liverpool born and bred, like Lily, she hadn't had much to do with the docks and the shipping that sailed in and out on every tide.

"The *Lily-Jane*, Mrs Quinn. My pa's schooner. It won't do her much good being tied up all this time at her berth." A look of excitement crossed her pale little face. "Unless Mr Porter's been taking her out. D'you think he might, Mrs Quinn?"

"Eeh, I don't know, child."

"Who d'you think would be the best person to ask, Mrs Quinn? If I was to go down to the docks, to the berth at Canning where she usually is, d'you think I might find out?"

"I couldn't say, lass. Wharrabout Mr Meadows? Don't 'e work at docks? 'Appen 'e'd know."

"What a good idea, Mrs Quinn. I'll go at once and ask him." Lily slipped down from her chair and immediately Villy stood up, ready to go with her wherever it might be, but Mrs Quinn had other ideas.

"No, yer don't, madam. Yer've ter be at school in 'alf an 'our an' beside, Mr Meadows will have long gone ter work."

The expression of bright alertness, which had been sadly lacking in the weeks since her pa's death, left Lily's face and she sighed deeply. The dog pushed her cold nose sympathetically into her hand, her devoted gaze turned up to say she fully understood, for hadn't they all been sad ever since the master had failed to return but surely it would do no harm to go out and have a game of ball or something to cheer themselves up.

"See, 'ere's a jug of 'ot water. You'd best go an' wash yer

'ands an' face, child, an' don't forget yer neck. Oh, an' say tara ter yer ma while yer up there. She's awake."

Was she though? Lily asked herself, her face screwed up into the worried, unchildlike expression that was becoming more and more habitual as the weeks passed. Carefully carrying the pretty, rose-painted jug, she trudged up the stairs, Villy at her heels, for Mrs Quinn had become much more lenient since Pa's death and even allowed the dog to sleep in Lily's room. Villy sat and watched her as she washed her face and hands in the bowl that matched the jug, pondering on the state of her ma and when she would be herself again. Even when she was not asleep was her ma awake and with them? She didn't think so. It was becoming more and more apparent with every passing day that Ma would never be any different. She and Pa had been the two halves of a whole and when Pa went Ma could not seem to function without that part of her that had been Pa. She sometimes seemed to know who she, Lily, was, and even spoke to her, asking how she was doing at school but Lily knew she was not really listening to the answers. Ma allowed herself to be hugged and kissed, not knowing, not caring really, Lily thought, how much Lily longed to be held on her lap and comforted. Lily wanted to talk about Pa, to ask Ma if she remembered this or that, the trip they had taken to the Clyde in Scotland, the jokes Pa made and his laughter, the puzzles he set them, all the lovely things that had made up the man her pa had been. It would keep him alive in some strange way if she and Ma could share the memories both of them had of him, but she was afraid to mention his name again. She had done it once. She had told Ma she would like to go down to the docks to see Pa's ship and would Ma come with her, at the time not realising how deep was the affliction her ma had suffered. She had been frightened when Ma had turned, very slowly, to stare at her, her eyes so dreadful Lily thought she had completely lost her mind. They were wide and blank, as though Ma didn't know her at all and was wondering what this stranger was doing in her bedroom, then she had opened her mouth wide and out of it had come some appalling sound, like an animal caught in a trap from which there is no escape. Mrs Quinn had come running and she had given Ma some of the medicine the doctor had left for her, indicating with an abrupt toss of her head that Lily was to leave the room. Lily hadn't spoken of Pa since.

She rubbed the slippery, lavender-scented soap between her hands, squeezing small bubbles through her fingers, wondering where these strange thoughts she had came from. She had always known that Ma and Pa were special, to each other and to her, but now, with Pa's death, she had begun to feel that not only was Pa dead, but so was her ma. She had wondered idly whether Ma knew what was to happen to the *Lily-Jane* but it seemed unlikely and, naturally, she could not bring herself to ask her, not after the last episode. There had been no one near them since the funeral except the neighbours, of course, and none of them would know. She supposed she could try Mr Meadows as Mrs Quinn had suggested, but he was a wheelwright. Nothing to do with actual ships though he was involved with the waggons that worked on the dock. He might know, she supposed, reaching for the fluffy towel that was draped on the rail beside the washstand.

"I think I'm going to have to find out for myself, Villy," she told the dog, who cocked her head enquiringly. "If you want a job doing properly, do it yourself, as Mrs Quinn says, and this is important. I want to know who's going to look after the *Lily-Jane* until I'm old enough, you see, though I don't know who's going to teach me now that Pa's gone, do you? Perhaps Mr Porter, or maybe I could persuade Ma to let me go to one of those schools like the Mechanics Institute where they teach navigation, astronomy and naval architecture." She sighed deeply, since she did not hold out much hope of that happening. It was such a long time before she would be considered old enough to go to sea and what was going to happen to Pa's ship until then?

She was allowed to walk to school on her own now. Or rather Mrs Quinn had no option but to let her, for Mrs Elliott couldn't be left, not just yet and the Goodwin School for Young Ladies was only at the bottom end of Walton Lane where it joined Everton Valley.

Grace and Evie were waiting for her at her gate, dressed in the plain brown calf-length dresses and elastic-sided boots, black, of course, their mothers thought suitable for school. Their skirts were fully gathered and calf-length, and beneath them six inches of modestly frilled pantaloon showed. Over this outfit they wore a simple pinafore, fastened at the back, frilled over the shoulders and a warm, hooded cape in a sensible navy blue.

Not so Lily Elliott. Her mother had laughed at the very idea of her daughter, who was so like herself, wearing such hideous garments and Lily was dressed in lavender blue velvet, apple green muslin, blossom pink shantung and primrose voile which was a very fine wool. In winter she wore a scarlet cloak of velvet lined with dove grey wool and a hood of white rabbit fur and in summer a dashing little jacket like the ones soldiers wore. She even had one trimmed with fur. She had a wide straw leghorn hat that tipped over her eyes and had long streamers of ribbons at the back, and pretty poke bonnets, the brims lined with white lace. She wore grey kid boots with stockings to match her dress, or boots made of coloured cloth with shiny leather toecaps and heels, frilled petticoats and pantaloons. All totally unsuitable, of course, for a child of ten, as her headmistress often remarked to the other teachers, but what could she do when Mrs Elliott insisted upon it and was so punctual with the not inconsiderable fees that were demanded. Lily was the envy of every girl in the school, though to tell the truth she would much rather have been wearing a pair of sea boots, a cap and a sailor's gansey! Today she was in her outdoor costume of misty blue, the jacket trimmed with buttons and cross-bands of velvet of a deeper blue. The full, gathered skirt reached the top of her kid boots and as it swung a fraction of lace petticoat showed above her lace-trimmed pantaloons.

When they reached the school gate Grace and Evie were flabbergasted when Lily coolly told them that she was not going to school today and if anyone asked they were to say she was not well.

"We can't do that, Lil," Evie quavered. "You know you have to have a note from your mother," then fell silent, remembering the state of Lily's mother.

"You could say you'd lost it."

"What, tell a lie?" Grace answered primly.

"It wouldn't be the first time, Grace Watson, and I'm sure it won't be the last. Go on. I'll . . . I'll make it worth your while."

"How?"

"Well, what have I got that you want? Whatever it is, you can have it."

"There's your new fur muff and bonnet that you got for Christmas."

Lily's face became stiff and her eyes frosty. "My pa bought me that before he . . . died. You know I can't give you that. Besides, your ma would notice," even if mine didn't, her manner implied.

"Well, that's all I want."

"You can want, then, because you're not getting it. I'll do this on my own."

"Do what?" Both girls edged closer to her, their eyes enormous in their fresh pink faces. "Where you going?"

"Never you mind. If you can't help me then you can go to hell for all I care."

"Lily Elliott!" they both gasped, then stood and watched her in awed disbelief as she stepped out in the direction of the town. Her head was high and her back straight and as she walked her long, silvery plait, so thick and heavy it lifted her chin, bounced vigorously between her shoulder blades. To be honest she was alarmed at her own daring, but there seemed to be no other way of easing the worry that had been plaguing her for weeks now. As she had said more than once, if you wanted something doing right, do it yourself, so she was.

It was a long walk down the length of Kirkdale Road, New Scotland Road, Scotland Road, Byrom Street and into Dale Street which led to Water Street and George's Dock. The *Lily-Jane* was usually tied up at Canning Dock Basin and this was where she was headed. It took her a long time to get there, for there was so much to see on the walk that she found herself stopping at every street corner. Naturally she had seen organ grinders before, and street musicians, hawkers, knife sharpeners and dancing bears, monkeys that jigged and dogs that did a polka on their hind legs but always from the hansom cab in which she rode with Ma and Pa, and she found her steps slowing continually as she stared at close quarters at the performers, human and animal. A blind man with a penny whistle pierced the air with a hauntingly sweet tune and round the hurdy-gurdy man, whose music vied with the penny whistler, a dozen ragged children danced in bare, calloused feet. She could have clapped her hands and joined them, it looked such fun but it soon became obvious that she herself was an object of their curiosity and she thought it might be wise to move on.

It was a grey February day, with a raw wind coming off the river but it in no way hindered Lily's enjoyment of this unexpected day out. It was a serious errand she was on, of course, but really, could you fail to have your heart lifted with joyful intoxication when your spirit rushed to meet the energy and vitality and noise which were all her young heart dreamed of? As she always did, and she had been here many times with her pa, she marvelled at the surge of humanity which sang and whistled and sawed and hammered on every spare bit of space on the docks. There were enormous men who carried bundles as big as themselves on their brawny shoulders, tipping them with ease on to waiting waggons. There were men with huge hammers striking blow after blow on some metal object, the sound of which made her head ring and she wondered why they stopped to stare as she went by them. They took off their caps and scratched their heads and muttered to one another.

"Good morning," she called out to them, enjoying herself for the first time since Pa died.

"Mornin'," they answered hesitantly, watching her as she tripped along towards the bridge that would take her into Canning Dock Basin. The river was a crowded highway carrying ships in and out of the estuary and she stood for a while watching them, dwelling on where they were going to and where they were coming from. She drew great breaths of the salty sea air into her lungs, turning her head to catch the sluggish breeze that carried it to her.

Her attention was caught by a great, almost totally silent crowd of people who were patiently waiting on the dockside. A uniformed policeman accompanied by a dock official in a peaked cap surveyed them, as though prepared to subdue any sign of the trouble that sometimes happened among these crowded and emotional farewells. Not that there seemed to be a spark of anything that might be called energy in this crowd. They were a mixed group, ladies and gentlemen, some of them, the ladies in elegant skirts edged with braid and wearing what was known as a "jacket-bodice", over which was worn a velvet-fringed, pelerine mantlet. Their bonnets tipped over their foreheads and were attached to a snood, or net, to hold their hair tidily, presumably for when they got aboard where the wind would be frolicsome. The gentlemen were stern, with long drooping moustaches, a wide-awake hat of felt and long greatcoats. But these passengers were rare, keeping themselves to themselves, for the rest of the crowd were of the working classes, shod in boots and gaiters, rough check trousers, ill-cut jackets, caps and mufflers. The women were in shawls, most of them with an infant tied into it and several poorly clad children at their rough skirts. The children grizzled fretfully and the women looked worn and haggard as though they hadn't had a square meal for a month. These would be steerage passengers, Lily decided, envying them even that; there was nothing she would like more than to be going with them, for she knew nothing of the perils of the high seas, among them disease and shipboard fever which often claimed more lives than accident or shipwreck. They sat about on boxes and crates, waiting to be told where they were to go which, it seemed to Lily, must be on the steamship that was berthed there. It had a name painted on its bow, the SS *Canadian*, and was to go to St John's in Newfoundland and Halifax, Nova Scotia, a passing dock labourer told her, obviously staggered to be accosted by such a pretty, daintily dressed child, looking round him as though to search out where she belonged. Newfoundland! Nova Scotia! The very names were exciting and she envied with all her heart these people who were to steam to these magical places. Mind you, she wouldn't care to go by steam. No, she would take the *Lily-Jane* and let the wind fill her sails, making her fly across the Atlantic Ocean until they came to the great Canadian seaports.

There were orange sellers moving about the crowds, cap merchants, Everton toffee sellers, vendors of ribbons and lace, nuts and gingerbread, ready to swarm all over the deck of the ship until the very last moment of departure. A man began to play a flute and as if it were a signal the women started to weep and, seeing their mothers in tears, the children joined in. It was a haunting little melody, one that Lily did not know and she found her own heart straining with sorrow, thinking of her pa who had gone and was never to return, as these people were going never to return.

She watched it all, unable to drag herself away until every last passenger was aboard and with a sudden lamenting wail from the women, as though they knew this was their last sight of everything that was familiar, the ship shuddered and began to pull away from the dock, edging into the river with a couple of little tugboats to assist her. Lily watched her sliding away into the February chill and mist, moving the silvery grey waters before her until, at last, she disappeared into the murk.

Lily sighed, then, finding to her surprise that her cheeks were wet with tears, she wiped them away and turned to the reason she had come here.

She knew every inch of the way. She had approached the docks down Water Street, walking along the strand until she reached George's Dock, cutting through a narrow passage at the side of the transit sheds and idling along the dock road which was intersected by railway lines. She had studied every ship tied up in George's Dock, all of them sailing ships and had been tempted to walk on into Strand Street to do the same at Canning Dock, but she had wasted enough time and must get to the other side of the bridge. By now it would have been discovered that she was not where she should be at school and Miss Goodwin would no doubt have contacted her ma. Or at least Mrs Quinn. There would be a great flurry of questions and answers, with poor Grace and Evie, who were known to be her particular friends, probably in tears and it was not their fault. She knew she should not be here, not by herself, but then none of them knew she had come. Nevertheless they would still be in a tear wondering what had happened to her. She must find out about the *Lily-Jane*, perhaps have a word with Mr Porter if he was around and then get right home before Mrs Quinn caused a commotion that might upset her ma.

Briskly she walked between the high walls of the warehouses, dodging the wheels of a portable crane which was lifting some heavy articles of machinery on to a berthed schooner. For a joyous moment she thought it might be the *Lily-Jane* but as she drew closer to the water's edge she saw the ship was called *Elvira*.

There were men discharging a cargo with a hand winch, neatly stacking bales of what smelled like coffee beans on to a waggon. The horse pulling it stood patiently between the shafts while from behind two more were being led by a couple of men, one astride the first horse's back, towards another waggon which was being got ready to receive a cargo of packing cases. A dog sat by a stack of crates, yawning and idly scratching itself, giving her a friendly wag of its tangled tail as she passed. A man shouted something, she didn't know what, or to whom but suddenly her arm was clutched savagely and she was lifted clear off the ground and thrown, there could be no other word for it, on to a pile of timber which stood waist-high to her left. Her hat fell over her eyes and her skirts flew up over her head so that she was temporarily blinded which made it worse and when she finally and indignantly disentangled herself she was more than ready to give a piece of her mind to whoever it was who had manhandled her.

Whoever it was spoke first.

"Yer wanner watch where yer walkin', queen, or there'll be a nasty accident. Didn't yer see them 'orses? One crack wi' one o' them feet'd knock yer senseless. I dunno what yer were thinking of, wanderin' around wi' yer 'ead in th'air. Any road, what's a lass like you doin' 'ere? It's norra place fer the likes o' you."

"Excuse me," she interrupted him tartly, "that is nothing to do with you and I'd be much obliged if you would lift me down and let me get on. I really haven't time to stop and talk—"

"Talk! I'm not talkin' ter yer, queen, I'm tellin' yer to go on back ter yer ma. This is no place fer a little lass like you. I can't think what yer pa's thinking on."

"My pa is dead."

"Oh, well, I'm sorry to 'ear that burrit mekks no difference. Yer shouldn't be 'ere. It's dangerous at best o' times but fer a girl like yersen . . ."

"Oh," she said airily, standing up in readiness to be lifted down, "I'm quite used to the docks. I've been here many times."

"Is tha' so?"

The man who had lifted her on to the pile of timber, apparently out of harm's way, or so he seemed to be telling her, had a face the colour of amber and in it his eyes were the palest blue she had ever seen, just as though years in the sun had bleached the colour out of them. He was a big man, heavy in the shoulders and chest, and his hands were quite enormous. He made no attempt to lift her down and their faces were almost on a level, for he was tall. His hair was like the colour of the corn that grew in the field opposite her house. He was dressed in the casual gansey, drill trousers, sea boots and a peaked cap like the one Mr Porter wore and she knew he was a sailor.

"Well," he said. "Are yer gonner tell me what yer up to?"

He smiled into her face, his hands on the stacked timber, one on either side of her so that she could not get down. She was not frightened of him though.

"That's my business," she told him haughtily.

"Is tha' so? Well, yer'd best mekk it *my* business an' all or I'm fetchin' 't nearest copper. If yer up ter no good it'd best be reported." But there was a gleam in his eye that told her he didn't really mean it, not about the copper. With a lithe jump he was up beside her, seating himself and then inviting her to do the same, with their legs dangling over the edge of the stacked timber.

"Yer a lovely little lass, queen, an' them duds yer've gorron . . . well, I've never seen the like, but yer 'adn't oughter be wanderin' round 'ere on yer own. Where yer from?"

"Well . . . you'll promise not to fetch the copper?"

"Right, if yer'll tell me wha' yer doin' 'ere an' then let me tekk yer back ter where yer belong. Me name's Liam, by't way. Liam O'Connor."

Gravely she turned and put out her hand. "How do you do, Mr O'Connor." He smiled and took it, swallowing it up in his own enormous one.

"An' what's your name, child?"

"Lily Elliott."

"Well, I'll call yer Lily if you'll call me Liam."

Lily was intensely gratified. She had never addressed a grownup by their christian name before and somehow it made her feel very grown up herself. Her face glowed into an enchanting smile and her silvery grey eyes turned at once into what was almost lavender. The man caught his breath, for he had never met anyone quite like her. She was as exquisite as a dainty bit of a flower, her name very appropriate, for she was like the wild lily of the valley which grew in the woods around his home in West Derby, or a piece of lace, the sort his grandmother made and which was as fine as gossamer. But what the devil was such a child doing here on these rough docks where men swore and relieved themselves with no thought for any of the niceties a child like this would be used to?

"Right then, Lily, now p'raps yer'll tell me wha' yer up to?"

She sighed deeply, gazing with those astonishing lavender grey eyes, which had become cloudy with some deep-felt emotion, at the dog that had now come to sit at their feet as though hoping for a titbit. She shook her head and her hat, which she had replaced to its correct position, bobbed precariously.

"I'm looking for the *Lily-Jane*. She's a schooner and—"

"Aye, lass, I know 'er. Lovely little ship, she is, an' I'd be glad ter sail in her meself."

"Would you, Liam?" She nearly knocked him off his perch with the brilliance of her smile.

"I would tha', Lily. Tidiest little schooner this side o't channel."

"Oh, isn't she, that's why I must find her. D'you happen to know where she's berthed, Liam? I would be so grateful."

"Eeh, Lily, she's not 'ere any more."

"Not here?" Her face paled dramatically, then cleared as a thought occurred to her. "Has Mr Porter taken her out then?"

"Nay, lass, I don't know owt about a Mr Porter. I only know Mr Crowther took her a few weeks back."

"Who's . . . who's Mr Crowther?"

"He's her owner, lass."

6

Mrs Quinn had been afraid she would hurt herself, or if not herself, her ma, and had it not been for the big man who brought her home, she would not have managed.

The cab had drawn up at the front door just as Mrs Watson was saying she thought Mrs Quinn had better send for the police. Lily had been missing for five hours. God only knew where she might have got to, or into whose hands she had fallen. Mrs Watson shuddered dramatically, for they had nothing to go on but the statements made by her Grace and Evie Meadows. Lily had walked to school with them as usual, the girls told them, then she had calmly announced she wasn't going in and asked them to lie for her to Miss Goodwin. Naturally, they wouldn't, Grace told them self-righteously, and it was not until the register was called and Lily was found to be missing, with no explanation of why, that she had told Miss Goodwin what Lily had told them. They had been brought home, both Grace and Evie, Evie in a flood of tears, for she could not be comforted, nor reassured that Lily was bound to be found soon, and was thought to be better off at home. Naturally, Mrs Elliott could not be consulted, Mrs Quinn made that very plain to Miss Goodwin, since her health had been very delicate ever since Captain Elliott had died, but she would let Miss Goodwin know the moment that Lily came home. Mrs Quinn had a fair idea where she might have gone, of course, particularly after the discussion they had had only this morning about Captain Elliott's boat.

They had a terrible shock when the child burst in on them, closely followed by an enormous man who was a total stranger. Mrs Watson was seated at Mrs Quinn's table in Mrs Quinn's kitchen, which was how they had both come to think of her place in the Elliott household since the captain had gone. Not that Mrs Quinn would presume to take over if Mrs Elliott were any different. If she came downstairs, for instance, or showed some renewed sign of interest in the affairs of her own home, which she didn't. It had become a sort of habit for Mrs Watson to take a cup of tea with Mrs Quinn on most days. Mrs Quinn was glad of her company since it was a bit of a humdrum sort of life with no one to talk to but a mindless woman and a ten-year-old child. Mrs Elliott had once been a sweet-natured lass with a good sense of humour, ready for a bit of a gossip as long as it was not offensive or likely to hurt anyone. And when the captain was home the house had been filled with laughter and music, since Mrs Elliott played the piano, encouraging him and the child to sing. The house had rung with "Are You Going to Scarborough Fair?", "Cockles and Mussels" and "Greensleeves"; noisy, cheerful, a lovely place to work but now it was like a bloody morgue and though she knew it was not quite right to invite Mrs Watson in to a house which was not, strictly speaking, hers, she was right glad of a bit of ordinary conversation. She was not a garrulous woman. She did not fraternise with anyone back at Brooke Alley but she missed the general bustle, the noise, the whistling and even the cursing, and it was not the same when Victoria, Mary or Alice came here to Walton Lane, which they were now forced to do on their days off. It was as though there were someone with a dread, even fatal illness upstairs and the girls felt the need to speak in whispers almost. They drank a cup of tea with her and told her what had been happening in the kitchens of the grand houses in which they were employed, but she noticed they always appeared to be glad to get away and could you blame them? They were young, attractive girls with their daddy's colouring, lively, and on their day off did not really want to sit in what they obviously felt to be a house of mourning, which it was. Well, there was nothing to be done about it, not until Mrs Elliott picked up, and Molly Quinn was sadly aware that that was very unlikely.

When the back door burst open they both gaped at the child as she erupted into the kitchen. Her face was the colour of dough, and her eyes were huge and glittering. Mrs Quinn had been about to put on her coat and slip down to the police station on St Domingo Road to tell them of Lily's disappearance and her belief that she would be found at Canning Dock Basin where her pa's boat was supposed to be moored, leaving Mrs Watson to hold the fort, and for a moment she stood there, her right arm in one sleeve, the other behind her back. The dog, frightened by the sudden clatter, since she had been peacefully sleeping on the mat before the kitchen range, sprang to her feet and began to bark hysterically and when, a second or two later, the big man came through the door, his hat in his hand, his face working with some emotion neither of the women cared to recognise, it was all they could do not to scream out loud.

"Dear God in heaven." Mrs Watson rolled her eyes in the direction of her own home next door, wondering if her Alf was back from work yet and if so could he get here in time to prevent all their throats being cut. She placed her hand on her heart, which threatened to stop beating but the man put out both hands in a placatory manner.

"I'm that sorry, ladies," he gasped. "I thought I 'ad 'er but she slipped out o' me 'ands like she were a little fish. She's that mad wi' 'er ma an'—"

"Oo the 'ell are you?" Mrs Quinn was beginning to say, ready to pick up a handy frying pan, for big as he was she'd clout him one if he proved dangerous, but the child began to yell, incomprehensible words bubbling from between her lips. Her face changed from mushroom white to a fiery red and spittle flew from her mouth in what seemed to be rage so hot and uncontrollable Mrs Watson stepped back out of range of it.

Words began to be recognised. "She's sold Pa's boat. I'll never forgive her . . . how could she? . . . knew how much I loved it . . . mine . . . mine. Pa would have wanted . . . for me . . . knew I loved the sea . . . and now what shall I do? I hate her, hate her . . . never speak to her again as long as I live. I loved the *Lily-Jane* . . . loved her. What shall I do? Oh, what shall I do?" she finished on a wail of torment. She jerked and trembled, her arms flinging about like a puppet whose puppeteer has lost control, her head snapping convulsively on her neck, her teeth beginning to chatter, and to the astonishment of the two women the man stepped forward and, with a sort of tender murmur, lifted her up and drew her into his arms. He held her to him, her arms about his neck, her face tucked beneath his chin, her cries of anguish muffled against his strong brown throat.

"There, lovebud, there, there. Yer mustn't tekk on so. I told yer in't cab there'd be a good reason an' yer've not 'eard yer ma's side yet. There'll be a decent explanation, you'll see. Yer must consider yer ma in this. What use would a schooner be to 'er? She'd 'ave no choice but ter sell 'er."

Without a by your leave, or even a glance at the two frozen-faced women, he sat down in what was considered to be Mrs Quinn's own special chair and, settling her on his lap, held Lily to him, brushing back her dishevelled hair from her flushed face with a big, gentle hand, and even kissing her forehead. She wept inconsolably, and once struggled to get away from him, declaring that she was going upstairs to tell her ma exactly what she thought of her, but the big man shushed her and patted her shoulder, quietening her until she lay still, hiccuping gently on to his chest.

It was then Mrs Quinn found her voice.

"Right then, we'll 'ave an explanation, if yer please, 'ooever yer are, an' I'd be obliged if yer'd 'and tha' there child over ter me. I don't know what the 'ell's bin goin' on 'ere burr I mean ter find out. See, purr 'er down an' get yer bum off my chair. Mrs Watson, run 'ome, if yer please, an' get yer 'usband ter fetch police, and you, Lily, come over 'ere."

The man looked up and smiled and really if she hadn't been a married woman Mrs Watson would have gone weak at the knees. She actually *did* go weak at the knees, for she'd never seen anything like it. His face sort of lit up, the eyes in it turning from the palest blue to an unbelievable violet just like those that grew in the woods on the far side of the front field. From round them fanned out deep creases which were duplicated in a slash down each side of his mouth. His teeth were a startling white against the sun-bronzed tint of his skin but it was the sense of good humour, of patience and yet strength, of easy-going tolerance which she knew would draw both men and women to him, and which was drawing her now, and she a married woman of thirty-five with two children. She had not thought him a handsome man when he had stood so alarmingly enormous in the doorway, but his male attraction was a tangible thing and one she could sense even Mrs Quinn felt. His hair was like corn silk, falling in an untidy tumble of short curls about his head. He continued to smile, a curious whimsical smile as though he knew this was a little out of the ordinary but he had a perfectly reasonable explanation which he was about to give them.

"Me name's Liam O'Connor, ladies, an' I 'ope you'll forgive this intrusion inter yer 'ome but I found this little lass down't by Canning Dock and I brought 'er 'ome. As yer can see, she were right upset an' I couldn't let 'er wander off an 'er own, could I? I reckon she'd be best in bed, wouldn't yer, lovebud," bending his head to Lily's feverish face. "She's 'ad a bad shock but she's calm now."

"I need . . . to ask . . . Ma why she . . . sold Pa's boat, Liam. Please, I need to ask her why she would . . . do such a thing . . . a cruel thing."

"No, yer don't. Yer need ter be in yer bed, that's where, an' this lady," bowing courteously in Mrs Quinn's fascinated direction, "will put yer there. Tomorrer'll do fer questions."

Lily sat up and stared tearfully into Liam's face, calmer now, but still inclined to tremble. He kept his arm about her, just like her pa used to do, Molly Quinn remembered thinking, as the child looked up at him earnestly.

"Will you come tomorrow, Liam, will you?"

"Nay, lass, I'm sure these ladies'll look after yer."

"No . . . no . . ." Her voice rose again dangerously and he shushed her gently, looking up apologetically to Molly Quinn and Lizzie Meadows. He gave a little shrug as though asking them what he should do. Though neither of them could have explained why, they both nodded acquiescently, trusting him. After he had gone they did their best to reason it out with one another but could come to no logical explanation as to why. He was a seafaring man, that was pretty evident, but they knew nothing about seafaring men, only Captain Elliott and this chap was nothing like that, but though they had never clapped eyes on him before, they found themselves agreeing that he should come tomorrow. The child was happy with that. Well, not exactly happy, for her devastation over the loss of her pa's boat so soon after the loss of her pa would be a sorrow she would carry for a long time, you could see that. Her narrow shoulders were slumped and her head bowed most pathetically as though she were being asked to shoulder a burden too heavy for her fragile strength. Poor little blighter. What was to happen to her?

She wanted Liam to carry her upstairs but he was firm with

her, telling her to be a good girl and go with Mrs Quinn, who had by now introduced herself, and promising to come back tomorrow. He didn't know what for, his helpless shrug and wry look told Mrs Quinn, but if it helped the child in her grief how could he refuse? That's if it was all right with Mrs Quinn, Lily must realise that, he told her. He was to sail tomorrow on the evening tide. No . . . no, they could not talk about that now. She must go to her bed this minute and tomorrow he would tell her all about the vessel he was to sail in, where she was to go and . . . yes, all right, when he would be in Liverpool again.

Without another word, she went, good as gold, believing him, trusting him, satisfied that he meant what he said.

She turned on the stairs as he watched her go, her hand in Mrs Quinn's. "What time will you come, Liam?" she asked him, her face tranquil for the moment.

"Well, I'm not sure . . ."

"Please, Liam, then I can look out for you. I shan't go to school, shall I, Mrs Quinn?" looking up resolutely into Mrs Quinn's face.

"Well, I don't know . . ."

She began to twist about on the stairs, the tranquillity gone and at once Liam O'Connor, recognising what was in her as no one else had, even Molly Quinn, smiled reassuringly.

"Will ten o'clock be too early?" looking enquiringly at Mrs Quinn.

Lily answered him. "No, come at nine if you want, Liam. Come for breakfast, if you like. He can, can't he, Mrs Quinn?"

"Well . . ."

"Please, Liam."

"No, lovebud, I can't. I'll be 'ere at ten. Now go on like a good little lass an' do as Mrs Quinn tells yer."

Mrs Quinn, who was not sure this perfect stranger, agreeable as he was, should be calling the captain's daughter "lovebud", frowned, then sighed, for if it helped the child to get over this second dreadful blow, did it matter? Who cared what happened to her now, except herself? And all that about the captain's boat being sold must be sorted out, for she knew for a fact, none better, that there had been no one to this house to discuss it, or even, now she came to think about it, to discuss *anything* to do with money. Surely a . . . a solicitor – was that right? – should have been round to talk about the captain's affairs and all the dozen and one things that needed to be discussed when someone died. Well, someone with property, that is, or money or something like that. It was six weeks now and the tin box on the kitchen mantelpiece, which the captain had called the "housekeeping box" and in which he left enough money to tide them over until he came home, was nearly empty. He had paid all the bills, she knew that, and Mrs Elliott had an allowance from which she bought her clothes and any personal thing she might need. She never went near the housekeeping box since she took no interest in the housekeeping, leaving it all to Molly Quinn who, she had said laughingly, knew far more about that kind of thing than she did.

Lily slept the clock round plus several hours and it was almost eight thirty when she woke. For a while she lay there, burrowing into the warmth of her bed, her eyes on the ceiling where shadows danced, created by the sunlight in the leaves of the beech tree outside the window. Villy slept curled up in a ball at her side and Lily put a hand out of the blankets to smooth her rough fur. The dog lifted her head at once and in her eyes was the look of devoted adoration she kept for her young mistress. It comforted Lily. No one loved her like Villy did. She supposed Ma still had some affection for her, deep down under the layers of suffering Pa's death had encased her in, but somehow, today, though she remembered that the *Lily-Jane* was no longer hers, for that was how she had thought of the schooner since Pa died, hers, she had the feeling that something nice was going to happen today. At once a pair of smiling blue eyes shone through the murk which her life had become and she sat up eagerly and swung her legs out of bed. Ten o'clock! He was to come at ten o'clock and for the first time since Pa died she would be able to talk about ships and all the things that had interested her to do with the docks and cargoes and ports and tides and every other fascinating subject which had been sadly lacking all these weeks. Liam was coming. Liam would be here for ten o'clock and she must be ready. She could hear Mrs Quinn talking to Ma in the next room while she coaxed her to wash and dress and she wondered if perhaps Ma might be persuaded to come downstairs to meet Liam; then, quite surprisingly, she decided she didn't want Ma to come downstairs and meet Liam, though for the life of her she couldn't have said why. Of course Ma wouldn't be interested in all the things that she and Liam would talk about, would she, so she would be much better off where she was.

She was hopping about at the window at nine thirty, driving Mrs Quinn to distraction, she said, and poking her nose against the window glass which Mrs Quinn had just cleaned wouldn't make him come any faster. Molly Quinn was having second thoughts about the advisability of letting a common seaman into the Elliott home, a common seaman they had none of them ever seen before. He might be a rogue or a bully or, worse, a despoiler of women, though he had brought the child home safely enough which many men would not have bothered to do. She had forgotten the effect Liam O'Connor had had on her and Mrs Watson yesterday or if she had not forgotten it she could not believe she had ever experienced it. She had forgotten the pleasing shape of his firm mouth, the brown smoothness of his shaved cheek and his odd, slanting smile that had so mesmerised them, and it was not until she saw him come striding down Walton Lane from the direction of town that it come flooding back to her. Lily was out of the parlour, across the shining black and white squares of the hallway and, flinging open the door, was halfway down the garden path and would, if she, Molly Quinn, not restrained her, have thrown herself into his arms. What on earth was the matter with the child? she asked herself in amazement, then fell, like Lily herself, under his spell again. But "spell" was not really the right word to describe what he had, she decided, as he wished her a pleasant good morning. He was not a charmer, one of those men who set out coolly to please a woman. Whatever he had it was natural and though she was not a woman to take to strangers in the first moment of meeting, she'd taken to him. Though he was not a gentleman, far from it, he was gentleman*like*. That was the only way she could describe him. He had been polite with her and Mrs Watson, and firm with the child and though he might have taken advantage of what had been a strained and awkward situation, he had not done so. It was not his choice to be here this morning. In fact he had refused at first and it was only Lily's obvious distress that had brought him. A good heart then, and intelligent enough to know that he was out of place here, out of his depth really, with a little girl who had apparently taken him into her heart like a small kitten that needs a loving hand to comfort it.

"Come in, Liam. I've been waiting for you," Lily told him artlessly, her eyes enormous with excitement in her pale face, putting her small hand in his big one and drawing him into the parlour. "Mrs Quinn has made some scones and jam tarts. Won't you take off your coat and sit here by the fire. Mind, Villy, get out from under Liam's feet. She does love to lie almost in the hearth," she explained, "and if we didn't watch her she can get singed. Now I'll sit here," indicating a pouffe at Liam's feet from where she evidently thought she would get the best view of him. She smiled and put her elbows on her knees and her chin in her hands and waited for him to begin.

Liam O'Connor looked down into the lovely, expectant face of the child who apparently was waiting for him to divulge some stupendous news about the *Lily-Jane* and wondered how he was to tell her what he had been told yesterday afternoon. How was he to advise the woman in the kitchen, the housekeeper it seemed she was, and the child's mother, who he had not yet seen, what they should do now, and he wondered why he should feel so protective of this child who, this time yesterday, he had not even known existed.

"Now, Liam," Lily began gravely, "I want to know all about your life as a seaman, like where you are to sail to today, what's the name of your ship and what sort of ship is she? How long have you been at sea and where you learned to be a sailor and did you know that the only thing *I* ever wanted to do is to be a sailor? I meant to go with Pa . . . when I was old enough but now . . ."

She cleared her throat and blinked, determined not to weep, for she wanted him to know that she was not a child who cried for nothing. She must convince him that she was a sort of half-grown-up kind of girl who must be taken seriously.

Mrs Quinn came in with a tray and set it on the round, chenille-covered table, then poured out the tea, handing a cup to the big man and inviting him to try one of her scones. Today he wore a decent grey jacket over a spanking clean white shirt, a neat black tie, a waistcoat, also grey, and a pair of check woollen trousers in a mixture of greys and black. He had taken off his short overcoat and placed it on a chair. She noticed he wore no hat. He looked smart and clean, not exactly fashionable, for gentlemen today, real gentlemen, wore top hats and frock-coats, but he was very presentable. You knew he was a man from the labouring classes who had come up in the world, the way he spoke told her that, and she wondered how he had done it and what his position in life now was.

Liam O'Connor was twenty-one years old and was a self-educated man who could neither read nor write until, at the age of ten, he had made the decision that if he was to get anywhere in this world he could not do it if he was illiterate. He had gone wherever a bit of learning could be found. Mostly Sunday School, and once, when his grandmother, with whom he had then lived, had a few bob to spare, to the village school in West Derby. It didn't matter what it was, an old newspaper, a dog-eared racing journal, a page out of a magazine found wrapped about a piece of fish from the market, he pored over it, deciphering every word even if the word made no sense to him. Within a year he was being loaned books by the teacher at the Sunday School he attended in West Derby, simple, easy-to-read and understand books at first, but as he soaked it all up, everything he was told, and retained it, he was started on *Masterman Ready* by Captain Frederick Marryat, *Waverley* and *Ivanhoe* by Sir Walter Scott, all heady stuff to the young lad who had spent the first ten years of his life in total ignorance of what went on beyond the perimeter of West Derby.

He was employed by then as a dock labourer, since he was as big as a fully grown man and could do a man's job, but the ships, the river, the smell of the cargoes and the seamen's talk on the docks fascinated him as nothing had ever done before and he wanted to be part of it. The same Sunday School teacher, on learning of the boy's wish to go to sea, had enrolled him in evening classes at the Liverpool Mechanics Institute where he was taught the rudiments of navigation and seamanship and on 22 November 1844, at the age of thirteen, he signed an agreement with Captain Oliver Jenkins to become an apprentice seaman for a period of five years. The indenture was crowded with the activities he should not indulge in, which included frequenting taverns, the games of dice or cards or gambling of any kind, and in return Captain Jenkins would teach him the business of being a mariner, would feed him and give him medical or surgical aid should he need it and would pay him the sum of £30 for his five years of apprenticeship.

He was intelligent, shrewd, conscientious, hardworking, ambitious, tough, the latter essential in a world where young boys were thought to be fair game in the absence of women. His size was a great advantage. He learned to fight, dirty at times. He had to if he wanted to survive, and survive he did and at the age of twenty-one he had his Master's Certificate. He was now first mate on the British and North American packet ship *Caledonia* which carried the Royal Mail, sailing from Liverpool to Boston and on to Halifax. The *Caledonia* was a passenger ship sailing on the 3rd and the 18th of every month – unless these dates fell on a Sunday – and in the winter months, December, January, February and March, only one mail, that of the 3rd, was despatched.

It was 3 February today and if he was not on board within the next two hours he would be in trouble.

Lily listened with rapt attention, her eyes like huge saucers filled with floating stars, her rosy pink mouth dropping open in awe as he told her of his life and how he had got to the position he had and all the time he was wondering how he was to get Mrs Quinn on her own to give her the news that Captain Richard Elliott had been so heavily in debt when he died that the chances of his widow having any sort of an income were absolutely nil. Indeed, his informant had told him, she would soon be asked to leave this house if the rent was not immediately paid. Captain Elliott had paid it up to the end of January but there was a distinct possibility that the bailiffs would be in by the end of the week. The schooner had been taken as part of his debt, but it seemed there were others. Liam was aware now that there was something seriously wrong with Lily's mother, for why was she not here when her child needed her?

He sighed deeply and turned to Molly Quinn.

73

7

She had no choice but to take them to Brooke Alley. She had refused the loan Liam O'Connor had offered her, appalled at the thought of borrowing from a man she barely knew, and though he had begged her to take it, to "tide her over" until he got back from America, she declined so coolly he knew he had offended her. Of course, she had not known what was to happen then. He had been unable to persuade her and, having to get back to the *Caledonia* unless he wanted to lose his job, he had had to leave.

Lily had been white-faced and stunned when he left, though she had understood that he had no choice. For twenty-four hours it had been almost like having Pa back again, bringing with him all the vigour and excitement and the special feeling of rightness that anything to do with the dockland and the ships berthed there gave her. She did not wonder, like Liam O'Connor did, about what had drawn them together, for, with a child's acceptance of matters which might seem curious to an adult, it had not appeared at all strange. After all, he was a seafaring man, like Pa, and it seemed only natural to her that he and she were in accord about so many things pertaining to what was the most important thing in both their lives. Ships! She had his promise that the moment he docked he would come and visit her again and so she settled down to make the best of things until that day.

Mrs Quinn was upstairs with Ma when the front doorknocker rat-tatted noisily the following Saturday morning.

"Answer it, will you, lass?" Mrs Quinn shouted down the stairwell, her voice sounding somewhat strained, for she was having a more than difficult time persuading Jane Elliott to wash herself and dress in the gown Molly had laid out for her. Her mistress was sitting, as usual, in the rocking-chair which was where she spent most of her day, staring out of the window into the lane where children were playing, and not for the first time Molly came to the conclusion that she was still watching for the captain to come home. Not that she said anything. She answered when she was spoken to, questions like would she fancy a bit of fish for her tea, what gown should Molly put out for her, didn't she think it was a lovely day and what about a bit of a walk to the end of the lane? She was vague and slow, deliberating on what the correct answers should be, just as though she were dragging herself painfully back from the world in which she had dwelled in merciful oblivion for weeks now, turning her head with an almost perceptible creak to look at Molly, then, with a polite smile and bowing of her head she would agree with whatever was said. She refused to go out of the house, though, and Molly was inclined to think that it was because she was afraid the captain would come home and not find her there. She did make a bit of an effort when the child came up, agonisingly clearing her mind, doing her best to take an interest in what her daughter said to her but Molly knew she was thankful when Lily left the room and she could drift back to the vacuum in which she existed. Molly had hoped that with the passage of time she might pull herself together, which was how Molly saw it, and wake up to her responsibility for the little girl who, it was beginning to appear, had lost not only her pa, but her ma.

There were two men on the doorstep, big men with expressions on their faces that said they expected trouble wherever they went and were well qualified to deal with it. They seemed somewhat surprised to be faced with a small, beautifully dressed little girl, but, as though it were a routine they had developed, one of them put his foot in the door so that it could not be closed.

"Is yer mam in?" he asked her, his face as blank as an unused sheet of paper.

Lily looked from one stony face to the other and a small frisson of disquiet ran through her. There had been so many bad things happen to her recently that anything a bit out of the ordinary, which these two men were, alarmed her. Villy was at her feet, ready to dart at anything or anybody that might threaten her young mistress and for some reason her snout drew back over her teeth and she gave a warning growl. Lily didn't know what to say, how to answer the question, for though her ma *was* in, she wasn't really, was she?

"She's not well," she answered vaguely, hoping that that would satisfy them and they would go away but apparently it didn't. She didn't know who they were or why they were asking for Ma but she didn't like them.

They exchanged glances, then the one who seemed to be the spokesman spoke again.

"Oo's at 'ome, then?"

"Pardon?"

"Don't tell me yer lookin' after yer ma all on yer own, queen. There must be someone in charge, like."

"Well, Mrs Quinn is—"

"Right then, we'll 'ave a word wi' Mrs Quinn," and before she could even shout up the stairs to Mrs Quinn that there were two men to see her they were inside, pushing past her and the snarling dog with as much concern as though two little birds stood in their path. They looked about them in an assessing sort of way, fingering the velvet curtain that was pulled over the front door at night to keep out the draught, running a hand over her ma's walnut hallstand, even lifting out one of the half-dozen walking sticks that were kept in it. It had a silver handle and the shaft was made of ebonised wood. It was a handsome thing and had been much loved by her pa.

"Don't touch that," she snapped, unable to bear the sight of it in the rough, calloused hands of this big . . . well, she could only call him a lout and what he was doing here she couldn't imagine. "That belonged to my pa and he wouldn't like it if it was broken."

"I'm not about ter break it, queen, believe me. It belongs ter't courts now, or will do soon as we get this lot sorted out." The men smiled at one another in an unpleasant way, then moved on to run a speculative eye over the framed pictures that hung on the wall, the rug that ran down the centre of the hall, the ornaments that stood on a small, rectangular table and the barometer that her pa had tapped every day he was home.

"D'yer mind tellin' me what's goin' on 'ere?"

The voice at the top of the stairs startled them for a moment but they continued with their appraisal of the contents of the hall before answering in a kind of casual way that seemed to say they had every right to be here, which it seemed they had.

"Bailiffs, queen. Appointed by't court ter collect monies owed by a certain Captain Richard Elliott, deceased. Now, if yer can produce what's owin' we'll be on our way an' that's th' end of it. Burrif yer can't then we 'as ter take what's owin' in kind, if yer get me drift. An' then there's rent which is two weeks be'ind, which means yer've ter be out right away, burrif yer can settle up now – see, 'ere's what's owed – then we'll leave yer in peace."

He showed his big yellow teeth in what was supposed to be a smile, and so did his companion, not friendly smiles at all, Lily thought, a bit frightening really, and what he had said about Pa owing money couldn't be right and Mrs Quinn would tell him so.

Molly Quinn came slowly down the stairs and took Lily's hand in hers, holding it protectively against her white apron. She did not speak. What was there to say? She did not even look at the papers the bailiff held out to her, for she hadn't more than a few quid in the whole world and neither had Mrs Elliott. She had nothing but what these men could see and some nice pieces of jewellery which, the moment she had a chance, Molly's stunned but slowly recovering mind told her, she meant to hide in her corset, for there was nothing more certain than the fact that what she had dreaded, what had niggled at the back of her mind for weeks but which she had kept firmly there, was about to happen. She'd known for certain as soon as the big man had told them about the boat. That had been taken and now the home and all its contents which the Captain and Mrs Elliott had gathered about them over the past eleven years were to go too.

"Can yer pay up, Mrs Elliott?" one of the men asked patiently.

"I'm not Mrs Elliott. I'm housekeeper." Her voice was hollow, totally without expression and Lily looked up at her anxiously.

"We'd best see Mrs Elliott then, an' can we 'urry this up? We've other folk ter deal with."

"Other folk ter turn out inter't street, yer mean?"

"Well, yer could purrit like that but we 'ave a job ter do so if yer'd fetch Mrs Elliott I'd be obliged."

"She's . . . not well. She in 'er bed. Anythin' yer want ter say, say it ter me."

"Well, there's nowt ter say. It's the cash in me 'and or yer'd best pack yer bags and bugger off."

Lily gasped, looking from one man to the other, waiting for Mrs Quinn to give them a piece of her mind for swearing. She still could not understand what was going on. These men seemed to be threatening Mrs Quinn and instead of standing up for herself, which she always did if argued with, she was backing away and taking Lily with her.

"I've ter go an' see ter Mrs Elliott," she was saying. "She'll be wonderin' . . ."

"Go wi' 'er, Bert. There's no knowin' what trick she's up to. We know 'em all, lady, an' if yer think yer can put one over on us, then yer can think again. Yer not gerrin outer our sight."

"An' if *you* think I'm allowing two thugs like you inter a lady's bedroom yer sadly mistaken. Mrs Elliott's not yet gorrover the death of 'er 'usband an' is still under the doctor. God knows what might 'appen to 'er if I was to let yer in, so you do wha' yer come ter do an' leave us alone."

"We can't do that, lady. We're 'ere ter see the law's done right, which means recovering the deceased's goods an' chattels an' escortin' yer from't premises an' if yer purrup a fight we'll 'ave ter send for't scuffers."

"Please yerselves but yer not goin' inter Mrs Elliott. Norrif I 'ave ter knock yer down these bloody stairs meself."

All the time she was speaking Molly was moving slowly up the stairs, drawing Lily with her, step by slow step, and following her, still hesitant, for she was like a spitting she-cat, was one of the big men. The other had started in a leisurely fashion to take down the pictures, to roll up the mat, to gather the walking sticks, piling them on top of the hallstand. He had opened the front door preparatory to carrying them out, revealing a small crowd of interested neighbours on the pavement beyond the gate. Behind them was an empty cart pulled by a sturdy horse.

With one hand Lily clung to Mrs Quinn while the other had hold of Villy's collar. It was awkward going up the stairs backwards and she and Mrs Quinn kept catching their heels in the hems of their skirts. The sunlight falling through the coloured glass in the window at the turn of the stairs fell on the menacing face of the man following them, changing it from red to green and blue, but at the same time it seemed to blind him and when he put up his hand to shield his eyes Mrs Quinn whipped up the last few stairs, dragging Lily and the dog with her. Like a flash she was in her ma's bedroom and the door was locked behind her. Ma never even turned round.

"Quick, lamb," Mrs Quinn gasped, calling her again by that name which Lily knew meant she was highly agitated, "open yer ma's jewellery box an' purras much as yer can in the pocket of yer drawers." Lily gaped at her, for surely she had gone off her head, but Mrs Quinn grasped her roughly, spinning her round to her ma's dressing-table where the jewellery box stood. As she was speaking and tossing Lily about like a rag doll she was opening the front of her own modest bodice, pulling it out at the bottom from the band of her skirt. Her apron got in the way and with a muttered oath she tore it off.

"Don't stand there gawpin', lass. Quick . . . fer God's sake, be quick. See, stuff some down 'ere," indicating the top of her corsets which she was loosening with fumbling fingers. Lily had begun to shake in fright, for she had no idea what was wrong with Mrs Quinn. In a daze she did as she was told, thrusting rings and bracelets and a lovely collar of clear red stones into the pocket in her drawers where her handkerchief usually went. Mrs Quinn was doing the same, only into the top of her corsets, but when the jewellery box was empty she sort of had a fit, or so it seemed to Lily.

"Dear God, wharram I doin'?" she moaned. "They'll know if it's empty, that we've took 'em. Put some back, for Christ's sake," and with a swift movement, as the man began to hammer on the door, she flung a handful back into the box. She was muttering to herself as she did up her bodice and fastened her apron about her curiously swollen figure. "If I'd known . . . if I'd just known I could've sorted 'em out. Dear God in 'eaven, go an' sit wi' yer ma an' say nowt . . . *nowt*, d'yer 'ear me, an' shut that bloody dog up, will yer or I'll chuck it outer t' winder."

Lily was past speech she was so terrified but she still had enough strength to pick up the frantically barking dog and go and sit on the bed beside her ma's chair, holding Villy's muzzle in an attempt to quieten her. By now Jane Elliott was turning blankly in her chair, a terrible wariness creasing her smooth face. The hammering continued, and with one last smoothing of her apron and her hair, Mrs Quinn moved in a dignified manner across the bedroom and unlocked the door, opening it so suddenly the man almost fell inside.

"What the 'ell d'yer think you're up to?" He glared about him, his gaze falling on the beautiful woman whose blank eyes, like pools of grey water in a mist, were fixed on his.

"Yer didn't think I'd let yer come in Mrs Elliott's bedroom an' 'er still undressed, did yer?" Mrs Quinn said to him icily. "Fer the sake o' decency I 'ad ter gerrer dressed. Now, if yer don't mind I'd be glad if yer'd gerron wi' it, wharrever it is yer've come ter do, an' lerrus get packed. I presume we can tekk a few clothes wi' us, or 'ave we ter go in our pinnies?"

"Well, I were told ter tekk everything what could be carried but . . . well . . ." He was staring as though mesmerised at the elegantly gowned woman in the chair. Molly had not had time to put up her hair into the neat bun which was all she could manage, for she was not a lady's maid, and it hung about her face and shoulders and down her back in a curtain of pale, silver gold. Her strange and fragile loveliness quietened even his ferocious need to be getting on with his job. You had to be tough doing what he did, not letting sentiment or pity get in the way and for the most part it didn't bother him overmuch. After years of turning out women and children and what little was left of the rubbish most of them had, he had become immune to it, but this woman, who looked like an angel from some far-off heaven he personally did not believe in, gave him the creeps and that was a fact. She didn't look all there, to tell the truth and the quicker this job was finished and done with the better. There were some nice bits in here that he and Bert might secrete on their persons and if that jewel box had anything in it, all the better.

He managed to tear himself away from the woman's blind gaze, striding over to the dressing-table and opening the box. He lifted out the few rings and a brooch or two that were all Molly had been able to get back into it, then grunted in satisfaction.

"Right, missis, pack yer things an' tekk yerselves off. An' yer'd best 'and over't keys afore yer go."

He nodded civilly in Jane Elliott's direction then clomped off downstairs to see how Bert was getting on.

Lily, who had been sitting in stunned silence beside her

mother, felt something begin to come alive and grow in her. The events of the last half-hour had sent her into a shocked state that had taken her speech and even her sharp mind, and she had dragged along at Mrs Quinn's skirt since she had not known what else to do. She had not understood what was happening, and even now it was not clear to her why these men were boldly helping themselves to Ma and Pa's things. She did know she did not like it and that was enough for the moment. Why didn't Mrs Quinn call for a policeman, or Mr Meadows? The man had said that Pa owed money but she wouldn't believe that, not her pa who had been the most honourable man in the world. There was a feeling of great resentment, anger even, welling up inside her when she remembered the way that man had handled Pa's walking stick, but mostly anger at the way her life had changed, had worsened, ever since the day Mr Porter had come to tell them that Pa had died. She didn't want to pack her things and leave the house in which she had been born and had lived all her life. She didn't want to do as Mrs Quinn said and obediently trot downstairs and place her bags by the front door in readiness for the cab that Mrs Quinn said was to take them somewhere else. She didn't *want* to go anywhere else. She liked it here. She wanted to stay where her memories of Pa were, where her friends were and anyway, Mrs Quinn was only the housekeeper and surely had no say in where she and her ma were to live.

She said so as she struggled downstairs with an overflowing basket.

"I don't want to go to live anywhere else, Mrs Quinn, thank you very much. I like it here and this is where Ma and I will stay. I'm sure it's very kind of you to—"

"Don't be daft, child, we've no choice," Mrs Quinn answered flatly, pushing her to one side as she hefted Ma's trunk on to the front step.

"Well, you may have no choice, but we have. I'll look after Ma until she's better but I would prefer to do it here, if it's all the same to you." She lifted her small chin, firmed her rosy lips and stared mutinously into Mrs Quinn's flustered face. Her own was a bright poppy red with her growing temper. For good measure she put her hands on her hips and took a stance in front of Ma's trunk.

Mrs Quinn sighed wearily. "Gerrout o' me way, queen,

there's a good lass. I've enough on me plate wi'out you kickin' up a fuss."

"Well, I'm sorry about that but we're not coming, me and Ma, and nothing you can say will change my mind. This is our home."

"Oh, give over, child, an' go an' fetch the rest o' yer things, an' yer'd best put that there dog on a lead an' fasten 'er ter't door 'andle. I don't want ter be lookin' for 'er at last minute."

"I don't think you heard me, Mrs Quinn." Lily's face had set into the obstinate mask of determination Mrs Quinn had seen before and she was aware that she really couldn't be bothered with it at the moment. She'd more than enough to see to without this little madam throwing tantrums.

"Yer'll do as yer told, lady, or yer'll feel t'back o' me 'and. See, run upstairs an' fetch—"

"I'm not going, Mrs Quinn, and as you are only my mother's housekeeper you can't make me. She's the one to say whether—"

Mrs Quinn had had enough. Really had enough. What with Mrs Elliott having to be forcibly removed from her chair and made to stand up in order to put her coat on, then led, resisting all the way, down the stairs, not to mention all that had gone before, she just felt like sitting down, throwing her apron over her head and having a damn good cry. But, of course, that was not Molly Quinn's way and she'd not let this little tinker – what on earth had got into her? she wondered in amazement – get the better of her. The child'd best learn right from the start who gave the orders, and who took them in the home that was to be theirs for the foreseeable future. God alone knew what was to happen to them but one day at a time she told herself steadfastly. But it was hard to think that she was to start all over again, or so it seemed, just like she had when Seamus died. This woman and this child dependent on Molly Quinn, but she'd done it once and, by God, she'd do it again.

First the child had to learn who was in charge.

"I think there's summat we'd best get straight before we go any further, young lady, an' that's that I'll say what's ter be done, or not ter be done, not yer ma. Until she's well enough ter look after 'erself an' you, then, I'm boss, see, an' you'll do as you're told, or else."

"Or else what?" Lily answered rudely, glaring at Mrs Quinn.

"I'll paddle yer bum, that's what."

"You wouldn't dare."

"An' 'oo's goin' ter stop me? Certainly not yer ma," glancing in the direction of the woman who was drifting about the hall with her head cocked in that way that had become so familiar and which seemed to say she was listening for something.

Lily wanted to kick Mrs Quinn. She wanted to kick and scream her frustration and anger and fear, but something in Mrs Quinn's face made her hesitate and before she had decided what she might do next there was a shout that the cab was here. Mrs Quinn took her arm, whisked her down the path and had her in the corner seat before she had time to say another word.

The worst part, or at the time what seemed the worst part, had been coaxing Jane Elliott to take her arm, walk through the front door, down the path and into the cab which Finn Flanagan had obligingly run to the corner to acquire for them.

"Where'll you go, Mrs Quinn?" her neighbours had asked her in turn as each had come to find out for themselves, not satisfied with second-hand news, what was happening in the Elliott household. They were agog with it, sorry for the widow, naturally, and the silently defiant child who didn't seem to know what time of day it was, let alone what was happening to her. Mrs Watson had helped Mrs Quinn to pack as much as she could into a lady's basket trunk, covered in dull canvas and bound with black leather and belonging to Mrs Elliott, a leather portmanteau belonging to the captain and several sturdy baskets for the child's clothes. The bailiff, or "bum-bailiff" as Bert Meadows contemptuously called him, watched every item of clothing being packed, only objecting when Molly tried to cram in Mrs Elliott's furs, since they would be easy to sell, which was what Molly had intended. The house seemed to be heaving with people, though in fact it was only Mrs Watson, Mrs Meadows and her husband who had offered to heft the luggage on his brawny shoulders from the house to the cab.

Mrs Watson cried as they did their best to persuade Mrs Elliott that she really must get into the cab and it was not until she had somehow got it into her head that she was going to meet Richard, which she had often done in a hansom, that she allowed herself to be tucked in beside her daughter.

How would Mrs Elliott manage, Mrs Meadows begged Mrs Watson to tell her, her the picture of charm and elegance, in the basement cellar from which Mrs Quinn had come ten years ago? Brooke Alley off the Vauxhall Road and they all knew where that was, and though they were perfectly sure Mrs Quinn's place would be like a new pin, what about the rest of the slum-dwellers with whom she would be surrounded? What on earth was to become of them, the lovely woman and child who would be as out of place as fragile violets on a dung heap? And how was Mrs Quinn, who would be called on to support and protect them both, to cope with it? Dear God, it didn't bear thinking about, they told one another as they went sadly up their own garden paths, to their own warm and comfortable kitchens. The captain and his wife had been a bit above them in the way of things but they'd been grand people and lovely neighbours and they'd be sadly missed.

Grace and Evie stood in the lane and watched the hansom cab until it turned the corner and disappeared from view.

"Never mind, Evie," Grace said kindly to her friend, who was crying as she always did at any sadness. "We'll see Lily at school, won't we, Ma?" to her mother's back as she walked up the path.

"I doubt that, chuck. The school fees'll be too much for the likes of Mrs Elliott now, I reckon."

"Well, we can go and play with her, can't we, Ma?"

Mrs Watson turned on her daughter with a force that made the child take a hasty step backwards.

"No, you cannot. I'll not have you going into that part of the town under any circumstances, d'you hear me? Slums, that's what they are in that quarter and no child of mine is going to mix with slum kids, so think on. Lily Elliott's lost to us now. Eeh, chuck, I'm sorry," as Grace began to cry as pitifully as Evie. "I know Lily was your friend but she's going to another world, child, and not one you're ever likely to see."

It *was* another world and even Jane Elliott seemed to become vaguely aware that she was in a place she did not know, or like. The cab ride down Kirkdale Road and into New Scotland Road had not been so bad. It was when the vehicle turned down Portland Street and into Vauxhall Road that Lily shrank back into the corner of the cab, seeing for the first time what she had not even known existed. The place seemed to be swarming with half-naked children, so coated with grey filth it was difficult to determine their sex. Slatternly women lolled on doorsteps watching the cab go by, while the children ran after it, screaming words Lily could not understand, and inside the cab Villy began to bark her head off. There were old women, dressed like mummies, sprawling in the gutter and young girls holding out their hands to every passing male. Dogs quarrelled over bits of rubbish and a crippled youth sat huddled up against a wall holding a painted board on his knees on which was painted a ghastly picture. It seemed to represent a human figure caught up in some appalling, whirling machinery. Next to him was another man, cadaverous as a corpse with a filthy bandage about his brow. His sign read: *I have had no food for three days. My wife and children are dying.*

The arrival of the hansom cab caused a sensation at the end of Brooke Alley and the cab driver almost flung them and their baggage into the overflowing gutter that ran down its centre in his eagerness to be rid of them and get away to more salubrious quarters. It appeared that every dweller in the tall, teeming houses that lined the narrow alley had got wind of their arrival and they were all outside to greet them. Unemployed and apathetic men in caps and mufflers leaning their shoulders on the walls, women in shawls nursing puny babies, whining toddlers, yelling children who were so undernourished they appeared not to have a yell in them, barking dogs and slinking cats. A man came out of small building in the centre of the courtyard ahead of them, casually buttoning his trousers, apparently unaware of the slimy ooze which crept about his feet.

"Come along in, lass," Mrs Quinn told her in mock cheerfulness, appearing not to be at all dismayed by the state of things. "'Old yer ma's 'and while I get this lot in. Afternoon, Mrs Maloney," she called out, nodding to an old woman on the opposite step while Jane and Lily Elliott held their breath so as not to taste the appalling stench that filled the alley, their nostrils, their head and lungs and to which they were to become so accustomed they did not even notice it.

8

The first setback, and there were many, occurred on the day they arrived at Brooke Alley, when Mrs Quinn slipped down to the shop on the corner to buy something for their supper. She had nothing in her cupboard except stuff that would keep, sugar, flour, tea, candles and things like that, and if they were to have a meal, which of course they must, though she had never felt less like eating in her life, she told herself – since there was no one else interested – the child needed something inside her.

Their faces were quite blank. She had become used to Mrs Elliott looking as though the life had been snuffed out of her but just at that moment the child was an exact miniature of her mother. The same strange sense that she was somewhere else and not here in Molly's dim and dusty basement room. The same fragile beauty, the same massed tumble of pale silken hair and ivory, rose-tinted skin, the same velvet grey eyes surrounded by long, drooping lashes, the same softly tremulous rosy lips, but where, before this devastation had come upon them, Lily had been bright and lively, with vivid life in her face and brilliance in her eyes, now she was as lifeless as her mother. They sat side by side where she had put them at the table, their hands folded in their laps, their eyes looking at nothing, both stunned, especially the child, by the disaster that had overtaken them.

It was searingly cold in the basement room. It was several weeks since Molly had been home and there had been no fire lit in the meantime. That was the first thing to be done and it was clear she would get no help from these two. Not that she expected it, for neither of them had ever lit a fire in their lives and even if one of them offered to help, which was unlikely, it would be quicker to do it herself.

In no time a good fire was crackling cheerfully in the grate, putting a gleam in the slightly dusty surface of the blackleaded oven and casting flickering orange and gold and rose shadows on the white walls and ceiling. It touched their faces to a more healthy-looking hue and Molly saw Lily begin to glance about her with a faint glimmer of that interest anything new evokes in a child.

"Come up t't fire an' gerra warm," she invited them with as much cheerfulness as she could manage. "See, Mrs Elliott, tekk off yer cloak an' come an' set yerself in th' armchair," a rather resplendent piece of furniture which was Molly's pride and joy. It was a wing chair, upholstered in a plain wool fabric in a pretty pattern of flowers and birds and had carved walnut legs. She had picked it up in one of the markets many years ago when her finances had taken a turn for the better and though it had been badly worn, the stuffing hanging out in places, she had patiently patched it with scraps of material bought from the same market. The different shades where the patches had been sewn on in no way detracted from its attractiveness, but rather gave it the appearance of homely comfort, of being a much loved and cared-for part of Molly's home. The one opposite in which she placed the silent child was not as comfortable, the original old rocker she and Seamus had bought for a few pence when they were first married. There were cushions on it and at once Lily sank back in them and began to rock. The bewildered dog crouched at her feet.

Molly studied them for a moment or two. They seemed settled enough, she thought, both of them staring as though hypnotised into the fire, and with a bit of luck she might just be able to slip to Mrs Nelson's at the corner and get a bit of corned beef and a few potatoes for their supper. She'd be back before they noticed she'd gone. She'd need milk too, for the child, and a tin of chocolate, that's if Mrs Nelson stocked such a thing; if not it would have to be cocoa. She chewed her lip and frowned and wished one of her girls was here to keep an eye on things until she got back, but they weren't so that was that and she'd just have to get on with it best she could.

"I'm just goin' t't corner shop," she told them brightly, doing her best to act as though this situation was nothing out of the ordinary. "I'll not be more'n five minutes. I've put kettle on," which was beginning to hum in the centre of the fire, "an' when I get back we'll 'ave us a nice cuppa tea."

Neither of them answered her. She had not removed her own old but decent black cloak, nor her bonnet, and so, with another anxious look at her guests, she opened the door and climbed the steps into the alley.

"Got visitors then, Mrs Quinn?" a voice accosted her and she turned in irritation to the direction from which it had come. It was the old woman to whom she had spoken earlier.

"Aye, I 'ave, Mrs Maloney," she answered shortly, unwilling to elaborate, though she knew Mrs Maloney was longing to know who they were. She turned away, prepared to move on, since she'd no time for gossiping. She could see several slatternly women propping up the door frames of their homes, arms akimbo, their faces worn and old, though in years they were neither, getting ready to challenge her. It was not often something exciting happened in their lives and none of them had missed the arrival of the cab and the two angelic visions who had descended from it. They all knew that Mrs Quinn had a grand job up Walton way but what on earth was she doing here in this sordid world of theirs, bringing with her these creatures, the likes of which they had never before seen. They knew they existed, of course, in some fairytale world beyond their knowledge, for they had heard tell of them being seen in Bold Street where they shopped, so it was said, but they had never actually clapped eyes on one, and they couldn't wait for another sight of these two.

They had not to wait long.

Mrs Quinn was barely out of the door when Lily leaped from her chair and reached for her cloak, swinging it out and about her shoulders where it settled in swinging folds. She could hear some woman address Mrs Quinn but when she stood on a chair and peered out of the small window, the bottom half of which looked out on to the basement steps, the top into the alley, she was just in time to see her hurrying towards the corner.

"Quick, Ma, put your cloak back on and let's escape while we can," she said briskly, while she pulled her mother's mantle about her and buttoned it under her chin. "If Mrs Quinn thinks we're going to stop here she's sadly mistaken. We'll go down to the docks and ask for Liam. He should be in port any day now and if he's not docked yet we'll go back to Walton Lane and see if Mrs Watson or Mrs Meadows will take us in until he comes." Her voice had been filled with optimism but it dropped to a sad murmur as she twitched her mother's cloak more warmly about her unresisting shoulders. "I know we can't go back to our own house because I saw Mrs Quinn give the keys to those awful men but we'll find somewhere to live until Liam comes. He'll help us, I know he will. Now just wait there a minute while I see if the coast's clear."

Jane Elliott stood obediently by the door, automatically adjusting her bonnet which her daughter had jammed on her head, while Lily popped her head above the level of the area steps. The afternoon was almost at an end and though to the west where the river placidly ran out to the bay the sun still shone low in the sky, in this deep valley of decaying stone and brick it was almost dusk. Children still played games but with none of the energy Lily and her friends employed. Others sat with their bare feet in the filthy, clogged water that ran in the central gutter, splashing one another aimlessly. She had got no more than a glimpse of them as she and Ma stepped from the cab and were hurried down Mrs Quinn's area steps and into her home and as Lily took her first good look at them and the alley they played in, she was shocked by the litter that lay about, by the dirty, ragged children themselves, by the unkempt, uncombed appearance of the women who leaned listlessly in their doorways. And what was that small building in the centre of the court further up the alley from which some dreadful noxious slime seemed to be seeping and what was that appalling stench that made her want to gag? There was a pile of rotting garbage against the far wall; at least she thought that's what it was but it seemed to be moving. She bit back a desire to scream and on top of that a great need to get back into the warmth and safety of Mrs Quinn's clean little room but she must be brave. Whatever it was and whoever these people were they were nothing to do with her and Ma and the quicker they got away from here the better. She couldn't understand why Mrs Quinn had brought them in the first place. She must have known that she and Ma were not used to such places. Dear Lord, what *was* that moving among the pile? It . . . it was an animal, a small animal, a kitten perhaps and when a rat ran across the alley she almost fell down the steps in her madness to get out of its way.

But they had to go, she and Ma. They couldn't stay here, could they, and if there were nasty things out there in the alley then they would just have to avert their eyes and hurry by. She'd best get Ma to hold her scented handkerchief to her nose until they got out into the better streets of the area. They would ignore the filth, the mud, the pools of stagnant water and what she was pretty certain was a dead cat and, leaving all their stuff since there was no way she could carry it, make for the river, and Liam.

They caused another sensation when they crept slowly up Mrs Quinn's area steps and moved out into the alley. Everyone in it froze and there was a deep and stunned silence. Lily had on her red velvet cloak. She had pulled the hood up in the hope that it might keep out the worst of the stink, and the fur edging it framed her face which peeped out like a pale flower. Her ma had on a deep blue woollen three-quarter-length mantle, shaped to the waist but flowing loose behind and under it her pale grey woollen dress soon had six inches of brown filth about its hem. Their dainty, pale kid boots skidded in the mess and Jane nearly fell and it was perhaps this that brought her momentarily to her senses.

"I want to go home, Lily," she moaned. "I don't like it here." Her already pale face took on the sheen and tint of bleached bone and her eyes widened to an incredible size in her terror. She clutched Lily's arm and when the noise started, the noise of men and women and children calling out in derision, for it is human nature to deride what is beyond their possessing, what is different to them, what they do not understand, she cowered away and began to babble senselessly.

"It's all right, Ma. There's not far to go and then we'll be out of this. We've only to get down to the docks and then Liam will help us," she said through gritted teeth, for by now she had convinced herself that the big man would be there.

Clinging to one another like two shipwrecked mariners in a storm-tossed sea, with Villy's nose almost attached to the heel of Lily's boot, they reached the end of the alley, but to her consternation she found their way was barred by what appeared to be a canal. Across the canal was some spare ground which was strewn with mouldering rubbish and bits of rusted machinery, of what sort she didn't know, and then beyond that was another narrow sheet of water across which a railway line ran. Towering over all this was a forbidding building with turrets and high walls which must be some sort of castle, Lily thought despairingly, not knowing that she was looking at the silhouette of the Borough Gaol. She could smell the sea now, the familiar smell of the river and the ships and their cargoes and see the gulls wheeling against the sky, but how was she get there, for there was no sign of a bridge and besides which, she thought Ma was about to faint. She was dragging Lily down and if she did how were they to get up again? She could feel her heart lurch in panic, for it was getting dark and if they didn't reach some sort of safety soon her instincts told her she and her ma would be in terrible danger. There was nothing for it but to go back and try to find another way out of this maze of horror into which they had descended. Oh, Pa . . . Pa, how are we to manage without you? What am I to do? Where am I to go? she begged in her ten-year-old terror. She could feel the tears gathering in a lump in her throat but she swallowed them resolutely and, lifting the almost dead weight of her mother, retraced her steps along the alley through which she and Ma had just dragged and when Mrs Quinn's voice demanded what the bloody hell she thought she was doing it was almost a relief.

"We're going home," she said defiantly. "If you would just show us the way."

"Home, is it? Well, Lily, you'd best get used ter the idea that fer the time bein' *this* is yer 'ome." There was no way but to be brutal. "Yer pa's gone an' left you an' yer ma in a birrof a pickle an' I'm th'only one yer've got to 'elp you out of it. Yer should just thank God we've a roof over our 'eads an' a bit o' food ter purrin our mouths fer there's many a family what 'asn't." Her face softened as she put her arms round the wilting figure of Jane Elliott and began to guide her feet back to Brooke Alley. "Yer only a lass," she went on, trying to take Lily's hand in hers but it was twitched angrily away, "an' yer don't understand."

"I understand that you are keeping us here against our will, Mrs Quinn. That's called kidnapping and you can go to prison for it." She was very near tears but she held her head high and clenched her jaw.

"Well, think wha' yer like, lass, but yer've no one but me an' yer'd best mekk most of it. What are you lot starin' at?" she demanded savagely of the crowd who had gathered to see the woman and the kid come back to them.

"Is it bloody Queen yer've got there, Mrs Quinn?" one called out mockingly. "Are yer to 'ave a tea party fer 'Er Majesty, cos if y'are I'm right willin' ter be a guest."

They hooted with laughter, those who heard the exchange, and began to crowd in on the trio as they approached Mrs Quinn's basement steps. They had always had a grudge against this neighbour of theirs, a feeling that she thought herself a cut above them, that she looked down on them in their abject misery. She kept herself to herself and was for ever fetching water from the standpipe, water which was just as available to them as it was to her but somehow they resented her use of it. She was for ever scrubbing and polishing and no matter how many times the kids scrawled on her whitewashed outside walls she continued to paint them again, so in the end they had given up and let her alone. Now they were vastly entertained by what she had brought into their world and were going to make the most of it.

"Gerrout o' my way," Mrs Quinn screeched, doing her best to force a way through the press of unwashed, foul-smelling bodies and at the same time trying to protect her two charges. The women meant no actual harm but they sensed a bit of "fun" with these two glorious creatures who, they supposed, were from where Mrs Quinn worked. They didn't know why they were here and didn't care really, but they had lost their usual apathy and listless acceptance of their lot and were intent on brightening up their lives with what promised to be a bit of unusual and welcome entertainment.

But they not reckoned on Lily Elliott who had stood up to Finn Flanagan and Jack and Charlie Meadows in the defence of the dog who pressed against her skirts. Villy was beginning to sense the danger and was prepared to stand up to it, as she was. She had trailed at their heels all the way down to the canal, her eyes following all the darting things that captured her attention, lifting her muzzle and growling in the back of her throat. When Lily stepped forward and elbowed aside a scraggy woman with a bundle which turned out to be a silent baby at her breast, then another who stood in her way, the dog snapped viciously and they stepped back hastily before she sank her teeth into their leg.

"Let my mother through," the beautiful little girl told them imperiously, "and get off Mrs Quinn's steps. This is a private area and if you don't remove yourselves I'll call for the police."

She tossed her head and her hood fell back. Her hair shone like silver gilt in the darkening alley and her eyes were translucent with anger, turning to the lavender grey which, if they had known it, meant trouble. "Come along, Mrs Quinn, take no notice of them," she said loftily. "Come along, Ma, mind the steps. Villy, it's all right now, you can stop snarling like a jungle beast," and while they watched in total disbelief she ushered Mrs Quinn and her ma through Mrs Quinn's door and out of their sight, slamming the door behind them. They were so astounded they let her do it without another word. One of the children threw a lump of something nasty at the window but by that time Mrs Quinn had the curtains drawn and it slid harmlessly off the glass.

They drank the hot milk she put in their hands, both of them shivering uncontrollably with the memory of the experience they had just gone through, even Lily who had seemed unafraid at the time. They changed into their nightgowns without a murmur, then snuggled down together in Mrs Quinn's bed, clutching one another and the stone hot-water bottle she had wrapped in a towel and thrust in between them. Villy lay at their feet, her nose on her paws, her eyes watchful, for it seemed she would need to be on guard in this place her beloved young mistress had brought her to.

Molly Quinn wept after they had fallen asleep, for this escapade – if you could call such a serious thing an escapade – of Lily's had brought home to her as nothing else had done the true reality of what was ahead of her. She wept, indulging herself, she knew that, as she crouched over her fire in her comfortable chair, but it would be for the last time, she told herself, wiping her eyes on the edge of her apron.

She had a cup of tea, washed the mug and was about to empty the teapot when a thought occurred to her and with all the care she had used in the old days when she had been so hard up she put the used tea leaves into a basin and covered them with a bit of cloth. They would stand a second brew, she told herself, knowing that until she had pulled herself together and decided on a course of action they would have to watch every penny and practise many little economies.

She pulled out the truckle bed in which one or other of her girls sometimes slept. Drawing it up to the fire she undressed in its warmth and pulled her voluminous nightgown over her head. Drawing the blankets about her she prepared herself for a sleepless night, but to her surprise she slept well and woke refreshed to start the first day of their new lives.

The next time Lily tried something on, she planned it more carefully. They had been at Mrs Quinn's for a fortnight and in that time had not once been outside the door, though Mrs Quinn made little forays to the corner shop for food. When she did that she locked them in!

"Why don't we have a walk down to the seafront, Mrs Quinn?" she asked artlessly. "We haven't had a breath of fresh air in all this time and I'm sure it would do Ma good," looking across the table to where her mother sat like a pale and lovely statuette. "Put a bit of colour in her cheeks, and perhaps give her an appetite." Jane Elliott picked at the nourishing food Molly prepared for her, not complaining but not eating much of it either. Her clothes hung on her slender figure and she had lost weight she could ill afford to lose. She no longer had the lovely breasts and rounded hips that had once been hers. She looked ethereal, insubstantial, as though the smallest breeze might have her over. Perhaps the child was right. Perhaps a smell of the sea and a saunter along the Marine Parade would do her good. Molly would keep a firm hold on her, for she herself was as strong as a horse and the child was not likely to run away and leave her ma behind, was she?

Jane took a bit of coaxing to get her up the steps and into the alley. Molly had kept an eye on it, waiting until it was empty of the slum-dwellers who lurked about there on a mild day.

"I don't think I care to go out today, Mrs Quinn."

"Now, lamb, it's just the day fer a walk. Only ter't river an' back. It'll do us all a birra good."

"I think I would prefer to stay by the fire and . . ." Jane seemed to cast about as though looking for something that desperately needed her attention but her empty mind could not remember what that might be.

"Nay, we'll wrap up warm an tekk dog fer a good run. She an't bin out fer a decent run fer weeks now," which was true.

There were no catcalls or interference today. It was cold with a bite in the air which kept the inhabitants of Brooke Alley indoors, huddled together under their few pitiful rags, but Molly's two were well wrapped up in the good winter clothes she had thought to pack. They'd come to no harm in the keen wind that blew off the river and even before they had got to the corner of Vauxhall Road and turned into Leeds Street which led down to Bath Street and Princess Dock – Lily memorising every step of the way – there was a faint flush of pink in Jane's cheek.

They were about to turn north in the direction of the Marine Parade when Lily suddenly darted away, the dog at her heels, in the opposite direction.

"I promise I won't be long, Mrs Quinn," she shouted over her shoulder as Mrs Quinn made to run after her. "God's honour, I'll not go far but I must just go and enquire for Liam and you and Ma would hold me up. Why don't you—"

"You come back, yer little divil," Molly screeched after her, afraid to leave go of Mrs Elliott, who might be frightened if Molly's strong arm was removed. "Come back, yer limb o' Satan, or I'll scorch yer drawers for yer." Her tone turned to one of pleading. "Lily, child, don't run off like that. Yer don't know 'oo might gerrold o' yer. Oh, please, child, come back." But she was shouting into the wind as the little, scarlet-cloaked figure disappeared across the lock gate bridge which barred Princes Dock Basin and headed towards the landing stage off Princes Parade. Mrs Elliott was beginning to show signs of distress, as though Mrs Quinn's raised voice of fear was disturbing the dreadfully shattered equilibrium of her mind. She had begun to pull away as though she were in the grip of a stranger and with a muttered oath Molly set her lips in a grim line and began to walk as fast as Jane would go in the direction Lily had taken.

The *Caledonia* had not yet reached port, an astonished gentleman in a uniform and a peaked and braided cap told her. He was obviously an official of the dockyard which was why Lily had picked on him. No, he couldn't say when, though he did admit she was expected on the 11th which was the day after tomorrow. There had been severe storms in the Atlantic which was unusual for this time of the year, he heard himself explaining to his own amazement to the exquisite child with the steady eyes who had accosted him.

"Anyroad, what d'yer want wi' the *Caledonia*, lass?" he asked her. "Is it a relative yer lookin' for?" beginning to glance about him for someone who might be in charge of her.

"No, a friend. Liam O'Connor he's called. He's first mate," she told him proudly, as though Liam's achievement had had something to do with her. "He's been to North America. I forgot to ask him what his cargo was, or what he was bringing back but I'm sure it's something important."

"I'm sure it is, chuck, burr I've gorra gerron, so if yer'll excuse me," for she was the sort of child, earnest and well mannered, who seemed to command his respect.

"Of course. I know how busy anyone who works on the docks must be. I do envy you."

"Oh, 'ow's that then?"

"Working here where the ships are." Her smile was dazzling and he was dazzled.

"Yer like ships then?"

"Oh, yes, my pa was a sea captain, you see."

"Retired, is 'e?"

"No." Her small face seemed to crumple. "He's dead."

"Well, I'm sorry to 'ear that, lass."

"Perhaps you knew him. He was the best sailor who ever sailed the oceans. His name was Captain Richard Elliott of the *Lily-Jane*."

His face broke into a smile and he leaned down to her. "So you're Captain Elliott's little lass, are yer? Aye, I knew Captain Elliott an' yer right, he were a good sailor. 'E knew 'ow ter 'andle a ship better'n any man outer this port."

Lily was enchanted and she looked up into the man's face as though he had just given down the word of God Himself.

"He did, didn't he?" she breathed, waiting for this man to say some other wonderful thing about her pa, but at that moment Mrs Quinn caught up with her and when the man turned at her high-pitched shriek, caused by fear, he was again knocked sideways by the amazing likeness of the child to the pale and lovely woman on her arm.

"It's all right, queen," he told Mrs Quinn soothingly. "She's only asking about some ship she's expectin'."

"God strewth, I'll give 'er lookin' fer ships when I gerr 'er 'ome. Yer frightened me ter death, Lily Elliott, runnin' away like tha'.

Mrs Quinn might not have spoken for all the notice Lily took of her. She was fishing about in the pocket of her cloak and with a triumphant air she produced a pencil and a piece of paper.

"Now, I've written my name and address – my *present* address – on this piece of paper, sir and I'd be obliged if you would do me a great favour and when the *Caledonia* docks ... You will know, won't you?" she added anxiously and when the official said he would she smiled the smile that would warm any heart as she handed it to him. She curtseyed, showing off her very best manners and the man found himself returning her smile in what he knew was a daft and foolish manner as he watched her walk away with her hand in that of her mother.

"Liam will be here soon, Ma," he heard her say, "and everything will be all right then, you'll see."

9

"I've gorra find a job, chuck. I've sold all t' bits of 'er jewels. Not tha' I got much for 'em. I know nowt about such things an' I reckon that chap at shop did me. I couldn't argue, yer see, knowin' nowt, an' I were afraid if I kicked up a fuss 'e might start askin' me where I gorrem. Yer can see 'ow I'm placed burr unless I put pair of 'em in't work'ouse, wharrem I ter do?"

"Mam, wharrelse *can* yer do? They're not your responsibility. Oh, I know they've bin good to yer, the Elliotts, I mean, but at your age yer don't want ter be saddled wi' . . . well, look at 'em."

Molly and Victoria Quinn both turned to look at Jane Elliott and her daughter who were perched side by side on two chairs at the table. Jane Elliott might have been in the drawing-room of some lady from the gentry class, her simple gown of pale grey broadcloth falling from her tiny waist in symmetrical folds, her hair shining in the neat chignon Mrs Quinn had recently mastered, her face placid and her manners perfection. Her back was straight and yet graceful as she held a saucer in one hand and a cup in the other, sipping her tea in a ladylike manner, her eyes unfocused as she stared into some place no one else could see. A little to the right of her on the scrubbed deal table was a tray covered with a lace cloth on which delicate china was placed, a milk jug, a sugar bowl with silver tongs and a teapot, the china decorated with pale pink rosebuds. The child had a mug of something on the table before her and it steamed in the chilly air but she was not drinking. As she cut out the figures from what looked like a fashion magazine, her mouth opened and closed as the scissors did.

"An' where in 't name o' heaven did that lot come from?" Victoria went on, nodding at the tea tray. "Don't tell me yer fetched it from Walton Lane?"

Mrs Quinn turned a somewhat apologetic look on her daughter. "An' why not?" she said defiantly. "She's used ter nice things. I managed ter tuck it inter't child's little bag."

"Eeh, Mam, yer barmy, that's all I can say," her daughter told her in exasperation. "An' 'ow yer ter manage I don't know."

"Well, if I could get summat, I dunno, p'raps at laundry in Banastre Street, just until we gerron our feet, like, then—"

"Gerron yer feet! Mam, yer'll never earn enough ter keep three o' yer. On yer own yer could likely gerra job livin' in: 'ousekeeper or summat. P'raps doin' cleanin', norr 'eavy, burr enough ter put food in yer mouth. An' yer know me an' Mary an' Alice'll not see yer wi'out but wi' these two round yer neck, well, I know our Mary an' Alice'll not give their 'ard-earned wages ter support *them* an' neither will I. It's not fair, Mam. On you or on us. Yer do see that, don't yer?" Victoria leaned forward and put a hand on her mother's knee.

Molly sighed deeply, studying the pair at the table.

"Drink yer cocoa, child," she admonished Lily absently, "before it gets cold." Lily took no notice.

"Me mam ses yer ter drink yer cocoa, Lily." Victoria's voice was as cold and cutting as an icicle, since she was well aware that her mother had gone out specially to buy the milk and it infuriated her to see it go to waste.

"I don't want it," Lily answered haughtily. "It tastes funny. Not like the milk we get from the farm."

Victoria gasped. "Well, yer ungrateful little beggar. Yer want a good 'idin' an' if yer were mine yer'd gerrit."

"Well, I'm not yours, so there, and I'm glad. My mother and I didn't ask to come here, did we, Ma?" She did not wait for a reply since she did not expect one. "In fact, we want to go home, don't we, Ma?" She glared ferociously at Victoria, drawing down her eyebrows and screwing up her mouth into a tight bud.

"That'll do, Lily," Mrs Quinn said tartly, then turned to resume her conversation with her daughter, speaking quietly so that Lily wouldn't hear her.

"She's bin like tha' fer weeks now. She was expectin' some chap she met down at docks—"

Victoria gasped. "Some chap she met down at docks! Mam, what're yer sayin'?"

"Oh, don't be daft, our Victoria. It were nowt like tha'. 'E were a nice lad, big chap, 'oo brought 'er 'ome when she went lookin' fer 'er pa's ship. Ever since then she's bin expectin' 'im ter come an' . . . well, I dunno what she expects 'im ter do. Tekk 'er an' her ma back ter Walton Lane, I reckon. Anyroad, 'e never came an' she's bin a little bugger ever since. Cheeky, disobedient, and she were once the best-'earted little lass yer could ever wish ter meet. Well, you knew 'er in't th'old days," meaning when Captain Elliott had been alive and Mrs Elliott in her right mind. "Oh, I know she were lively an' liked, 'an got 'er own way but she were never nasty. She keeps wantin' ter go out an' look fer this chap burr I can't lerr 'er wander about, can I? God knows what'd become of 'er. When I go out ter't shops I 'ave ter lock 'em in. Yer can see wharr I mean, can't yer?"

They both turned again to look at Jane and Lily Elliott. The child and her mother were totally out of place in the dim basement cellar, for they both looked as though they had stepped out of the pages of the very fashion magazine from which Lily was cutting out figures. It was early April now and though the sunlight was laying a golden sheen on the river and polishing the windows and wet roofs of the buildings to copper, none of it reached into the chasms of tortuous alleyways and courtyards that laced the poorest parts of the Liverpool slums. The sun had a bit of warmth in it where it reached but here in the deep and rancid back streets it was damp, raw, bleak, even though a small fire burned in the grate of Molly's blackleaded oven. The oven was a handsome affair, the fire held in by iron bars, on one side a full oven and on the other a half-oven on which a kettle stood. Above the mantelpiece and down each side were numerous shining pans. Just below the mantelpiece was a brass rod on which items of underclothing were airing. There was a brass fender on which Molly and her daughter had their feet propped and along the mantelpiece were lined Molly's cheap but attractive ornaments. So far she had not been forced to sell any of *her* stuff but if something didn't change soon, and God knows what she meant by change, she would have to do something drastic, again not quite knowing what that might be. As Victoria said, she was too old now to do the hard, drudging work she had managed eleven years ago. Though she had been busy from morning till night in the house in Walton Lane, she had gone at her own pace. She had had it easy all these years, she admitted it, soft, luxurious even, for she had eaten the same food as the family, had a decent wage – the savings from which were almost gone – and had lived in a fair degree of comfort, there, and here in her own snug little place. She could only thank God she had kept it on, for only He knew where they would have ended up if they hadn't had Brooke Alley to come back to.

So how was she to find work that she could manage that would support her, Mrs Elliott and the child? And if she found it how was she to go off and leave a small girl and a mindless woman by themselves all day? God, she was worn out with the worry of it going round and round in her head, but there was one thing that remained clear and shining and steadfast within her and would always do so and that was that Jane Elliott and her child would not finish up in the poorhouse, no matter what their Victoria had to say about it.

"Is there nowt up at Silverdale ter suit me?" she asked her daughter diffidently. "You know me, I'm norr afraid o' 'ard work, scrubbin' or summat, an' if you was ter vouch fer me they might tekk me on," despite my age, she appeared to be saying. Her daughter worked as parlourmaid at Silverdale, the home of the Hemingways in Garston, a lovely old house set on the shore of the river in several acres of ornamental gardens and lawns sweeping down to the gliding water, the whole set about by a thick stand of trees. There were terraces leading in steps from the house, each one edged with flowers in due season. Molly knew this because one day, several months after their Victoria had been lucky enough to be taken on as skivvy there, Molly, holding their Mary – who was just about to go as scullery maid at High Cross, another grand house on the shore – by the hand, had walked along by the Pottery Shore, past Dingle Point and Jericho Shore, to stand on the little sandy beach that edged both properties. She and Mary had crept up between the trees, having been told all about it by Victoria, and had a good scen up the slope where the roof of the house was just visible. They couldn't see the house itself, of course, which Victoria said was grand inside with wonders they could not even imagine, but it had given Mary, who was only ten and of a nervous disposition, some idea of what she might expect.

They had been lucky, the two sisters, working so close together, for it meant that if the servants above them gave them an hour off, not long enough to get home, of course, they could have a walk on the shore together which made it more comforting for the two lasses.

Victoria shook her head sadly, looking into the glowing coals of the fire. There was a pan of stew, scrag end of mutton with carrots, turnips, potatoes and barley, bubbling gently in it, the evening meal of the Elliotts and her mam, smelling delicious and making her mouth water. There was no doubt about it, Mam was a decent cook and could make one penny do the job of two. She had been a good housekeeper, as well, though she was sure the Elliotts had not realised it. Oh, she had been well thought of, she was aware of that, trusted and depended upon and what they'd have done without her, Victoria didn't know. And her loyalty to them, to the two at the table, was unbelievable. She was a strong woman, she and her sisters had always known that, for had it not been for her they might have ended up in one of the terrible situations children with their background got caught up in. Probably in the clutches of the workhouse keeper who would have sold them to some unscrupulous middle man who found children to work in the cotton mills of Lancashire. Mam needed work, decent work that was not too demanding, work that was suited to her many and excellent qualifications and where was she to find such a position and see to the pair at the table at the same time?

Her face was screwed up in thought and then, slowly, her face cleared and she turned to her mam. There was a hesitant look about her and she chewed her lip thoughtfully.

"Well . . ."

"What is it, chuck?" Molly leaned forward eagerly.

"We 'eard only yesterday the 'ousekeeper at Oakwood Place, yer know, the place between me an' our Mary's . . ."

"Aye." Molly hitched herself closer to her daughter so that they sat knee to knee.

"Well, she's givin' up. Retirin'. She must be seventy if she's a day, poor old soul, an' 'ow she's kept goin' all these years, I don't know. There bein' no mistress an' all. Mr Crowther's a widderman so 'appen 'e's not fussy. Men aren't, are they? An' the daughter's too young. Anyroad the groom there . . ." For a moment her face turned a rosy pink and she lowered her lashes, a gesture that would normally have set all Molly Quinn's maternal instincts quivering but she was too transfixed by what her daughter was hinting at even to notice.

"Wha' . . . wha'?"

" 'E said they was goin' ter advertise fer a new 'ousekeeper. Now whether the old man'd consider yer, seeing as 'ow yer'd 'ave no references, like, I don't know. Well, she's not gonner give yer any, is she?" turning her gaze on Jane Elliott. "Though 'appen if I was ter 'ave a word wi' Mrs Taylor" – who was in charge of the kitchens at Silverdale where Victoria worked – " 'oo's friendly wi' Mrs Jackson at Oakwood Place, she might purrin a word for yer. Knowin' yer were my mam, like, yer might 'ave a chance." Her face fell. "But then yer'd 'ave ter live in, so what yer'd do wi' these two, again I don't know. Eeh, Mam, it'd be ideal for yer if yer didn't 'ave them."

"You don't have to bother about me and Ma," a casual voice from the table said. "When Liam comes we'll go home, won't we, Ma? I don't know why we were forced to come to this horrid place at all."

Victoria turned in fury, her face livid, for did this bloody kid not understand what her presence here meant to her mother? Victoria's mother. If it wasn't for them she was pretty sure Mam could get this job at Oakwood Place as easy as falling off a log but there wasn't a hope of it as things were and she didn't really know why she had mentioned it in the first place.

"You shut yer gob, yer little madam. Yer know nowt about it an' why me mam keeps yer on 'ere, I'll never know."

"Me neither and if you'll just unlock that door, Mrs Quinn, we'll be off. You've no right keeping us prisoner here, has she, Ma?" turning for a moment to her mother. "There's no need to call us a cab, we'll walk," she added loftily. "I'm sure I can find the way to Walton Lane."

"Will you shurrup, yer daft little cow. 'Ave yer any idea—"

"Hush, Victoria. The child's bin through a lot an' doesn't know wha' she's sayin'."

"I don't give a damn about tha', Mam. I can't stand ter 'ear 'er talk like tha' after all you've done for 'er an' 'er mam. Listen 'ere, you," spinning round to face Lily who was still unconcernedly clipping away at the page of the magazine.

"This bloody mess me mam's in is your fault. No, I tell a lie, it's that pa o' yours 'oo's at fault. If 'e 'adn't chucked 'is money about like a man wi' no arms none o' this woulda 'appened. Borrowed it like there were no tomorrer, so I 'eard, no doubt buyin' yer mam all the fal-de-lals she tricked—"

"That's enough, our Victoria. Norr another word or I'll crack yer one, old as you are. It's no good shoutin' at lass, she's don't understand."

Lily was standing up by now, her face as red and bursting as a ripe tomato, her eyes glittering with venom, her fists clenched. She swung round the end of the table and stuck her face close to Victoria's.

"Don't you say things like that about my pa. He was a good man who loved us and he was honourable, and . . . and . . . decent and . . ."

"E'd a gone ter gaol if 'e'd lived," Victoria jeered, incensed past the stage where her usual good sense would have told her she was arguing with a child.

"How dare you . . . you . . . liar . . ."

Mrs Quinn stood up swiftly and before Lily could land one on the end of Victoria's nose, which she clearly intended to do, she pulled her into her arms and on to her lap. Lily struggled, her face like bleached bone now, but in her eyes was an appalling expression which said that though she didn't want to, she knew Victoria was telling the truth. Not that she would admit it, not to anyone, but her own common sense told her she and Ma would not be living here with Mrs Quinn if Pa had left them any money. Liam had said that Pa's boat had gone to pay a debt, which was a bit hard to understand but if Liam said it was so then it must be. She didn't know why Liam had not come in answer to her note, for it was long past the time for the *Caledonia*'s docking but he would come and if he didn't then she meant to go down to the docks to try to get to the bottom of it, that's if she could escape Mrs Quinn's vigilant eye. But she couldn't help but feel that . . . well, perhaps this awful Victoria girl might be telling the truth, about Pa, that is.

"I refuse to believe it," she hissed across the rag rug, almost spitting in Victoria's face, but Victoria was sorry now that she had lost her temper and her face had softened.

"I'm sorry, kid, I shouldn'ta said wharr I did about yer pa. My daddy died when I were a little kid burr I know 'e were a good man and anyone 'oo said different would a gorr a smack in't face from me."

"Really? I didn't know that." Lily leaned against Mrs Quinn's soft breast and felt better. It was nice to have someone's arms about her. It was nice to have someone who cared about her, which it seemed Mrs Quinn did, but really, when Victoria had gone she must have a good talk with Mrs Quinn about what was to happen to them. They couldn't go on hanging around here, could they? Somehow she must find the means to get herself and Ma back to Walton Lane and the house where they had all lived so happily. She wasn't sure how it might be accomplished. If they were very careful surely they could manage it, though again she didn't know how. If only Liam would come.

She was only half listening as Mrs Quinn and Victoria talked, making arrangements about something that seemed to concern Mrs Quinn getting a job somewhere. Perhaps she and Ma might do the same. Ma was so pretty and bright . . . well, she had used to be bright and would be again, Lily was sure, when she had recovered from Pa's death. She just needed a bit of time. She was good with her hands. Pa had always said she was good with her hands. She could knit the most beautiful jumpers, remembering the sea gansey which was packed in the straw basket behind the curtain, and her sewing was exquisite. She made all her own and Lily's undergarments, of the finest lawn and trimmed with lace, and her embroidery, done on the finest and most delicate of fabrics such as net and gauze and from her own design, was the most beautiful that Lily had ever seen. She had tried to teach Lily, just the simplest stitches like stem stitch and satin stitch but it had been hopeless. Lily wanted to be a sailor not a seamstress. She'd stitch sails if she had to, which sailors did, but not petticoats and pantaloons.

As though her thoughts, dreaming and insubstantial, had drifted on the cool, quiet air from her mind to her mother's, she suddenly spoke and they all turned, even the dog which lay before the grate, to look at her.

"Where is my sewing, Mrs Quinn?" she asked in what seemed to be a sensible voice. "I seem to have mislaid it. Do you happen to know where I left it?"

For a moment nobody spoke. It was the very first time she had addressed them without being addressed first. At other times she had hesitantly answered questions but this was different. This had come into her mind without prompting from them and Molly Quinn could feel her shoulders lifting and her back straightening as though a load had been lifted from it. There was no sewing, of course. Mrs Elliott had not done any sewing since the day the men came to tell her her husband was dead and whatever it was she had been doing was put away, or lost in the general upheaval of the day they had left Walton Lane.

But Molly Quinn's quick brain leaped to life and without thinking she put Lily from her and stood up.

"'Old on, I'll gerrit for yer, Mrs Elliott. I seen it somewhere . . . aah, yes, I know."

Both Lily and Victoria watched her with fascinated attention as she moved to the chest of drawers where she kept what little bed linen she had, all much patched but clean and still used, of course.

"Ah, yes, 'ere it is, my lamb." The endearment came from somewhere deep inside Molly Quinn, somewhere that was ready to weep with joy that this beloved woman appeared to have come back from the dead, so to speak. It was a start. It might not be much but it was a start and if Molly Quinn could keep it going, then she'd bloody well do it. She was to call her "my lamb", at least in private, for the remainder of their lives together.

She laid a folded sheet on the table. The Lord only knew where it had come from; she couldn't remember, probably the second-hand stall in Paddy's Market, but it was fine linen edged with lace. The lace was torn and the centre of the sheet was so thin you could have spat through it, in Mrs Quinn's parlance.

"Now you gerron with that, my lamb. You'll know better'n me what wants doin'. Middle ter edge, would yer say and then that lace needs a stitch or two."

"Indeed it does, Mrs Quinn. Now, if you'll hand me my sewing box I'll make a start."

Her sewing box! Dear God, what had become of her sewing box? But if Mrs Quinn's mind went cold and blank, Lily's didn't.

"It seems to be mislaid, Ma, but if Mrs Quinn gives you a needle and thread to be going on with, I'll have a look for it for you."

"Thank you, darling, that is kind of you."

Threading a needle with some hastily unearthed thread, Jane Elliott began to sew, her face tranquil.

It was two days later when the note came. It was delivered by a fresh-faced young lad in what could only be called "country" clothes. Well, it was country where he had come from, he told Lily later. He had taken exception to the jeers and whistles that had followed him through all the back streets and alleyways ever since he had left Chapel Street to venture into the maze of the dockland slums. He had been given precise instructions by Miss Quinn on how he was to get to her mother's house – if you could call it that, his freckled nose wrinkling in disgust. Follow the docks along the river, he had been told, along the Cast Iron Shore to Strand Street until he reached St Nicholas Church and he wasn't to stand gawping at the ships but to go straight there. At St Nicholas Church he was to turn right into Chapel Street to Key Street and Leeds Street and Brooke Alley was dead ahead of him. He was to put the note into Mrs Quinn's hand. Mrs Quinn was Miss Quinn's mother and this was a very important task. Very important indeed.

His rosy-cheeked face, his air of being well fed from the moment his infant mouth had fastened on his mam's nipple, his sturdy limbs, his sturdy boots and gaiters and corduroy breeches, his best jacket and peaked cap, come to him from his master's son who was grown up now, all gave him the look of a toff to the children he encountered and had he not been a lad who was handy with his fists, and with his tongue as well which gave as good as he got, he might have fared ill. As it was he was relieved to find the house, terrible though it seemed to his country-bred eyes, where Miss Quinn's mam apparently lived.

"Me name's Dick," he told the old lady who answered the door, "an' I've come from Silverdale. Miss Quinn gi' me this note an' I've ter wait for an answer. I work there," he added importantly.

He was quite flabbergasted when, on being asked to enter and sit himself down and would he fancy a fresh-baked scone, which of course he did, being a healthy lad with a healthy appetite, he found himself face to face with the most exquisite little girl he had ever come across in his life. She was sitting at the table writing on a bit of paper. He was impressed not only with her beauty and the way she was dressed but by the fact that she could write! Next to her, sewing on something, was a lady who was exactly like her, with silver hair and the softest smile just like the angel in Mam's picture which she directed right at him.

The girl didn't smile though. "Haven't you been told that it's rude to stare, boy," she said to him, without appearing even to look up from her writing.

"Now, Lily, haven't you been told it's rude to make personal remarks to people?"

"He's not people, Ma. He's only a boy."

Mrs Quinn, though her daughters could all read and write, thanks to her, could not and it was Lily who read the letter to her. It was from Victoria and in it she wrote that Mrs Jackson of Oakwood Place would be glad if Mrs Quinn would present herself for an interview for the post of cook/housekeeper on the following day.

"And Victoria says you've not to be late, Mrs Quinn."

"No, I realise that, child," Mrs Quinn answered absently, her mind twisting and turning on the problem of how she was to get from here to – where was it? – Oakwood Place, leaving Mrs Elliott and the child all on their own. It was only two days since Mrs Elliott had picked up her sewing again, stitching serenely from morning till night so that Molly wondered how she was going to keep her supplied with all the materials necessary, not to mention something actually to sew! She had finished the first sheet and was doing some fancy lace work round a pillowcase, but at the rate she was going that would soon be finished. All she could think of was that she would have to tear their clothes deliberately in order that Mrs Elliott could then mend them. She had been down to the pawnshop yesterday afternoon to see if there was a sewing box, complete with needles and threads and a thimble and had been in luck, though it had cost her the last of the savings she had put away for a rainy day. Good God, if it wasn't a rainy day now, when would it be!

"I'd best be gerrin back," the boy said uneasily, since he didn't fancy walking through these lurking streets after dark. He'd a long way to go, all the way to Silverdale and Miss Quinn would be waiting for an answer and would give him what for if he was late. He was the boot boy at Silverdale, not much of a job for a lad with his ambition, but he meant to get on and you had to start somewhere. His pa was a groom for Mr Hemingway and his mam helped with the laundry, but with a cottage filled with children of all ages from toddlers to himself who was the eldest at twelve, he was glad to be out of it and allowed to sleep above the stable with the grooms and stable hands.

Lily wrote the answer in her best handwriting, saying that Mrs Molly Quinn would be pleased to attend Mrs Jackson at Oakwood Place at the time stated, and after Dick had darted away down Brooke Alley all Molly had to do was rack her brains on the best way of going about it.

10

She took them with her in the end. Well, what else could she do? Mrs Elliott seemed calm enough, endlessly sewing on anything Molly put in her hands, simply sitting by the fire, or at the table with no thought in her head but putting in one tiny stitch after another, but Molly didn't trust the child and that was the truth of it. She could lock them in, of course, as she did when she went to the corner shop, but she had no idea how long she would be and she wouldn't put it past the little madam to break the window and climb out in her determination to go down to the docks and find that big chap. She appeared to be obsessed with him, positive that in him lay the answer to all the problems that plagued her and her ma. When he got back he would come. It was as certain as that and even the fact that they had been at Brooke Alley for going on eight weeks now and he had not turned up seemed to make no difference to her, and Molly was reluctant to burst the bubble of hope the child carried almost visibly around with her. It was as though he had taken her pa's place in her young mind and would find the perfect solution, as her pa had always done, for the continuation of Lily and her ma's life as it had been. Molly had even considered whether she might perhaps leave the pair of them with Mrs Meadows or Mrs Watson but something held her back. If Lily found herself back in Walton Lane among her friends she would expect to "play out" with them and Molly could not ask either of their previous neighbours to stand guard over her, or Mrs Elliott for that matter, and naturally there was no one in Brooke Alley who was even vaguely capable of watching over them.

"Are we going to Oakwood Place?" Lily asked her as Molly pulled her little jacket round her and fastened the many tiny gilt buttons that marched up the front to the high, military-style neck. It fitted snugly into her waist and was edged with midnight blue braid. With it she wore a full, gathered, midnight blue skirt which just reached the top of her black-buttoned kid boots. Below the hem hung half an inch of her petticoat which was edged with frilled lace. On her head was perched a jaunty pill-box hat, tilted above her forehead and secured beneath her chin with narrow velvet ribbon. Her thick silvery plait was looped under itself and secured with a knot of scarlet ribbons, for if it was left it hung below her waist. Afterwards Mrs Quinn was often to wonder why she had dressed the child, and her ma, in their best finery, for they were only to sit in the cab and wait for her!

"Ask me no questions an' I'll tell yer no lies," she replied tartly.

"Well, that's the silliest answer I've ever heard, and if you don't tell me I'm not going," Lily told her disdainfully, then her imperious expression changed to one of wild hope. "Is it to the docks? Have you heard that the *Caledonia* has moored? Is Liam coming, is he?"

"No, it isn't an' no, I 'aven't 'eard from him an' I wish yer'd give over worryin' about 'im. Chuck, 'e's got more to think about than . . . well, fer all we know 'e might 'ave a family, a wife an' children of 'is own an' e'll norr'ave time ter come 'ere. Yer know wharra seaman's life's like. In port one day an' out again the next nearly. Yer pa . . ."

But Lily didn't want to be reminded about her pa and she twitched herself away from Mrs Quinn's busy hands, her face mutinous, and Molly wondered despairingly what she was going to do with this lovely but increasingly naughty child who only last night had thrown Mrs Elliott's good china teacup at the wall, smashing it to pieces and making the blasted dog bark its silly head off. Lily had howled that she would go out, she would. She didn't care if all those horrid children outside called her names and threw lumps of shit . . . yes, she had screamed, that was what it was called, she had heard one say so. She'd run away and find Liam or Mr Meadows or Mr Watson or . . . or . . . Here she'd run out of people she knew. She had stamped her feet and wept bitter tears, saying she wanted her pa, so distraught she had upset Mrs Elliott who had begun to cry too. Lily had been sorry then and had hugged her ma and kissed her wet cheek but there was nothing her ma could say to comfort her, and neither could Molly, for the situation seemed hopeless. She couldn't keep them locked up here for much longer, even if it was for their own safety. This job would be a life-saver, if she got it, but then, if she did, what was she to do with these two while she was out? It was a huge dilemma; well, more than that, it was a bloody impossibility and she despaired of ever getting round it. It was her wildest hope that she might be able to persuade them at Oakwood Place to let her go home at night, that's if she got the job, though she didn't hold out much expectation of either: getting the job or of being allowed to live out. Housekeepers and cooks were often required to work until late, so she had heard. The gentry did a lot of entertaining, dinner parties and such and it was hardly likely they'd allow her to take off her pinny at six o'clock and tell them she was off home now, was it? Dear God, she'd finish up in an early grave, she knew she would if this thing wasn't resolved soon. In fact she was beginning to believe that their Victoria was right and that she'd have to put the pair of them into some place of safety, perhaps the Ladies of the Society for Bettering the Condition and Increasing the Comfort of the Poor might be able to guide her to the right place but it had better be soon or they'd all three starve.

Refusing to tell Lily or her ma where they were going, she led them through the stinking streets, beseeching them to hold up their skirts out of the filth, until they reached the corner where Vauxhall Road met Tithebarn Street. There was a hansom cab just discharging a passenger and with a fluttering heart and a dry mouth Molly put up her hand to get the cabbie's attention.

"Where to, ma'am?" he asked her politely, for it was very evident in his eyes that at least one of the females was a lady and the child her daughter. The woman who had hailed him must be the child's nanny, he had decided, or the lady's companion, for she was dressed in respectable black, a good quality cloak and bonnet, her boots well polished and her face well scrubbed.

He had seen a great many pretty ladies, real ladies, in his time but the one who climbed gracefully into his cab was a real head-turner. She was dressed in the palest duck egg blue with a skirt so wide she had the greatest difficulty manoeuvring it into the cab. It was flounced, each flounce edged with blue velvet. The bodice was slightly too large for her, he had time to notice as he handed her in, though it in no way detracted from her elegance and fragile beauty. Draped about her shoulders and hanging over her arms was a large cream shawl, fringed and very fine, embroidered with blue to match her dress, and on her incredible silver blonde hair was what was known as a cream straw "round-hat" – though he was not aware of its name – with a wide flexible brim and a low flat crown. It was mushroom-shaped and trimmed with pale duck egg blue ribbon round the crown with floating ends down her back. It was tied to her head with matching ribbons under her chin from beneath its brim. She carried a dainty drawstring reticule.

It was the woman in black who answered him.

"Oakwood Place on Holmes Lane. D'yer know it?"

"Can't say I do, ma'am, burrif yer was ter direct me I reckon I can find it."

"Are we going about the job, Mrs Quinn?" he heard the child say, but the woman hushed her and the child's mother seemed to drift off into some dream world of her own, taking no notice of the child, her companion or the route they were taking.

It was a Wednesday and as it was on any weekday the streets were bursting with pedestrians dodging smart carriages coming from and going to the fine shops in Bold Street where the wives of the wealthy and influential men of Liverpool had their gowns and bonnets and boots created. The sun broke through clouds which had gathered all morning but which were now drifting out to sea on a mild breeze. The golden light shone brightly on the glossy coats of the fine horses that pulled the carriages and on the equally well-groomed backs of the gigantic, patient Shires that plodded beside them, pulling a completely different kind of equipage: waggons loaded with goods for the docks, with barrels of beer from the brewery, with crates and boxes of every shape and size, lumbering in and out of wide gateways, causing hold-ups and tangles of traffic above which could be heard the curses of the drivers as their wheels seemed in great danger of becoming locked. There were boys on every corner, barefoot and as filthy as the streets they cleared of the droppings of the hundreds of horses that passed by. There were other children, not so apathetic as the ones Lily had become used to seeing from Mrs Quinn's basement window, ready to jeer or throw stones, and there was a policeman, resplendent in his dark blue coat, red waistcoat and tall black hat who chased them away. There were dozens of vehicles, drays and milk carts and hansom cabs, horse-drawn trams, all doing their best to push through the press of people and conveyances and get to where they were going no matter what the risk.

Jane Elliott looked impassively out of the window but when the hansom cab reached the southern outskirts of the city and began to pass pleasant terraced houses and small villas Lily, who had watched with great interest the throbbing scene beyond the cab's window, began to show signs of excitement. She didn't know why really, because it was a suburb of Liverpool she didn't know but it was away from that appalling place where they had lived, like pampered prisoners in an underground cell, for the past eight weeks and surely it promised that some change was under way.

"Oh look, the river's just over there," Lily squeaked excitedly, pointing to her right. "Oh, please, please, won't you tell us what is happening? Are we going to enquire after the job Victoria told us about? Are we Mrs Quinn"?

Her head turned constantly from side to side as the cab driver whipped the horse up to a brisk trot round Princes Park, along Belvedere Road and into Aigburth Road. They were well clear of the city now with open fields on either side cut here and there by high walls with fine gates in them, newly greening trees arching over smoothly raked gravelled drives that led away to some great house probably belonging to a ship-owner or a merchant prince, for there were many such in Liverpool and this was where they chose to live.

The fields, those that were not ploughed into pleasing brown furrows, were a living canvas of golden cowslips and primroses, the pale white and lilac of cuckoo-flowers and the delicate green of new grass in which cows stood knee-deep, turning their slow heads to watch the cab go by. There was a little spinney about halfway along the road beneath whose trees was a carpet of golden daffodils trumpeting the arrival of spring, nodding as though in welcome as the breeze moved their glorious heads.

They came to a sign that told them they were entering Holmes Lane and, turning into it, Lily was enraptured at the sight of pale yellow ox-slips growing on the banks side by side with the sweet purple of dog violets and the striking pink of cranesbill, the hedges themselves already in bud for the explosion of pure white of the hawthorn blossom that would come in May. Lily had her head out of the lowered window by now, and she drew in deep breaths of pure country air, which she had missed for so long, craning her neck to watch a formation of swallows flying high. A blackbird sang madly in the hedge and the sky, now that they were away from the smoke pall of Liverpool, was clear, achingly blue and cloudless.

And she could see the river! It was there, just across the fields, the sun sparking ripples of silver off the water. There were ships, dozens of them, small and large, iron ships, full-rigged, topsail schooners, brigs, three-masted barques, trawlers, tugboats and a ferry boat bobbing up and down on the swell as it made its way from Liverpool to Eastham. Coastal ships and deep-sea ships, every kind of ship, and Lily felt her heart, which had been buried in the deep alleyway where Mrs Quinn had taken them, lift with joy and excited anticipation. Something was afoot. Mrs Quinn would not bring them all this way in a hansom cab, which she knew she could ill afford, having heard nothing but how they must economise for weeks now, just for a casual jaunt.

There was a pair of stone pillars set in a high stone wall and between the pillars were two glossily painted wrought-iron gates, both of them closed. On the other side of the wall, which stretched for as far as Lily could see in both directions, was what appeared to be a small woodland. The river could not be seen from here and Lily had the idea that whatever was behind the wall must run down down to the water.

Mrs Quinn rapped on the roof to attract the attention of the cabbie who at once brought the horse and cab to a halt.

"I think this is it," she told him, staring doubtfully at the rather forbidding gates, "though there's no sign ter tell yer."

"Gentry don't purrup signs, ma'am," he told her through the small window in the roof, "but this is 'Olmes Lane so I reckon this could be't place. Shall I go an' open 't gates?"

"No, I'd best gerrout an' see," she told him firmly. He had leaped down from his seat ready to fling back the gates but at her words he turned back and opened the cab door instead, surprised that the ladies were proposing to walk the length of the drive to get to the house instead of letting him take them there.

"Shall I not tekk yer up there, ma'am," he said politely to the lovely woman, since she must be the mistress of the other but she stared at him in dismay and cowered back in her seat.

"She's not comin'," the lady in black told him shortly. "In fact I want yer ter stay 'ere an' wait fer me. I'll not . . . not be long."

"But wharrabout me fare? I can't afford ter 'ang about 'ere . . ."

"Yer'll be paid wharrever goin' rate is an' a bit beside when yer've gorrus 'ome."

"I thought this were—"

"Yer not paid ter think, lad. You just wait 'ere fer me. 'An don't let these two outer yer sight, d'yer 'ear me."

"'Ere, I'm not paid ter be a nursemaid," though he had to admit it would be pleasant to chat to the lady and the little girl for a few minutes while the older one went and did her errand, whatever it was.

Molly reached back into the cab and took Jane's hand in hers. "I won't be long, lamb. If yer want ter gerrout an' stretch yer legs then I reckon it'll be all right, but don't go outer sight o't cab. See, Lily, look after yer ma, there's a good lass. I've a birra business to attend to burr I'll not be long. Now I'm trustin' yer ter look after yer ma, Lily."

"I will, Mrs Quinn, I promise." Lily well knew by this time that her ma needed a lot of looking after, that the smallest thing upset her. She loved her ma and was passionately protective of her which she knew her pa would approve of. This was turning out to be a grand day and she and ma were going to enjoy it so she must behave herself or it would be spoiled, for her and for Ma.

Mrs Quinn cautiously opened the well-oiled gates and stepped inside, then swung them to behind her with the haunted look of a prisoner taking a last look at the world before going to the gallows. With a last nervous wave at the two faces that peeped at her from the cab window she began to walk up the drive, disappearing from view round a bend.

Lily had persuaded her ma to step out of the cab and come and smell the blossoming buds which were spread like icing sugar on the hedge opposite the gates. It was pleasantly warm and as quiet and tranquil as only a deserted country lane can be. There was no sound but birdsong and the hissing whistle of the cabbie who was becoming increasingly impatient with the situation. He had been disappointed when the woman shrank back when he attempted to engage her in conversation and his irritation showed in the way he slapped the reins on the horse's back. He wasn't awfully sure whether or not the woman had abandoned these two and if so what was he to do, marooned out here in the middle of nowhere with no chance of getting a fare back to the city and nothing to show for the journey he had already made. On top of that he'd been sitting on his bum for half an hour now while the lady and her child wandered further and further out of his sight down the lane.

At last he could stand no more. He jumped down from his high seat and began to walk after them. The horse, unhindered now by the reins, moved in a leisurely plod towards the hedge and began to eat the vegetation with great smacking sounds of appreciation.

"Aay," the cabbie shouted. "'Ow much longer am I supposed ter 'ang about 'ere? Is t'other woman comin' back or wha'? I've a livin' ter earn, yer know."

Lily, who was carefully holding her ma's hand, turned back. She had been enjoying herself for only the second time since Pa died, the first being on the day she walked down to the docks, and she knew Ma was too. Ma had picked a little bunch of wild daffodils which were growing on the bank and was sniffing about her as though the fragrance of the fields and hedges and trees, none of which either of them had known for weeks, was a pleasure to her.

"Well, I don't know. She did say she wouldn't be long."

"That were 'alf an 'our ago, queen." He was beginning to look seriously aggrieved and it was then that Lily had the delightful idea that if she was to go up the gravelled path that Mrs Quinn had taken and enquire for her at the house, which she supposed was where Mrs Quinn had gone, she might get a closer look at the river and the ships.

"Well, I suppose I could go and see if I can find her. That's if you don't mind waiting a few more minutes."

The cabbie, who had already wasted a whole morning, or so it was beginning to appear, told her sullenly that a few more minutes would make no difference to him, resisting the temptation to curse and say she'd best look lively or he'd be off back to town.

"Very well, I'll be as quick as I can and I'll tell Mrs Quinn what you said."

"You do that, queen," he told her truculently, watching as she opened the gates and in a way that surprised him coaxed the woman through them.

"Come on, Ma," she was saying, "there's nothing to be afraid of, God's honour. Just look at those daffodils under the trees, aren't they lovely? Yes, I'll hold your hand, dearest," which she had begun to call her ma because that's what Pa had called her. "We'll just go and find Mrs Quinn and then we might have a walk down to the river, would you like that?"

"I think I would, darling," the mother answered, the first words the cab driver had heard her speak since he had picked them up.

It was not going well, she knew it wasn't. For a start the cook/housekeeper at Oakwood Place was a cantankerous old biddy who, Molly decided, would not be satisfied with anyone, even if she had references from the Queen herself. She had ruled this kitchen for twenty years, ever since the master had brought his young bride home; the kitchen *and* the house for ten years ever since that same young bride had died. She had absolute power over everyone in it, except for the master and the family, of course, and she was furious that her age and increasing infirmities were forcing her to give it up. She could barely walk what with her rheumatics and the pain in her joints, which again put her in such vile moods she had all the housemaids in tears at least once a day. It took her half an hour to get on her feet in the morning and stagger to the chair by the fireside where she remained for most of the day, and though she had managed for almost a year now with the help of Maggie, who was head housemaid, to guide her here and there, it had come to the notice of the master and that was that, of course. She would have a snug cottage and enough money to live out her days, the master had told her that, but it wasn't the same, was it.

Mrs Quinn was the sixth woman she had interviewed and not one had suited her, and she told the master so as each one left. Too old, not clean enough for Mrs Jackson's liking, references not good enough, couldn't cook to save her life in

Mrs Jackson's opinion, though how she knew she wouldn't say, too high and mighty, too meek and mild which attitude wouldn't rule the servants in her care, and so on and so on and it looked as though this one was going the same way. For a start, though she was scrupulously clean and respectable-looking, she hadn't the experience needed in a house like this. She'd been cook/housekeeper for a Mrs Elliott for ten years so she must have been suitable, but it turned out there were only three in the family and no other servants so what use was that to anyone? This house had nine indoor servants not including herself and eight outside and though the outside men were in the charge of the head groom and the head gardener, the housemaids had to be supervised by the housekeeper. And this woman had never been in charge of other servants in her life, it appeared.

"What kind of meals can you prepare, Mrs . . . er . . . Quinn?" she asked Molly, who did her best to think of something that might sound difficult. The sort of meal that might be eaten by a family who lived in a house like this. Even the kitchens overwhelmed her in their grandeur, not just one room but several in which it seemed different tasks were performed. If the kitchens were like this, all gleaming and spotless and containing objects and pieces of machinery whose purpose was a mystery to her, what was the rest of the house like? She had been struck speechless when she turned the bend in the drive and saw the house for the first time, a great towering place with turrets and tall chimneys and what seemed like hundreds of windows, all glittering in the sunlight. The front door was enormous with steps leading up to it from beneath a kind of pillared porch and there were men about in the garden, doing things with trowels and hoes and clippers and when one spoke to her she nearly turned round and fled for her life back down the drive.

"Round the back, queen," he said, evidently recognising her as a person of the lower orders, but smiling kindly just the same.

Now she stammered and stuttered as she did her best to answer Mrs Jackson's probing questions and when a bell jangled somewhere on the wall she nearly jumped out of her skin.

"See what the master wants, Maggie," Mrs Jackson told a woman who was polishing something at the table. Mrs

Jackson had her feet propped up on a stool and every now and again she winced as though struck by a sudden pain.

"Right, Mrs Jackson," the woman, one of six all busy at some task, answered submissively, going through a door which led, Molly supposed, into the house.

She was back in two minutes, shaking her head, her white frilled cap bobbing, her face alight with excitement, barely able to get the words out and it was plain that Mrs Jackson was irritated. Mrs Jackson looked the sort of woman who would become irritated often and very easily.

"For God's sake, woman, speak up. There's no need to stand there gibbering like a halfwit. What did the master want?"

"Oh, Mrs Jackson . . ."

"Yes?" The expression on Mrs Jackson's face was becoming more and more treacherous and Molly had time to think that she would rather work in the laundry in Banastre Street than for this woman.

"There's a woman, Mrs Jackson."

"A woman? Where, in God's name? Pull yourself together, Maggie, or I shall be forced to slap you."

"In the garden, Mrs Jackson, and there's a child with her."

"A child?"

"Yes." The whole of the kitchen had come to a jarring halt, hands poised over bowls and dishes and trays and Molly felt her heart begin to bang against her breastbone. Before her eyes flashed a picture of Mrs Elliott and the child, for who else could it be, either being hauled off to gaol for trespassing or being dumped in the poorhouse for want of anyone to look after them, for she certainly couldn't, not the way things were going.

Mrs Jackson seemed somewhat undecided what her part in this drama, if that was what it was, was to be, but Maggie managed finally to tell her.

"Master says she's to be fetched from the garden and shown in."

"Shown in! To him?"

"Aye, that what he said. 'Go and get that lady from the garden and bring her to me,' he says, 'and ask Mrs Jackson to send in tea.'"

"Tea!"

Molly nearly laughed out loud and had she not been so

frightened for Mrs Elliott and the child she might have done so. Mrs Jackson was acting as though the master, and the woman in the garden, whoever she might be, were in conspiracy to put her day totally out of joint and just when she was enjoying herself, probably for what could be the last time, chucking her weight about with Molly and the servants in her charge.

"Well," she said at last. "You'd best do as he says."

11

Lily was not afraid though she knew her ma was.

They hadn't got as far as the river, which was a shame, for she would have liked to stand on the shore and watch the ships skimming the water but Ma kept being distracted by something she spotted in the truly wonderful garden they had entered and wanted to go and have a closer look. Lily hadn't the heart to stop her, though her whole being, her very heart and soul, was crying out to get down to where the ships where.

The drive curved away from the wrought-iron gates which Lily closed carefully behind her, turning to the right, both sides of it shaded by closely packed trees and huge bushes which were coming into bud in glorious colours of flaming pink and purple. The dense woodland thinned out as she and Ma got further from the gate. The grass beneath these trees was starred with golden clumps of wild daffodils, nearly finished now but still vividly bright and graceful. Rough paths of mown grass meandered off into the stand of trees and Lily would have liked to follow one of them to see where it led but she supposed it would be more sensible to find the house and enquire from someone the whereabouts of Mrs Quinn.

The house, when it came into view, took them both by surprise. It was quite enormous, built of mellow, honey-coloured stone with a turret at each corner and a great pillared entrance to which the drive curved. There were wide steps, some from the great stretch of immaculate lawn which sloped up to the porch and others from the porch up to the front door. There were no trees here except for two ancient spreading oaks, one on either side of the house, but there were flowering shrubs and clipped hedges and bushes that looked like animals and birds and other things that Lily could not identify. Edging the drive were neat rows of narcissus and primula and other spring flowers Lily did not know the names of, ribbons of colour which led away along paved walks to a lake half hidden among the trees and on which swam several ducks. Against the house on either side of the porch and beneath the windows were terraces edged with stone pillars and flowering urns and on them were white-painted wooden benches and vast terracotta pots filled with massed bright and colourful flowers, all carefully tended. Though it was only April there was colour and fragrance everywhere and Jane Elliott was enchanted. She drifted from one lovely plant to another, bending her graceful head to sniff their fragrance, her shawl slipping from her shoulders, the hem of her gown trailing on the close-cut grass and it was in this lovely setting and this enchanting pose that Joshua Crowther saw her for the first time.

He had been considering a business deal with another gentleman which he thought might be rewarding to both of them. Joshua Crowther never did business deals that were any other, which was why he was so wealthy but he did not always work *just* to become wealthy. Sometimes it was the challenge of pitting his wits against another man's which speeded him on and the deal he was mulling over was one of these. He was not in any particular line of business. There was no need to be in this thriving port where so much was going on that any man with his wits about him who was prepared to take a risk had as good a chance of making money as the next. There was shipping, manufacturing, exporting and importing, railways, the building of houses as the city spread outwards, the lending of money to speculators at enormous rates of interest and he had a finger in all of them.

He had been sprawled out before his study fire, his long legs stretched out before him, his feet propped on the fender and crossed at the ankle, his chin resting on his steepled fingers, his thoughts clear and concise as always. Feeling the need to move about, which often helped him to crystallise something in his mind, he stood up, pushed his hands into his trouser pockets and strolled across to the window which looked out over the front lawns.

She was the most exquisite thing he had ever seen and his wife had been considered a beauty but this woman was like nothing he had ever known before and what he felt was like nothing he had ever felt before. He stood for several minutes at the window, watching her, her hand in that of a beautifully dressed little girl. The sun glinted on her hair which was the incredible colour and had the polished sheen of a newly minted silver coin. Even from here he could see the bloom of her flawless skin, cream and rose, and the grace of her long neck which seemed to bend like the stalk of a flower. He was stunned and speechless, incapable of thought, or even wonder at who she was. She looked so exactly right there. So totally in the place that was meant for her, that had been made for her and in that moment Joshua knew he must have her. He hadn't the faintest idea who she was or what she was doing in his garden but it didn't matter. It didn't matter if she was the wife of some other man and completely out of his reach, he must have her and with the same direct ruthlessness with which he dealt with everything from the running of his business interests to the bringing up of his children, he took the shortest route to getting what he wanted.

He rang the bell.

Lily was alarmed when the maidservant appeared at the front door, getting ready to run for cover dragging Ma with her. She was doing nothing wrong, though she supposed they were trespassing, but she had come for a good reason and that was the searching out of Mrs Quinn who was somewhere in this house.

"I'm sorry," she began politely. "I know we shouldn't be here but you see—"

"Never mind that, girl, the master wants to see you." The maid had a sharp face, pointed and foxy but her eyes were not unkind and she was smiling.

"We weren't doing anything bad, God's honour, only Ma loves flowers and I couldn't—"

"It doesn't matter, girl. You come along with me and I'll take you to the master."

"Oh, please, he won't frighten Ma, will he?" Lily pleaded, for already her mother was dragging at her hand in an effort to get back to where they had come from, back to the hansom cab at the gate.

"Nay, lass, he won't hurt you or your mother but you'd best hurry up because he doesn't like to be kept waiting."

"Well, I will if I can get Ma moving."

For the first time Maggie noticed the confusion on the face of the beautiful woman. She had wondered why the child did all the talking instead of the woman but it seemed she was not right in the head or else why should she be so frightened, which is what she appeared to be. She was obviously the girl's mother but she looked so disturbed Maggie glanced about her as though searching for someone to help her. She'd have to get a move on or the master himself might come out and he could be a tartar when he was crossed.

"Dearest," the child was saying to the woman, "there's nothing to be afraid of, really. We are to go inside this lovely house and . . . and have a look round. Wouldn't you like that? The gardens are splendid but I'm sure the inside of the house will be just as wonderful and this lady" – indicating the wondering maid – "has invited us . . ."

"To take tea," the servant finished daringly.

"I'm not sure I should, darling," Jane Elliott quavered, for, as usual, anything that was out of step with the tempo she had got used to frightened her.

Lily looked about her in much the same way that the maid-servant had done, then her mind fastened on the one person who would have this little problem sorted out in a trice.

"Is Mrs Quinn about?" she asked the woman on the step hopefully.

"Mrs Quinn?"

"Yes, she came to see someone here but I don't know who or where she might be."

"You mean her in the kitchen with Mrs Jackson?"

Lily looked baffled, beginning also to look somewhat dishevelled as she struggled to hold on to her mother.

"I suppose so."

"Well . . ."

"I'd be obliged if you'd fetch her," she said in her most grown-up manner. "She knows how to handle Ma, you see."

The maid looked bewildered. Handle Ma! What on earth did the child mean? She hadn't the faintest idea but she'd better get a move on or the master'd be out here to find out what was happening to the order he had just given her and he could frighten the wits out of the most courageous!

It took almost fifteen minutes before the order Joshua Crowther had given to his housemaid was executed and the trembling figure of Jane Elliott was led into his drawing-room which he had decided was more appropriate for entertaining a lady. If he was astonished when she came in on the arm of a decently clad woman who was obviously a servant he did not show it. The lovely child trailed behind them, her face a picture of bright interest.

Joshua Crowther could be kind, charming, gentle, gracious when he chose, showing a side of him that none who did business with him would have recognised. He was not a sensitive man but he was intuitive and his intuition told him that he must tread carefully here.

He rose from the chair where he had seated himself after watching the antics on his lawn, a pleasant smile on his handsome face, but he did not move forward to greet Jane Elliott as he would have done with any other lady. Again his instinct was at work.

"Good morning," he said, "or is it good afternoon. Time gets away from you sometimes, doesn't it? Do you find that? Is it a sign that we are happy, or just forgetful? I have been reading and became so engrossed in my book I did not notice the time. Now please, won't you sit down?" indicating a chair near the wide French window from which she would see the garden she had just been exploring. "I've ordered some tea. May I offer you a cup, and your companion, and perhaps the little girl would care for some . . . some lemonade?"

"Yes, I would, please," Lily said, turning to smile at him from a table crammed with the loveliest things which she had been examining.

"And perhaps some biscuits . . . or . . ." What in hell's name did females like on occasions such as this? He hadn't the faintest idea since he had never attended one.

"Cakes would be nice," Lily told him simply, unafraid and supremely confident.

He passed on Lily's order to the hovering maid who couldn't wait to get back to the kitchen to tell them of the extraordinary goings-on in the drawing-room. Mrs Jackson had nearly thrown the teapot at Mrs Quinn when she was summoned to the front of the house. Mrs Quinn was *hers* and had no right to tread the carpeted hallway that led from the servants' quarters to the family's. What on earth was going on when a woman who had no qualifications, no status, no possible need or reason to be there, could go and sit in the master's drawing-room and drink tea, which Mrs Jackson's staff would have to make for her. It was beyond all comprehending and there was one thing for sure, she'd not step into Mary Jackson's shoes when she retired!

The tea was brought and for a dithering moment Maggie didn't know where the trolley should be placed. It was hardly a man's job to pour, was it and yet these two women were visitors and what the protocol was she couldn't fathom. She put it near Mrs Quinn who seemed the most likely, the most sensible of the two and waited deferentially for further orders. Perhaps she was to pour and hand round the teacups. She hoped so, then she could report back to them in the kitchen what was going on. She was to be disappointed.

"That will be all, thank you, Maggie. I'm sure we can manage nicely. I'll ring if I need you."

He waited until the door was closed behind the maid before he spoke.

"Perhaps we should introduce ourselves first," he said gently, smiling at the troubled face of Jane Elliott. He was glad to see she had calmed down somewhat now that she had the hand of the woman in black to cling to. "My name is Joshua Crowther. May I ask yours?"

It was the woman in black who answered. "I'm afraid my mistress 'as been ill, sir. She . . . she lost 'er 'usband a few weeks back an' it's tekkin' 'er a while ter gerrover it. She's very . . . shy."

A widow! He had always considered himself to be a lucky man, though he firmly believed that a man also made his own luck but this was more than he could have hoped for. No man standing between himself and what he wanted. A woman still in the throes, one presumed and didn't her actions verify it, of grieving. Vulnerable, ready to fall like a sweet, ripe peach into the hands of the first man who was kind to her and Joshua Crowther could be very kind when he chose. He wasn't sure how he was going to get her into his bed but he knew he would eventually. Even if he had to marry her. Which was not a bad idea, for she would grace any man's table.

"I'm so sorry. I know what it's like to lose a loved one."

Jane Elliott's eyes, which had been wide and frightened, became clear and soft and she smiled tremulously at him. Incredibly, he felt his heart stir with something he did not recognise but it made him even gentler with her.

"May I know your name?" His voice was as smooth as silk and Jane Elliott was reassured.

"Jane . . . Elliott." It was said in almost a whisper but it was a good start, he thought. At least she had answered him.

"Mrs Elliott, it is a pleasure to meet you. And you, madam?" turning courteously to Mrs Quinn. Joshua knew exactly who it was, in any deal, who should be deferred to.

"Mrs Quinn, sir. I'm 'ouskeeper ter Mrs Elliott. I've bin lookin' after 'er since the captain died."

"The captain?"

"Mrs Elliott's 'usband."

"Not . . . Richard Elliott?"

"Yes, sir."

"I think we should go home now, Mrs Quinn." Jane began to clutch at Mrs Quinn and Lily moved towards her with the instinct of a mother protecting her child. "It's . . . I think . . . it would be better if . . ."

Joshua knew he had made a mistake in mentioning the name of this woman's husband. She was obviously not herself, in fact she was beginning to struggle with her shawl and her reticule, doing her best to get the housekeeper to her feet and lead her from the room and the child was helping her. He was aware that if she went it might be tricky getting her back again. He had to win her trust *now*. It was unfortunate that he should have blurted out the man's name, the man whose ship he had taken to pay back some of the money Richard Elliott owed him. He had known the man had a wife and child and when the bailiffs were called in to see what could be rescued from the mass of debts he had incurred he had given no thought to what would become of these two. It was a fact of life. Men got into debt and women suffered, but now he could put that right. It was not, of course, the reason for doing what he was determined to do.

"Please, Mrs Elliott, I beg your forgiveness. I'm a crass idiot and deserve to be horsewhipped for upsetting you. Please, don't go. Drink your tea – if you would be so good as to pour, Mrs Quinn – and rest before you go home. I saw you in the garden and noticed how much you enjoyed it and perhaps, when you've finished your tea, you and your companion might like to see the plants in my winter garden. It's a glass conservatory and my wife, sadly gone now, I'm afraid, put in cages of birds and . . . well, when you have finished your tea, if you feel up to it, we shall have a look. It's only through those doors."

The room was on a corner, the front overlooking the gardens but on the second outside wall a conservatory had been built. There were wide doors leading into it and from within could be heard the cheerful twitter of birds. Jane Elliott stopped her tussle with Mrs Quinn, with Lily and her reticule, lifting her head to listen intently to the sound and a look of interest passed across her face, smoothing it, erasing the confusion and grief Joshua's word had aroused in her. She stood up and Mrs Quinn stood up with her and without looking again at Joshua she began to walk towards the open doorway. Lily went with her and, rising to his feet, so did Joshua. Mrs Quinn threw him an apologetic glance but he nodded at her to show her it was all right.

Jane hesitated in the doorway, her lovely eyes which Joshua couldn't decide were grey or violet, looking about her. An expression of wondering delight lit her face. The conservatory, or winter garden as it was known, had been built by the previous owner of Oakwood Place and it was very evident that whoever had lived there had loved the cultivation of flowers. It was a very grand affair, built entirely of graceful fretwork and glass, stretching from the drawing-room at least thirty feet along the side of the house and it was entirely filled with exotic plants. There were small palm trees, plants known as birds of paradise in vivid orange, a monkey-puzzle tree, limes and bleeding heart vines in a delicate white and scarlet, hibiscus with frilly petalled crimson flowers, sweet-scented jasmine, passion flowers, magnolia, all growing in pots of every size and colour. From the high glass ceiling hung baskets with trailing ivy and among them half a dozen pretty cages, each one containing a singing bird. Set in groups on the tiled floor were white-painted basket chairs with brightly coloured cushions, round tables with lace cloths thrown over them and beneath the lace another cloth of deep green. All very inviting. Lying in a patch of sunlight was a black and white cat.

"Ooh . . ." Jane put her hands together as though in prayer, her fingers to her lips. She stepped hesitantly through the doors and slowly began a tour of the garden, touching with tender fingers this bloom and that, bending to smell the jasmine, moving slowly as though in a dream, watched by Molly Quinn and Joshua Crowther. For some reason they turned to smile at one another as though in shared triumph. Jane bent to run her hand over the cat's glossy coat then picked it up as it purred rapturously.

"Look, Lily, is she – or is it a he – not handsome? And did you ever see such a glorious room? Listen to the birds sing and the warmth from the sun would make you want to spend all your day here. It's . . . it's heavenly . . . so peaceful and . . . and safe."

"Perhaps we could have our tea here, Mrs Elliott," Joshua suggested, "if Mrs Quinn would like to bring the trolley through."

"Oh, that would be lovely, Mr . . . ?"

"Crowther. Joshua Crowther."

"Mr Crowther. How lucky you are to have such a lovely place. We can appreciate it all the more after . . ." For a second she became confused again and Lily, who was poking her nose into one of the bird cages, trying to decide what kind of bird was in it, for she had certainly never seen its like before, turned to her and began to stroke the cat in her arms which sounded as though it had an engine rumbling inside it.

"What's its name, Mr Crowther?" she asked. "I have a dog named Villette but we usually call her Villy."

"Have you indeed? It seems we have something in common then, Miss Elliott. I have three dogs out in the stables. Two black labradors and a golden retriever. Henry, Wally and Alex after my three favourite authors."

"Really? Who are they, then? I don't know of an author called Wally."

He laughed and thought what a taking child she was. He would have no trouble assimilating her into his household.

"Well, there's Henry Fielding, Sir Walter Scott and Alexandre Dumas. But I must confess that I don't know the cat's name. I think it must have sneaked in from the kitchen."

While he was talking to the child he was watching her mother as she drifted peacefully about his winter garden. She still held the cat in her arms, her long, slender hand smoothing its fur and he could see she was totally herself now, or as he imagined she would be in normal circumstances. Relaxed and . . . yes, at home in this room which some lady who had once lived here had created. The house was Georgian and he had loved it from the first moment he had set eyes on it, knowing it was the perfect setting for himself, who was then an up-and-coming force in the city, his lovely young bride and the many children they would have. To some extent his dream had been fulfilled but now it seemed it was to be made perfect.

Molly Quinn wheeled in the trolley. She had removed her black cloak, though not her bonnet and with a confidence that amazed her, for she had never been in a place like this before, guided Jane to a seat, told Lily to stop messing about with those birds and sit down, poured the tea with an expert hand and passed a cup first to her mistress, then to the extraordinary Mr Crowther. She was astonished at the way he seemed able to draw out her mistress, speaking softly as though she were to be treated with the greatest respect and courtesy, asking her simple questions that did not tax her fragile grasp on this new experience. Lily behaved impeccably, drinking her lemonade and though she ate half a dozen dainty cucumber sandwiches, five of the little fancy cakes which were sent in at the master's command, two freshly buttered scones and a slice of rich pound cake – and could you blame her, the poor food she had been eating these last weeks – she was as dainty as a little cat about it. Molly's mind was in turmoil, for what was to come out of all this? She hadn't a cat in hell's chance of getting the job of housekeeper, that was for sure. She had seen the expression of venom on the old biddy's face in the kitchen when she had been summoned to the front of the house, but really, had you ever seen a man as taken with a woman as Mr Crowther seemed to be with Mrs Elliott and where might that end? She didn't dare hope. She didn't dare even think about it as she sipped her own cup of tea, hot and sweet and strong just as she liked it.

Lily, with her prettiest manners, just as though she knew she must be on her best behaviour, asked to be excused and might she have a look round the drawing-room at all the lovely things Mr Crowther had on display? She was given permission and as she stood up, so did Jane, drifting off vaguely to sniff a blossom, touch a leaf, gaze out of the window at the men who were working in the garden, the cat still cuddled in her arms.

Joshua Crowther turned politely to Molly Quinn.

"Mrs Quinn, I can see you are troubled about something. Won't you tell me your story, and theirs," indicating the woman at the window and the child who had disappeared into the drawing-room.

Molly drew a deep breath. Perhaps there was a chance for her after all, and if for her, then for them.

"Well, sir," she began, "it started when Captain Elliott died in an accident at sea."

"Tell me about it."

So she did, from that first day when they had been told of his death, the dreadful effect it had had on Mrs Elliott, the bailiffs who had turned them out on the street, their flight to Brooke Alley . . .

"Brooke Alley?"

"Aye, tis off Vauxhall Road and norr at all wha' they're used to."

She could see the appalled shock on his face at the idea of the flower-like Mrs Elliott being forced to live in such a terrible area. He knew what it was like. He had property there.

"I 'ad ter keep 'em locked up. Well, I couldn't lerrem roam t'streets, sir. Yer've no idea the sort what live round there."

"And yet you did, Mrs Quinn."

"I 'ad no choice, sir," she answered him grimly. "I were a widder wi' three girls an' it were all I could afford. Burr I brought 'em up decent."

"I'm sure you did, Mrs Quinn. Go on."

"Well, we was runnin' outer money. I 'ad ter get summat ter put food in our mouths, an' fer't rent so I asked about an' . . . well, I come 'ere terday ter see if I could 'ave 'ousekeeper's job . . ."

"What a splendid idea, Mrs Quinn. I think you would make an admirable housekeeper. The job is yours." What a perfect solution, he was thinking, again marvelling on the luck that seemed to be falling once more into his lap. Get the old woman here, fit her up with some job or other, and surely some reason could be found for Jane Elliott to follow. It couldn't be better and with that direct and compelling way that was his it would be all arranged right this very minute.

"There's a snag, Mr Crowther." Molly Quinn's voice was steady and her face composed though inside she was boiling over.

Mr Crowther frowned and his eyes grew flinty and she realised that this man was not one to be crossed, a lesson she was to learn again and again.

"Yes?"

"I can't live in, sir. I've them ter think on. I can't leave 'em."

His face cleared and broke into its most charming smile.

"Of course you can't and until some suitable arrangements are made you must bring them with you."

Molly's jaw dropped. "Bring 'em wi' me?"

"Yes, I shall arrange for you to have your own quarters and Mrs Elliott and her daughter will live there with you. Now I want no argument, Mrs Quinn, since I'm sure it can only be for the best. Look at her," turning to gaze tenderly at the woman who, an hour ago, he had not known existed. "See how she has responded to the atmosphere here. Perhaps you had not considered that the very place where she has lived with you lately might have been holding her back. She needs light and air and beauty in which to recover her spirits. Wouldn't you agree?"

Molly could feel her own spirits beginning to soar. Yes, she would agree. She had never seen Mrs Elliott look so . . . so content, not since before the captain died, and what a wonderful place for the child. She could roam these gardens and be free from the stink and danger of Brooke Alley and perhaps regain that lovely strong sweetness she had known before her pa died. But . . .

"There's just one thing, sir."

His face hardened again. "Yes?"

"I can't cook."

He grinned like a boy as he leaned to take her hand.

"Don't worry about that, Mrs Quinn. Cooks are easy to find," but lovely women like Jane Elliott were unique, though he did not utter this last.

12

How she got through the next few hours she was never to know, she was to tell Victoria later. It was like being in a lunatic asylum with the inmates all determined on their own way and fighting like tigers to get it. And he was the worst, the master, as she was now to call him apparently, for he wanted to ride roughshod over every suggestion made to him. Mind you, it was sheer heaven to know they were safe, not only her in her grand new job, but Mrs Elliott and the child as well, even if it was completely unorthodox.

And it was worth every unquiet thought in her head over the strangeness of it all just to see that old biddy's face when they were taken, by the master, if you please, into the kitchen. It seemed to be crammed with more servants than before, all busy with some task or other and as the four of them, her and Mrs Elliott, the child and Mr Crowther, entered the room every face became slack with shock, especially that of Mrs Jackson who struggled valiantly to get out of her chair.

Molly had hold of Mrs Elliott who had withdrawn again now that she had been removed from the lovely calm of the winter garden and though it was clear that Mr Crowther longed to offer her his arm he restrained himself, allowing her to cling to Molly even though it did look a bit odd. She peered about her, nervous as a cornered animal until she caught sight of the kitchen tabby which was lying on the rag rug before the fire, its tail curled neatly about itself.

"Oh, how lovely, you have another cat and exactly like the one in the other room. What handsome creatures they both are. Hello, puss," she went on, crouching down in so graceful a manner her wide skirts ballooned about her. She scratched the animal behind its ear and at once it stood up and began to rub itself against her. "Oh, look, Lily," she exclaimed delightedly to her daughter, who was staring about her with the same bright interest she had shown in the drawing-room, "I think it likes me."

The maidservants watched her with silent fascination. Their eyes spoke their thoughts though and it was evident what they were. Who in the name of God was this lovely woman, this beautifully dressed woman who had not only invaded the master's garden but was now in his kitchen playing with the bloody cat? What was she to him and what was she doing here? What was he up to? And what about the child? She was obviously the woman's daughter and would you look at the lovely outfit she had on which must have cost a pretty penny. They had seen the other one, of course, the one who had had hopes of taking Mrs Jackson's place but what was her connection with these two fairy-like creatures?

"Of course it does, Ma," the child said. "I think you must be a cat person. I prefer dogs myself, though I wouldn't mind a kitten. Have you any kittens, Mr Crowther?"

Joshua Crowther came to with an almost perceptible start, for he had been as spellbound as the rest.

"I don't know, Lily. Have we? Does anyone know?"

There was a lad in a glassed-off room who had stopped to stare with the rest of them. He was vigorously cleaning his master's riding boots but at this he popped his bright orange head out through the door. For a moment Lily thought he might be one of the Meadows boys and a shaft of home-sickness for Walton Lane stabbed her but when he stood, a brush in one hand, his other arm inside his master's long riding boot she could see it was not.

"There's plenty in't stables, sir. That there ginger tabby what belongs ter Mrs Arnold the groom's wife 'ad a litter only last month."

"There you are, Lily, perhaps Mrs Arnold will give you one of those." Joshua Crowther was eager to get this over and the child's sidetracking had irritated him. He walked over to where Jane was still fondling the cat and with great gentleness lifted her to her feet, but it seemed Lily had not yet done.

"Well, I'd like a kitten, sir, thank you, but you see I'm not sure Villy would. She's never had anything to do with cats, you see."

"Villy?"

"Yes, I told you about my dog, remember."

"But you—"

Suddenly Joshua pulled himself up short for he had just been about to tell her that her dog would be confined to the stable with his, since he did not allow them in the house, when he realised she was not even aware that she was to live here. And neither was Jane.

"Of course, but first I must make an announcement to the servants. We can discuss dogs and kittens later."

"But—"

"Later, Lily." His voice said that was the end of it.

For some reason Lily did as she was told, closing her mouth though it was thinned to a mutinous line. She frowned, took her ma's hand in hers and waited.

Joshua continued. "This lady here, who I believe you have already met," nodding his head in Molly's direction, "is to be our new housekeeper." There was an audible gasp from the maidservants and Mrs Jackson sat down heavily in her chair as though to say to hell with respect for one's betters. "Her name is Mrs Quinn and she is to start at once which I'm sure will be a great relief to Mrs Jackson. Mrs Quinn is not a cook but she has my permission to engage one. I think that's all, so if you, Mrs Jackson, would ask one of the yard men to help you move your stuff to your cottage I would be obliged. I know you were hoping to go as soon as a suitable replacement was found for you. You will, of course, be paid until the end of the month. Oh, and one more thing. Mrs Elliott here," putting a hand on the one that rested quite trustingly in the crook of his arm and which miraculously he had managed to keep there, "and her daughter are to be my guests, so if a room could be got ready for them at once. The best guest-room, Mrs Jackson, if you please. I think that's all except that I shall need the carriage in half an hour. Will you inform Bentley. Mrs Quinn will be back shortly to make herself known to you, I'm sure, but there are one or two matters to be attended to first. Now then, Mrs Elliott, if you would like to come with me . . . yes, my dear, Mrs Quinn is coming too." This last remark was addressed to Jane who was looking confused.

But Joshua Crowther had reckoned without Lily Elliott who was used to speaking her mind and at the moment it was absorbing what Mr Crowther had just said about her and Ma staying with him. Not that she would mind that. It would be grand to be able to walk down to the river and watch the shipping. It would be grand to be able to play with Villy in the woods they had come through on the way up here. It would be grand to be away from Brooke Alley and the confinement of Mrs Quinn's cellar but she did think this should have been discussed with her and Mrs Quinn before a decision was made. For a start Liam wouldn't know where to find them when he came home, which she was sure he would soon. And, if Mrs Quinn was to be housekeeper here . . . oh, yes, she had not missed *that* even if Ma had, then what was to happen to her and Ma, especially Ma, when their visit with Mr Crowther was over? Where would they go then? In fact, why was Mr Crowther inviting them, perfect strangers, to be his guests? These were all questions Lily would like answered, for, after all, with Pa gone she was responsible for Ma, wasn't she?

"What d'you mean, Mr Crowther?" she asked him, her small face serious as though she were considering his offer and found it wanting. "About me and Ma staying here?"

Joshua, who had been just about to lead Jane Elliott from the kitchen, turned impatiently to the child, then looked to Mrs Quinn as though to say this must be dealt with by her. She knew what he was about, or in part she did, and anything to be said must come from her, but Lily stared at him defiantly, waiting for an explanation.

Mrs Quinn took her hand and tried to prise her loose from her mother but short of a tussle before the spellbound gaze of the servants there was no parting the two of them. Still holding on to her mother Lily had swung round to face Mr Crowther, waiting for an answer.

Joshua's face tightened ominously but he kept his voice smooth, for he did not wish to alarm this child's mother.

"Would you not like to have a holiday, Lily?" he asked her. "Do you not think it would do you and your mother, especially your mother, a power of good to come and stay here for a while? The sea air and the rest, the peace here by the river and—"

"But you don't know us, so why are you asking us to stay with you?"

The servants hung on her every word, for that was what they would like to know, too.

Joshua gritted his teeth. "I think that is for your mother

and me to decide, Lily. And Mrs Quinn, of course. Mrs Quinn will be housekeeper at Oakwood Place and since you have been *her* guests for quite a long time and when she starts here will have nowhere to stay, so she tells me, it seems only sensible for you and your mother to come with her for the time being." As he spoke he wondered why in hell's name he was explaining to this persistent child what was essentially none of her bloody business, and in front of the servants too. It was not his custom to explain his actions to anyone and certainly not to a small girl. But he couldn't afford an upheaval at the moment, for God only knew what Jane Elliott, in her present precarious state, might say or do.

"Well, all right, but can we bring Villy?" Lily interrupted him. "I know she might chase the cats but I'd keep her on her leash when we're out," which was a fib, of course.

"Yes, er . . . Villy can come too."

"And then there's Liam."

"Liam?" For a dreadful moment there flashed through his mind the image of another man making free with what Joshua had earmarked for himself and he could feel the angry blood surge through him. As though she sensed it the woman on his arm slipped her hand from his and moved towards Mrs Quinn, her face taking on that strange expression in which doubt and uncertainty were mixed and he could have cheerfully wrung the child's neck. She was staring at him boldly and he wondered why he had thought her such an engaging little thing.

"Oh, please, sir," Mrs Quinn cut in, almost savagely, for if the little madam spoiled their chances of a good home and herself a good job she'd gladly take a whip to her, which sometimes she wished the captain had done. She was far too knowing for her own good and certainly far too talkative. "'E's some lad 'oo brought 'er 'ome one day when she were lost."

"I was not lost."

Mrs Quinn shook her soundly. "Be quiet an' speak when yer spoken to." She turned eagerly back to the master of the house. "'E's a sailor. We 'ardly know 'im."

"I see, well . . ." Conscious of the avid interest of his servants he turned and opened the door for the two women and the child to go through to the front of the house. "We can talk about that later. Now, don't forget the carriage, in half an hour, if you please."

There was total silence in the kitchen after the door swung to behind the child who was the last to leave, for she had loitered for a moment to have another look at the cat. "It's a nice cat," she told them, "but I like dogs better. Mine would chase this one. That's what dogs do, you see. Chase cats."

The hand of Mrs Quinn appeared round the door and dragged her out!

"Well . . ." Maggie let her breath out on an explosive sigh, hardly daring to turn to Mrs Jackson. The old lady had as good as been given her notice and in no uncertain terms and it didn't seem fair, but then when had Mrs Jackson ever been fair to any of them? A cow was what she had often called her under her breath so perhaps this one – Mrs Quinn – might be an improvement. She exchanged a look with Betsy who was the under-parlourmaid and second to Maggie. She could see everyone was waiting for her to make some comment, but while Mrs Jackson was about she thought it prudent to keep her lip buttoned.

"It seems I'm to be chucked out on me ear," Mrs Jackson said, her voice ice cold with rage, "so I'd best go and get me things packed." So great was her bitterness she threw caution out of the window. "You, Dora," who was her kitchen maid, "can come and help me and if he thinks I'm making dinner for that lot he's got another think coming!"

It had been Joshua Crowther's intention to send Mrs Quinn in his carriage back to Brooke Alley to fetch their things, since he didn't want to let the delectable Mrs Elliott out of his sight, but it seemed Mrs Elliott had other ideas. She would not be parted from Mrs Quinn under any circumstances, it seemed. There was no way of keeping her here short of tying her up; no, not even if her daughter remained with her, which was suggested to her. She said so vehemently and it began to dawn on Joshua Crowther that he must be patient with this lovely, damaged woman if he was to bring her back to full health, which he had every intention of doing.

"Very well, Mrs Elliott. Please, don't upset yourself. I couldn't bear you to be upset, really, so instead I'll come with you and help with the . . . the packing. We'll all go, how would that be?" But even that seemed to cause her some anxiety. So much had happened this day that the vacuum in which she had existed since the death of her husband seemed to have been invaded by demons of some sort and yet at the same time, for the first time, she had known a few minutes of pleasure in the loveliness of the winter garden. She understood that Mr Crowther had invited them to be his guests for a while and as long as she had Mrs Quinn, her child and her sewing, in that order, she thought it might be rather nice to spend time in the warm peace of the glassed room. And she had liked the cats, too. Stroking their silky fur had calmed her in some strange way. But in the back of her mind, in some place that had not been used for many weeks, was the thought that she would not care for Mr Crowther to see that dreadful locality which had dimly filtered into her mind recently.

"Oh, no, no, I don't think so." She shook her head emphatically and several silver blonde curls, which had escaped Mrs Quinn's ministration, bobbed enchantingly about her ears.

"Mrs Elliott, I'm sure . . ."

"Oh, no . . . no . . ."

"P'raps it'd be best if we went on our own, sir," Mrs Quinn told him diplomatically. "She's 'ad a lot ter think about terday an' I must say she's done right well. She . . . I think she trusts yer, sir, if yer don't mind me saying so, but if we was ter move slowly, lerrer come 'ome wi' me an' pack 'er things 'erself she'd take to it better. She's made up wi't idea of 'avin' a 'oliday 'ere burrit's gorra be done right. She loves sewin' an' such an' when she's gorrer bits an' pieces about her she'll settle nicely. Well, why shouldn't she in a lovely place like this."

So, to the consternation of the outside men, and the maid-servants who peeped from upstairs windows, the new house-keeper, the lovely woman and her child went off in style in Mr Crowther's splendid carriage, driven by Mr Crowther's splendidly attired coachman. The carriage was a midnight blue with gold engraving, the inside a darker blue buttoned velvet. The coachman wore a jacket to match with gold buttons, a top hat and magnificently polished boots over his beige breeches. He carried a long whip which now and again he flicked over the backs of the beautifully matched chestnut mares which pulled the equipage and which, since it was such a pleasant day, had its hood down. Beside him, similarly dressed, sat a groom.

The cab had long gone. The driver, disgruntled and tired of sitting on his bum waiting for the ladies to come back, had ventured up the long drive to the house, knocking deferentially at the front door and, after explaining to the astonished housemaid, who had gone to inform her master, had been paid and sent about his business.

To say the residents of Brooke Alley were struck dumb by the magnificence of the carriage, the wonder of the glossy horses that pulled it, the two impeccably turned-out men on the box and the sight of their neighbour climbing down from it, was a vast understatement. It was as though an icy hand had come down and frozen each and every one of them to the spot, at least for the space of ten seconds, then the place erupted. They poured from their crumbling doorways. They rose from their recumbent lounging on doorsteps, they pulled themselves away from the greasy walls on which they had been leaning and, accompanied by a horde of screaming children, surrounded the carriage like the hordes of Israel. They jostled the horses, making them rear and fall back in terror, shook the carriage with the force of their excitement and for a moment it looked as though disaster were to strike. Bentley, who was Mr Crowther's coachman, was to say later that had it not been for the big chap the mass would have overturned the coach and stampeded the horses. Even with Jimmy up beside him it was looking decidedly perilous and he wished despairingly that he had brought the pistol he sometimes had about him when Mr Crowther was out at night. The lady in the back began to moan as the elderly lady, who had stepped down without waiting for Jimmy to open the door for her, was swept away into the crowd. Neither he nor Jimmy fancied leaving the comparative safety of the box but it was at that moment that a roar like that of a maddened bull surged down the alley and what seemed to be the bull itself charged through the crowd. They melted back like magic as the figure reached the carriage. The child in the back began to squeak with what seemed like delight, mouthing a name Bentley could not catch but by now, with reinforcements at hand, both he and Jimmy were in command again. Bentley cracked the whip about the thin shoulders of those within reaching distance and they fell back further.

The elderly lady had gone down some steps and was at the door of what appeared to be a cellar, just the top of her black bonnet visible and before you could say "knife" the big chap had the terrified woman out of the carriage, the child tucked under his arm and with no more ado had them down the area steps of the basement, through the door and tucked away safely inside.

"You all right?" he shouted back to them.

"Aye, but don't be bloody long."

"I knew you'd come, I knew you'd come," Lily kept repeating, her face like a little star in the gloom of the cellar. Mrs Quinn was dashing about the place like a whirling dervish, stuffing things in bags and boxes, stopping frequently to check on Jane Elliott, who sat like a graven image, patting her shoulder and reassuring her that they would be away soon, but Lily was not concerned with anything except the wonderful sight of Liam who had promised to come back and here he was. She did not question why she felt as though her world had suddenly become a lovelier place, why her heart felt as though it would burst with joy, it just did and her feelings shone from her brilliant silvery grey eyes as she knelt at his feet with her arms round Villy's neck.

Liam sat in Molly Quinn's old chair and smiled down at the child. What a lovely little creature she was. He had not given her much thought during the weeks he had been away and had not really meant to look her up again since he was perfectly certain she would be settled now and safe in her home in Walton Lane. But after the *Caledonia* had docked and the dock official had passed him the grubby note which had been in his pocket for weeks, Liam had felt a compulsion to make his way to Brooke Alley to find out what had happened to her and her ma. He had been appalled when he had stood in the alley, himself an object of great curiosity in his good suit of clothes and the jaunty wide-awake hat he wore tipped over one eye. What could have brought that lovely child and her equally lovely mother to this? He knew Richard Elliott had been deeply in debt but surely there must have been something, some insurance which a responsible man would take out to look after his widow and fatherless child. It seemed not and this was where they had landed and now it appeared they were to be off again, and into more salubrious surroundings than these by the look of the carriage waiting for them at the end of the alley.

"I'm sorry, lovebud, but we were held up in Halifax. The ship was damaged in a storm, a right bu— er, corker it was, and it took a while ter get repair done so that's why I'm late gettin' back inter Liverpool. As soon as I got yer note I came straight here."

"See, I told you so." Lily shot another look of triumph at Mrs Quinn. "And what a good job you came today, Liam, or you would have missed us." Her expression was one of horror at how close they had come to missing one another.

"An' why's that, Lily?"

"Oh, please, do call me lovebud. I like it."

His smile deepened and into his mind came the thought that what a joy it would be to have a daughter like this one. Bright and beautiful and innocent, intelligent and honest and open. A child who had not been twisted into the shape of many young girls of good family today, though he supposed she was not really what you would call of good stock. Her father had been a working seaman and her mother's people had been in trade. Perhaps because of this she had been allowed to develop into her true and delightful, if somewhat unconventional and outspoken self, brave in the face of adversity, trusting and with a great capacity for loyalty.

"Lovebud," he said, earning a sharp look from Mrs Quinn.

"Well, Mrs Quinn is to go as housekeeper to a gentleman called Mr Crowther," Lily continued, "and we are to go with her. He lives in a lovely house down by the river and I shall be able to watch the ships and take Villy on to the shore and play in the woods. There's a lovely garden for Ma and you should see what Mr Crowther called the winter garden. Ma loved it, and the cats, though I'm not sure how Villy will take to them. She's not used to cats, you see. It's absolutely splendid, Liam, and when you are in port you'll be able to come and see us. I'm sure Mr Crowther won't mind, will he, Mrs Quinn?"

He exchanged a look with Mrs Quinn, who shook her head slightly as though to say take no notice, but on his face was a look that told her he was not awfully sure if he liked the sound of this. A total stranger who employs a housekeeper was all well and good, and Mrs Quinn must be relieved to have found work, but what was he doing taking on the widow of a sea captain and her small daughter as well? Jane Elliott was a beautiful, defenceless woman, vulnerable in her present state, so could he, Liam O'Connor, put any interpretation on it but the worst?

Lily was still speaking, so enthralled with his arrival just in the nick of time she failed to see the quizzical look

Liam gave Mrs Quinn nor the defiant one she gave him back.

She was still babbling on. "I knew it was something like that, Liam. I was sure it must be a storm or even a shipwreck. I told Mrs Quinn, didn't I, Mrs Quinn," turning a rapturous face to Molly who was still galloping round like something gone mad.

"That yer did, child, but I'd be glad if yer'd gerrof yer bum an' 'elp me wi' these things. That there coachman'll not be 'appy sat out there wi' 'alf o' Brooke Alley 'angin' about 'im an' Mr Crowther'll be waitin' on us."

"Oh, he can wait, Mrs Quinn. I've so many things to ask Liam and I might not see him for a while. Now, Liam." She sat back on her haunches, gazing earnestly up into his face. "What was it like in Halifax? That's in Novia Scotia, isn't it? Did you see any polar bears? What was your cargo? Timber, I expect. One day when—"

"Lily, Lily." Liam held up his hands in mock horror, then bent to cup his calloused palms round her small, pointed face. "Stop . . . stop and let me speak."

"Well, go on then."

"Lovebud, this isn't the time nor't place. Can't yer see that? We can't leave them fellers in that carriage fer much longer or they'll have wheels stripped off it an' them lovely horses whipped away an' carved up fer their Sunday dinners. Now, go and help Mrs Quinn while I go an' give them a hand. I promise I'll not go without . . . well . . ." He was not sure what he meant to say to this child whose face had begun to fall into lines of serious distress. She obviously meant them to have a long and interesting talk about the sea, the ships, his life, where he was to go and when she would see him again, so what was he to do? She missed her father, that was very evident and because he was a mariner, as her father had been, she had transferred something of her pa to him. But this was none of his business. Mrs Quinn was an honest, respectable woman and surely would not allow her mistress to get into some situation that would not be right for her, or the child. From what he could gather they were in dire circumstances right now and this job would give her at least a breathing space.

He stood up and drew Lily to her feet. The dog began to prance, obviously expecting some game, or perhaps a walk.

On an impulse, Liam gently pulled Lily to him so that her cheek was resting on his broad chest. Putting his own cheek on her silky hair, watched by the suddenly still figure of Molly Quinn, he put his arms about her. Hers went instantly round his waist and she appeared to nestle, like a homing pigeon, or a small, abandoned kitten, against him.

"Yer must go, lass, an' so must I, but if yer like I'll take a walk on this shore yer talk of an' we can have us a good old chinwag." Though he wanted to he did not tell her that it might not be advisable to inform Mr Crowther about this meeting. He knew of a man called Mr Crowther and if it was the same one, which he thought it might be, he would not like a common seaman meeting any "guests" of his. He felt uneasy and could you blame him? And for some odd reason he felt responsible, though God knows it was *not* his responsibility. He was in port for a week while the ship was checked over, their cargo unloaded and another, with the Royal Mail, taken on. If he could have a few private moments with Lily, make sure that for the time being she and her mother were safe, he would sail away with an easy mind.

"When, Liam?" Her voice was muffled in his waistcoat.

"How about the day after tomorrow?"

"What time?" having no notion of the routine of the big house where she was to be a guest, and neither had he.

"How about two o'clock?"

"You promise to be there?" She pulled away from him for a moment and peered up into his face. He felt a great desire to drop a comforting kiss on her smooth white forehead.

"I promise, lovebud."

13

Lily was never to forget that day. It was a milestone in her life, though she was not to know it then. The beginning of something that was to test her endurance, to challenge her courage, to subject her childish but resolute will to its very limits and it began the moment she stepped for the second time that day into the wide and gracious hallway of Oakwood Place.

Mr Crowther was waiting at the top of the steps as though he had been watching for them. It had begun to drizzle on the way out of the city and the coachman had stopped to put up the hood. As she got out of the carriage Mr Crowther ran down the steps with an umbrella to hold over her ma, urging her up them, holding her arm solicitously as though she were an invalid, which Lily supposed she was really. She had been ill ever since Pa died, hadn't she, at least in her mind. She was not as strong as Lily but she was recovering slowly and it seemed she had taken to Mr Crowther which was good.

"Come in, my dear, come in out of the rain," he was saying. "Let me take your cloak," which he threw carelessly to the hovering figure of the maidservant. "There's a good fire in the drawing-room and Maggie shall bring us some tea. Dinner won't be for a while," unaware that he would be lucky if dinner arrived at all, since Mrs Jackson had already gone stumping off through the stable yard and across the vegetable garden to the cottage that was now her home.

Lily saw Ma hesitate, waiting for Mrs Quinn, who was directing a couple of maids who had appeared from somewhere or other in the unloading of their bags.

"Nay, don't you touch them, Mrs Quinn. We'll see to 'em. Yer rooms'r ready," one of them told her as she took a basket from the groom which Lily was glad of, for Mrs Quinn looked worried, tired, and could you blame her really? It was Liam who had put such a thought in her head, since up to now what Mrs Quinn had done for her and her ma had not been much considered.

"You'll help Mrs Quinn, won't you, lovebud," he'd told her as they had said goodbye. "She's got a lot on 'er plate wi' you an' yer ma. You must try an' see to yer ma, look after her until she's well again. Will yer promise?" And looking into his concerned face, willing to do anything to please him she had said she would.

"We've put yer on't first floor at th'end an' yer next door to one another fer't minute, not being sure what—"

"That'll do, Rosie." A chilling look from the maid who had taken Ma's cloak cut off the flow but Lily turned to smile at her. For some reason the maid, who seemed no older than herself, winked at her and her soaring spirits soared even further. She had a feeling she and Ma were going to enjoy this holiday, wondering, as the thought struck her, how long it would be for and what would happen when it was over. But it didn't really matter now, for Liam was back and that was all that mattered.

"Thanks, lass. If yer'll show us t'way I'd be grateful," she heard Mrs Quinn say. She took Ma's hand in hers, since it seemed to her that it would be best to get her settled somewhere. Somewhere she could begin to feel at home in. She could see that Mr Crowther didn't like it, though. He didn't want Ma to go to her room. He wanted her to go with him into the drawing-room, pour the tea, engage in conversation of some sort and Lily was surprised, since couldn't he see that Ma wasn't up to it? It all looked so lovely and Ma had gasped in pleasure as they had driven up the drive. It was growing dusk and every lamp in the place seemed to be lit, shining from every window like small bursts of sunshine, warm and welcoming. The hallway was the same, with lamps glowing on tables and even fixed to the wall so that there were circles of soft colour and softer shadows filling the hall and illuminating the staircase. But Ma was not easy, you could tell that.

"I'm sure Mrs Elliott would be glad of a cup of tea, Mrs Quinn," Mr Crowther persisted. "You and Lily go up and . . . well, unpack if you wish. Make sure everything is to your liking," meaning to Jane Elliott's liking he was telling them. "Then perhaps you might like to take over in the kitchen."

She was his servant now and as his servant he was dismissing her.

As they had hovered in the hallway waiting for the housemaid to go before them up the wide curving staircase, Lily had wanted to look about her. This was the second time that day she had entered Oakwood Place. She had been too nervous to notice anything the first time but now, especially since seeing Liam this afternoon and having the secret knowledge inside her that the day after tomorrow she was to see him again, she seemed to float in a stream of joy and well-being. She could feel it inside her, warm and comforting, like the hot toddy of honey, glycerine and lemon Ma used to give her when she had a cough. She could tackle anything now, now that she had Liam again. She could look about her in this lovely house and see things that had gone unnoticed before, but if Mr Crowther didn't leave Ma alone, let her rest for a while, there would be ructions. Today had been a big step for her and she'd done wonderfully well, but she needed to be left alone for a while until she had got used to this new place.

She told him so. "I think Ma would be best having an early night, Mr Crowther." She used her very best manners, polite as Ma and Pa had taught her to be, but Mr Crowther didn't like that either.

"I think your mother and I are the best judge of what she should or should not do, Lily. Now, off you go upstairs with Mrs Quinn. Perhaps it might be wise if *you* were the one to have an early night. Maggie will bring you a tray to your room. Oh, and" – turning to the hovering servant – "see to the dog, will you," eyeing Villy with some misgivings. Villy was excited. She was a young dog and as young dogs do she was busily exploring her new surroundings, sniffing energetically at every table and chair leg, poking her sharp little nose into corners and even jumping up for a moment against Mr Crowther's immaculate trouser leg. "Ask that lad in the kitchen to come and get her. Give her a feed and settle her in the stable with—"

"Oh, you can't do that, sir." On to Lily's face had come an expression of horror and she swooped down and lifted the wriggling dog into her arms, closing them protectively about her. "She sleeps with me, you see," and had done ever since her pa died. She and Villy would both be upset if they were separated now and Mr Crowther must be made to see it.

"Well, she must be taught her new place, Lily," as you must be taught yours, his expression said. "I have never allowed my dogs into the house. They are working dogs, retrievers which go with me on a shoot. I'm not quite sure what use . . . your dog will be but I'm willing to allow her to stay if you keep her—"

"Oh, no, I'm afraid not. If Villy can't stay then neither can I." Her young face was red with indignation. Her eyes flashed their message of defiance and her head tilted imperiously. She was not afraid of him her look told him, and for a moment he had it in him to admire her spirit. But it wouldn't do, of course. "We've never been parted," she went on fiercely, "not since I got her. She'd be frightened in the stable all by herself."

"She would be with my dogs, Lily. Dogs will usually settle down together, especially if one is a bitch."

Lily set her chin at a truculent angle. "I'm sorry, Mr Crowther, but it wouldn't work. She'd pine, you see, and cry all night, wouldn't she, Ma?"

It was as though she knew, through her mother, she had the upper hand of Joshua Crowther. He had taken a great shine to Ma and it seemed to her that whatever her ma wanted, Mr Crowther would provide. She hated to upset her mother, to put her in the position where she must . . . well, stand up for her but she could not have Villy howling away the night in a strange stable. Lily had never been in a stable but she knew you kept horses there and Villy was used to a bed, a proper bed, and would not take kindly to sleeping in straw!

Jane Elliott could feel the dreadful tension begin to paralyse her and, still hanging about at the foot of the stairs, Molly Quinn was ready to seize Lily and box her ears. The servants, clutching this and that ready to take it all upstairs, were frozen to the spot, only their eyes moving. No one, *no one* ever argued with the master and here was this slip of a girl, all big eyes in her flower-like face, tall but slender to the point of thinness, telling him that she would have her own way or she and her ma would be off, presumably taking their new housekeeper with them.

"Dearest?" the child asked her mother questioningly.

"Well, she does sleep on your bed, darling, and I'm not sure . . ."

Lily turned triumphantly to Joshua Crowther. "There, you see. I told you so."

It was in his eyes, not that the child could see it, nor her mother, but the servants who knew him watched, coiled tense as springs, for if he struck her as it seemed he longed to do what in heaven and earth would the mother do?

He gave in. It was the very first day. There were weeks, months, years in which to show this impertinent, obstinate child who was the master of this house but tonight it was in his own interest to keep Jane Elliott calm, happy, settled in and at home in what was to be her home if he had anything to do with it. Let them go upstairs to the suite of rooms he himself had inspected. Let them dine up there, the three of them and the bloody dog, but let the time come when the beautiful woman was totally his and things would be different then.

He was charming, gracious, courteous, the soul of consideration, wanting only their comfort, he told them, even the dog, making himself stroke Villy's rough coat and at once he could see the child was satisfied. Not only with her victory but with him. She believed him again. She trusted him again and if she trusted him, so would the mother.

He did not notice the strange look his new housekeeper shot in his direction. Not that it would have concerned him if he had.

"Sleep well," he told them. "Let the servants know if there is anything you require and we will meet again for breakfast when I shall introduce you to my daughter."

Their rooms were so comfortable, luxurious even, so tastefully decorated, so exquisitely appointed, both Jane and Lily gasped with delight as Maggie and Rosie ushered them in. The bed was the focal point, a large four-poster draped with curtains of cream muslin which were tied back with cream satin ribbon. The dressing-table was layered with the same cream muslin and ribbon and the floor was fitted from wall to wall with a delicately patterned Brussels carpet in peach and cream. The fireplace had a plain marble surround and in the heart of it a glowing fire cast dancing shadows of orange and gold on the plain walls and ceiling. The wardrobe and the chest of drawers were simple in design and of the best mahogany, glowing and satinlike in the light from several pretty lamps. There were flowers, a great vase of pink roses mixed with the misty white of gypsophila placed on a shining table where candles in silver candlesticks had been lit. Maggie moved across what seemed to be a vast amount of carpet and drew the curtains, which matched those of the bed, then beckoned to them to follow her through an open doorway to another room which was just as elegantly furnished, just as warm and comfortable, but smaller. Again there were flowers and a leaping fire and when Lily put Villy down the animal went at once to the rug in front of it, turned a couple of times until she had found the right spot, then lay down and closed her eyes in exhausted sleep. They all smiled, even Maggie.

"Well, someone's settled in at any rate," she said, then went on, "Mr Crowther thought yer might like to have yer own sittin'-room, ma'am. Fer when yer want ter be quiet. An' he ses you're ter make free with his library which yer'll see tomorrow. Now the little miss is ter sleep on that little day bed in't bedroom wi' you, an' Mrs Quinn is right next door."

She sniffed, evidently not agreeing with a housekeeper sleeping in the family's quarters but if Mr Crowther said so, then that was that. What he was up to was anybody's guess but time would tell. They did hope he was not going to take advantage of this lovely frail woman, but then who were they to interfere? What he did with himself, and with others, was nothing to do with them. They had decent jobs, a fair wage, good grub and comfortable quarters. What else could a servant ask for?

The next hurdle came when, after unpacking their bags while the child and Mrs Elliott drifted round like two children in a toyshop, exclaiming over this and that, Mrs Quinn told them briskly that she was off to the kitchen to see about something to eat.

"I'll come with you, Mrs Quinn," Mrs Elliott said at once, hurriedly putting down the slender figure of a shepherdess she had been examining.

"I think it'd be best if you was ter stay wi' Lily, Mrs Elliott. Mr Crowther might not like it if we was ter wander round in 'is 'ouse uninvited, like. You settle down 'ere an' I'll fetch yer up a bite ter eat. Now, what d'yer fancy?" having no idea what might be found in the household's pantry. "'Appen a nice coddled egg an' some toast ter be goin' on with. Look, 'ere's yer sewin' an' while I'm down there I'll see if there's owt else wants mendin'. Bound ter be summat in a place this size, wouldn't yer think?"

Distracted, Jane smiled tentatively. "Yes, indeed. Then . . . then you want me and Lily to stay here," looking round the lovely, firelit, lamplit room and, finding nothing to alarm her, sat down in the small sewing chair by the sitting-room fire. She leaned down and smoothed Villy's rough fur. Villy lifted her head and gently licked her hand, then rested her head on her knee. The child sprawled on the rug at her feet, her arms round the dog's neck and they all three stared placidly into the flames.

Letting out her breath on a long sigh of relief and telling them she wouldn't be long, Mrs Quinn slipped from the room.

She quite enjoyed the atmosphere of the enormous kitchens which were as warm as the rest of the house and smelled of the bread Mrs Jackson had baked that morning. The maids scuttled about as she opened the door and walked in, not sure whether she was to be a harridan like old Mrs Jackson, but Mrs Quinn had decided on a slow, undemanding approach to this new challenge in her life, at least until she'd found her feet.

"Now then, ter start with p'raps it'd be as well if you was ter tell me yer names an' wha' yer duties are."

They were Maggie and Rosie, whom she had already met, Betsy who was second-in-command to Maggie, Jenny who was eleven and general skivvy, Dora who was kitchen maid and the one Mrs Quinn thought would be most useful to her, and Maggie number two, called simply "Maggie Two" to distinguish her from Maggie, the head parlourmaid. There was a Mrs Ambler who was the laundry maid but she had gone home for the night, and Jackie, the boot boy who had been so helpful on the question of the kittens.

Which gave her an idea but first things first.

"Now then, lasses, yer may remember Mr Crowther sayin' I were to employ a cook, which I will, but while one's found we'll 'ave ter mekk do wi' me. A plain cook, that's wharr I am burr I reckon this lass 'ere," indicating Dora, "will give us an 'and. 'As owt been prepared fer ternight?" And when a beautiful piece of roast pork was produced, crisp with crackling and seething in its own juices she was triumphant. There was nothing to making a bit of decent gravy, roasting a few potatoes and steaming the fresh cabbage which it seemed the gardener had left at the kitchen door only an hour since. Rice pudding, what did they say to that? she asked them, plain fare but wholesome and well cooked and could the Queen herself ask for more than that. If Dora'd be so good as to begin on the vegetables, potatoes first to roast in the oven, the magnificence of which overwhelmed her, then she'd just slip up with a tray for Mrs Elliott and the child.

But first she'd like a word with Jackie. The lad's face fell when she called him out, for what could he possibly have done wrong in the short time she had been in the kitchen? He'd been carefully scraping the mud off Miss Eloise's boots, for she had been riding that day and they were in a right mess. He was sure she did it on purpose. How could someone get mud on their bloody boots when they were sitting on a bloody horse, he asked no one in particular, and got no answer, for none of the women in the kitchen gave him the time of day.

His face fell into a delighted smile as she whispered in his ear and he scampered off across the kitchen and out of the back door with great enthusiasm.

They were still sitting by the fire when Molly returned. She wore the voluminous white apron she had found in one of the kitchen drawers and looked every inch what she knew she was going to be, an efficient and well-respected housekeeper. The girls in the kitchen had not exactly jumped to do her bidding but there had been no covert mutterings or a reluctance to obey her orders. They had set to with the vegetables, and with setting up the dining-room table for the master. Maggie had taken her through to see it when she and Betsy had finished and it had looked a real treat. Shining cutlery, silver by the look of it, an immaculate white cloth and napkins, flowers, glassware that gave off shafts of reflected light and this was all for one man. Well, that was how many places had been set.

She had a tray in her hands as she entered the sitting-room but the moment she came in the dog sat up and began to get excited.

"Are you hungry, Villy?" the child asked, taking the tray from Mrs Quinn and setting it on the table which was drawn up to the fireside chairs, but Villy was sniffing at Mrs Quinn's apron pocket, not sure whether to growl, and when Mrs Quinn drew out a dainty kitten and placed it in Mrs Elliott's lap they all burst out laughing since Villy looked so bewildered.

Jane Elliott was enchanted. The kitten blinked in the lamplight, disorientated by its bumpy journey from the kitchen in Mrs Quinn's deep apron pocket. It craned its neck and peered about it, flinching back from the interested face of Villy who put her black button nose on Jane's knee. It seemed she had decided that this strange creature was no threat to her, or to her family and might even be the source of a good game.

Jane laughed in delight. She picked up the tiny, pretty animal, cradling it against her own bright face. It had a black and white patchwork body, a pair of transparent, saucily winking green eyes set in a pointed, triangular face and was as soft and smooth as the finest velvet.

"Aah, Mrs Quinn, Mrs Quinn, isn't he lovely?" she exclaimed, like a child who has just been given an unexpected present. "Is he for me?"

"Aye, lamb, 'e's all yours. Or should I say 'she'. That lad downstairs fetched 'er specially for yer."

"I must go and thank him at once." Jane stood up, the kitten on her shoulder but Mrs Quinn sat her down again.

"Nay, my lass, termorrer'll do. Now I only 'ope that dratted dog tekks to 'er," though in Mrs Quinn's sad opinion that dratted dog would soon be relegated to the stable, since Mr Crowther had struck her as a man who got his own way, one way or another, sooner or later. She'd not missed the twist to his mouth nor the gleam in his eyes when he had given in to the child.

"Can I hold her, Ma?" Lily begged, her eyes shining, her face rosy in the firelight. She took the wriggling body from her mother's shoulder who reluctantly let it go. She kissed its face, then, reaching for a small ball of wool from her ma's workbasket, she put the kitten down, rolled the ball of wool across the carpet and watched the small animal chase it. When the kitten caught the ball, it pawed it delicately, then rose to its back legs in a fierce battle with it. Both Jane and Lily, laughing as they had not laughed since Richard Elliott's death, were on their knees now with Villy an interested spectator but ready to join in at some point. They were giddy with the fun of it, even Molly, and did not hear the knock at the door.

Joshua Crowther, getting no reply, opened the door and

came upon a scene which, even in his wildest, most hopeful imagination, he had not expected. Perhaps a hesitant acceptance of the loveliness he had had created for her. A shy bobbing of her exquisite head, an uncertain smile of politeness, but this merry intoxication, this almost childlike glee, this sense of bewitchment and all over a bloody kitten, filled him with deep satisfaction. Nothing had prepared him for it and he was struck dumb for a moment. He was not awfully sure he cared for her undignified sprawling about on the floor, nor her squeal to the child to "Catch her, darling, before she climbs the curtains," but it was infinitely better than downstairs in the hall when she had clung to Mrs Quinn and a vast improvement on the blank-faced creature she had been this morning. Christ, was it only this morning? It seemed as though weeks had gone by since he had first seen her drifting about his garden, burying her face in his spring flowers, holding the hand of the child beside her. His whole life and what he wanted from it, demanded of it, had been refocused at that moment, to his own astonishment, for he had known many beautiful, desirable women before, during his marriage and after the death of his wife. He had had no wish to marry again in those ten years. He had children. He was a sociable man who did a lot of entertaining, managing it very nicely without a hostess, though there had been many who would gladly have taken up the position. He was entertained in his turn by his many business acquaintances and their wives. He had no friends, not close friends, and needed none. He was perfectly satisfied with his life, wanting for nothing.

Until he had seen Jane Elliott wandering in his garden. He was a man who did not act on impulse, though he could make a snap judgement, or decision in business, but all his senses, all his male instincts, as they had never done before, had become concentrated on this one woman and he must have her for his own as soon as possible. It would have to be marriage, of course. She was too closely linked to her child and the old woman, who had risen respectfully to her feet as he entered the room. They had great influence over her and were fiercely protective of her and if he alarmed her in the slightest she would be whisked away out of his reach.

"What have we here?" His voice was soft with a smile in it as he squatted down beside them. It did not do to tower over a group one wished to join.

Jane turned her velvet grey eyes on him. They were warm with emotion and he was bowled over by the luminous quality of radiance that shone there, not at all concerned that it was not directed at, or for him. He had not known her before her husband's death and so had no conception of how she had been then. No conception of the strength of love that had lived in her, of the sweetness of her spirit, the constancy, the humour and sparkle and yet gentleness which she had given to just one man. If he had he might have paused to consider, but he did not and so he moved gently forward, longing to bulldoze, since he was not a man for waiting.

Here, captured by the absurdity of a black and white kitten, the spirit of Jane Elliott had momentarily returned and he was bewitched by it.

"Look, Mr Crowther, look what Mrs Quinn has found for me. Isn't she darling?" She looked anxious for a moment, a frown dipping her delicately arched eyebrows. "I may keep her, mayn't I? I have quite fallen in love with her."

He could quite cheerfully have strangled the damn thing which, he found to his own annoyance, he felt jealous of. As *he* could not have done, the kitten had brought her back to life again, but he smiled, resisting the temptation to push a shining curl that had come adrift from her neat bun behind her ear.

"Of course you may, as long as she and the dog get along."

"Oh, I'm sure they will." Then, as though suddenly conscious of the unseemly sprawl of her position on the floor, she attempted to rise, trapping her feet in the full skirt of her gown. He rose swiftly and held out his hands to her and with no more than a second's hesitation she took them. He was wise enough to let go of her immediately they were both on their feet, and when she sat down in the fireside chair he lowered himself uncomfortably into the one opposite her.

She was grave now but there was still a small residue of laughter in her eyes as she watched the kitten leap dementedly over the back of the bemused dog.

"I just came up to see if you had everything you need," he told her, doing his best not to stare too long or too fiercely at her glowing face.

"Thank you, I'm sure we have. It is most kind . . ." She stopped as though some sense of the strangeness of the circumstances between them had stirred in her mind, but the child laughed and the dog growled in mock ferocity and she turned back to him, the thought gone.

"We are very comfortable, Mr Crowther, thank you."

"You are more than welcome, Mrs Elliott. I . . . I was just about to dine and wondered . . . ?"

"Yes?"

"Whether you would care to join me? There is no need to change."

He could have kicked himself as the look of confusion and self-doubt clouded her face. He had gone too far and too bloody fast again and just when she was doing so well in her acceptance of the situation, which a woman who had her wits about her would have realised at once was not correct. Not even proper in this world where the "look" of the thing was all-important.

"Or perhaps we might leave it for a day or two?" he went on smoothly, making a great effort to be casual about it and was at once rewarded by her look of gratitude.

"Yes . . . thank you, Mr Crowther."

"Well, I'll leave you to your fun. Perhaps you and your daughter will breakfast with me and my daughter in the morning."

She appeared surprised. Evidently his words earlier had gone unnoticed by her, by her child and by his new house-keeper, for it had not been remarked on.

"You have a daughter, Mr Crowther?"

"Indeed I have, Mrs Elliott. And a son."

"Well . . ."

Seeing that she did not know how to reply to his declaration, he went on smoothly, "My son is away at school at present. His name is Nicholas and he is sixteen. My daughter, who is ten years old, is called Eloise."

"What a pretty name. And your wife?"

"My wife passed away ten years ago when Eloise was born, Mrs Elliott," doing his best to arrange his features into a suitable expression of sorrow. Hadn't he told her this earlier? he asked himself but then she placed her hand on his in great sympathy and every thought wheeled from his head like a flock of starlings swooping over a roof, leaving it empty of anything but the determination that this woman would be his by the time summer came or he would know the reason why.

14

Joshua sat at the head of the breakfast table, his daughter on his left hand, Maggie and Betsy standing self-effacingly at the serving table against the wall. He was not aware that he was almost holding his breath as he waited for her.

The breakfast-room faced south and the sunlight, which was a blessing after the drizzle of the previous afternoon, fell through the two tall windows, clear and bright, burnishing the mahogany of the rectangular table to a mirror-like sheen in which the faces of the father and daughter were reflected. Against the third wall was a delicate Georgian sideboard of varied mahogany veneers on which stood a big Chinese vase painted with deer and little fir trees in brown and green on a white background. The walls were painted a delicate green and the velvet curtains, which were pulled back as far as possible to allow in the light, and the carpet were a much darker green. There was a fireplace with a basket grate in which was banked a coal fire though it was not a cold day. The coal was kept in a bright copper scuttle and next to it on the hearth were a substantial poker, tongs and a shovel. Behind the serving table was a curtain of washable silk on a brass rail to prevent the splashing of grease on the wall. Around the wall were a dozen watercolours of rural landscapes.

When she finally came, the one he was waiting for, he had no idea of the time and patient persuasion it had taken Lily and Mrs Quinn to get her there. It seemed that Jane did not want to leave the safe, calm haven of the room and go through the comfortably solid doors which protected her and had begged to be left here with Beauty, the name she had given the kitten. She would prefer to have breakfast here, she had told them tearfully and all the while Mrs Quinn got her into the simple morning dress of the palest apple blossom unwatered moire she had pleaded in such a pitiful manner Mrs Quinn had almost decided to let her have her way.

"Well, I'm going down, Ma," Lily told her stoutly. "I want to explore the gardens for a start and then I mean to walk down to the river. I know Villy would love it and I'm sure you would too."

"D'you think so, darling? It certainly sounds very pleasant." Her mother sounded doubtful.

"And then it would only be manners to be introduced to his daughter. You know how important manners are. You've always said so."

Clever little thing, Mrs Quinn thought admiringly. She had hit on the very thing that would persuade Mrs Elliott that to go downstairs was the only correct and courteous thing to do. A few days ago not even this would have penetrated the barricade of Jane's grief and tearing sense of loss, but this house, this lovely room, the splendid view of the river which Lily was in raptures over, the conservatory, the kitten, they had all served to draw her from her prison, or at least persuaded her to peep through the open door that had been presented to her.

He stood up as she entered the room, her hand clasped tightly in Lily's. He was not to know that she had clung to her daughter all the way down the stairs. He took in every detail of her gown, the colour of which brought a faint pinkness to her cheeks, and the perfect shape of her mouth, a soft rose. His only criticism was her hair which had been dragged back quite severely from her white brow. He would have liked to see a looseness, perhaps a careless tumble of curls, ribbons of apple blossom twined in it, but quite evidently Mrs Quinn was not up to that sort of thing and one of the first things he must do was to get her a lady's maid. Someone to look after her appearance and her clothes, to dress her hair and present her as the lady, the *wife* he meant her to be. Thank God she was not wearing black as widows were expected to do for God knows how long, wondering why for a moment, then forgetting it as he moved towards her.

Joshua was casually dressed in a tweed jacket and sand-coloured breeches. He was to go riding later and his boots were a credit to the lad in the boot-room off the kitchen. His shirt was immaculately laundered and about his neck was an equally faultless cravat. He looked very distinguished, tall and lean, his dark hair with a touch of grey at the temples, his deep blue, almost black eyes searching hers in a way she did not understand.

"Mrs Elliott, and Lily. We're so glad you felt able to join us, aren't we, darling?" He turned to the young girl at the table who stood up politely as her governess had taught her to do when addressing an adult. "This is my daughter, Eloise. Eloise, this is Mrs Elliott and *her* daughter, Lily. As I told you earlier they are to be our guests for a while."

To Lily's great astonishment Eloise curtseyed prettily to Ma.

"Mrs Elliott," she said, then looked at Lily and in her eyes was something cold and slithery which seemed ridiculous since they were a beautiful hyacinth blue and as innocent as the day. She did not speak and neither did Lily, just looked assessingly as though each were measuring the strengths and weaknesses of the other. Joshua watched them for a moment as though he too were measuring something then he turned back to Jane.

"Come and sit here by me, Mrs Elliott," taking her limp hand and leading her gallantly to the chair opposite his daughter, "and perhaps Lily will sit next to Eloise."

Lily did as she was told, seating herself at the table where a place had already been set for her, or at least for someone. Ma looked as though she longed to sit beside her, as near to her as possible, in fact, but Mr Crowther was holding her chair for her and she had no option but to sit in it.

"Now, what would you like, Mrs Elliott? We have . . ." He turned to Maggie enquiringly.

"There's porridge, sir, or fruit. Peaches and melon and grapefruit. Or perhaps a mixture of all of them." She smiled kindly at the frightened-looking lady who appeared to have lost her tongue. "Shall I bring you a small portion of each, madam?" and with great relief Jane nodded.

"And you, Lily?"

"I'll start with porridge, thanks, then I'll have some fruit." Her pa had always told that porridge set you up for the day and so, though she didn't care for it, that's what she'd have. She shook out her napkin and placed it on her lap, turning to beam at Maggie. She needed a good breakfast, since she meant to be off the minute it was over, though she didn't tell them that.

"Would you care for some coffee, madam?" Maggie began, again speaking in a kindly fashion, for you could tell the poor lady was quite bemused. Maggie didn't know why since she seemed to be a person who would be accustomed to the ways and manners of the gentry, but even last night when they had taken her up to her rooms you could tell she wasn't quite . . . quite right. And her so beautiful and fragile somehow. Mrs Quinn, their new housekeeper, was saying nothing, though while she had supervised the breakfasts this morning they had all tried to get her to divulge something about Mrs Elliott and the child. Well, not *all* of them, for Jenny and Jackie, the skivvy and the boot boy counted for nothing and would no more question those above them than they would speak to Mr Crowther.

"Ma doesn't like coffee, do you, Ma? She'll have tea."

"Of course, madam. With milk or lemon?"

"She likes it with milk for breakfast," Lily told them as she spooned her porridge into her mouth. The girl next to her as yet had said nothing and it seemed she was not going to. Stuck-up little beggar in Lily's opinion but she didn't care. She didn't want to make a friend of anyone who might interfere with her plans for the day, and especially tomorrow.

As though he had read her mind Mr Crowther turned to her mother. "And what do you and Lily plan for today, Mrs Elliott? The weather is so lovely it might be pleasant to show you about the gardens and then, if you feel up to it, we could go up to the paddock and have a look at the horses. I'm to ride later and I could introduce you to my hunter whose name is Ebony." He smiled. "You will see why when you meet him."

"He must be black," Lily offered pleasantly enough, doing her best to make up for Ma's silence and the girl next to her sniggered.

"What's funny about that?" she asked, turning to glare at the dark and dainty prettiness of Eloise Crowther.

"Well, I would have thought it very obvious that he must be black with a name like Ebony," Eloise said loftily, smiling at her father as though to ask had he ever come across such ignorance. The smile slipped from her face when he frowned at her.

"That is not a kind thing to say, Eloise. In fact it was rude and we are not rude to guests. Apologise at once."

It was plain that Eloise was flabbergasted. "But, Papa, it *is*—"

"That is enough, child. Apologise to Lily."

She mumbled something in Lily's direction and Lily smiled triumphantly as she passed her empty bowl to Maggie and began to tuck into a heaped plate of colourful and deliciously smelling mixed fruit.

"And will yer 'ave bacon ter follow, Miss Lily?" Maggie asked her, pleased to see someone at this table tuck in. "There's tomatoes or eggs or mushrooms or—"

"I'll have all of that, please, Maggie. What about you, Ma?"

"Oh, I think not . . ."

"Perhaps a slice of toast with marmalade, or honey, madam?"

"Yes, that would be lovely." Jane smiled up at Maggie, then turned to Joshua who caught the tail end of it and was again pole-axed by the loveliness of it.

"So, would you like to see the gardens, Mrs Elliott?" he asked her patiently.

"We would, wouldn't we, Lily?" she asked her daughter.

"Aah . . ." Joshua smiled in what he hoped was a reassuring manner. "I thought while she was here Lily might like to join Eloise in her lessons."

"What!" Lily's head came up swiftly and she swallowed a piece of melon, almost choking.

Joshua ignored the interruption. "From what Mrs Quinn told me Lily has missed a great deal of schooling since . . . well, lately, so I was positive you would agree with me that she should attempt to catch up. Miss Kaye is an excellent governess and would be happy to welcome Lily to the schoolroom."

"Ma, please, you can't . . . oh, please, Ma . . ."

"Lily, I'm sure your mother will agree with me."

"This is nothing to do with you . . . sir," Lily added belatedly. "This is to do with me and Ma. I don't want to be shut up in a schoolroom with" – she turned and gave Eloise a scornful look – "with . . . with anyone. This is supposed to be a holiday, you said so."

"Mrs Elliott, what do *you* think? Is Lily's education important to you?" His smile was gentle, soothing, persuasive.

"Oh, yes, most important . . ."

"There, that is settled then."

"No, it isn't," Lily said desperately. The very idea of being shut away in some schoolroom with only this disdainfully smiling girl and her governess for company was appalling. She intended gathering Villy, and Ma, if Ma wanted it, and finding her way down to the river. To explore every inch of the gardens, which appeared to be extensive. From the bedroom window she had caught sight of neat avenues, ornamental ponds, long paths leading, she was sure, to some wild, exciting place in the woods and even, just beyond the woods and outlined against the sky, a peculiar little building with turrets. She meant to investigate every nook and cranny, every clearing and tree in the woods. Even to climb a few. She wanted to know the exact layout of the property so that tomorrow she could find Liam without delay.

There was a deep, implacable sigh from Mr Crowther.

"Really, Lily, you must learn that children—"

Rescue came from an unexpected quarter and it was a measure of Jane Elliott's slow journey to recovery and her frail courage that made her aware that her child, for the first time, needed her support which she knew had been sadly depleted since Richard's death. She would never, never recover from it totally, she knew that, but something in Mr Crowther's manner, his assumption that he could order Richard's child about as though she were his own, put a fragile and unexpected stiffener in her back. It would not last long, for it meant she had to emerge from the quiet place in which she had felt safe for the past few months, but while it did she must give Lily what she needed, what she was appealing for, from her. From her mother.

"I believe Lily is . . . would like a day or two to get used to things, wouldn't you, darling, as I would, before she is included in . . . whatever plans you might have for her, Mr Crowther. If you would be . . . patient with both of us for a while we would be most grateful. You have been so kind . . ."

It was the longest utterance she had made and both the maids held their breath, wondering what the master would say. Not only the child but the mother defying him, and in front of them as well. Not that there was a lot he could do about it, since she was a guest in his house. He had no influence over her, no rights as a member of her family might have, or a husband, for instance. She was perfectly at liberty to pack her bags and leave as spontaneously as she had come. The little lass was splitting her face in a huge smile of loving approval directed at her ma and you could see Miss Eloise was tickled pink by the whole ruckus and was dying to see her papa's enormous temper let fly.

But Joshua Elliott had learned self-control and patience in his years as the astute businessman he was and though he longed to take the child by the arm and haul her off to the schoolroom with instructions that she was to have a good thrashing for her insolent disobedience, he showed nothing of it in his expressionless face. Inside him was the smouldering fire of anger which was lit when he was crossed but he did not show it to the frail creature beside him. Not yet!

"Of course, my dear, you must do just whatever pleases you, and so must Lily. I want you to feel as though you are in your own home. If you wish to wander about, in the house, or the garden, then you shall. But my offer still stands. Perhaps when I go up to the paddock you might like to accompany me, but if not then I will quite understand."

She even went so far as to put a grateful hand on his sleeve, causing his desire for her to leap like a salmon in a river. Dear God, had any woman ever affected him as this one did? And though he racked his brain he could think of none. Not even as a hot-blooded youth.

Eloise Crowther had listened to this exchange between her father and the interloper, which was how she thought of the girl, with total astonishment, not only that she dare argue with him but that she should get away with it. But now she saw that not only was the girl a trespasser on her father's time, which had up to now been exclusively hers, but the woman had a hold on him too. She was ten years old, the same age as the girl, her father had told her, and for the whole of those ten years she had been his pet, spoiled and indulged by him. And he was the centre of her universe. She knew exactly how far she could go with her coaxing and wheedling and her charming little ways that laughingly persuaded him that this or that was something she must have. He did not often refuse her and she supposed that was because all she had wanted from him in the past had been easily granted. But she knew him to be implacable in his passionate certainty that he was always right, turning away any man's challenge of his authority. Her own brother was an example, for Papa did his best to stamp out any defiance shown by Nicky which was why she was amazed that this girl had so easily overcome him. She was too young to know that it was not Lily who had bested her father but Lily's mother.

Though it was sunny there was a nip in the wind which blew straight from the river and both Lily and Jane were well wrapped up. Villy, released from her overnight prison, went mad with delight, chasing her own tail and generally playing silly beggars, as Lily called it. She ran on ahead of them, eager to be off to whatever waited for them in this wonderful dogs' paradise.

Lily linked her arm in Ma's, stepping out from the side door of the house which Maggie had shown them and which led to a small, sheltered but overgrown garden. Across the neglected garden, and let into a high stone wall, was a handsome wrought-iron gate. They opened it with the excited daring of two travellers in a foreign land, peeping out to see what lay beyond, which turned out to be a vast lawn on which an elderly gardener was steering a lawnmower pulled by a small pony. There was a boy with him who was carefully raking up the sprinkling of grass cuttings and putting them in a wheelbarrow. The lawn already looked immaculate, as did the rest of the garden and the neatly clipped hedge that divided it from whatever was on the other side. Villy instantly disappeared from view.

"Good morning," Lily piped up, smiling at the boy's look of total amazement. She supposed they were a bit of a surprise, her and Ma, for neither of them possessed what might be called country clothes. Her scarlet cloak and Ma's elegant town mantle in which she had arrived yesterday looked entirely out of place but it didn't matter. She had had the foresight to make sure they both wore their stoutest and plainest boots.

The gardener turned, for a moment losing the graceful symmetry of the line he was following on the downward slope of the lawn. He whoa-ed the pony to a stop which it did with great willingness, putting its head down to crop the grass not yet cut.

Both the gardener and his lad stared with respectful admiration at the two lovely females who had been the talk of the servants hall last night. After the new housekeeper had gone up, of course. Who were they and what were they doing here were the two questions that were constantly asked and there had been no answers. Now, here they were, walking briskly through his domain and would they stop and speak? Both of them doffed their caps in readiness.

"Mornin', miss, mornin', ma'am," the older gardener answered.

They stopped at once, the child's eyes bright with interest, the woman's a bit shy, he thought, but ready to smile.

"What a lovely place you have here," the child said artlessly, as though it all belonged to him. "Do you and" – she nodded at the boy who was struck dumb – "do all this by yourselves?"

"Bless yer, no, miss. There's me an' Will 'ere, and then there's Mr Roddy an' 'is lad Benjy."

"And what is your name, sir?"

"I'm Mr Diggle, Miss."

"My name's Lily, Mr Diggle, and this is my ma, Mrs Elliott, and that was my dog Villy who's just vanished behind the hedge. We're guests of Mr Crowther's," she added grandly.

"That's nice, Miss Lily," the gardener answered awkwardly, wondering what to add to this, but Mrs Elliott cleared her throat and at once the man and the boy turned to her.

"Mr Diggle, I wonder . . ." she began hesitantly.

"Yes, ma'am?" he said reverently.

"Could you tell me the name of that lovely yellow bush in the . . . the other part of the garden?"

"Yer'll be meanin' the forsythia, I reckon. It's right bonny, int'it?"

"Oh, yes," Jane breathed.

"Trouble is, it don't last long, the blossom, I mean."

"Doesn't it, Mr Diggle?"

"No, ma'am, more's the pity."

"Oh, indeed. And could you . . . I do hope you don't mind my asking but . . . ?"

"Yes, ma'am?" his expression saying she could ask till the cows came home and he wouldn't mind.

"That little garden," turning to point at the high wall and the gate through which they had just come. "Why is it so neglected? You have the rest so beautiful, I wondered . . ."

"Oh, that were Mrs Crowther's garden, Mrs Elliott. She were

a rare one for herbs, was Mrs Crowther. When she died I wanted to keep it up but Mr Crowther said no. I couldn't tell yer why, ma'am." Then, as though he might have said too much, he clamped his lips together tightly.

Both he and Will waited for the heavenly being to speak again but it was the child, obviously her daughter, who chirped up.

"We thought we would just go down to the shore, Mr Diggle, if you could direct us." She was so excited at the thought of getting down to that magical place where her heart had always lain, her cheeks had flamed to poppy and her eyes were diamond stars in her vivid face. Mr Diggle was hard put to decide who was the more lovely of the two. The slender swaying grace of the woman who made him think of the sweet-scented white jasmine in the winter garden, or the vital colour of the bonny child. They both had the same cloud of silver pale hair, for neither wore a bonnet, but really, he was getting daft in the head and him a bloody grandfather!

"Just follow this path, miss," pointing with a gnarled, soil-encrusted finger along the edge of the lawn to a gap in the hedge. "Go right past the kitchen garden and the greenhouses then turn right. There's an orchard. The ground might be a bit rough. Then yer come to a birra woodland. Just keep on an' yer'll hit the shore."

"Well, thank you, Mr Diggle," the child beamed.

"Thank you, Mr Diggle," the mother echoed and for quite a full minute he and Will stood as though transfixed until they had disappeared through the gap in the hedge.

Mr Diggle hummphed. "Well, don't stand there gawpin', lad. Get them clippin's over ter't compost 'eap," he growled, knowing he was being unfair since he had gawped just as much as Will.

Lily and Jane, with Lily in the lead, followed a dim, chequered tunnel through the narrow strip of woodland described by Mr Diggle. The sun shone through the burgeoning branches already shivering with a light burden of leaves. The grass was soft and starred with wood anemones. A finch chattered in a holly bush, only to fall silent as Villy caught up with them, skidding to a stop as she plunged from the stand of trees to the narrow strip of rough grass that edged it and on to the long stretch of golden sand which lazed away in both directions. It was completely empty as far as the eye could see, which was due, of course, to the fact that the men who owned the houses that lined the shore owned the shore itself, right down to where the little waves trilled on to the sand.

And there they were, the ships, plying busily up and down the great highway of the River Mersey. Ships of every shape and size, some with lilting, graceful lines, dipping through the silver grey waters like birds in flight, others as sturdy and ponderous as the elephants at the Zoological Gardens on West Derby Road. They were on their way to Garston Dock, serving the rapidly growing export trade in coal, to Widnes and Runcorn to discharge cargoes and take on others in the never-ending traffic that had made Liverpool the second biggest port in the country.

Lily sat down on the lightly warmed sand and Villy flopped down beside her but her ma wandered off, bending to pick up shells and stones, perfectly content, it seemed, in the total peace and emptiness that surrounded them. Gulls wheeled dizzily, following in the wake of ships that were discharging rubbish. Ships' sirens hooted. The sun shone and the child and the woman breathed deeply of the sudden sweetness that had come into their lives, lives that had been torn apart so savagely when Richard Elliott died. Sweetness mixed with the salt tang of the sea, the river, the tiny fragrances that came on the ships from faraway places and eddied about them, familiar fragrances to them both, for they had both been born and bred in this great seaport.

Lily sat with her knees drawn up and her arms clasped about them. The old spell of the sea worked in her as she dreamed about what it would be like to sail away on the tide, to go to places with exotic names such as Rio de Janeiro, New Orleans, Trinidad as these ships before her were doing. One day it would be her turn. She just knew it. She didn't know how, she only knew with a certainty that settled in her like the soothing touch of her pa who had comforted her babyhood and young childhood that it was her destiny. She did not know where the *Lily-Jane* had gone to. She had disappeared as Pa had disappeared, but one day she would find her and her life would be complete, rounded, perfect.

In the meanwhile, there was Liam!

15

She did not take Villy, since she thought she might interfere with the important discussions she and Liam were to have. It would not do to be constantly interrupted by the dog who liked to have sticks thrown for her, so she had been left with Ma and Beauty in the quiet of the sitting-room. She hadn't liked it.

Lily saw him coming from a long way off and the pulse of excitement and gladness inside her seemed not at all unusual. It was how she had felt when Pa came home. A great surge of happiness, bliss even, and the certainty that for the period she was with him she was understood, protected, wrapped about in a devoted care that would never let her down. She trusted him as she had trusted her pa and it did not occur to her to wonder why. He had given her back what she had lost with Pa, right from that first moment at Canning Dock when she had gone to look for the *Lily-Jane*, and her heart lifted and her mind sang and her sturdy boots took wing as she sprang to her feet and began to race towards him.

He had not seen her. He had his head bent, looking down at his own feet as he trudged through the sand which was soft and fine. He had walked from the Custom House along Wapping Street at the back of Canning Dock, Salthouse Dock, Wapping Dock and Queen's Dock until he reached Sefton Street, then, when he came to the bathing sheds that served the swimmers, dropped down on to Pottery Beach. From there he continued above the high-water mark round Dingle Point to Jericho Shore. It was here that the mansions of the men of wealth and consequence began. Silverdale, Ladymeadow, High Cross and Oakwood Place, none of which could be seen from the beach. There was a strand of trees edging each property which screened those who lived there from the rude stares of trespassers.

It was another soft spring day, the arch of the sky a pale and lovely blue with a feathering of gauzy clouds away across the river above Birkenhead. As he had walked along Sefton Street, on his left he had passed meadows criss-crossed by footpaths and carpeted with cranesbill, a shimmering lilac-blue carpet moving in the slight breeze. There was lady's bedstraw like delicate lace of the palest yellow tangled with the brilliant green of new grass. Sycamore and beech had sprung, almost overnight in the stretches of woodland that lined the shore, into full-leaved grace and beyond the swell of a dune, through the spread of oak and ash, he could see orchards studded with fruit trees, in a froth of pink and white blossom. It was warm and he had removed his jacket and tie, carrying his jacket over one shoulder, letting the sun and wind brown the already amber skin of his strong throat. The sunshine caught in his short curly hair, turning it to gleaming gold. He lifted his head and his pale blue-grey eyes studied the water to his right. There was shipping of every kind in the river, their movement keeping the waters constantly on the swell and sending wavelets of white foam up on to the beach before sinking back into the sun-gilded river. Several oystercatchers were searching for cockles at the water's edge, their black and white plumage and orange beaks distinctive against the pale sand. Their call was loud and strident, frightening away a more timid grey plover.

He looked away and ahead then and saw her and felt his face split into a huge grin of delight, but, unlike Lily, he was surprised by the strength and strangeness of his feelings. She was skimming the sand as lightly as the gulls rode the breeze over the river, the shining silver weight of her plait thudding between her shoulder blades. She wore a white dress of some light material with a strawberry pink sash of satin about her waist and a bow of the same colour and material tied at the end of the plait. She was laughing, her teeth white and perfect between her rosy lips, her eyes narrowed and gleaming like newly minted silver through her dark lashes. He stopped and held out his arms and when she flew into them he swung her round and round until they were both dizzy, losing their balance to fall in a crazy heap on to the sand. It seemed they couldn't stop laughing though neither knew at exactly what.

It was a lovely day. They were both young with life stretching away ahead of them, hidden perhaps for the moment but certain to be exciting, for they were neither of them willing to settle for the blandness of conformity. He wanted his own ship, and, though it struck him as an odd thought to have, so did she. She wanted her own ship, her father's ship which had been stolen from her by some cruel twist of fate and though he could not see how she could possibly do it, he knew she would try her damnedest. He had learned that much about her in the short time he had known her.

As though she had caught a sense of what was in his mind her first words were of the *Lily-Jane*.

"You haven't seen my pa's ship, have you, Liam?" she asked him wistfully. "I know someone has her, *stole* her, more like." Her voice was sad and bitter, strange in one so young. "When I get the chance I'm going to go down to the docks and have a good nosey round." This was one of Mrs Quinn's expressions. "Someone must know who has her. What about the Mersey Docks and Harbour Board? Don't they keep records of ships moving in and out of port?"

"There are records, yes, lovebud, but whether they'd let yer get a look at 'em, I couldn't say. I've not seen her though," which was not a lie.

"She must be trading, mustn't she, Liam? In the coastal trade like my pa did?"

"Aye, I suppose she must."

"One day I'll find her and when I do I'm going to the police and tell them about her being stolen and when they've gone to gaol, whoever pinched her, I'm going to get Mr Porter and Johnno and Mick to sail her for me. Just until I'm old enough to do it myself." Though she was naïve in her belief that as a woman she would become a sea captain, she was also intelligent enough to realise that she must grow up before that could occur. "I'm going to ask Ma if she'll go with me to the Mechanics Institute in Mount Street and enrol me in the navigation class and all the others I'll need to sail a ship. What d'you think, Liam?"

His heart ached for her. Should he tell her not to set her hopes too high? Should he tell her that the boat had not been stolen as she believed but had been taken legally as payment of a debt? Should he warn her that the chances of her becoming a mariner were so slim as to be non-existent or should he let her go on dreaming her childish dreams and hope to God that, as she grew and became a young woman she would turn to more womanly pursuits. Marriage and children, which were really all that a girl of her upbringing could expect? He was that fond of her he couldn't bear to hurt her, for hadn't she been hurt enough by the death of her father? So he remained silent.

They sat for over an hour, their backs to the grassy bank that lined the shore, their knees drawn up, their shoulders touching, talking, talking, neither of them aware that their talk was of nothing but the sea until, at last, he came to the subject that had been worrying him ever since he had seen her and her mother drive off in the splendid carriage that he knew to be Joshua Crowther's.

"How did yer come ter be stoppin' with Mr Crowther?" he asked her cautiously. "Is . . . was he a friend of yer pa's?"

"Oh, no, nothing like that. It was Mrs Quinn really. She needed a job, you see" – which Liam could see she would with the child and the mother to support – "and when Victoria, that's Mrs Quinn's daughter, came to tell her there was a housekeeper needed at Oakwood Place, that's Mr Crowther's house, she decided to try for it. She got it too," she added proudly.

"An' Mr Crowther . . . didn't mind you an' yer ma goin' too?"

"Oh, no, he was very kind to Ma. He's given us two lovely rooms in his house and says we're to stay as long as we want."

Her innocence was frightening, and so was her mother's. He knew she had been out of her mind when her husband was killed and, had it not been for Mrs Quinn and this lovely child beside him, might have chucked herself in the Mersey. But surely she must know that what she was doing was going against the code of ethics that polite society demanded? And if she didn't *he* certainly did, so what was his game? A young widow in the home of a widower with no female chaperone, no relative except a small girl, and when it became known, as it invariably would, would be the talk of Liverpool. Jane Elliott's reputation would be ruined and he could not stomach the idea of her being exploited by some smooth-talking, apparently quixotic philanderer. She was the most beautiful woman Liam had ever seen and he had been in places where women were dusky, exotic, young and ripe and luscious, glorious in their dissimilarity to their northern sisters but she had about her something that was almost not of this world. Ivory and rose and silver. Sweetness, unworldliness and gentleness combined with a look about her of innocent sensuality which no man could resist. She had been protected by her husband, coming straight from her parents' care and now, when she was at her most defenceless, she was the *guest* of a man whose own reputation was far from spotless. In the world of shipping, indeed any business connected with it, Joshua Crowther was highly respected but he was known to be a gambler and a lover of fast horses and faster women. For which no gentleman criticised him in the least. No, any slur would be laid at the feet of the woman he compromised!

"An' yer ma is happy?" He didn't know how to phrase what he really wanted to say, which was, "Does your ma know what in hell's name she's doing or is her mind so wounded she doesn't know the difference?"

"Oh, yes, she's settled in nicely, thanks. It was the winter garden that did it, and the kitten. She loves that kitten. She calls her Beauty and she loves the garden too. The outside garden, I mean. I think she's going to try her hand at growing a few things herself. Mr Diggle said he'd help her. She loves flowers, you see."

"Mr Diggle?"

"Mr Crowther's gardener."

"An' what about you, lovebud? D'you like it?" He did his best to keep his voice neutral. He wanted to warn her, or at least to make her aware without frightening her that it might be best if she and her mother made other arrangements, but where would they go? From what had been discussed back at Mrs Quinn's cellar home the Elliotts were totally dependent on her. She had done her best for them. She had fed and housed them all these weeks so what else was she to do? And what could he do?

"I like the house and the garden and being down here on the seashore and it's lovely having somewhere to take Villy. She hated being cooped up in Mrs Quinn's place, and so did I."

Lily leaned forward and picking up a small twig began to make squiggles in the soft sand. She shaped some initials, two letter Ls, forming a pattern about them of leaves, but Liam was staring out across the estuary and did not notice, and really, neither did she.

"But I don't like the girl," she added.

"What girl?" He leaned back on his elbows, turning to peer into her face. Her plait had become unravelled slightly and a loose fall of hair covered her face, hiding her expression. He sat up again and, leaning forward, gently pushed the hair back, tucking it behind her little pink ear.

"What girl?" he asked again.

"She's his daughter. She's called Eloise," she said scathingly.

"What's wrong with her?"

"Oh, she's a stuck-up little prig and the worst thing is I'm to have lessons with her in the *schoolroom*."

"What's wrong wi' that?" Dear God, it sounded as though Crowther had long-term plans for Jane Elliott and her daughter or was it just a way of keeping Lily out of the picture while he seduced her mother?

"Liam! How can you ask? Of course, you haven't seen her or you'd know what I mean." Her face fell into lines of deep brooding. "I wish I could see Grace and Maggie and Evie. They were my real friends. They were good at hopscotch. I bet this one doesn't know what it is even. We used to have some good games of hopscotch, me and Grace and Maggie and Evie." She sighed deeply and he smiled as he put his arm about her and drew her head to his shoulder. She was like some tragedy queen in a play!

"An' you will again, lovebud. Why don't you ask yer ma if she'll take yer for a visit? I'm sure yer old neighbours'd like to see yer both."

"Oh, I don't know, Liam. She's better'n she was but I don't think she could cope with . . . well, you know, cabs and that sort of thing. And anyway, we've no money," she finished simply.

"Well, that's easily remedied." He took his arm away, though she continued to lean against him. Fiddling in his trouser pocket he withdrew some coins. Selecting one he put it in her hand, closing her fingers about it. She unfurled them. It was a sovereign!

She gasped, staring down at it, then back at him and, since no one had ever told her that you did not accept money from people you barely knew, she clasped it in her hand as though it were more precious than a precious jewel.

"Oh, thank you, Liam, thank you. You're so good to us. This will be a lovely surprise for Ma."

"No, lovebud, don't tell yer ma. Make this our secret."

Her eyes shone, for there was nothing she liked better than the idea of sharing a secret with Liam.

"Of course, our secret."

"An' there's something else I want ter promise me."

"Anything, Liam," hoping it would be something tremendous and hazardous and hard to do. Her face gazed up earnestly into his.

"If . . . if yer should . . . I don't know how ter put this . . ."

"What is it, Liam?"

"If you or your ma are ever in . . . trouble . . ."

"Trouble?"

"Aye, in need o' somewhere ter . . . stay, like . . ."

"To stay? But what about Mr Crowther?"

"I know, lovebud, but if . . . well, yer never know . . ."

"Know what, Liam?"

"Will yer be quiet a minute an' let me finish. I've an old granny . . . she brought me up—"

"Did she? What happened to—?"

"Let me finish, Lily." She knew when he called her Lily that it was serious.

"Sorry, Liam."

"She lives in West Derby. She's a cottage in Lower Breck Lane. Her name's Mrs Earnshaw. I stay wi' her when I'm in port. I . . . well, I told her about you an' yer ma so if you were to turn up unexpected like, she'd be right glad ter give yer a bed. Until I'm home, that is. She's a grand lady an' I say that in the proper meanin' of the word. She's working class just like me but she's a lady all the same." His face was soft and his eyes gazed backwards to where he obviously had known much loving care. "If it wasn't fer her I don't know where I'd've fetched up. She made me work at me readin' an' writin' an' me sums. While other lads were driftin' along doin' nowt with their lives she encouraged me to keep me nose in a book so that when I came to be taken on by Captain Jenkins for a five-year indenture I was a fairly well-educated lad. I can pay me granny back now I've me Master's Certificate an' I'm earnin' a better wage an' when I've me own ship, which I hope won't be too long away, I'll—"

"Can I come with you then, Liam?" she begged him eagerly. "When you've your own ship. Like I used to do with Pa?"

"Yer ma might have something ter say about that, lovebud." Again he smoothed the heavy fall of hair back from her forehead, smiling down into her enraptured face.

"No, she wouldn't mind, God's honour. She really likes you, I can tell."

"Well, that's as maybe but I think it's time you were on your way, an' me too. We'll talk about it another day. I sail on the tide tomorrow."

At once her face fell and the mutinous look of a child refused something dear to its heart crossed her features, the look that asked why it was grown-ups always said they would think about it another day, or they would go somewhere another day. It was always tomorrow, never today and she was disappointed that Liam had turned out the same.

He saw it in her. He seemed to be able to see everything there was to see in her, to read her mind and know her heart and he wished he had time to think about it, to wonder at it, to go over this strange feeling he had for her but he must be off and so must she. He had the idea that Joshua Crowther would not take kindly to some stranger, and especially a man, sitting close to the child of the woman who had taken up residence in his home. Liam was nothing more than a common seaman even if he had got his Master's Certificate and if Joshua Crowther was displeased he had it in his power to damage badly the career of any man who offended him.

"But I don't know when I'll see you again." Her strained face was close to his and in her eyes was such a lost look he wanted to hug her to him and tell her everything would be all right. She was to be a good girl and do as her ma or Mrs Quinn told her, not mentioning Joshua Crowther, and to do her lessons because if she didn't she would never be a sea captain. Something held him back. She was a girl child and must be treated with suitable restraint but, God's teeth, she was becoming as dear to him as if she were his own.

He put up a big hand and cupped her chin. She looked so comically pathetic, as though the world, *her* world, were to come to an end, that he smiled. He bent his head so that their foreheads touched and she squinted in an effort to keep his face in her vision.

"Now give over," he told her firmly. "I'll be home in three or four weeks' time, perhaps less an' we'll see each other then."

"But three or four weeks is *for ever*, Liam," she wailed.

"No, it isn't. Now just get this date in your head, 14th May, got it? An' every day after that you come down here an' see if I've arrived. About the same time. Now cheer up an' give us a smile. Oh, an' I'd keep this just to ourselves, lovebud. Not even yer ma or Mrs Quinn must know. They . . . we might be stopped from seein' one another," and I might lose my career if it became known that I'm meeting a ten-year-old girl, no matter how innocent it is.

She put her arms about his waist and buried her face in the middle buttons of his shirt, hugging herself close to him and without thought he stroked her silky hair and murmured some soft endearment before turning away and striding off down the beach.

She watched him go, her childish face wet with tears, for it was like those days when Pa had left them, her and her ma, both of them bereft without him.

She could find no fault with Mr Crowther during the following weeks. He was so kind and careful with Ma, gently guiding her through the days, days in which he scarcely left her side except to go in to town on urgent business. As spring moved slowly towards its summer blooming he could be seen at any hour of the day walking along the neat gravel paths, Ma's hand in the crook of his arm, his head bent to hers, sometimes pointing out a plant of interest, or standing with her to breathe in the heady scent of the lavender bushes which were coming into bloom.

He sauntered with her up through the kitchen gardens, for she had evinced an interest in the growing of herbs and vegetables, through the white-painted gate that led into the orchard, a breathtaking picture of apple and pear blossom at this time of the year. Beyond were the paddocks where the horses, led up there from the stables by Arnold and Jimmy, the grooms, with Mr Bentley, the coachman, were going mad in the soft, warm sunshine. Even the staid carriage horses kicked their heels and frolicked like the skittish young foal that had been born six weeks earlier to a lovely chestnut mare which was intended, when she was tall enough, for Joshua's daughter. There was Ebony, his coal black hunter, and Star, the pony ridden at the moment by Eloise; the paddock alive with expensive and well-bred horseflesh, except for the lawn-mower pony. His name was Tub, and he cropped amicably among the thoroughbred nobility, unaware that he was not of their class. They didn't seem to mind either, flirting and kicking their heels as though they too welcomed the coming of summer and the pleasure of being out of the stable and in the paddock.

The master and Mrs Elliott were reported by the housemaids to having been seen sauntering down by the lake, stopping to admire the swans which were a recent addition since Jane had admitted a fondness for them. The woods were a misted haze of bluebells, so lovely and delicate Jane said she could not bring herself to walk on them, and so ardent was his passion for her and his need to please her he led her along mossy paths through the woodland, solicitous in his understanding of her fragile hold on the realities of life. He even suffered the kitten which often nestled against her breast. His own dogs, big, gentle creatures who padded obediently at his heels, became her friends, even, like their master, tolerating the kitten. It opened its infant mouth in a wide snarl whenever it saw them, its tail lashing furiously from the safety of Jane's shoulder but if it kept her from falling again into the almost mindless state she had been in when she arrived, Joshua Crowther was prepared to put up with it. For now!

Jane Elliott was regaining her grip on life, trusting the man who, it seemed, was so like Richard in his endeavour to bring peace and a measure of content into her life. It did not occur to her to wonder why, as it did not occur to her daughter, but Molly Quinn was not so easily satisfied.

She had settled in to the routine and the intricate pattern of being housekeeper to Joshua Crowther with remarkable ease, bringing with her her own qualities of honesty, industry and vigilance, particularly where Jane Elliott was concerned. She spent as much time as her duties allowed with her, since the master had told her she was to consider herself Mrs Elliott's companion, and she was elated by the great strides "her lamb" made in her recovery from the loss of her husband. She would never fully recover, Molly knew that, for he had been the linchpin of her life and when a linchpin goes the wheel comes off! Jane's wheel was still treacherously frail but it was working again and moving the vehicle onwards. Molly was aware, if Jane was not, that the master was courting her, with what in mind she could not be sure, and with the utmost delicacy and tact, and if she had been a praying sort of a woman – which she was not, for everything she'd ever obtained in life had come not from some distant God, but from her own perseverance and hard work – she would have prayed that it was marriage. She knew, as she was sure he did, that already there was talk of the woman he had tucked away in his home, but he was the soul of circumspection with Jane Elliott and that, for the moment, was all she could hope for. She had a Mrs Kelly now, recommended by the cook at Highcross, where Alice worked, who was a clever cook herself, and between them, consulting one another politely on what was to be served, the food brought to the master's table had improved beyond recognition. The other servants, after an initial skirmish or two, testing her, she was well aware, worked well under her supervision and though she had never dealt with servants before, since all the houses she had worked in had employed only one, herself in fact, had found that she had a way with her that showed them fairness with firmness in equal measure. The house was polished and scrubbed, dusted and brushed to the perfection of cleanliness she herself required and had it not been for the constant nagging anxiety over what was to happen to her mistress, she would have been made up with her new position in life.

Which could not be said of Lily Elliott. Each day after breakfast she and Eloise would be forced into the schoolroom – not that Eloise needed any forcing – where the underpaid and under-qualified Miss Kaye endeavoured to push a little learning into the head of her master's daughter. From the first day Lily became aware that not only was Miss Kaye woefully ill-educated herself, but she was as unconcerned as Joshua Crowther with the academic range of Eloise's accomplishments. As long as she could read, which she did at a painfully slow pace, speak a little French, sing a song and pick out a tune on the piano in the corner of the schoolroom, paint sweet little watercolours and sew a sampler, that was all he required of his daughter. Miss Kaye was a lady come from good stock, the impoverished and plain daughter of a distant cousin of Joshua's. She knew how to dance, and how to hold a simple conversation, which was all that a gentleman required. How to behave in company, how to be a well-bred member of good society, that was all she passed on to her pupil. They liked one another. They liked the simple routine of their day which included pleasant walks in the garden and woods, and the occasional trip into town to look at a picture or two in the art gallery. Miss Kaye believed that if a young lady could mention a book she had read or a picture she admired, that was enough for any gathering where eligible young men might be looking for a wife. Her pupil was only ten years old but it did not do to waste time when many girls were married before their seventeenth birthday.

She knew from the start that this changeling child who had been cast among them was going to be trouble.

16

It was the end of June when Joshua Crowther announced
that he and Mrs Elliott were to marry, causing shock waves
to reverberate throughout the house. Molly Quinn, who had
been called to his study and informed privately by the master
yesterday, breathed a silent prayer of thankfulness. It was
official then. They were safe. She and her mistress and her
mistress's child were safe. Mrs Elliott had said nothing to
her last night when they sat placidly sewing together in Mrs
Elliott's sitting-room. Well, she wouldn't, would she, she was
so childlike in the twilight world she lived in, and Molly
wondered if she really knew what was happening to her.
Molly thought it best for her lamb to speak of it first and so
she herself had said nothing.

"Well, who would've believed it?" When those in the kitchen
were told the news Maggie spoke for them all. They were
staggered and almost, but not quite, rendered speechless as
they begged one another to give an opinion on the wonder of
it all. Work came to a halt as they gathered round Maggie who,
as head parlourmaid had been informed by the master. Tell the
others, he had said, and then tomorrow he and his bride-to-be
would speak to them about the future, whatever that might
mean. Would they get the sack under the new regime? they
asked one another apprehensively. Surely not. Mrs Kelly and
Mrs Quinn had only been employed at Oakwood Place a
matter of weeks and the new mistress would hardly get rid
of them, would she, and the rest of them had worked here
for years. No, she wouldn't do that to them, not her.

But a wedding! They could hardly believe it. They had seen,
since they weren't blind, were they, that the master was very
taken with their lovely guest, and in the privacy of the kitchen,

when Mrs Quinn was not about, they had speculated on what he had in mind for her but it had never once occurred to them that it was to be wedding bells. She was the sweetest lady with a shy word for anyone she met, but surely she knew what was being said about her in the mansions up and down the river, and in Mr Crowther's social circle. News got about so quickly and so efficiently on the servants' grapevine and the scandal of it was all over Liverpool and she had only herself to blame, after all. To live in the same house with an unmarried gentleman and no female relative to chaperone her was asking for trouble, but it seemed the master was to do the right thing by her. This would silence the wagging tongues and no mistake. They could not say they were displeased, providing no sweeping changes were made and that was hardly likely, was it? they asked one another anxiously, for she was so pleasant and gracious. Yes, that was the word, gracious, and with Mrs Quinn and Mrs Kelly in the kitchen to look after things for her she need hardly stir from her fireside, doing nothing except work on the endless bits of embroidery and fine sewing she always had in her hands.

Both Lily and Eloise were not only stunned, they were appalled. Mr Crowther had summoned them to the drawing-room to break the news to them and for the space of ten seconds neither spoke.

A small fire flickered in the fireplace though it was a warm evening, still light beyond the windows which faced west over the gardens. The sun was setting across the broad stretch of the silken river, soft as though draped in gauze, the sky orange and red, gold and apricot. Seagulls floated on the slight wind, flushed underneath with rose and in the drawing-room a stray beam of dying light lit Jane Elliott's hair with a halo of pure silver. She was placidly sewing, her back straight, her lovely head bent gracefully and on the arm of her chair the kitten perched precariously. It was scrabbling with a ball of wool from her workbasket. It took a sideways step as though blown by a sudden gust of wind and nearly fell off but Jane rescued it and held it for a moment to her face. It was as though she had no part in this moment of drama and merely happened to be there when it was announced.

The silence stretched on. Lily's face, which had lost every vestige of colour as Mr Crowther spoke, leaving her eyes enormous murky pools of horror, suddenly rioted with a high colour and she exploded into enraged life.

"Marry Mr Crowther! But you can't do that, Ma," she babbled, the words barely decipherable as they fell from between her rosy lips. Her voice was high and frightened. "What about Pa? He's . . . he's only been gone seven months and anyway, how can you consider marrying this . . . this man after being married to Pa? You know how we loved him, and he loved us and he'd not like to think you were . . . were being so disloyal to his memory, and neither do I. You can't do it, Ma. I won't let you. We must leave here at once and find somewhere else to live."

Both she and Eloise were dressed almost identically in dresses of white tarlatan, each with a broad sash of a different colour about their waists. The necklines were high, the sleeves short and puffed and their soft, full skirts came midway between knee and ankle. They wore cream kid boots and white stocking and both looked as pretty as a picture, one so dark the other so fair. The dresses had been made for them by the dressmaker who had been coming to the house to "do" for Miss Eloise ever since she came out of her baby clothes and a new dress for Lily had been thought appropriate. There was constant consternation over the way she seemed to wear out everything she had on, coming home from goodness knows where with tears in her skirt and rips in her drawers, her boots and stockings wet through and her plait unravelled. She had been told time and time again by Miss Kaye that she was to behave as a lady should, as Miss Eloise behaved, but it did no good, she continued to go off on her own without anyone's permission, let alone Miss Kaye's.

She suddenly became unfrozen from the bit of carpet she had occupied when the news exploded over her, darting to her mother's side and kneeling at her feet. She threw the sewing to the floor and took her mother's hand in hers.

"Please, Ma . . . please, don't do this to Pa," she pleaded, looking up into her mother's alarmed face. It was just as though her mother was considering marrying another man while her husband still lived, but by this time Joshua Crowther had had enough. He had expected something like this, for the child was as rebellious as an unbroken colt. He had let her have her say, but this was as far as he was prepared to go. He had been lounging against the fireplace, one hand in his pocket, the other busy with a cigar, but with a muffled oath he threw the cigar into the fire. He was still careful, though. Until they were married he had to be careful.

"Come now, Lily, let's have no more of these histrionics. It will only upset your mother. Do you not want her to be looked after? Do you not want her to live a life of comfort and luxury which, as my wife, she will get? And you will be as another daughter to me."

"No, I will not," Lily shrieked, springing to her feet to face him. "I already have a father, even though he's dead." Her face was passionate in its fury. "I don't know how you persuaded Ma to this . . . dreadful thing but I won't let it happen, I won't. My pa—"

"As you said, Lily, your pa is dead and I think if your mother is willing to . . . let him go, then so should you."

"*Let him go!* We'll never let him go, never, and if you hadn't . . . well, I don't know how you made her do it."

"Made her do it! Lily, your mother agreed to marry me of her own free will, didn't you, my darling?" turning to take her mother's hand and, bending his head, bringing it to his lips with great gentleness.

Jane continued to look somewhat confused. Sometimes the warm chocolate that she and Joshua – as she had been told to call him – drank together two or three times a day did that to her. It made her feel pleasantly drowsy, relaxed and unconcerned with the day-to-day battle she had with her desolate sense of loss. She grieved continually for Richard and always would, but Mr Crowther, Joshua, was so kind, so solicitous of her comfort, so thoughtful, making her feel at ease in his lovely house, making no demands on her except that she be at peace. Somehow, she had found herself agreeing to become his wife, hardly knowing how it had come about. It would be so much better for Lily, he had told her and she had been forced to agree with him, for how could she, a penniless widow, give her the things Richard's daughter was entitled to. She would never love again, she had told Mr Crowther, Joshua, that, but he had smiled and said she was not to worry about it. He would be her friend and she would be his. His daughter would be a sister for her daughter. And of course, she must realise that living under the same roof with an unmarried man was not really respectable, not proper and the only way to put it right was for her to become his wife. Didn't she agree?

She knew he was right, though now and again her soul fought against it, longing to fly free and join Richard, to find again that wonderful sense of totally belonging, of being one half of a whole person, of being in total loving communion with the man whose death had left her only half alive.

She did not say this to him, of course. She did not want to hurt him, for one thing, and for another she felt so muddled at times she would not have known how to put it into words. On their frequent walks about the gardens and woodland, the paddocks and orchards and even on their occasional carriage drives out into the country beyond Old Swan, he had been so persuasive it had seemed to her that it would be only sensible and so much easier to do as he wished. He did not touch her, though now and again he held her hand, the casual clasp of two friends and she had not found it distasteful. It would be such a relief not to have to worry about money, about Lily's education and even about Mrs Quinn who had been so good to them. Mrs Quinn often came to sit of an evening – when Joshua was not about – not saying much but you could tell she was happy here at Oakwood Place, and if all it took to keep them safe was to marry this kindly man, then how could she refuse?

"Lily, dearest, you must not speak to Mr Crowther like that. It is most rude. I know you miss Pa, and so do I but . . . but . . ." She seemed to lose the thread of what she meant to say, her voice trailing away to nothing, like a drift of smoke that vanishes on a breeze. She stroked the kitten's velvet head, her eyes unfocused, and the little creature mewed with pleasure.

Lily turned this way and that, like a trapped animal looking for a way out, her eyes travelling round the elegant and charming room which Joshua's wife had put together so many years ago. A lovely room, a lovely setting for the beautiful, sense-bereft woman who was her mother. It was right for her, this room and this house, but some instinct, a child's instinct that has not been blunted with the years, seemed to be telling her, warning her that it wasn't right, there was danger here though she didn't know in what way.

Still in the same spot where she had received the news about her father and that woman, Eloise Crowther's eyes burned like hot blue coals in her paper white face. For once she and Lily were in total agreement. They had fought like two cats tied together in a bag for the past few weeks, spitting and clawing at each other throughout every lesson, much to Miss Kaye's distress. The schoolroom which had once been so pleasant and peaceful as she and Eloise pottered through bits of this and that, a poem that was suitable for a young lady's ears, one that taxed neither of them, a sum or two, reading aloud from a child's primer, again not too taxing, had blown up in their very faces as Lily Elliott challenged every word that was spoken.

"One, two, buckle my shoe, three, four, knock at the door . . . Lord, I used to say that when I was about four years old." Lily's voice was derisive. She sprawled at the schoolroom table, refusing to sit up straight no matter how many times Miss Kaye beseeched her. "How about 'Christmas at Sea' by Robert Louis Stevenson? It goes like this:

"The sheets were frozen hard, and they cut the naked
    hand;
The decks were like a slide, where a seaman scarce
    could stand,
The wind was a nor'wester—"

"That will do, Lily," Miss Kaye told her icily, badly affronted that a word like "naked" should be spoken in the presence of ladies. "I will decide what we are to read."

"I don't know why you don't report her to my father, Miss Kaye," Eloise said spitefully. "He'd soon make her behave."

"It'd make no difference if she did, clever clogs. He's your father, not mine and I've no need to take any notice of him. Only my ma can order me about."

"Your *ma*! Honestly, did you ever hear anything so ill-bred. Only the underclasses call their mothers *Ma*. Isn't that so, Miss Kaye? In our circle we say Mama, or Mother."

"Well, as you've neither I can hardly see that it matters."

"How dare you, you . . . offensive, vulgar . . ."

"Well, I may be all those things but at least I can read and write. What on earth you call that scribble you do I can't imagine. It looks as though a spider fell into the inkwell and then crawled across the paper."

"You are the rudest, most ignorant—"

"Girls, girls, please, stop it at once."

"And as for the other things you do, well, all I can say is

who wants to learn to sew and paint and play the piano? Where I'm going none of these things matters."

"Oh, yes, and where might that be?" Eloise sneered.

"I'm going to go to . . ." It was at this juncture that something always stopped Lily from revealing her dream – no, not her dream, her *intention* – to these two simpering, silly females. She could just imagine Eloise saying casually at breakfast, which was the only meal they shared with Eloise's father, that Lily Elliott was going to be a sea captain and what a furore that would cause. Besides upsetting Ma it would infuriate Mr Crowther, though how she knew that was a puzzle to her. The less anybody knew, except Liam, of course, about her ambitions, her future plans, the better. When Ma was more recovered Lily was going to beg her to go with her to the Mechanics Institute and enrol her there. She had noticed in a newspaper Mr Crowther had left lying about that not only did the institute teach English, writing, mathematics, mechanical philosophy, navigation, astronomy and naval architecture, but drawing, painting, French, German, Spanish, the classics, vocal music, rhetorical delivery, whatever that might be, perhaps something to do with speaking, and dancing, and surely all these last must be for girls as well as boys? What was she doing sitting here in this dreary room listening to Miss Kaye droning on about buckles and shoes when she could be out in the real world, learning real things? She was wasting her time in this sedate schoolroom when she could be going into Liverpool every day to finish her education at the Mechanics Institute. And when her wonderful day at the institute was over, or at the weekend, she would spend her time off up to the meadow, rolling down the grassy banks with Villy, or down on the seashore, her shoes and stockings discarded, her feet in the cold rippling wavelets of the River Mersey, or curled in the fine sand that edged it. She thought it might be rather nice to ride a pony, as Eloise did, then she could gallop away like the wind and go to all kinds of places where no one could find her. She loved the paddock. The larks would be singing, the horses frisking on their lovely fragile legs, Villy would bark that high, excited bark of hers and even Mr Crowther's dogs, so placid and well behaved when they were with him, would be tempted to high jinks when she secretly let them out of the stable and led them down to the beach. There were so many grand spots to explore or simply lie down in at Oakwood Place, the sun on your face, the dogs panting at your side. She had enjoyed their stay here, apart from the schoolroom, and would have been glad to stay for ever, or at least until Liam came for her and took her to sea, but not with Ma married to Mr Crowther.

She had met Liam several times in the last couple of months, down on the empty seashore and it had all poured out of her, all the things she could tell no one else. Sometimes she wondered what she would do without Liam to listen to her. She was like a bottle that was kept tightly corked, which, when the cork was pulled out, erupted in an endless spray of – what was it Mr Crowther drank? – aah, yes, champagne. Or a volcano like the one she had seen in one of Mr Crowther's books she had "borrowed" from his library. Well, there was nothing to read in the schoolroom, was there, unless she fancied *Through a Needle's Eye* which was about clerical life in an English village, or *Sunday School Romances*, which Miss Kaye thought suitable reading for a young girl. In Mr Crowther's book, called an encyclopedia, there were many things of interest to read about and the best thing was that there were a dozen of them from "A" to "Z". She was halfway through the second one already! She and Liam discussed what was in it and he told her he had actually seen a volcano on his travels. Not erupting, of course, like she felt like doing, he had smiled but a wonderful sight just the same. Would he take her to see it, she had begged, one day when he had his own ship and he had turned her face to his and looking deeply into her eyes had said he would. When she was older and with her ma's permission, he had told her and she had believed him as she believed everything Liam told her.

She tried again. "Ma, dearest, please listen to me. You don't have to marry this man." If she had been looking at Joshua Crowther and not her mother the expression that came and went across his face might have alarmed her. "We could . . . I suppose we could go back to Mrs Quinn's place. Now that you're more yourself you and Mrs Quinn could find a job and I could go to the . . . well, to school. You're a lovely sewer, Ma, and Mrs Quinn's very strong and a good cook. Even I could get work . . . somewhere—"

Mr Crowther's silky voice interrupted her.

"Come, Jane, you're looking tired. I'll ring the bell for Mrs Quinn and you shall go and have a rest. I'm sure all these arguments are very upsetting for you and the last thing I want is for you to be upset."

"Please, Ma, think about it for a while. I can't bear to think of . . . of Mr Crowther taking Pa's place." Her face was wet with tears now and it was this that made itself felt in Jane Elliott's bemused mind. She could not bear to see her little girl upset and for a moment she turned a set face of implacability towards Joshua Crowther. It did not last, that feeling that she must listen to Lily, for Joshua's kind face loomed over her, smiling and speaking of a cup of hot chocolate and a rest before luncheon, shutting out Lily's tears, and when he gave her his hand she allowed him to help her from her chair. He rang the bell and then led her into the hall where Mrs Quinn, steadfast, comfortable Mrs Quinn was there to take her to her room.

There were few guests at the wedding. A business acquaintance or two and their wives, carefully picked not only for their discretion but their usefulness to Joshua in business. They would come back to the house for a glass of champagne and a piece of the exquisite wedding cake Mrs Kelly had made for them. All very circumspect and calm. Nothing to alarm his bride nor wake her up from the dreaming state of suspended animation in which she existed. Joshua Crowther had wisely decided that the quieter the event and the fewer people who came to it, the less chance there was of Jane Elliott baulking at the last moment. Perhaps some memory of her first wedding and her first husband might slip into her confused mind and God alone knew what she might say or do. Right up to the last moment the bloody child had been at her, pleading with her not to go through with it until he had begun to think he might have to lock her up until it was all over. He kept them apart as much as he could, or at least spent as much time as he could with Jane but it didn't stop her. Even with him in the room the bloody kid kept on about it, about her pa and how he must feel up in heaven, weeping most distressingly at times. Not that it distressed him, but he had the devil's own job with Jane when the child was sent up to the schoolroom, or the bedroom she shared with her mother. So the sooner they were married the better.

It took place in July in the tiny church of St Anne's on Aigburth Road. A mild sunny day and in the hedges on the short ride to the church were tangles of wildflowers, dog roses and festoons of black bryony and honeysuckle, pale pink blackberry blossom. Climbing up the banks to meet them were the purple splashes of foxglove and the nodding heads of grasses heavy with pollen. On the far side of the hedges were fields of growing wheat and among the gold, vivid splashes of large red poppies. It was all so beautiful, the larks piercing the air with their sweet song, and yet Lily's heart, as she and Eloise, with Ma and Mrs Quinn drew nearer to the church where Mr Crowther waited, was heavy with desolate despair. Pa, oh, Pa, how has this come to be? it asked over and over again. Ma looked simply glorious in a new dress of pearly pink silk, very simple, the bodice fitted to her small breasts and the skirt enormous. She carried a tiny posy of white rosebuds and under the brim of her bonnet, made from the same material as her gown, was a cluster of the same flowers. The Misses Yeoland in Bold Street had been called out to design and make her dress and to fit her and it was a measure of Joshua Crowther's great wealth and influence that they should extend such a service, since they were much in demand among the fashionable of Liverpool. Lily and Eloise had been fitted into demure little dresses, identical, of white muslin, tiny wreaths of pink rosebuds and ivy in their hair, both of them as obstinate as mules about it. They were to walk behind Jane Elliott as she glided up the aisle towards her groom.

Jane seemed to be unaware of anything, even her own devastating beauty as she approached Joshua Crowther, and the wife of one of the guests was of the opinion that she was drugged and told her husband so afterwards.

"Don't you repeat that remark to anyone, d'you hear?" he had thundered, but he had to admit the bride certainly seemed to be of another world.

The wedding feast, if such it could be called, was as simple as the ceremony, and very short, and the gentlemen of the party agreed among themselves that they would be as eager as Joshua to get rid of them all and take his bride to his bed. He and his new wife, the picture of loving domesticity, stood at the top of the steps, he with his arm about her waist, which somehow did not seem to please her, waving them away. They had noticed that he could not keep his hands off her, which was natural enough, and during the afternoon what had seemed to be docile acceptance on her part had slipped imperceptibly into what might be called distaste, even fear.

That evening the two girls were not present at the dinner table. Maggie and Betsy were hard pressed to keep up with the master who was throwing his food down his throat so quickly it was a wonder he did not choke. He drank a lot of champagne, too, toasting his wife again and again, filling her glass and begging her to drink up, for was this not a special occasion. His hand was constantly on her, fondling her bare neck and shoulder, her arm and hand and Maggie felt herself go hot with embarrassment for a dreadful moment when she thought he was about to thrust it down the front of her bodice.

At last he stood up and held out his hand to his wife. She shrank away from him and in her face was the dawning realisation of what she had done, of what was about to be done and she tried to pull away. She had had no cup of chocolate since just before she left for the church.

"Come, my dear, it is getting late," he said to her, ignoring the cringing presence of the two embarrassed parlourmaids.

"No . . . please . . ."

"No, to your husband?"

It was clear Betsy was about to burst into sympathetic tears, so without being given permission Maggie took her hand and pulled her from the room, almost running with her up the hall and into the kitchen where the maidservants waited, among them Mrs Quinn whose heart was beating thick and sluggishly in her bosom.

"They're . . . they're off," Maggie told them faintly, nodding in the direction of the hallway. It was not even dark outside the kitchen window.

"Poor lady," one of them whispered, waiting for God knew what to happen. They had moved all her things while she and the master were at church into the master's bedroom, on his orders, and what would she think to that, they wondered in the depths of their women's hearts which knew she was, or had not been, in her right mind when she agreed to this.

The screaming began ten minutes later and for half an hour Molly Quinn stuck it out, covering her ears and bending her body as though she were suffering her mistress's agony with her. It was intermittent, the crying, the screaming, the agonised calls that none of them could answer, but at last Molly could bear it no longer.

"I'm norr 'avin' this," she screeched, making them all jump. "'E's treatin' her like a bloody animal an' I'm norr 'avin' it."

The furious knocking at his bedroom door interrupted Joshua Crowther's immense satisfaction and enjoyment of the naked woman in his bed. He had stripped her methodically, his eyes slits of reddened lust, thrown her on the bed and raped her. He hadn't hit her. He was a gentleman, after all. She had fought him, which had been a great surprise and had given an added and pleasurable dimension to the whole exercise. He hadn't expected it, neither had he expected any of his servants to have the temerity to interrupt him on his wedding night.

He should have known, of course. It was that woman, the one who had stood over his wife, before she had become his wife, like some protective knight in armour. The one who was where she was in his household simply because it was the only way he could get what he now had in his bed. At the moment his wife was lying senseless and spreadeagled on her face where he had placed her but when he had got rid of this woman he would . . . well, he had many fancies and she would satisfy them all!

Molly Quinn squared up to him like some small farmyard hen facing the fox.

"Sir, please . . . Mrs Elliott . . . we heard . . ."

"You mean Mrs Crowther, don't you, Mrs Quinn?" he asked her smoothly.

"Yes . . . yes . . . Mrs Crowther. Can I . . . ?"

"You can do one thing, Mrs Quinn, and that's get the hell out of here and if you try to interfere in my household again you will find employment elsewhere. My wife and I have retired for the night . . . *for the night*, do you understand? And you'd best go to that brat and shut her up or *both* of you will be out on your ear by morning."

He shut the door in her face and Molly Quinn, her heart broken, and her spirit as well, moved heavily along the passage to the room that Jane and Lily Elliott had shared and where Lily was doing her best to knock the door down. Molly was not surprised to find it locked!

17

Joshua and Jane Crowther had been married a month when Nicholas Crowther came home for the long "vac".

The deep sense of sadness in the house, the misery that pervaded every corner of it, even out into the gardens where Mr Diggle worked silently alongside young Will, oppressed them all. Mr Diggle had not seen the new mistress since her marriage to the master but he knew, as who did not in the Crowther household, of what the master did to her in that locked room, though they did not speak of it, of course. Well, to say they *knew* was not strictly true but they could only come to one conclusion on what went on there, couldn't they, and they were shocked that a man who had always been perfectly decent to them, if somewhat distant as the gentry are, could treat his new wife as he was doing.

It was often a mystery to those involved how these things became known, since not one of them would shame the lovely Mrs Elliott by discussing her sad plight with one another, but hadn't they all heard those anguished screams, even the stable lads and the gardeners, on the night of the wedding. Of course it was a man's right to take his wife to his bed and to do with her there what he wished and Mrs Crowther was not the first to suffer it, nor would she be the last in this world where a woman was her husband's property, just like his horse or his dog, to do with what he liked. It was a crying shame but what could they do?

She had never cried out again.

Lily did not see her mother for nearly a week after the wedding and though she begged and pleaded, almost on her knees, to Mr Crowther, to let her go into her he would not allow it, saying Lily would upset her.

She had lost her temper then. "*Me!* Me upset her! Tell me what you're doing to her and why did she scream like that in your room? And why does she have to sleep in your bed?" Though she knew that married ladies and gentlemen shared a bed, just like her ma had once done with Pa. "I want to know what you do to my mother," she had shouted defiantly, "and why won't you let me see her? Or Mrs Quinn? Why are Maggie or Betsy not allowed in, tell me that? Even her food is left outside the door. I'm going to call the police if you don't let her out. You can't keep someone prisoner like that. It's against the law."

She was too young and ignorant to realise that it titillated Joshua Crowther's sense of powerful male sexuality to know that the lovely creature who was now his wife was in his bed, naked and dead-eyed, waiting for him, at his own leisure, to go and unlock the door and let himself in, to do with her what he liked, when he liked. It was a new game that he would tire of soon, but not yet, not until he was totally satiated with the body he had craved and denied himself all these months. He would let her out then, when she would take up her duties as his wife, in his bed and out of it. He was looking forward to showing her off to his acquaintances. He would dress her in the finest the Misses Yeoland could provide, deck her out in the jewels that had once been his first wife's, and display her like a trophy to the admiring, covetous eyes of other men. In the meanwhile she stayed where she was and if this bloody child didn't bugger off he would do her a serious injury.

But Lily Elliott was not like Mrs Quinn. She was not afraid they would lose their place or that Mr Crowther might do her ma a serious injury. She was not revolted, disgusted, horrified by what was being done to her mother, since she didn't know what it was. The other women in the house did, or could half guess at it, but Lily was a child with no knowledge of the terrors of sexual abuse and she believed if she made enough of a nuisance of herself Mr Crowther would have to release her ma, or at least let her go into the bedroom and see for herself how she was.

"I mean it," she told him stubbornly. "You've no right to lock her up. I'm going to fetch the police constable from the corner of Aigburth Road and he'll make you let her out."

She faced him rebelliously, her hands behind her back, her chin stuck out at a truculent angle, her eyebrows drawn down in a ferocious scowl and if he had not been so damned fed up with her he might have laughed. He had it in him to wish her mother had a fraction of her spirit, for after that bitter struggle in the first half-hour, his wife was as submissive, as pliant as a rubber doll. She made no objection to whatever he did to her, allowing herself to be pulled this way and that, arranged into the most perverted poses and positions to please his fancy, but this one would be a tiger when it was her turn. The thought startled him, for he was not sure he knew what he meant himself since the girl was only ten. Or was it eleven? He seemed to remember she had a birthday recently. He was in a good mood, since all his bodily senses were deeply satisfied so he was prepared to humour her.

"Your mother is my wife now, Lily, and she and I . . . do things that as a child you will know nothing about." He smiled quite roguishly, a smile Lily did not understand.

"What sort of things?" She frowned even more and stuck her lip out.

"Really, child, the questions you do ask; one day I will answer them but in the meantime go and . . . and do whatever it is you should be doing at this time of day. I'm sure Miss Kaye must be looking for you."

"Miss Kaye and Eloise have gone for a walk and I—"

"You should have gone with them. That is why I employ Miss Kaye. To look after you and—"

"I'm worried about my mother and if you—"

"There is nothing to be worried about, Lily, so you'd best go and join—"

"I want to see my mother. You've no right—"

Suddenly he had had enough. He slapped the newspaper he had been reading when she burst into his study into a crumpled heap on his lap and glared at her with eyes that had gone a furious red.

"Will you get out of my sight, or must I lock you up too," he snarled at her, shaking out the newspaper in readiness to resume his reading.

"That's what I mean. You're not allowed to lock people up."

"Will you get out of my sight."

"Not until you—"

With an oath he sprang to his feet and from him came a roar of rage that made even Jane, in the comatose state into which her husband's attentions had flung her, lift her head to listen. The servants in the kitchen stopped as one what they were doing and Molly drifted slowly to the kitchen door to listen. She opened it a crack and was just in time to see the master dragging his step-daughter up the stairs, not by the hair as he would have liked, but by the arm. Lily was doing her best to struggle free, her voice high with indignation as she told him what she would do to him if he didn't let her go, but he continued up the stairs and along the passage, throwing her into the bedroom she and her ma had shared and where, for now, she still slept, locking the door and pocketing the key.

The maidservants all shrank back as he came down again but he went into his study and banged the door.

It was then, or at least the next day, that Lily began to plead with him. She had found that with a bit of effort and a great deal of slipping and catching herself on sharp sticky-out bits of branches, she could climb down the tree that was directly outside the bedroom window, but when she had done it she wondered why since she could go nowhere, could she? She did reconnoitre under the window of Ma's bedroom, or rather *his* and Ma's bedroom but there was no handy tree there, so, reluctantly, she had climbed back to her own room for it he came and found her gone her means of escape, which might come in handy another time, would be discovered.

It was nearly a week later when Mr Crowther summoned Mrs Quinn to his bedroom, telling her casually that his wife would be down for dinner and she was to instruct Cook in the preparing of a splendid meal. And could she make sure there was a suitable wine to serve with the meal, and, as though it were an afterthought, she was to get his wife ready. He was off to the stables in half an hour and would she send a message to Arnold to saddle Ebony. Oh, and he thought the children might be brought down to dinner since this was a celebration. There was just one more thing. Mrs Crowther was in need of a decent lady's maid since Mrs Quinn's job was to be housekeeper and nothing else from now on, so would she ask around for a suitable woman. Servants always knew these things.

With a brisk nod he left the room.

Hardly daring to move her head for what she might see there, Molly Quinn turned to the lifeless figure propped up in a chair by the window. It wasn't looking at her, that figure, but at something beyond the window, not even in the garden but somewhere way on the horizon, further than that even and Molly could only call it eternity. It was Jane, of course. She could not bring herself to call her Mrs Crowther, or even Mrs Elliott, the poor broken woman by the window, and so she called her by the name, and herself by the name, she had always used that were to be theirs with each other to the end of their days.

"It's Molly, me lamb. I've come ter see to yer," she murmured softly, since it appeared to her that the slightest noise or movement might send her lamb spinning off into that eternity she was studying with such longing. "I'll ge' yer a bath and wash yer 'air," for it was obvious her mistress had had no such attention since her wedding day. "Then our Lily'll come an' see yer. She's bin that worried wi' yer bein' so poorly, like."

She was not really aware that she had called the child the possessive "our Lily" which was only used to speak of or to a member of the family. She was concerned only with putting some excuse, some reason into her lamb's mind that might be used to explain the days she had spent locked in this room. She looked unkempt, her hair in a snarl, the flimsy wrapper which Molly had never seen before and through which her nipples and the triangle of hair between her legs could clearly be seen, crumpled and torn. But at the sound of her daughter's name she turned her head and looked at Molly with eyes that had seen and known things no woman should ever have to know or see. There was desolation of her spirit in her eyes, a great tearing shame, a devastation of the soul which had once been clean and loved by Richard Elliott and which the man who was now her husband had done to death in the cruellest way. She moaned low in the back of her throat, like someone who has been tortured beyond endurance and knows it has not yet come to an end. Her face was a travesty of the serene face Molly Quinn had loved for years, gaunt, hollow-cheeked, the eyes fallen into the sockets below her forehead, the mouth bitten and torn.

"Oh, Molly." It was said so forlornly, like that of a child who has been punished for something it does not understand, and yet with a memory in it of an act so shameful it could be told to no decent woman.

With a cry of pain and rage so great it almost choked her,

Molly flung herself across the room and gathered her into her arms.

It was Lily who got her through those dreadful hours and days and weeks, for of them all in the house and in the garden her innocent child was the only one who did not know the truth. And it was perhaps the horror of what had been done to her by Joshua Crowther that brought her back from the precipice on which she had teetered ever since her husband, her *real* husband, had been killed. Though she could not reason the why of it, Lily gave her a small measure of strength to shore up the barricade that protected her and behind which she hid her real self from the man who shared her bed. He shared her bed. He took her body in any way he fancied but he no longer took *her*.

She kept Lily by her side during the day and Joshua, who cared nothing for the child's education, which was doubtful she got from Miss Kaye anyway, allowed it. He was too busy with the grouse-shooting season which had just begun and as long as she was in his bed at night did not seem to care what she did. Jane renewed her interest in the garden, reassured by the quiet kindliness of Mr Diggle, who treated her as though nothing had happened in the space of time since they had last met, nothing that need matter to them, at any rate. Even Will, who was a simple, uneducated lad, and was not sure what ailed her, only that something did, found the words to speak to her, showing her how to dead-head the roses, to plant geraniums on a south border in the sandy soil, how to sow what were known as "ten-week" stock, how to pot those that would be needed for spring planting. She could be seen kneeling on a cushion planting out pinks, double wallflowers and pansies, her ravaged face at peace for the time being as she put her hands in the life-giving soil. Lily sprawled on the grass beside her, her nose in the latest encyclopedia, waiting patiently for her mother, who she knew depended on her at this moment in her life, walking slowly back to the house with her hand in hers, or up to the potting shed, the enormous hothouses, admiring the vegetable garden and the fruit which burgeoned on the apple trees, the plum and pear trees. These growing things, these simple, God-given things seemed to give comfort to Ma and so, though she longed to be away to more exciting pastimes, Lily curbed her impatience.

On fine days Lily took her down to the seashore where they

sat for hours on end in the warm August sunshine, watching the passing ships, not talking much, for what was there to say between the badly damaged woman and her innocent child? But they held hands and it was as though, for that peaceful moment, Pa was back with them in this world that had been his. The world of the river and the oceans beyond, the lovely sailing ships, the rippling highway of dancing, gold-streaked water which he had loved and which had been passed on to his child.

It was there that Lily found the courage to speak of the Mechanics Institute. She bent her head and stroked her mother's hand with the tenderness a mother might show her child. As though their roles were reversed which, in a way, was true.

"Ma, can I tell you something?" she asked her, looking up to meet her mother's gaze, which had become more tranquil during the last few days, especially since her work in the garden.

"Of course, dearest. What is it?"

"I want to go to school, Ma." Her voice was low and hesitant and she bent her head again as though to hide the desperation in her eyes.

"To school? But what about Miss Kaye? She's teaching Eloise."

"No, Ma, she's not. Oh, she can just about read and write and sew a sampler and play the piano but I don't want that." She looked up again, her face passionate in her sudden determination to let her ma see what Lily Elliott needed and it wasn't sewing a bloody sampler. "I want to learn what Pa learned. Dearest, I don't want to hurt you any more than . . . well, I know you're not happy here and neither am I with . . . with *him* and that damned Eloise is a stuck-up little bitch."

"Lily!"

"She is, Ma. All she does is try to get me into trouble with Miss Kaye. Not that that matters, for I don't give a fig for Miss Kaye but one day she'll tell *him* something and that would mean . . . well, if she found out that . . . that . . ."

"Found out what, dearest?" Jane looked troubled, turning to gaze over her shoulder as though her husband might be lurking over the green bank.

"It's a secret, Ma, but God's honour," she added hastily, "it's nothing bad. You see . . . well, it might get someone into trouble if I told anyone or it got back to . . . to Mr Crowther."

She could not forget Liam's tense entreaty that she must tell no one of their meetings.

"Oh, Lily, please don't do anything to make him angry. He can be very . . . very forceful when he's angry." Jane's distress was growing but Lily continued to stroke her hand, doing her best to calm her, beseeching her to believe that it was nothing dreadful and if she could she'd tell her ma but it wasn't her secret, did Ma see?

"But it's about going to school that I want to talk to you, dearest. To learn properly what I need for . . . for the future."

"Do you mean go back to the Goodwin School for Young Ladies, dearest?" Jane looked doubtful. "Oh, I don't think Mr Crowther would agree to that. Not when there is a governess here in the house to teach you."

"But she teaches us nothing, Ma, don't you see? I want to learn what *Pa* knew. I want what he had. I want to find the *Lily-Jane* and become a mariner like Pa was and the only way I can do that is to go to the Mechanics Institute. Look, I've cut this piece out of the newspaper to show you," pulling the crumpled cutting from her pocket. "They teach all kinds of things, see. French and Spanish and singing, not just the art of seamanship. There will be other girls there, probably not learning what I want to learn but that wouldn't matter. I could go into the boys' classes and . . . oh, please, Ma, say yes. Let me go. Talk to him and make him see . . ."

Even as she spoke Lily felt despair creep over her as she watched her mother retreating towards that barricade she hid behind to escape her husband. Her eyes took on a curiously blank stare as though there were nothing remaining of Jane Elliott inside her head. She had gone, retreated to the place of safety which was the only way she could deal with her situation. Her soul did not even attempt to peep out in case he should notice it, and her, and until the danger had passed over she would remain as still as a bird in a bush when the hawk flies over.

"Ma . . . please, Ma . . . I can't do it without you." Tears slid down Lily's face as she saw her only chance of becoming the sea captain her father had been slip away. She had counted on her mother being able to persuade Mr Crowther to allow her to go to the school and yet when she gave it proper thought, which she was forced to do now, she could see what a fool she had been. Her mother had been almost destroyed by the death of Pa and now, when a man with tenderness and sensitivity might have restored her to her self, her true self, she had married a brute like Mr Crowther who cared for nobody but himself. She did not exactly think in these terms, for she was a child of ten years but she knew with a different man her mother would have been a different woman. A man like Liam, for instance. She had no idea what Mr Crowther and Ma did in their bedroom, nor why he had locked her up for nearly a week, but whatever it was it had certainly made her mother even worse. She was not as vague, as lost as she had been, but she certainly was not capable of demanding the education her child needed, of standing up to him, of arguing that Lily was *her* child and would go to the school *she* chose. That was what Lily had hoped for but she knew she had been sadly, badly mistaken.

There was a sound from further up the beach, the sound of footsteps crunching on seashells and they both froze into stillness. They were afraid to turn to see who intruded on their moment of peace and the youth who approached them was startled by the rigid fear that showed plainly in both still figures.

It was Lily who turned towards him, for into her mind had come the wild hope that it might be Liam, but the tall, dark figure who sauntered towards them was not that of her friend but strangely familiar just the same. Jane sat like a flower petrified by time, her gaze fixed and unblinking, her hand like ice in that of her daughter and when Lily struggled to her feet she rose too, incapable of thought except that it might be *him*.

"Good morning," the young man said, lifting his hand to his head as though expecting to find a hat there which he intended to raise politely. "A lovely day, isn't it?" He smiled and made to pass them, wondering, you could see it in his face, what had caused the strange expressions, the strange stillness in the woman and her daughter, then he stopped.

"I do beg your pardon, ma'am, but aren't you . . . ? I know it sounds foolish but I do believe you might be my new stepmother, and, of course, step-sister."

They both looked at him as though he were a cobra about

to strike and he wondered what sort of a woman his father had married. Very beautiful, he could see that, though she looked as though she were recovering from an illness, but the child was an exquisite replica of her, or of how she must have been herself as a girl. She was dainty, tall and slender, nearly as tall as the woman, with silver-streaked hair in which shades of gold could be seen, silken and curly just like her mama's. Her skin was a fine ivory and rose and her eyes a deep unfathomable grey, almost lavender in the reflection from the lapping water.

Lily cleared her throat and Jane, like some old woman near to death, turned her head slowly to look at him, almost as though she were afraid he might do her an injury.

Lily spoke. "This . . . is my mother. Her name is Jane Elliott . . . No, I beg your pardon, Jane Crowther and I am Lily Elliott. Are you . . . ?"

He gave a merry smile and though his likeness to Joshua Crowther was uncanny they could not help but relax a little. "Then it's true. You are my new mother and sister. I'm Nicholas Crowther but my friends call me Nicky."

"Nicky." Lily cleared her throat again and Jane did not speak.

"Yes, I got home no more than an hour ago but the first thing I always do is to come down here. I love it, the river, and one day, whan I go into my father's business I mean to have my own boat."

"Ship."

"Pardon?"

"You should say ship."

"Well, I never, a girl who knows the difference."

Lily bristled. "And what's strange about that? Some girls are interested in things other than . . . than dolls and embroidery, you know."

He looked startled, as though a kitten he had put out a hand to stroke had turned out to be a full-grown and infuriated tabby.

"I'm sorry. I do apologise, but it is so seldom that anything that interests a male, interests a female."

"Well, it does."

"I can see that. Now are we friends again?"

"Well . . ."

"Please . . ."

"Well, all right."

He sighed, satisfied, and sat down on the warm sand and they sat down beside him, though Jane kept a firm hold on Lily's hand. He did not *feel* like Mr Crowther, nor did he *sound* like Mr Crowther, but this was how Mr Crowther must have been when he was a boy, a young man and until he had proved otherwise she would not trust his son.

"I was sorry I could not come to the wedding," he was saying politely, just as though urgent business had kept him away, though the truth of it was he had not been invited. He had known nothing about it until his father had written to him a week or two back informing him that he had a stepmother and sister and he was to behave himself and remember his manners when he came home. That was how his father talked to him, cuttingly, contemptuously, since they were both aware that he was not the son his father would have liked.

For once Lily was at a loss for words. Like her mother she did not trust anyone with the name of Crowther. If he was anything like his sister or his father she was prepared to loathe him, but at the same time it was hard to tell him so when they had only just met. She was usually forthright, she had heard it called rude, saying whatever came into her head but she had her ma to think of now and if what she said was repeated to *him* and hurt her ma she would never forgive herself. She was learning to watch her tongue. Mr Crowther had absolute power over her mother since she was now his wife and though this last week or two he had been amazingly pleasant at the breakfast table, not only to her and Eloise but to Ma, she would not depend on it to last if he was displeased. The maids, their faces set in the blank mask of the well-trained servant, had exchanged glances, when the master wasn't looking, of course, at his aimiability, reporting back to the kitchen that he was like the cat who had swallowed the cream, which they thought was true though they pitied the poor woman who was providing it. Mrs Quinn said nothing. As soon as he had gone, which he did every day now he no longer had to butter up her mistress, she would slip up to the sitting-room attached to the bedroom her lamb shared with Joshua Crowther, and they would enjoy half an hour together in private, drinking a cup of tea and saying little but being a comfort to one another. There was to be a lady's maid starting next week, a nice little thing, sweet-faced and pleasant and very well trained by some titled lady in Yorkshire and who had been hand-picked by Molly herself. She'd have no grim-faced, hard-hearted, stuck-up biddy looking after her lamb!

He walked back with them, Nicky Crowther, talking pleasantly of this and that. What he meant to do in the "vac", the prospect of a bit of shooting and riding. Did she ride? What a pity, and what about Mrs . . . Mrs Crowther, hesitating over what to call her mother. His eyes were the deepest chestnut brown, soft with anxiety as though he knew what was behind her mother's silence. His gaze was clear and steadfast and his expression earnest. He was sixteen, Lily knew that, but he was still a boy. There was a warmth within him and about him that Lily liked but was not sure she could trust, for hadn't Mr Crowther been just like that to begin with? When they reached the gardens and her mother hesitated beside a bed of lavender, he stopped, bending to crush the flowers between his fingers.

"What a glorious smell," he murmured, "and what a glorious sight, that wall of lavender mist. D'you not think so, Mrs Crowther?" He turned courteously to Jane.

She looked into his eyes and, seeing nothing there of his father, smiled.

Part 2

18

He was waiting for her where he had said he would be, on the steps of the Custom House in Strand Street and for a moment she allowed herself the pleasure of just watching him without him being aware of it. He was leaning gracefully against one of the pillars, his arms crossed, looking directly across the street to the backs of the transit sheds that lined Salthouse Dock, and the plantation of gently swaying ships' masts beyond, from which penants of every colour flew. Many of the ships were square-riggers but a three-masted barque had almost finished loading her cargo and on deck work was under way getting ready for sea. The sails had been roused out of the sail locker and sent aloft and he was scrutinising the activity with keen interest, probably comparing what was taking place with that of his own capable crew. Amid the bowsprit rigging the barque had a finely carved figurehead in toga, tunic and sandals, which was not unusual since all the ships, and unique to each one, had a figurehead. Many of the carved figures, executed in the workshops of Liverpool's carvers, came in a variety of forms, human figures that reflected the name of the ship, or the portrait of their master, or masters' wives or daughters, and docks like Salthouse had been likened to colourful outdoor sculpture galleries.

He still had not seen her. The cab had dropped her at the corner of Canning Place and Strand Street and though she attracted many admiring glances herself, she did not see them, for her whole attention was taken up by Liam O'Connor. For some surprising reason it was as though she were looking at him for the first time with another woman's eyes. That's if you could call Lily Elliott a woman at sixteen. She liked to think so. The sun seemed to be captured in his unruly tumble of wheat-coloured hair which, she noted absently, needed cutting again, striking gilded sparks from it which contrasted agreeably with his dark, sunbrowned face and the sharp intensity of his narrowed, hyacinth blue eyes.

He was frowning slightly as though he were critical of the seamen's performances and he shook his head as a rope ran haphazardly through careless hands. He turned away in what seemed to be scorn for their seamanship and saw her and at once his face lit up, opening into a warm, sweet smile, revealing his excellent teeth and he began to stride towards her. Even then she could not help but be aware of his great height, the breadth of his shoulders and the tapering leanness of his hips and long, well-muscled legs. He was dressed in a well-cut frock-coat of dark grey worsted reaching to his knees, with narrow trousers to match and a pale grey waistcoat. It was what the fashionable young gentleman of growing means would wear but, particularly as he was carrying his hat, he managed to make the suit look casual, informal, as though he were off to a country fair instead of a day in town. He had loosened his necktie since it was a warm day, but his boots were polished and his face well shaved and he drew every female eye to him which, again for some strange reason, did not please her.

A strange moment, then it was gone and he was her dear, familiar Liam again, loved, trusted, depended upon for comfort and support and sympathy when circumstances at Oakwood Place overcame her. Her friend who had never let her down and whom she loved dearly. Her face expressed her feelings, and her eyes glowed like a candle just lit in a darkened room.

"You're late," he told her cheerfully, not at all put out, "and if we don't look sharp we'll not get a decent place. She comes in in half an hour and most of Liverpool seems to be making its way down there. Where've you been, anyroad?" He had taken her arm and was hurrying her across the dock road in the direction of Princes Dock which afforded harbourage for the largest class of vessels. The road was a continuous motion of horse-drawn vehicles, carts and team waggons shifting goods to and from quaysides, from warehouses to the holds of ships tied up alongside the low transit sheds and they were in mortal danger of being run down. Drivers cursed, but the patient plodding Shires that pulled the waggons did not even flinch, fully expecting the small scurrying human creatures to get out of their way, which they did, thanks to Liam.

"Well, if you'll let go of my arm and give me a chance to draw breath I'll tell you." Her voice was tart and as she almost ran to keep up with his long-legged stride her feet barely seemed to touch the ground.

"Can't you talk and walk at the same time, lovebud? Or shall I pick you up and carry you?" He grinned down at her. "It wouldn't be the first time. Remember when we walked all the way from Pottery Beach to Canada Dock and then when we turned to go back you said your boots hurt you and I had to sling you over my shoulder."

"Liam O'Connor, you did no such thing and besides, I was only a child then." Her mouth drew into a prim line and she did her best to toss her head but it was hard to do when you were being propelled at great speed along a pavement crowded with people all going to the same place and intent on getting there before anyone else. Liverpool folk did love ships and they were keen to be the first to get a look at the one that was just about to steam into the Mersey.

Strand Street was almost impassable as people from every walk of life headed towards Princes Dock but with the help of Liam's powerful bulk which shouldered aside those who would have stood in his way, and those who would have argued with him over his methods, they came to St Nicholas Church and the walkway that led down to Princes Landing Stage which was so crowded Lily said she knew how a sardine felt in a sardine tin.

"Get behind me and hold on to my coat," he ordered her, "and don't leave go for anybody. I'll see if I can get us down to the landing stage."

Besides the ordinary men and women who had come to see the biggest ship in the world steam into port were dockers leaning upon the handles of hefty sets of wheels which they would use to trundle the ship's cargo to the warehouse, stevedores, tally clerks, porters and casual labourers, for this was a sight never before seen and no one wanted to miss it. Most of them had a pipe gripped between their stained teeth and smoke wreathed about their heads, mingling with the richer aroma of cigars smoked by gentlemen who had come down to see the fun. And mixed with the smell of tobacco was the pungency of the sea, of tar and coffee beans, of rum and raw brown sugar, of linseed and cocoa and every conceivable cargo which was being unloaded, or loaded, along seven miles of dockland.

Lily was enchanted, wondering why it was she never failed to feel like this whenever she was here. The river was beautiful, the sun glinting on its moving waters and the ships standing silently in their own shadows. Ferries beat out towards New Brighton and Birkenhead, for business must go on despite the arrival of such an important vessel. In the far, far distance she could see the mountains of Wales and behind her rose the bustle of the town, and about her was the clang of hammers, the hoots of the sirens greeting the great ship. She leaned against Liam's shoulder, his arm protectively about her, and knew she had never been so happy as she was on this day. Pa had been gone for six years now but in Liam she had found what she had lost when Pa died.

She beamed at her old friend the piermaster, as she now knew him to be, remembering the day, long ago now, when she had entrusted a note for Liam with him which he had faithfully delivered for her. He was in his smart cap and uniform and was an important man, for he controlled the movement of ships in and out of the docks, helped by a team of dock gatemen. His job was an arduous one because he was expected to attend the opening and closing of the gates into the river before and after each high tide. He had his own house right on the waterfront by the Dock Board which Lily envied enormously and, in the early days, when it began to look as though Mr Crowther was not going to let her go to the Mechanics Institute as she had hoped and learn to become a sea captain, she had thought she might like the piermaster's job. She and Liam had even been to take tea with him and his wife and they had become firm friends.

"A fine sight, Lily," he said to her now. "I've seen some ships come and go in this river but I do believe this is going to be the finest."

"Oh, no, sir, we can't agree, can we, Liam? What could be more beautiful than a clipper ship under full sail? Steam will never replace them, never. Great unwieldy things with all that filthy smoke belching out and the noise of the engines."

Liam and the piermaster exchanged amused looks over her head but just then a great shout went up and there she was.

She came upriver like a queen, regal and if not exactly

beautiful, a sight that filled the crowd with awe. The incredible length of her as she glided over the gilded waters, momentarily quietened them all to open-mouthed silence, even Liam who had known of her dimensions. She was painted a sleek black and had a massive side paddle. She had six masts and five funnels and how they were to fit her into her berth was a mystery to the onlookers. The *Great Eastern* had made the passage from New York with a large cargo and 212 passengers – though she was equipped to accommodate four thousand – in the record time of nine days and eleven hours which was a marvel in itself and the sight of her was a bloody marvel, as one old salt said to another in Lily's hearing. She and Liam were crammed together with men and women from all walks of life, hundreds of them, who were in love with the sea and had come to watch the biggest ship in the world make her stately way upriver towards her berth and if Lily's toes were stepped on and her new bonnet knocked askew, what did it matter? They cheered and shouted and Liam threw his brand-new bowler hat into the air and never saw it again, which didn't matter in the least because they had both agreed that it didn't suit him!

It was a lovely day which, of course, it always was with Liam. Now that the *Great Eastern* was safely berthed and after they had gawped with the rest at her tremendous size close to, they made their way arm-in-arm, along with the now relaxed and sauntering crowd, back up the walkway towards St Nicholas Church. They strode up Chapel Street, their strides matching now, for Lily was tall, cutting through the Exchange Flags behind the Town Hall which was a regular meeting place for cotton brokers, merchants and ship-owners to do deals and exchange gossip. It was packed today with a multitude of gentlemen who had been to see the *Great Eastern*, all dressed in what was almost a uniform of top hat and tails. They came out on Castle Street and then turned at St George's Church into Lord Street.

"Now you can tell me why you were late, lovebud. Not that it matters, but you know I worry if you're not on time. I get it into my head that your stepfather has—"

"Don't call him that, Liam. You know I hate it." She turned a mutinous glare on him and he sighed and shrugged his shoulders.

211

"Well, that's what he is, Lily, and if he were to say you couldn't leave the house you would have to obey him."

"No, I wouldn't. He has no rights over me. And it wasn't him, anyway, it was Ma. You know she's expecting?"

"Yes. Is she . . . pleased?" He had nearly said *resigned* to it, since he had the impression the coming child had been a shock. He was not quite sure how to approach the delicate subject of Jane Crowther's pregnancy after six years of marriage, since he was uncertain of Lily's feelings about it. She had not told him until her mother was in her fifth month and he had the distinct feeling she was ashamed, or felt it in some way to be disloyal to her dead father for his wife to be having a child that was not his. Lily was unpredictable and sometimes, when he least expected it, she took up arms on some point or other and argued until he could have put her over his knee and spanked her.

"I don't know, really," she answered him gloomily. "She is thirty-five and I heard Maggie telling Mrs Quinn that it was a great age to be having a child. Mrs Quinn should know, since she's now a grandmother as well as a mother. Her daughter Victoria married Arnold, the groom, did you know?"

"No, lovebud, I didn't. How could I?"

"Of course. Well, they have a couple of children but Mrs Quinn refuses to say anything about Ma being too old to have a baby. Do you know, Liam? Is it right?"

"Lord, don't ask me. I know nothing about children, only you, and you've always been a handful." He grinned down at her and squeezed her hand which rested in the crook of his arm.

"I meant about . . . well, Maggie seemed to be saying there might be . . . danger, though Mrs Quinn soon saw her off. Mad as Beauty when she fell into the water butt, she was. I thought she was going to hit Maggie and they're best of friends, really. So it was Ma who held me up. I wanted to make sure she'd be all right while I was out, but Mrs Quinn said she'd sit with her until I got back. *He'd* gone off somewhere on business, after having told me I was to stay close to the house, which he has no right to do so I just ignored him as usual."

"It will get you into trouble one day, lovebud, this determination you have to disobey him at every turn."

This was an old argument, and one they had whenever they met. She did her best to convince him and herself that her mother's husband had no claim on her, as a parent would, and that consequently she could do as she liked. For the most part it was true, for the fact was Joshua had not the faintest notion what she got up to half the time. Neither did Miss Kaye who was supposed to have her in her charge. She had long since given up trying to keep Lily in the schoolroom, or on the tedious walks she and Eloise took up and down the garden paths. She had long since given up coaxing her to accompany them to the art gallery or the museum or the Zoological Gardens.

At first it was a regular occurrence to be hauled up before her mother's husband and an explanation demanded as to where she had been all day and when she refused to say, which she *always* did, she was locked up in her room on a diet of bread and water, or threatened with the strap. It had not the slightest effect. Usually she had been no further than the seashore, the paddocks to see the horses and talk to the grooms, the kitchens where she counted the maidservants as her friends, eating Mrs Kelly's marzipan biscuits and angel cakes, helping to mix the batter for her batter pudding, or reading to Jenny, for whom she felt inordinately sorry, while the scullery maid peeled the spuds. She spent hours in the woodlands, where she took the dogs, including Mr Crowther's so that he complained they were getting out of hand, but she didn't care. She derived great pleasure out of crossing him which, if he had not been somewhat indifferent to her and her whereabouts, might have led to trouble.

Sometimes it was a day such as this, one she spent with Liam when he was in port, walking the length of the parades that lay before each dock. Or up to the top of Duke Street to St James Walk where they would sit and talk and look out over the splendid views to the south-west where, on a clear day, Chester could be seen. To the right of Chester was Park Gate on the east bank of the River Dee and in a straight line dead ahead the smooth and beautifully indented chain of the Derbyshire Hills. There was Bidston Lighthouse across the river, like a slim finger of stone pointing into the sunshine, and on the dancing water the wonderful panorama of the ships racing to beat the tide out to sea. The ferries were busy with their passengers like fussy old ladies dressed in black and full of their own importance. In the distance was the dome of St Paul's with the sunlight glinting off it and circled with the endless crying of the seabirds.

These were precious days, days that made those first months of her mother's marriage to Mr Crowther bearable, at least for her, and she did her best not to jeopardise them. Now and again, mostly at Liam's coaxing, and to give the impression that she was learning to settle down, she spent an hour or so in the schoolroom, but it always ended up with her and Eloise having an argument and Eloise threatening to tell her father about some misdemeanour and Lily would swear she wouldn't come again. Both Eloise and Miss Kaye were as relieved about it as she was!

Ma seemed to have settled at last to being the wife of one of Liverpool's wealthiest men, probably because after the first few months of greedily devouring her every night in his bed, the novelty of it wore off and his demands lessened. Not that Lily was aware of this. She only knew Ma was better, in health and in her looks, especially as Mr Crowther insisted that she have her gowns and outfits made by the Misses Yeoland and, having perfect taste and wonderful style, Ma quickly became known as the most fashionable and best-dressed lady in Liverpool, which vastly pleased Mr Crowther. Lily and Eloise were similarly dressed, in garments suitable for their age, of course, and even Eloise didn't mind accompanying her stepmama, as she called her, to be fitted for her new outfits.

Now and again Nicholas Crowther showed his face, but as he and his father did not agree on anything, and in fact Lily was beginning to think the only one who *did* agree with Joshua was Eloise, she was not surprised. Contrary to his father's wishes he had not joined the family firm of shippers and merchants but had somehow managed to buy himself – with money left him by his mother – a commission in a fashionable regiment and had served in South Africa and Ireland. He had done well, promoted to subaltern at the age of twenty and had scarcely been seen since. Lily had been sorry, for of all the Crowthers he had been the best, in her opinion, and she had thought if he had remained at home they might have become friends.

She and Liam strolled up Lord Street, her hand in the crook of his arm, idly looking in shop windows and admiring the goods displayed there. Lord Street was well groomed, alert, brisk with traffic and pedestrians, like the rest of the town thronging with the vast population of peoples of the world who passed through it. Languages of all nations fell on their ears but they were so used to it it excited little interest. They crossed into Brownlow Hill, walking slowly up towards Mount Pleasant and the Adelphi where he was to take her to lunch.

Liam was conscious, if she was not, of the stir she caused as they entered the dining-room of the hotel. It was filled with the elegant and wealthy of Liverpool, most as fashionable and well turned out as she was. The influence of the Misses Yeoland who were considered to be the best and cleverest dressmakers in Liverpool, clearly showed. It was said they catered to the majority of the discerning wives of shippers, of merchant princes, men of cotton, men with influence and property, and it was all on display here in the dazzling array of jewels, silks, hats laden with lace and flowers, fans with mother-of-pearl handles and parasols with ivory or coral sticks which, when opened, would be seen to be made of costly silk and lace, with the very latest black fringes. It was not often that Liam brought her here, for it was very expensive and way beyond the means of a seaman, even if he had his Master's Certificate, but today was a treat, a wonderful ending to a special day.

All the women, many of them very attractive, appeared overdressed and showy, even coarse beside the delicate silver, ivory and rose loveliness of Lily Elliott. Though she was tall, taller than most women, she was slender and graceful as a swan, with a neck that was white and long. Her glorious hair, which had darkened slightly as she matured to a mixture of tawny gold and silver, was parted in the centre and drawn back into an enormous chignon which had no need of the false hair worn by many ladies. A ringlet or two strayed endearingly behind her ears and on to her neck. In her ears were pearl earrings given to her only last month for her sixteenth birthday by her mother. She wore pale cream lawn. Miss Yeoland had insisted on it, saying that there were only so many years when a woman could wear simple cream and that Lily was to take advantage of it. There was plenty of time for the rich poppy colours, the rose, the buttercup and shades of plum which her mother wore and which suited her so well.

The basque bodice was trimmed with honey-coloured satin ribbon about the neck and at the edges of the pagoda sleeves, and her bonnet was tied beneath her chin with the same coloured ribbon. It was very small, no bigger than a cake plate, called a puff-bonnet, just a scrap of lace and cream satin roses that perched precariously just above her forehead.

"You look very elegant, lovebud," Liam said to her, his eyes intent on her every movement, though he was smiling as she tucked in to her second whipped cream meringue. "And there really is no need to lick the spoon like that. I'm sure if you were to ask the waiter nicely he would fetch you another."

"Thanks, I will. They're lovely. Not quite as good as Mrs Kelly's but scrumptious just the same. Won't you try one?"

He shuddered. "Thanks, but no. I have enough difficulty climbing the rigging without adding extra pounds."

"When do you have to climb the rigging, I'd like to know?" she asked him, her eyes on her dish as she scraped her spoon round it, then popped the spoon into her mouth. He watched her, fascinated by the parted rosy lips, the small pink tongue that came out to give added power to the movement, then looked hastily away as she caught him staring at her.

"What?" she said. "Have I got cream on my nose?"

"Would you be surprised if you had, you greedy child?"

"You didn't answer my question. How many times do you climb the rigging?" for Liam O'Connor was the captain of a fine, fore and aft schooner now, a man of some importance and she knew he was looking about him for a ship of his own. "A captain doesn't do that sort of work."

He grinned wryly. "Well, not very often, I admit, but now and again I like to go up to show the men, and myself, that I can."

She sat back in her chair and carefully folded her napkin before placing it beside her empty plate. Her eyes had become misted and her mouth drooped as she fiddled with the spoon in the saucer of her coffee cup. The fine excitement of the day had vanished for the moment and he knew the reason why, of course. He knew what was in her mind as though he could see inside her head, which in a way he could. He had known her for six years now. They had met as often as he could manage, first down on the shore, then, as she grew and was allowed, or took, more freedom, in the city parks, the art galleries and exhibitions, the library and sometimes here where he brought her for afternoon tea. She had shared every aspect of her life with him, though he could not say the same to her since he was a grown man and she was a child. He knew of her stepfather's cruelty to her mother, not physical from what she told him but of the more sinister kind where a stronger will overpowers a weaker. And yet the man was generous to a fault, a generosity that allowed his wife and her daughter to dress like princesses. Lily had a mare of her own and on fine days met him out towards Speke or Hale Hall, pleasant leafy rides southwards to the point of land where the Mersey narrows and the lighthouse called the Dungeon Light stood.

Liam had done well. He had got on. He was ruthless, hardworking and ambitious and he had got on. He had done his share of scrubbing decks, coiling ropes, climbing rigging to reef and unfurl sails and now what he had always wanted was almost in his grasp. He had saved every penny he had earned, investing it wisely, since he had a good head on his shoulders and soon, when he found her, he would have his own ship.

And that was what his little lovebud wanted and had never achieved, nor was she likely to. He had never heard the last of her plans to enter the Mechanics Institute in her early years, when she had been a child who knows no better but, of course, it had not happened. Her mother, who would have died for her, had had the stuffing knocked out of her by her bullying husband, from what Lily told him, and though Lily herself had stood up to him and demanded that she be given a proper education, he had merely laughed at her and told her to get back to the schoolroom. That was when her education had ended.

He put her in a cab at the front entrance to the Adelphi, then set off at a brisk pace along Renshaw Street, Berry Street, turning into Upper Duke Street where smart town houses climbed the hill from the dock area up towards North Toxteth. It took no more than ten minutes. As he approached a house in the centre of a terrace and opposite a pretty garden area, he glanced up to the small, balconied window, tipping his hat to a woman who smiled at him from behind the nets.

The cab dropped Lily at the gate, for it was still ingrained in her to let Mr Crowther know as little as possible about her movements, even though she was aware that he didn't give a damn what she did. Now Eloise, that was different, but the whereabouts of the rebellious daughter of his wife was a matter of complete indifference to him. As long as she brought no scandal to his door, which he knew was unlikely since she loved her mother too much, she was virtually free to do as she pleased.

Her cream kid boots scrunched on the newly raked gravel of the drive. She waved her hand to young Will who was now a strapping lad of twenty and was surprised when he turned away and bowed his head over his spade. He had been digging so furiously it was a wonder he didn't break the damned thing, she had time to think as she mounted the front steps.

Maggie was standing in the doorway, her hand on the doorknob just as though she had been behind the door, which had been flung open the minute she had spied Lily.

"Well, that's what I call service, Maggie. Were you watching out for me?" She scowled. "He's not been asking for me, has he, because if he has . . ."

Her voice trailed away uncertainly as she stepped into the absolute quiet of the hallway.

Maggie's face was blank, white as paper and she held herself rigidly as though she were afraid she might fold up like a concertina.

"Ma . . . ?" Lily croaked, her expression anguished and was not surprised when Maggie began to cry.

19

They were to call the child Abigail and that was the end of it, he ranted at them, and if there was any more arguing he would knock their heads together. It had been his mother's name and it was to be the child's.

The child. That was how he spoke of his new daughter, how he was always to speak of his new daughter, for there was no doubt he considered her a poor exchange for his beautiful wife. He and his elder daughter, his step-daughter and the household servants had just got back from the funeral which had been gratifyingly well attended, though none of those who had come could really say they had known the dead woman. She had sat at the head of Joshua Crowther's dining table on numerous occasions, looking like some exquisitely dressed doll who only spoke when directly spoken to, but she had been gracious and inoffensive and what was wrong with having a speechless wife? They wished they might be so lucky. Pity it had rained so, though the weather certainly matched the absolute devastation of the dead woman's daughter. She looked like some tall, black, stick insect, painfully slender and completely quenched by her grief, standing somewhat apart from Joshua Crowther and his daughter and totally alone. The servants wept unreservedly, even a tall lad and an elderly man who were said to be the gardeners, and a woman, the housekeeper, they were told, who had come with Mrs Crowther to Oakwood Place, almost fainted dead away she was so distressed as the coffin was lowered into the wet black earth.

The daughter had disappeared after the interment and the drive back to Oakwood Place, heading, it was whispered, to where she had been ever since her mother's death which was the nursery where the infant resided. A bit odd, really, they were inclined to think but they had eaten a morsel or two, the kind that is served after a funeral, and drunk Joshua's excellent sherry and claret, and gone on their way.

"My mother didn't want her to be called Abigail, she told Mrs Quinn before she died. She . . . she wanted Celeste if she had a girl and Thomas for a boy." Thomas had been Pa's second name but she couldn't tell *him* that, could she? "She would have hated Abigail and as she's my mother's child, my sister, I absolutely refuse to allow her to be given that name."

"You refuse! By Christ, that's rich. I'll call my child any damn thing I please and with no help from you, miss."

"Doesn't what her mother wanted count for anything?" Lily asked him desperately.

"No, it bloody well doesn't," he snapped, as though Jane had deliberately gone against his wishes by dying and so had forfeited her right to any say in the matter.

Eloise hissed spitefully, "She happens to be *my* sister too, or hadn't you noticed, and Abigail was my grandmother. Besides, if Papa wants her called that it is surely up to him. Tell her, Papa."

They were all in the deepest black, even the nursemaid who cowered in a chair by the fire, the tiny daughter of Jane Crowther, which neither Jane nor Joshua had wanted, sleeping peacefully in her arms. The baby was like a little scrap of lace, or a perfect rosebud with the dew still on it. She was wrapped in a shawl which looked like a spider's web, or a square of gossamer, knitted by her dead mother, and on her head was a little cap of lace. Even so you could see the wisp of silvery curl beneath it and the length of pale brown eyelashes that rested on her creamy cheek. She had just been fed before Mrs Crowther's elder daughter had burst into the nursery and her rosebud mouth still sucked vigorously, even in sleep. She was a month premature but even the doctor had been surprised at her perfection, for that last month, which often made the difference between a sickly child and a healthy one, was sometimes sadly missed.

"I don't give a damn about that at the moment, Eloise. I just would like to enquire, miss," glaring at Lily, "what in hell you think you're doing coming up here and leaving our guests in such an ill-mannered fashion?"

"They're your guests, not mine, and I—"

"It was *your* mother's funeral they were attending, dammit," not noticing, or even caring, as she flinched from his cruel words.

"I saw my mother decently buried, sir, and I did not care to engage in ineffectual chatter with a group of people I didn't know. Now then, to get back to my mother's daughter . . ."

"You mind your tongue, my girl, or you'll find me a somewhat more watchful parent than I have been before. With your mother dead . . ."

"You are not my parent, sir."

"Thank God for that, is all I can say, though I *am* your guardian so just watch your step."

Ignoring this last she resorted to begging. "Please, Mr Crowther, will you not allow the baby to be called Celeste, knowing it was my mother's choice?" Her voice was desperate as though she would do anything to fulfil this last wish of her mother's. She would never, never forgive herself for not being here on the day the baby was born, and had almost convinced herself that had she been Ma would have survived, no matter what Mrs Quinn said to the contrary. It made no difference but if she could persuade Mr Crowther to call the baby as her mother had wanted it would go some way, a small way, to easing her guilt.

"Celeste! Where the bloody hell did that come from?"

"It's French and it means heavenly. Ma liked it."

"I want no child of mine being called some foreign-sounding—"

"What about Eloise, then?" she whipped back quick as a flash. "That's French."

For a second or two he looked confused. He had not named his daughter, his wife had done that before she too died, and he had not cared enough one way or the other, but this bloody girl had done nothing but stand against him ever since he had married her mother and, if only to deny her, he would call the child anything but what she wanted.

"Well, this one's Abigail which comes from the Bible so that should suit your mother wherever she's fetched up."

"I think Marguerite is nice, Papa," Eloise put in, though to tell the truth the baby meant nothing to her, since she did not associate Jane Crowther's child as being related to herself, despite what she had said to Lily.

Her father turned on her. "Don't you start," he snarled. "It's Abigail and that's that."

He opened the door noisily and left the room, banging it to with such force it made the sleeping child jump. The nurse was seen to heave a great sigh of relief, hoping, no doubt, that her charge's father would not be a frequent visitor to the nursery. She herself was new to the household, having been hastily summoned by Mrs Diggle, her mother's sister, who knew she was looking for a good post.

"There," said Eloise, malevolently, "I hope you're satisfied. You've upset my father and the baby's still to be called what he wanted so you've achieved nothing. I don't know what else you expected, really I don't," and she too left, leaving the nurse, whose name was Dorcas, looking at Lily with great sympathy. Dorcas hadn't liked Celeste, she had to admit. Abigail was much more suitable, but she felt so sorry for the dead woman's older daughter. It was as though she didn't know what to do with herself, where she should be, how she should be acting at this time of great grief. She wandered about the house like a willowy black ghost, turning up in the kitchen where she was received with great sympathy, then drifting off again as though what she searched for were not there. The housekeeper, Mrs Quinn, was lovely with her, holding her when she wept and in front of them all as well. In fact they all wept, for it seemed the dead lady was beloved of everybody except her husband and step-daughter. But her own daughter always finished up back here as though in the whole of her life there remained only this tiny scrap carried over from a life she had once known. Her own flesh and blood. Her *only* flesh and blood, and perhaps, if Dorcas could get the baby into her arms she might find a way to recover.

But there was no sign of it yet. Lily was desolate in her grief and when Mrs Quinn came up to the nursery and whispered in her ear that there was someone down on the seashore to see her, she turned and fled, and was still weeping when she flew into Liam's arms ten minutes later.

"I was there, lovebud, though you didn't see me," he murmured into her hair. "I was standing behind that big oak tree but, by God, I'd have given my right arm to be at your side." His voice had become savage and she turned her wet face up to his in surprise.

"What . . . ?"

"Bloody hell, you were all alone with no one but that bastard to stand by you. I wanted more than anything to stride over and put my arm round you and hold you safe and sure, but I couldn't, I bloody well couldn't. I would only have made things worse for you. I couldn't simply walk over and hold you as a friend should and it almost killed me. Lovebud . . . no . . . no, weep if you want to," when she began to stutter an apology. "I'm here now. I took a chance and called over a lad who was hanging about by the water looking as lost as you do so I reckoned he must have loved your ma."

"It would be Will. He and Mr Diggle adored her."

"Well, he promised to put a note in Mrs Quinn's hand without anyone seeing and . . . here you are. And why, in the name of all that's holy, didn't you put a cloak on? It's pouring with rain and cold enough for two pairs of bootlaces. See, come under my cape and let's shelter beneath those trees."

They stood face to face with his cape about them both. They were not exactly face to face, for hers was pressed into the curve of his neck where her tears wet his collar but he hugged her close and let her cry, though it broke his heart to hear her. Poor little bugger. First her pa and then her ma and who had she left now? And as though she had picked up the thread of his thoughts she pressed herself even closer.

"At least I still have you, Liam," she murmured against his throat and to his horror, as her breath caressed his skin and her young body moulded to his, he felt a stirring in the pit of his stomach and his manhood fought to get free of the restriction of his tight breeches. Thank God she was wearing the usual mass of petticoats and skirts that were the fashion and would not be able to feel it but he could and he was ashamed. He knew the bloody thing had no mind of its own. Put it close to any attractive woman's flesh and it would react in just the same way, but this was his lovebud, the child he had loved and sheltered as best he could ever since she was ten years old. She had been his little sister, his daughter even . . . well, not quite that for there were only eleven years between them, but she was still very dear to him.

But she was a child no longer. She was so slender he could feel the bones of her spine under his fingers and the sharpness of her shoulder blades, but in contrast the roundness of her breasts was pressed so tightly against his shirt front he could swear he could feel her nipples.

She had stopped crying and had gone quiet, leaning against him with that trusting innocence she had always shown him. She was warm now, he could feel the heat of her, for though it was raining it was mid-summer. Her heart was beating somewhat rapidly; he could feel it just below his own. She sighed, still disconsolate, but calm, and when she lifted her face to him, without thought, a purely male response to the closeness of a woman, he laid his mouth gently against hers and heard her sigh in what seemed to be great content.

"Liam . . . ?" she murmured questioningly, her lips still close to his.

"Lovebud . . . ?" He was ready to draw away now, confused, distressed even, as though what he had done were somehow shameful.

"Yes . . . ?"

"I'm sorry," he mumbled. "I don't know . . ."

"I'm no longer a child, Liam," she said, her voice trembling with emotion. Whether it was still grief for her mother or something else he could not tell. She huddled closer to him like a young bird looking for protection beneath its mother's wing, then lifted her face again and this time her lips captured his, parting slightly so that he could feel the bewitchment racing through him as her breath whispered into his mouth. He broke away, gasping, drowning in the sweetness of her, yearning to go on but something in him protested, something that had, for the past six years, known her as a child and was trying to tell him that this was wrong.

They stood for perhaps five minutes in a close embrace, her face cradled against his jawline, while his eager male body lashed him on to do more than this to her, and his cringing mind held it back. They did not kiss again and she did not seem to expect it and he thanked the gods for it, since he knew if she turned her face up to his again he would not have been able to resist. He could feel his love for her – what sort of love? his bewildered mind begged to know – welling up inside him, a protective love, strong and welded by the bond they had forged six years ago on the docks when she had been looking for her father's ship. It had never faltered. Many was the time when he had it in him to wish that he did not have to spend some of his precious time ashore with a child of eleven, twelve, thirteen, but he had never forsaken her, never let her down, he didn't know why even now.

Always he had come to this place and there she would be, her face aglow with joy and merriment, flying into his arms as a child will do with a father.

Strangely, even as she grew from a pretty child into a lovely young woman, he had scarcely noticed, for she was Lovebud, always the same: laughing, argumentative, self-willed, head-strong, good-hearted, bloody-minded at times. Though he had given it no thought at the time he had never been bored in her company. She was keenly interested in everything he did; indeed she had a mind that was inquisitive about matters that other young women did not care about. She read a great deal, all the books in Joshua Crowther's library, many of which had never been opened, and the newspapers he left lying about. She had continued her education without knowing it, without the guidance of a teacher and was far more aware of what was going on in the country, indeed the world, than many a man. Only a month or so ago they had exchanged views on the growing conflict in America and what impact it might have on the cotton trade of Lancashire and he had not been particularly surprised by her knowledge. But he had never once, even then, considered her to be anything other than a child. He was a sailor and though he did not boast that he had a girl in every port, he had great success with women and was not a man who lacked sexual gratification. There was a certain lady in Upper Duke Street, a widow somewhat older than himself, whose husband had left her well provided for. They each enjoyed what the other could give but with no romantic ties.

But now he was overwhelmed by this sudden startling revelation, not just of how much she meant to him, but of her loveliness, her femininity and what it had done to him in the last few minutes. Quite simply, he wanted her as a man wants a woman and what the bloody hell was he to do about it? She was sixteen, for Christ's sake. She had just lost her mother and was frail and vulnerable because of it, so how could he go on with this in the way she seemed to be encouraging him to do? Well, not exactly encouraging him, she was too inexperienced for that, but not unwilling just the same. He could not take advantage of it, not and still call himself a man.

He cleared his throat and removed his arms from about her, holding her by the elbows. His cape was draped about her, hiding the sweet lines of her body but her face was turned up to his expectantly and her lips were parted. She was waiting for him to go on, ready to smile, to continue in any way he told her, her expression saying she had liked the kiss and would not be averse to another but he was not ready to commit himself. Not yet. This was much too fast. Totally unexpected and something that must be thought about carefully, for the last thing he wanted, in fact he would cut off his arm to avoid it, was to hurt her now. She was hurt enough already.

"Lovebud . . ."

"Yes, Liam." Her lips quivered and she put out her tongue to moisten them and inside him that darting flick of pleasure struck him again.

"You must go now, and so must I. I sail on the tide . . ."

"Oh, Liam . . ."

"But I'll be back in three weeks," he added hastily, for her face had paled even further and her eyes filled with tears.

"I'm not sure I can manage without you, Liam. You see, I have no one else."

"You have Mrs Quinn, lovebud. She shares your . . . your grief, you know she does, and will comfort you. You will comfort each other."

"But it's not the same, Liam. You're—"

"Lily, you're used to me coming and going and besides, your new sister will need you."

"Oh, her."

"Yes, her. Don't speak of her as if she were nothing to you. I doubt she'll get much affection in that house." His voice was hard. "So you must provide it. Your ma would have wanted you to love her and you have so much love in you to give, lovebud."

She brightened. "Have I, Liam?"

"Yes." It was all he could manage to say, for he could see it there in her eyes. She didn't know, of course, what she was telling him, for she scarcely knew herself, but what he saw there almost made him drag her back into his arms.

At the last moment, as he bent to place a kiss on her cheek, she turned her head and their lips met with a warmth that shook them both. She clung to him for a moment but he gently loosened her hands.

"Goodbye, lovebud. Three weeks. Take care of that baby. Promise?"

"I promise, Liam."

And she did. Dorcas was quite amazed and not a little put out at the attention Miss Lily showered on her baby sister, almost taking over her job, she told her Aunty Mabel Diggle when she went across to her cottage for a cup of tea. On Miss Lily's instructions!

"She baths 'er an' feeds 'er an' wi'out so much as a by yer leave tekks 'er down ter't kitchen ter show 'er off ter't servants an' wha' can I say since she's the master's stepdaughter? She practically lives in't nursery an' wha' master'd say I don't know. Not that 'e ever comes, like, or t'other 'un, an' it fair beats me 'ow anyone could stop away from that babby. She's that bonny an' thrivin' an' all, even if she do 'ave ter mekk do wi' cow's milk."

"Yer mustn't grudge poor young lass, our Dorcas. She lost 'er pa an' . . . well, she'd norrad much of a life wi' . . . Well, I shouldn't say it, I suppose, an' yer not ter repeat it to a livin' soul, but 'e's norra *lovin*' man, Mr Crowther. 'E's tekken no notice o' that child."

"What child?" It was plain Dorcas was bewildered.

"Miss Lily, I mean. She's bin allowed ter run wild an' 'er poor ma . . . eeh, she were a lovely woman. My Ted thought sun shone out o' 'er backside, I can tell yer, an' if 'e 'adn't bin past such things I mighter felt jealous."

"Give over, Aunty."

"No, I'm tellin' yer. 'Im an' Will worshipped ground she walked on. Well, she loved flowers an' such an' were never outer't garden, but she were a sad lady, fer all 'er wealth. 'Is wealth, I should say. Dressed like a queen she were . . . you never saw 'er, but she 'ad nowt, not really, only Miss Lily an' I believe Mrs Quinn were right fond of 'er. Now there's this babby . . . eeh, I could cry, reely I could an' Miss Lily's got no one burr 'er."

The first Joshua Crowther knew of it was when his stepdaughter waylaid him about a perambulator, of all things, and he could not have been more astonished if she had begged him for her own carriage and horses.

The three of them, Joshua, Eloise and Lily always took breakfast together. It was a habit begun when Joshua married Jane and though she was no longer there it was still kept up. There was little said. Joshua might idly question his daughter

on where she and Miss Kaye were to go that day and she
would tell him. They might discuss the merits of Eloise's
new mare which she thought might make a good jumper.
A croquet party to be held at the home of one of Joshua's
business acquaintances to which Eloise had been invited.
The start of the grouse shooting which Eloise had shown
an interest in joining, expressing a desire to learn to shoot
which was a perfectly respectable pastime now for a young
lady. Neither of them once addressed a remark of any kind to
Lily who did not care anyway. She would eat a good breakfast,
for she had the healthy unfussy appetite of the young, not like
Eloise who was inclined to put on weight and so was careful
what she ate. Eloise was seventeen in October and was ready
for marriage and there had been interest shown by several of
her papa's friends with eligible sons.

When Lily had finished she would politely beg to be
excused and wish her stepfather and sister good morning,
to which they answered with an absent-minded nod, but not
this morning, for she had something she wished to say.

"If I might interrupt this . . . this conversation, Mr Crowther,
there is something I wish to ask you. That's if you can spare
the time." Joshua missed the irony in her voice. They both
turned to stare at her and at the serving table Maggie nudged
Betsy. She was going to do it then.

"Oh . . ."

"Yes. Abby . . . Abigail is nearly two months old now and
it is time she was pushed out in a baby carriage. While the
weather is still pleasant. With this in mind I have taken the
trouble to obtain a catalogue and would like your permission
to order her one. May I show it to you?"

Joshua Crowther noticed that his step-daughter had lost
none of her defiance. Her chin was lifted and the set of her
head imperious just as though, should he refuse, she were
ready to give him a piece of her mind. By God, she was
a feisty one, growing up as well, he thought, noticing the
soft swell of her breasts which her proud posture showed
off. The bloody image of her mother. Not that he had ever
seen her mother at sixteen – was she? . . . or seventeen? –
but he had often imagined what she must have looked like
then and here she was, alive again in her daughter.

He licked his lips. "I beg your pardon?"

"I asked if I might have permission to buy a perambulator

for . . . for your daughter. She needs to be wheeled out in the fresh air."

"Yes, I heard you."

"Well?"

"Don't take that tone with me, young lady. I swear you do it on purpose just to annoy me," which was not true. She did it because she loathed him. He was smiling as he said it, which to Lily was even worse than his black scowls.

She waited, aware that he was looking at her in a quite strange manner but not particularly concerned by it, for he was a very strange man. Abby, as she called her, was eight weeks old and in those eight weeks he had never once been near the nursery and neither had Eloise, but then, did Lily care? All she wanted for the next few years, until Abby was old enough to . . . well, here she stopped since she was not sure what she intended to do when Abby was old enough. She only knew it involved her and Liam and Abby. But Abby was Joshua Crowther's child and though he had not the slightest speck of feeling for her she knew he regarded her as one of his possessions. Just like Ma had been one of his possessions. Just like his dogs and his horses, this house even, were his possessions. She often wondered what he counted *her* as.

"Shall I bring the catalogue?" she asked him as he continued to study her. "The prices are in it." Her bold, unfearing eyes looked coolly into his.

Suddenly he lost interest, or that was how it seemed. Throwing his napkin to the table he stood up and with a nod at Maggie who ran to open the door for him, strode across the room.

"Do as you like," he growled, "but don't let me see you on the front lawn with the contraption. D'you hear?"

20

She could get down to the beach now, though it was bit of
a rough ride for Abby. The baby's little face looked out in
astonishment from her cocoon of wrappings as Lily struggled over tree roots, heaving and shoving the perambulator
through the rough grass, across hummocks and down shallow
dips until the shingle of the beach was reached. Even there
it was hard going but it was worth it when she saw the tall,
casually dressed figure of Liam coming towards them. She
wanted to let go of the handle of the baby carriage and fly
over the pebbles and shells and the ripples left by the tide
into his arms as she had once done but she knew and he
knew that it was different now. Not their great attachment for
one another but the make-up of it.

She often wondered why it was that no one ever questioned
her constant walks down to the beach, nor see who she met
there, but she was mistaken in her belief that it was a secret
she and Liam shared with no one. They had known for years,
all of them, and at first Ted Diggle, who had reported it to Mrs
Quinn, was not at all sure it was seemly, or even safe for the
mistress's young daughter to be consorting with a man who
was obviously not a gentleman. A seaman, in fact, who wore
a fisherman's outfit of gansey, waterproof pea jacket and stout
drill trousers. Just off to sea by the look of it, Mr Diggle had
told Mrs Quinn. A giant of a chap with a steady look about
him, not unfriendly, like, if Mrs Quinn caught his drift, but
with a resolute jut to his chin that seemed to say he'd stand
no nonsense.

Molly Quinn had been frightened at first. If the master heard
of it there'd be trouble, not only for Lily and Molly Quinn's
lamb, the master's wife, but for all of them. They would have

been expected to have watched over his wife's daughter, not because he feared for her safety but because the idea of a common seaman trespassing on his property would be like a red rag to a bull.

"Oh, that'd be an old friend o' Lily's pa, Mr Diggle," she managed to say calmly, looking up from the menus she and Mrs Kelly were going over. The whole kitchen had come to a halt as they all listened to this astonishing bit of news. They were right fond of Miss Lily who was in and out of the kitchen all day long and this was the first they had heard of any old friend. "He were a seaman an' all, Lily's pa, an' this chap often came ter't th'ouse. A lovely chap an' right fond o' Lily. Bu' . . . well, as yer could see, 'e's norra gentleman an' wouldn't be welcome in Mr Crowther's drawin'-room so't child meets 'im down on't beach when 'e comes inter port. Mrs Crowther knows all about it," which wasn't true, "but we'd best not lerron to anyone else. 'E's quite 'armless, Mr Diggle, so would yer ask the outside men ter keep their traps shut. Poor little beggar don't 'ave much an' she'd be 'eartbroken if the master stopped 'er seein' 'im."

Mr Diggle kept a watchful eye on her at first, quite startled when she showed such obvious affection for the chap, running into his arms like a homing pigeon, but gradually they all became used to Lily's "friend" and Lily's wanderings, which often took her out of their sight. Well, they couldn't watch her all the time, could they, particularly when the master bought her that pony, which she called Precious and which Arnold taught her to ride. They had expected her and Miss Eloise to ride together after that but no, the pair of them were, as usual, like cat and dog, scratching and snarling and agreeing over nothing, going off in different directions, Miss Eloise always accompanied by one of the grooms. She was, after all, the master's daughter.

The baby carriage was a grand affair, called a Victoria and though not exactly suitable for a small infant, since it had been designed for a child who could sit up, Lily and Dorcas thought it was wonderful. It was large, high-backed with four big wheels and a deep hood and with the help of several cushions and the ingenious use of blankets she and Dorcas had arranged Abby in it so that she was quite safe, venturing into the garden for the baby's first walk. They had taken turns to push her, both delighted with the freedom they could now enjoy when the weather was fine. Though she herself loved her little sister, doted on her, in fact, and would have liked to spend all day with her, Lily was aware that she must allow Dorcas to share the caring for the baby, which was, after all, what she had been employed for. When Lily went riding, or into town or somewhere she could not take Abby, Dorcas was there and so far it had worked well enough. They never, ever took the baby carriage to the front of the house, bearing in mind Joshua Crowther's parting shot on the day the purchase of it had been discussed. Because of this, which was a good thing in Lily's opinion, he was never to know who was out with his baby daughter and therefore was not aware of how much time Lily actually spent with her.

It was October now and this would be the fourth time she had seen Liam since the day of her ma's funeral. She would not forget that day. The kisses they had exchanged then had been very different to the ones they had given one another in the past. Childish kisses on her part, smacking kisses on the cheek, big hugs and passionate entreaties to be home soon, for she did miss him so.

Now they had become somewhat constrained when alone together. Those kisses had changed everything between them and though she longed to ask him why, since they had both enjoyed them, she held her tongue for the moment, talking quietly of his latest trip which had been to New York and the next which was to Nova Scotia. They met only on the seashore, for she was still in the deep black of mourning for her mother. She was a young woman who would gladly defy any convention she thought foolish, and did, but respect and love for her ma made her honour this one. She was still grieving and for now was no longer the high-spirited, defiant young creature who would have run away to sea with Liam if he let her. It was as though they were shy with one another, only just met, that is until the day she introduced him to Abby who could dissolve any reserve with one of her huge, toothless grins or her slow, baby chuckle.

"She looks just like you," was the first thing he said about her. And "Can I take her out of the carriage?" was the second.

He had done so, cradling her carefully against his broad chest, not the least bit awkward, pushing down her lacy shawl with a strong, brown finger the better to look more closely at her delicate rose cheeks, the curve of her puckered mouth, the arch of her fair brows, the wide-eyed wondering stare of her lavender grey, unblinking eyes.

"She's the loveliest thing I ever saw and the dead spit of you."

"No, she's prettier than me. She looks like Ma," Lily had answered just like a proud mama herself, still peering down at her sister, not seeing that Liam was looking, not at the baby, but at her.

"I didn't know your ma well, lovebud, but this is how you must have looked at the same age."

"D'you think so?" She was pleased, especially when he put his lips to the baby's cheek in a gentle kiss. It was essential that Liam should love this child as she did, since she knew with great certainty that their futures, the three of them, were inextricably linked.

They had walked that day as far as the Pottery Shore with Liam pushing the perambulator across the difficult bits, then up on to the parade which ran beside Egerton Dock and on to Toxteth Dock, crossing bridge after bridge from granite island to granite island until they came to Queen's Basin where they stopped to absorb the quiet, patient presence of the great sailing ships. They strained their necks to look up at the wrangling cranes perched on their high roofs and walked among the long transit sheds ringing with echoes of men and hammers and whistling cheerfulness.

Many heads turned to watch them go by, the beautiful young woman and the tall, protective chap at her side trundling the baby carriage. You didn't often see a father pushing a perambulator, that was women's work, but you could see it in their smiling glances that they thought they were watching a young husband and wife with their newborn child.

"We'd best turn back now, lovebud. I think this is far enough for one day."

"I want her to love it all as much as we do, Liam. I want her to be an Elliott, not a Crowther. If we bring her here whenever you're home I'm sure she will be. I can't bear to think that part of her is . . . from *him*."

"I know, lovebud."

They had been even more quiet on that day walking back across the Pottery Beach and on the days they had met since, for Jane's ghost, the fragile drifting memory of her came to haunt Lily as though to say look after my child. Love my child, for no one else will.

Sometimes they just sat on the shingle looking across the shimmering water to the training ship on the Cheshire side of the river, or watching the flats going up towards Garston to collect salt, not saying much, smiling down at the baby who lay on the rug between them, or Liam would hold her on his lap, talking down into her face which showed great interest. She would watch his mouth intently, then arch her back in a sudden smile while his curved over her in great tenderness. Lily waited. It was as though some great moment, some important crossroads had been reached in their lives and neither knew which way they should go. They were no longer Liam and Lovebud, the man and child who had loved one another for six years but a man and woman; those kisses had confirmed that simple fact and so Lily waited, for she knew, despite her own headlong wish to move on to the next step in their relationship, she must give Liam the time and the freedom to take it with her.

In the privacy of the room which she had once shared with her mother and which no one had thought to move her out of, she would sit in the window seat in the darkness and stare out over the dim shapes of the garden and wonder about men and women. With Villy twitching in sleep at her feet and Beauty curled up on the rug before the fire she would ponder on the strangeness, the *difference* which showed itself in Liam's reluctance to go forward when it was obvious to her, at least, that that was the only way they could go. In her heart was something so beautiful words could not express it. It ached because of it but she knew it for what it was and did wish that Liam would hurry up and accept it too. Oh, she knew he was still struggling with the image of a small girl with her lace pantaloons showing beneath the hem of her short dress, her bonnet hanging on a ribbon down her back and he was fighting what was in him because of it. She did hope it would not be left to her to bring it out into the open. She supposed she could do what she had always done which was run along the beach to meet him and simply fling herself into his arms and kiss him but something held her back from it. She didn't know what it was, for she had always been the sort of person who said what she thought, and acted on whatever was truth to her.

It was a mellow October day, perfect with that soft warmth that sometimes comes between summer and the onset of winter. The trees were fast losing their leaves and the yellow buttons of tansy bobbed their last blooms in the grass. Bright-eyed jackdaws swooped in and out of the almost naked branches. She did not take Abby with her this day and for some reason was disconcerted by her own feeling when he appeared to be disappointed.

"She has a cold," she told him tartly, "and Dorcas thought it best not to bring her out," which was a lie.

"Since when did what Dorcas say matter to you? I thought you were chief factotum in the nursery."

"Well, you thought wrong. Dorcas is her nursemaid and must be listened to."

He hooted with laughter. "Well, God bless my soul, I never thought to hear you admit that, since you know it's not true."

She turned on him, making a hole in the wet sand with her heel. The water was low and great sandbanks were revealed on which multitudes of seabirds had settled. The low water had left a long stretch of mud and wet sand along the shore and the hem of her black gown dragged through a pool.

"Watch where you're walking, you fool," he said, nettled by her attitude, "you'll ruin your dress."

"Don't change the subject and are you calling me a liar?"

"Don't be daft. Of course I'm not but ever since Abby was born you have decided what is right and wrong for her and now you're telling me Dorcas has forbidden you to bring the child out."

"I didn't say that at all."

"Then what did you say, for God's sake, and why the hell are we arguing like this?"

"I'm not arguing and anyway, you started it," which bit of logic made him laugh. He was ready to brush it aside, this strange mood she was in, not recognising it for what it was, but she wouldn't let it go. She was mad about something, though what in hell it was he had no idea. But, Jesus, she was beautiful. Not in the way of the child she had been, but as a woman. Alive, vibrant, overcoming the quenching effect of her black gown. He felt the pain of it spear him in his fierce masculine need to sweep her into his arms and into his heart where she had always been but that uncomfortable feeling of guilt gripped him and he kept his arms firmly pinned to his sides.

"So what is so humorous about that, may I ask?" Her face was a furious pink and her eyes were enormous in it, a deep lavender grey but glittering like the light on the water. The hot flash of her temper surprised them both. Her nostrils flared and her soft pink mouth had thinned out into a hard line, straining to find the words to hurt him as he had hurt her. Dear God, she had time to think. I'm jealous. I'm jealous of a four-month-old baby, but she was on a path that would not let her turn aside. She wanted him to pull her into his arms and kiss her. She had wanted it for months now and he had been hanging about like some shy schoolboy and, by God, she'd had enough of it but the trouble was she didn't know how to change it.

"Now then, lovebud," Liam managed to say mildly, "there's no need for all this and why you're in such a tantrum . . ."

He couldn't have spoken a word more likely to infuriate her. Tantrum! His look of good-natured tolerance changed at once to amazement as she lifted her hand and aimed it at his face. It did not connect, since he was quick on his feet and his own hand came up and caught her wrist.

"What in hell's name is the matter with you?" he was ready to snarl. He had seen Lily in many moods, most of them those of a thwarted child, a grief-stricken child, a frustrated child, a child who is bewildered by life and what it had done to her. But this was different.

"There's nothing the matter with me, Liam O'Connor," she told him imperiously, lifting her chin and turning away disdainfully, "but I can't say the same about you," wondering as she said it how she'd got herself into this foolish situation, and why!

"What the devil's that supposed ter mean?" In the last few years the rough Liverpool accent he had picked up as a child had gradually been erased from his speech. He had not done it purposely but somehow, on the trips he made and with the men from all parts of the country, and the world, he met, it had slipped away. Except when he was angry, as now.

"You know what it means," she told him, all reason gone. "And I'd be obliged if you would get out of my way. I must get back to the nursery to see how Abby is."

"I'm certainly no' keepin' yer, lass. Yer free ter go wherever yer please."

"Well, then . . ."

"Well, then, what?"

"I'll be on my way. I hope you have a good trip." She lifted her small chin even higher.

Liam pushed his hands through the thick crop of his curls in exasperation, then turned abruptly on his heel, walking a little way from her, keeping his back to her. She watched him breathing heavily. She was too young and inexperienced to know that she was trying to force a confrontation. She loved him, that was all she knew. She had always loved him but now it was not the same. It hurt her, this love, for she did not know what to do with it and Liam was no help at all. He should know. He was the man, older than her and therefore wiser in the ways of love. Why hadn't he kissed her again like he had months ago? Why did he continue to treat her like a child when it was very plain she was a woman now? Why . . . why . . . what should she do? How could she make him notice her again? Since that day they had been neither one thing nor the other. It was as though she had lost him, that man who had been her friend for six years and yet he had not moved on to become someone to replace him. God, she was so confused. So lost if she could not be something, *anything* to him. Why was he holding back like this and if he was, how was she to . . . to recover him?

Suddenly she turned and began to walk away from him in the direction of the rough path that led from the beach through the strip of woodland to the house. Her head was held bravely high and she moved like a young queen, holding her full skirts so that she would not trip on them.

Liam watched her go, knowing exactly what was in her mind, for the same thoughts were in his. But he was a man and could analyse them more easily than she could who still, on one level, thought as a child. A child woman who was simple and forthright in her approach and could not bear the shifting emotions, indeed did not even know of them; that worried him. Dear God, why could he not just accept what had happened to them, to him, and love her as he was meant to? For four months now he had been vacillating, running whenever he was in port to the widow in Upper Duke Street in the hope that she would solve his problems with some plain, unthinking, sexual pleasure. Even she had noticed a change in his performance as a lover and had asked him only last night if he was quite well. This child, no, call her what she is . . . this *woman* who was marching so resolutely away from him was the one who stood between him and other women and unless he did something about it, in one way or another, he would never recover from it. Did he want to recover from it? *Could* he recover from it? There was only one way to find out, but if it failed how was she to go on with the rest of her life? She was so bloody alone, so vulnerable. If he found he could not . . . could not possibly treat her as a woman after all these years of seeing her as a child, what could he say to her? The risk was too great, surely. Surely if he left her alone she would get over it . . . What in hell was he talking about? *Get over it* . . . His lovebud . . . his . . . his . . .

Every thought but one left his head as he began to race after her, his feet making no sound in the soft sand and grass. He caught his head on a branch as he ran, cursing under his breath as he felt the blood begin to flow but it did not stop him. He must catch her before she reached the edge of the trees where they thinned and the lawn began but she was still in the clearing which was about halfway through. Her arm was bent up against the broad trunk of an oak tree, her face pressed into it and she was weeping. The thick carpet of autumn leaves, wet from the rain that had fallen the day before, muffled his footsteps. The leaves still fell, drifting in spirals down from the branches and one fell on her hair, a brilliant copper against the silver.

His hands reached out and took her shoulders, then turned her towards him and with a combined cry they fell against one another. His mouth searched for hers and it was there. He kissed her so savagely he could taste blood on his lips, and he wondered vaguely whose it was, hers or his. He slid his mouth across her wet face, leaving a tiny smear of crimson. Her eyes were closed and she seemed to be ready to faint but he could feel the strength of her, the woman's strength of her as she pulled at him to hold her closer. They did not speak. He felt he should be appalled by his own behaviour, for he was not treating her with the gentleness her innocence and inexperience demanded, but his body urged him on since *it* knew this was no child in his arms but a woman. He could feel the peaked roundness of her breasts against his chest, with no more between them than the bodice of her mourning gown and his fine cambric shirt. His hands moved to her throat, stroking the soft flesh beneath her chin, cupping her face as his lips travelled across her eyes and cheeks and down again to her jawline.

"Oh, God," he moaned in the back of his throat, wanting her to stop him, begging her to allow him to go on.

"Liam . . . I love you, Liam." Her warm lips were against his chin, moving to his ear where she caught the lobe with her teeth and he groaned as hot desire flowed madly through him. His hands moved of their own accord to find her breasts and the hard nipples swelled into the palms.

"Dear God . . . Lily Elliott, I love you."

"Yes . . . love me, Liam . . . now . . ." She arched her throat, making some noise that spoke plainly of her own longing. His hands went to the buttons of her gown, a couple of dozen of them marching down the front of the bodice and here, as though it had been designed to repel the eager attention of any male, they defeated him. His hands shook with maddened longing and she was the same, doing her best to help him, both of them desperate to have her naked breasts in his hands but even as they struggled Liam's inflamed mind was cooling to reason.

Taking a deep breath he captured her hands which were still busy at her throat, bringing them to his lips in a gesture of loving tenderness.

"Liam . . . Liam," she moaned, "please . . ."

"Lovebud . . . sweetheart . . ."

"Don't stop, Liam, I want . . ." whatever it is that comes next, her anguished, flower-like face told him.

"Dearest heart . . . stop it . . . calm yourself . . . help me."

"No, I want to be yours, Liam. Please, I don't know what to do . . . please . . ."

He drew her fiercely into his arms, pushing her face into the curve of his shoulder, holding her trembling body close to his own which was doing its own share of trembling. Sweet Christ, this was the hardest thing he had ever done. This woman he loved had not learned to be subtle or artful. All her life she had said exactly what she felt or meant. Now she wanted him to make love to her and so she said so, but he couldn't. He bloody well couldn't. Not because he didn't want to, nor did he have any scruples left about their age difference, or the sudden shift in his emotions from loving the child to loving the woman. It was simply not the time. It was simply not the place. He had something to tell her that would shatter her slowly regained peace of mind and it could not be clouded with their bodies' needs. They must be practical and when the time was right, which he hoped to God would not be long, then they would be married.

"Come and sit down, lovebud. We must . . ."

But she would not let him be. "No, Liam. You love me. You said so. I heard you . . . and I love you. Don't turn from me."

"I'm not turning from you, my love. My love, that's what you are. My love, and when the time is right we will . . . go on from here, but I have something to tell you and I can't do it unless you calm yourself, and allow me to calm myself. This is not easy for me. My body is . . . it wants yours, sweetheart. D'yer know what that means? D'yer know what goes on with a man and woman? Did yer ma not tell yer?"

"No . . . but I've read the encyclopedias in the library and I . . . I think I have a rough idea. There was one about . . . human reproduction, you see." Her innocence enchanted him and before he knew what he was about he had kissed her and for several minutes they lost control again. Now that they were sitting down, their backs to the wide tree-trunk, the buttons on her bodice were more accessible but though his hand cupped her breasts, making her sigh with delight, he put her from him, sitting up and clutching himself round the knees, his head bent, his breathing fast.

"I must say this quickly, lovebud, then go."

"Liam . . ."

"No, darlin', let me speak. I have a present for yer. I was not goin' ter tell yer . . . for a while but now . . . I must. I want yer ter understand . . ."

She sat up and turned to look into his face, which was hidden in the curve of his arms.

"What?"

He lifted his head and in his eyes was a look of such joy she let out her breath on a gasp.

"What? Oh, Liam, what?"

"It's the *Lily-Jane*."

She could not speak. Her heart was bounding in her breast and her face felt suddenly cold as the blood drained away from it. He took her hands in his, turning to kneel before her.

"I've found 'er, lovebud. An' nor only that, I've bought 'er. She's mine . . . ours . . . and she'll be my wedding present to you."

She began to weep then tears of such joy she could not contain them, lifting her face to the pale stretch of blue sky above the autumn trees, her eyes streaming, her face awash.

"There's just one thing, lovebud," he said quietly. "It's taken every penny I've ever earned ter buy her an' ter restore her . . . she's in a right old mess, lovebud. I need to earn a lot more. The only way ter do that is ter go . . . long distance. I'm ter sail on the clipper ship *Breeze* tomorrow morning. To China."

21

Remember, I may be far away but I'll always be with you, were the last words he said to her, then she watched as he walked away towards the Pottery Shore, listening to those words as they tried desperately to soothe their way round inside her head. He did not turn, not once in the five minutes it took him to reach Dingle Point where he disappeared. Her heart was like a rock inside her breast, heavy with foreboding, for how was she to manage without him for so long, particularly now when they had just found each other? He had been a small part in the days of her life for the past six years, going away for weeks on end, but always there had been that bright light of expectancy illuminating the interval in between, the warm anticipation of the day of his coming back. While he was at sea she had led her own secret life, roaming the woodlands and the seashore, putting in the occasional appearance in the schoolroom to lull Miss Kaye into a belief that she was turning over a new leaf.

And when the day came he was always here waiting for her as he promised. He had never forsaken her, never made a promise he had not kept and though he had told her he would be home again in approximately 110 days, which was the time a fast clipper took to make the round trip to Foochow and back to Liverpool, he might have said 110 years, for that was how it would seem. February at the very latest, he had told her, crushing her to him in an agony of sorrow at their parting and she had been like a doll in his arms, numb with shock. Now he was gone. No longer to be seen and it was tearing her apart. It did not concern her that Pa's lovely little ship had been found and was to be brought back to life again. How could it when it was separating her and Liam for so long?

The dream she had nurtured for all these years was sterile now as she watched another dream, born only a few months ago, that of her and Liam spending the rest of their lives together, drift away with him. She knew in her mind where sense was that she was being foolish. That she was allowing her heart to distort out of all perspective what was happening but just now it felt as though he had gone from her for good. He was coming back, she knew he was, he had told her so, but not for months and she could not bear it.

She didn't sleep that night. She didn't even get into bed but sat on the window seat with Beauty on her lap and Villy at her feet and stared into the darkness towards the river where Liam still was. There was nothing in her head but pain which did not allow for coherent thought but there was one there, nevertheless.

At first light she let herself out of the side door and glided silently across the grass towards the gate. She had left a note for Mrs Quinn, for she and Maggie and the others would be alarmed if they found her bed not slept in. It was an ambiguous little note, saying nothing much about her destination, hinting that she might have gone riding, just in case *he* should see it.

She wore an ankle-length black cloak, lined with a rich wool, with a hood that framed her pale face, drowning her and yet enhancing her delicate beauty. She walked the length of Beech Lane, turning into Holmes Lane. There was a hackney cab just drawing up to the doors of the Aigburth Hotel from which a gentleman in a top hat and evening clothes was alighting. He looked at her in amazement, for it was barely six o'clock and the sight of a woman who was obviously not of the working class was uncommon at this time of the morning.

She ignored his stares, speaking to the driver who looked equally surprised.

"Can you take me to the docks, please. And as—"

"The docks, miss, at this time of the morning?"

She became the haughty Miss Elliott, her face set and cold.

"Is it any of your business where I go or at what time?" she asked him imperiously, while the top-hatted gentleman watched with great interest.

"No, sorry, miss, it's only that a young lady like you ought not to—"

"Please, spare me your lectures and take me as quickly as possible to the docks. I must catch the tide."

"The tide!"

"Dear God, will you please do as I ask and as quickly as possible."

Breeze was just about to set sail. There was a great bustle amidships, and in the rigging, as sails were unfurled, the men who clung precariously in a line along a lofty spar seemed to be in imminent danger of losing their footing and being dashed to the deck. The gangplanks were drawn away from the ship's sides and there was a last-minute flurry as two men, using thin iron bars, battened down a hatch cover. The mainmast swayed gracefully as *Breeze* began to inch her way out into the river, helped by a couple of tugs, a sliver of greasy water appearing between her and the quayside.

She could see Liam in the wheelhouse standing next to the master, a Captain Fletcher of the Hemingway Line. His face was set in lines of intense concentration and he constantly turned his head as though judging the distance between the ship, the tugs and the land they were leaving behind. He wore no hat and the light from the rising sun, which was still hidden behind the transit sheds, struck gold from his ruffled hair. He wore the dark coat and neat white necktie of an officer and his tall frame dwarfed the other man with him in the wheelhouse. It seemed Liam was at the helm since he was to be second-in-command to the captain. He had a Master's Certificate himself and had been master of a couple of ships since he had gained it, but in order to get a berth on a clipper he had been forced to sign on as first mate. It would be worth it, he had explained to her in those last appalling moments before he left her, for officers in the "Flying Fish" trade, as the China run was known, who had cash to spare were allowed to purchase goods on their own behalf and sell them at immensely inflated prices when they arrived back in port, thereby making a handsome profit. He had not much after the purchase of the *Lily-Jane*, but with what he had he meant to do the same. They would need it if they were to restore the *Lily-Jane*, he had told her, frightened of her icy control and hoping to warm her, melt her with hope for their future which included the schooner she had loved since the day she was old enough to understand her significance.

Imagine it, porcelain, silks, paintings, fans, dishes fashioned in delicate silver, ornate ivory, furnishings of polished wood, lacquerware and all manner of *objects d'art* to be brought back to a market hungry for such things. He had seen them himself carried back from the Far East by men serving on the swift and beautiful clipper ships, and now it was a chance for him to do the same. For them. *Breeze* would sail down the Atlantic, round the Cape of Good Hope and across the Indian Ocean to the port of Melbourne in Australia where they would discharge their passengers and cargo and sail on in ballast to Foochow to load up with tea and other profitable goods. Then it would be a race to be home with the first cases of the new crop of tea which was carried in beautiful ornamental chests, one of which would be her bridal chest, he promised her, smoothing her ice cold cheek with his lips, cupping her face and doing his best to take that look of dread from her eyes. And then there was that far more lucrative trade which concerned opium and from which a fortune might be made but he did not mention that!

Breeze was a newly built British clipper belonging to the Hemingway Shipping Line. She had a raked stern and a hollow bow overhanging the counter-stern. She was finer, and had more delicate lines than her American counterparts, with an improved sail plan which enabled the ship to "ghost" in light winds, and yet she was marvellously efficient in a gale and therefore was a much safer vessel. This was what Liam had told her as he had held her in his arms and as she watched the lovely graceful ship move away towards the centre of the river she tried to get comfort from this.

It was a fine morning, a rosy dawn turning the billowing sails of the clipper to shades of washed pink and rose and outlining the rigging against the lightening sky. It was all so beautiful it hurt her to see it and yet this was her element, hers and the ship's, and she must hold the truth to her, which was that in three months she would be standing here again watching *Breeze* bringing Liam back to her.

It took a long time for *Breeze* to fade from sight. The quayside, which had been crowded with hundreds of people, many of them emigrants sailing on her, the rest there to see them off, was almost deserted now. There had been barrels and boxes and bales, tin trunks and leather portmanteaux, all waiting to go on board but now the space they had taken up was empty and Lily was alone in a great echoing expanse which still held the sad notes of their goodbyes. The voices of the officers shouting commands, relayed from the captain who had stood beside Liam in the wheelhouse, had died away and a curious quiet fell as if, no matter how many times they saw it, the partings saddened the onlookers. There were porters and dock labourers about, leaning on the waggons that had brought the cargo of coal, salt and Manchester piece-goods to the ship. There were many waggons pulled by enormous Shires moving back to the transit sheds for their next loads, and, perched on a bollard, an old seaman was doing some intricate thing with a rope. From inside the transit shed dockers whistled and sang, the latter an old ballad which was popular in Liverpool:

> Come all you dry land sailors behold
> And listen to my song,
> There are but forty verses . . .

And standing on the edge of the quay, so close several dockers looked uneasily at her, Lily watched the vessel carrying her love fade slowly into the pink and gold morning mist in the mouth of the river. For an hour she stood there, a silent, slender figure in the graceful folds of her black cloak, her hood revealing nothing but the curve of her pale cheek and a silver glint of a curl which had escaped and blew across the wool of the hood in the lazy breeze which had got up. They watched her, the men who loaded the waggons which were all on the move now, men busy with the work of the great seaport, wondering what she was doing and why she stood so still and so silently gazing out to the mouth of the river and when one, encouraged by his mates, approached her, he was startled by the blank stare she turned on him when he gently touched her arm.

"Are yer all right, miss?" he asked her in the adenoidal tones of a true "Dicky Sam", a man born within a mile of St Nicholas Church. His face was rough and seamed with his years working in all weathers on the dockside, but it was kind and anxious.

"She 'ad a face like an angel," he was to tell his mates when he rejoined them, but she smiled at him and thanked him for his concern.

She began to walk then, past Albert Dock and the tobacco

warehouses, moving steadily southwards beyond Brunswick Dock, where large lengths of timber from North America were being unloaded through openings in the bows of several vessels. Teams of men and horses dragged them ashore, cursing and sweating as she moved steadily through the brisk activity, seemingly unaware of their presence, staring after her in amazement so that confusion reigned in her wake. She continued along the parade until she reached the Pottery Shore, striding on round Dingle Point, her boots wading through several inches of water, for the tide was high and fast. She did not notice, and it was not until she had reached the strip of sand that stood in front of Oakwood Place that she sank to her knees as though in prayer. Her hood fell back and she bent her head, then folded in on herself and wept brokenheartedly.

An hour later she let herself into the house by the same side door through which she had left, moving quietly up the stairs until she reached the privacy of her bedroom. Villy sprang up to meet her, licking her hand then running to fetch one of her soft toys to show her mistress how pleased she was to see her. Beauty arched her back and smoothed herself against her skirt, purring her own pleasure and when Lily had undressed and put on her nightgown, climbing into bed and burrowing under the covers, the dog and the cat came to lie alongside her. When Maggie popped her head round the door an hour later she reported that Miss Lily was back, and fast asleep in her bed, though God knew where she'd been. Not on her mare, that was for sure, since the hem of her gown and her boots, which she'd left lying on the floor in front of the fire, were soaked with what could only be seawater. Did Mrs Quinn reckon she'd been down to the shore to meet that friend of her pa's then?

"Aye, she coulda done," Molly Quinn answered absently.

"Shall I wake her, d'yer think?"

"Nay, lerrer sleep."

"Mebbe she's not well. It's not like her ter stay in 'er bed."

"Well, leave 'er fer a bit then I'll go up an' see 'ow she is. Sleep's a good 'ealer when yer badly."

It seemed Lily was "badly" for several days, only leaving her room to climb the stairs to the nursery to sit with Abby for half an hour or so. The baby greeted her with welcoming smiles which warmed the cold and distant reaches of her heart which had been empty ever since Liam left.

"Is she all right, Dorcas?" she had asked, peering anxiously into Abby's face.

Dorcas was seriously offended, she told her Aunty Mabel. Anyone'd think the poor little beggar was being neglected without Miss Lily to oversee her and, as Aunty Mabel could see, putting the good-natured baby on to her Aunty Mabel's capacious lap, there was absolutely nowt wrong with her. It was Miss Lily who looked to have something wrong with her and no wonder she had kept to her bed. She only hoped it was nothing catching.

"Where is she now, our Dorcas?" her Aunty Mabel asked her, bouncing the baby on her knee and making her laugh with delight.

"She were back in 'er bed when I left."

Which was where Joshua Crowther found her when, for some reason, scarcely recognised even to himself, he knocked on her door and entered her bedroom.

She was asleep. Her hair, which she had tied carelessly back with a ribbon, was spread like a silver and amber shot cape on the pillow about her head, ruffled into tumbled waves that glinted in the firelit room. One arm was flung above her head and the covers, which she'd pushed down, showed the roundness of her breasts and the high peaks of her nipples beneath the fine cambric of her nightgown. Her eyes were closed, her long thick lashes forming a half-moon on her flushed cheeks and her poppy lips were moist and parted, showing a tiny portion of her tongue and white teeth. She was breathing deeply but when Villy, who had lifted her head at the man's entrance, raised her muzzle and began to growl, she woke with a start.

Joshua Crowther, whose hand had been stretched out to touch her, perhaps her hair – or had he intended something more pleasurable? – jumped back as though a wasp had alighted on his flesh and sunk its barb in him. He recovered quickly, smiling urbanely as though to say there was nothing amiss in a man visiting his unwell step-daughter. Lily reared up on her elbows, pulling the covers up to her chin, then flinched away until her head rested on the headboard. Villy huddled up closer to her, her muzzle still raised though no sound came from her, which was somehow more telling.

"What d'you want?" Lily quavered, her eyes wide and barely focused, not frightened, more astonished, for what in hell's name was he doing in her bedroom? For six years he had taken no interest in her, save a threat now and again if she did not settle down to Miss Kaye's rule, but even those had stopped years ago. Since Ma died they had barely exchanged a word, even at breakfast, the only meal they shared. After Ma died Lily had taken her evening meal in her own small sitting-room, eating off a tray in front of the fire, sharing titbits with Villy, but gradually, over the last month or two, she had begun to eat with Mrs Quinn and the rest of the maidservants in the big, cosy, cheerful kitchen. They had been somewhat surprised at first, for she was one of the daughters of the house, but then they had grown used to it, telling one another that the poor little beggar must be lonely now her ma was gone. She was a lively young girl with a good sense of humour, making them laugh, or at least she had done before Mrs Crowther died, and would again, they were sure, when she had become more used to her loss.

"There is no need for alarm, my dear. Can a man not come to see how his daughter is faring?" he asked smoothly, smiling down at her in a way she did not like. "We missed you at breakfast and when I enquired after you was told that you were unwell so I thought I would see if there was anything you wanted."

He had stepped back from the bed when she woke but now he moved closer, his hands in his pockets. They seemed to be scrabbling for something, shifting about in his pockets in a most odd way and she found her eyes hypnotically drawn there, then back to his face which was smiling. His gaze drifted over her and Villy's hackles rose even more.

"Does that dog have to lie on the bed?" he asked, dreamlike, his eyes narrowed to dark slits in the dim light from the fire. "You know my views on animals in the house. I must ask one of the yard men to come and take her to the stable where she belongs."

"You do and I shall go with her. And I am not your daughter."

"Now then, you are being silly. There is no need for that. You *are* my daughter now, or at least my ward and as for the dog, I'm sure we could come to some agreement about it that suits both of us."

What on earth did he mean by that? her confused mind asked as he sat down on the end of the bed, pushing aside the angry cat. It was a dreary day, the rain beating on the window and the tree outside it lashing against the glass, not a day for sailors at sea, she remembered thinking as Mr Crowther's agreeably smiling face loomed more closely over her. She was reminded of the time when he was wooing her mother. This was how he had been then, smiling and speaking in that deceptively gentle voice. Ma had been taken in but Lily Elliott, who had loathed this man ever since he married her mother, was not so easy to deceive. He wanted something, that was why he was like this, and though she still felt weak and lost without Liam, it would not be for long. She would be strong again very soon and she would show this bugger that though she might look like her mother, inside she was vastly different. How dare he come in here. How dare he!

"I also came to say that the moment you feel well enough I hope to see you at the dinner table with Eloise and myself. It has come to my notice that you are eating with the servants and that will not do at all. Perhaps this evening?" He edged a little closer to her.

Her tone was almost conversational as she spoke. "If you come one inch nearer to me I shall scream the bloody place down," she told him and was amused to see the expression of amazement cross his face, amazement and annoyance. "And as for an agreement between you and me I'd sooner make a pact with a rattlesnake which would be easier to trust."

She spoke bravely. She was supremely confident, her blood pulsing hotly through her veins, believing in her innocence that she had nothing to fear from this man. Even when he smiled that slithery smile of his she was still not afraid. What could he do to her in this house full of servants who had only to call to the men outside and there would be a dozen of them cramming the room to defend her.

"Well, you are a fire-eater, aren't you? I only came to enquire after your health, my dear, so why you are taking this attitude I cannot imagine. But since you are unwilling to accept my offer I'd best go."

"And what offer is that, Mr Crowther?"

"For us to be friends, of course, my dear. This constant touchiness on your part is very tedious. So perhaps we may see you at dinner this evening. I'll leave the matter of the dog for the present. So get some sleep and tonight put on your prettiest dress, leave off that mourning since your mother has been dead for four months now, and come down and dine with us. I mean that, Lily."

When he left the room, turning at the door to smile back at her, she began to shake. She wasn't even sure what had happened. Mr Crowther had come to her room to enquire after her health which had never been anything other than rude in all the time she had been at Oakwood Place. On the face of it there was nothing wrong with that, was there, but she knew there was. He was threatening her with something, holding Villy over her as a lever. Dear God, why did this have to happen to her when she was feeling so low, when she felt as though the bottom had dropped out of her world for the moment? She knew, her sensible mind *knew* that she had only three, four months at the most to get through and then Liam would be back. They would be married and go and live in a house of his choice, perhaps even on the *Lily-Jane* while it was being restored to the condition it had known when Pa was alive. Only four months in this house which held so many special and yet so many unhappy memories. Memories of the peaceful times with her and Ma, with Will and Mr Diggle in the gardens, with Villy prancing beside them and Beauty doing her best to make them believe she didn't give a fig for any of them, but hanging about Ma's skirts just the same. Memories of Liam sprawled on the beach beside her watching the ships move along the busy swaggering river, a bustling highway dancing with eager craft, tall frigates swaying graciously out to sea and bursting into white sail bloom as they went. They had shared such joy, such laughter and yet she had known of her ma's deep unhappiness and could not get it out of her head that perhaps Ma was better off dead, for she would be with Pa now and not that monster who had caused her such pain.

She was sixteen and only this week had learned of the loveliness of being close to and cared for by a man. Liam's kisses, Liam's hands on her body had brought her such a feeling of joy, of racing, bubbling aliveness, if there was such a word, she had felt her senses become dizzy with it. She had wanted in some strange way to hold him so close to her it was as if she were doing her best to force herself *inside* him, to *be* him, or part of him and now that part was gone and she must learn to be patient and strong until it came back to her with

Liam. She loved him. *She loved him.* She was a woman who loved her man, for that was what Liam was, *her* man and she must find some way to get through the days and weeks safely until he came back. Now why should she have said that? she wondered. Why had she said *safely?* And when Mr Crowther's arrogant face swam before her eyes, that cruel, smiling face, she knew why.

She got out of bed and dressed herself in her newly sponged and pressed black gown, clicking her fingers to Villy to come with her, going down the back stairs, which she knew he never used, to the kitchen.

"Why, 'ere she is," Mrs Quinn exclaimed, her face lighting up at the sight of the child who now had the love she had once reserved for Jane Elliott. "Are yer feelin' better, queen? See, Mrs Kelly's medd some lemon curd tarlets an' Betsy were purrin' on't kettle. Sit thi' down an' try one."

She waited to see if Lily had anything to say on the matter of her indisposition of the last few days, but her lamb sat down and with the appetite of a child began to tuck into the lemon curd tartlets. The dog sat at her feet, her head cocked, her ears pricked, her mouth watering as she waited hopefully for some to come her way and when it did, throwing it down her throat without it touching the sides.

Lily licked her fingers and sat back in the kitchen chair, looking about her at the friendly faces, the smiles, the general air of approval, for these women were her friends. They had loved her ma and they were fond of her and surely, in an atmosphere such as this she could come to no harm until it was time for her to go to Liam. Mr Crowther was an evil, filthy old man, that was all, who had done his best to besmirch her mother with his filth but he had not succeeded, for the parts of Ma that were special, that had been loved by her father, could not be touched. She had heard the grooms, when they thought themselves to be alone, speak of their master's exploits – though that was not the word they used – with women, before and after Ma's death, but he could not touch her with his ugliness. He liked to play games, she was aware of that, even in her ignorant state of the ways of men, for she had seen him play them with her mother, baiting her with his "teasing" until she was reduced to tears. Well, he would not play the same games with her.

She felt better as she sat and dreamed before the kitchen fire in Mrs Quinn's chair, her stockinged feet tucked up beneath the hem of her skirt. Mrs Kelly was up to her elbows in flour, for she'd a fancy for a steak and kidney pie for their supper, she told them, though the family were to have Crimped Cod in Oyster Sauce followed by Veal *à la Jardinière*, Wild Duck and then Charlotte *à la Vanille*.

Lily had no intention of dining on the latter. She much preferred steak and kidney pie and tomorrow, she promised herself drowsily, feeling better than she had since Liam left, she would go and see her pa's schooner, *Lily-Jane*, where she was at berth in Canning Half Dock. She sighed and stretched and Molly watched her, her previous feeling of apprehension drifting away in the relaxed atmosphere of the kitchen that she had come to think of as hers.

22

He watched her from beneath hooded lids as she glided gracefully across the room, the hem of her full black mourning gown just brushing the carpet. Tall, slender, exquisite in her young loveliness. Even the way she walked and held her head – though Jane's had become disappointingly bowed latterly – the way she seated herself on his right-hand side opposite Eloise and shook out her napkin was so exactly like her mother she might have been her.

"Good morning," she said to no one in particular, looking at no one in particular, then turned to smile at Maggie who was at the serving table alone this morning.

"I'll have some porridge, please, Maggie, if I may. It has turned very cold and porridge is warming on a day like this." Her pa had told her that more than once.

"Yes, Miss Lily." Maggie beamed at her.

Joshua waited until the maidservant had placed the bowl of steaming, creamy porridge in front of her before he spoke.

"Good morning. I trust you are better, my dear? We have been most anxious about you, haven't we, Eloise?" not looking at his daughter who stared at him in astonishment but did not answer.

"Yes, thank you. I am completely well."

"We're glad to hear it, are we not, Eloise? And may I say we missed you at dinner last night. It seems you went against my express wishes and took your meal with the servants again. May I ask why?"

"It is quite simple. I prefer their company."

Maggie gasped then clattered a spoon against a serving dish to cover the sound. Blessed Mother, the child asked for trouble, saucing the master like that and when she got back to the kitchen she would have a word with Mrs Quinn, who should definitely have one with Lily! They all knew the master was as amiable as a babe when he was not crossed but to provoke him deliberately like that was begging for a box on the ears. Not that he had ever hit his step-daughter, as far as Maggie knew anyway, but there was always a first time. She held her breath and waited for the master's response but it was Miss Eloise who spoke.

"Well, I suppose it's understandable for like to prefer like," she sneered. "It must be easier for you to consort with servants rather than ladies and gentlemen since you were never used to the latter."

"If by the latter you mean yourself then you are right. I find the servants in this house, and outside it, are honest, truthful, warm-hearted and unaffected. They are kind. They are pleased to see me which gives me a warm feeling I have not found . . . elsewhere." Except with Liam, of course, though she did not voice this last.

"Is that so? Well, all I can say is that proves my point about your upbringing. Anyone who finds pleasure in associating with the underclasses can only be considered one of them."

Maggie was not at all sure what Miss Eloise was implying about the underclasses, of which she was one, she only knew it was not kind but she could do nothing about it, merely stand against the wall and stare blankly across the room as though she were not only deaf but half-witted.

"I would sooner count Maggie and Betsy, Mr Diggle and Jackie, the boot boy, as my friends than—"

"That is enough, the pair of you," the master roared. Maggie nearly jumped out of her skin, she was to tell the dumb-founded servants later when she recounted what had been said. It promised to be a real battleground this morning. And them usually so quiet, the master reading his newspaper, Miss Eloise dwelling, no doubt, on the outfits she was to have made for the coming season which included the Hunt Ball, several dances and parties to which she had been invited and the approaching pre-Christmas festivities. Miss Lily never opened her mouth except to put food in it since, up to now, neither the master nor the young miss had ever spoken to her.

"I will not have this bickering," Mr Crowther growled, "and I would be obliged if you would remain silent for the moment, Eloise."

Eloise subsided sullenly. Her father turned to Maggie and pointed to his plate. "I'll have some more bacon, if you please, Maggie, that's if you can drag yourself from that trance you appear to have fallen into."

Maggie jumped to obey, so flustered she almost dripped bacon fat in the master's lap.

"Now then, Lily," he continued when his plate was replenished to his satisfaction, spearing a forkful of bacon and mushroom and carrying it to his mouth. "Let us return to this liking you appear to have developed for consorting with your inferiors, rather than your family. I propose—"

"If by my family you mean yourself and your daughter then let me remind you I am not related to you in any way. Just because my mother was witless" – Dear God, she should not have used that word, she remembered thinking in some part of her brain that was still functioning coolly, for that was what Ma had been at the time – "enough to marry you does not mean you have any control over me."

She gave him cool stare for cool stare, but something inside her was beginning to quiver with what she recognised as dread. It was as though some instinct told her there was worse to come.

"Aah, that's where you're mistaken, my dear. When your mother died I made it my business to consult a lawyer with a view to . . . well, shall we say *adopting* you. You are legally my ward, or even my daughter in the eyes of the law. The legal documents arrived last week. So you see, you are as much my . . . my responsibility as Eloise here and the infant in the nursery. I may do with you . . . and *to* you, as I please. You and my other daughters are my property, you might say, and will obey me as a father expects to be obeyed. You have run wild in recent years but that, I'm afraid, is to end. You will—"

She stood up with such an eruption of violence her chair crashed backwards to the floor. Maggie squeaked, she couldn't help it, putting her hand to her mouth in horror, but Eloise smiled, a smile of triumphant satisfaction as though to say she had been waiting for this day for a long, long time.

High colour rushed to Lily's cheeks, a fierce flame of anger and her eyes glittered like grey ice with the sun reflected in it. She clenched her hands then brought them down with such force on to the table everything on it jumped an inch into the air. Eloise was just as flushed as she was but with excitement.

She looked from her father's face to the girl who had been pronounced her sister – which she did not care for – then back to her father, unaware that she was holding her breath. There was something odd about the way her father was acting but she was too young and ignorant to recognise the sexual undertones in his manner.

"You can go to hell," Lily hissed, "and I hope you fry there. I belong to no one, only my ma and pa and they're both dead." And, of course, one other but it would not be prudent to mention him here. "I'd leave this house and find work rather than be beholden to you. You'll never be my father, never, nor this trollop my sister. I have one sister and she is in the nursery."

"Where she will remain, naturally, no matter what course of action you take, my dear." Joshua Crowther sat back, wiped his lips on his napkin and smiled up at her. She was quite magnificent, despite her youth, the exact replication of her mother, but younger, and spirited. A fighter, and how he would enjoy taming that wildness, putting a curb on that defiance, knocking the rebellion out of her one way or the other. It might take a long time, for she had had her own way for years but how pleasureable it would be. The truth was, he was bored. His business ventures flourished, needing the minimum of attention. His social life, which had picked up when Jane died and he became an eligible widower, was the same old round where nothing new ever happened. He needed something to stimulate his jaded palate and forcing this new daughter of his, which legally she now was, to conform to the social manners and customs of his class and of his generation was just what he needed.

Lily took a deep breath as the truth of what Joshua Crowther had said filtered into her enraged mind. It would be a simple matter to pack a bag and run away from Oakwood Place. Find a room and some work to keep her until Liam came home, though she was not certain how easy that would be, since she was trained for nothing. But if she left she would have to leave Abby behind and Abby was her ma's child and how could she desert her? If she did she knew her sister would not be ill-treated, far from it. She would be brought up as Eloise had been brought up. Eloise who had also lost her mother at birth, a mother who might have had a softening influence on her. From infancy Joshua's eldest daughter had been in the custody of nurses and governesses, raised to believe she was a little princess. She had been given everything the child of a wealthy man can be given, everything but his attention. Everything but the special hours spent with a caring parent which are necessary to a developing child. The feeling that she was cherished. Oh, Dorcas was carelessly affectionate with Abby, giving her a cuddle, dandling her on her knee, making sure she was clean and well fed but Dorcas was a nursemaid, probably the first in a line of nursemaids until a governess took over. Exactly the sort of childhood Eloise had known and look how she'd turned out! She'd been given none of the loving warmth Ma and Pa had wrapped about her, Lily, and though Eloise had been moulded into a perfect young lady, fit to be a gentleman's wife, she was deeply flawed, spiteful and small-minded. But then when Lily left to go to Liam would she not have to leave Abby behind? The thought speared her through the heart, going straight for the place her little sister had settled into. In her recent dreams she had visualised herself, Liam and Abby living together in some pleasant place, no doubt a cottage with roses round the door, she supposed bitterly, realising what a foolish child she had been. Abby was this man's child. She belonged to him and what could Lily Elliott, who was sixteen and only Abby's half-sister, do about that?

Of course she had not known about the *Lily-Jane* then! She lowered her eyes so that he could not see the expression in them and he smiled triumphantly.

"I see you believe me, Lily. I see you finally realise that I am the master here and that my word is law. I am the guardian of three daughters who will remain in my care until they leave it to pass into that of a husband. Believe it, Lily. Now, won't you sit down and eat your breakfast. And do please tell us where it is you are to go on this cold morning and why you seem to feel the need to stoke up with porridge?" His voice sharpened. "Oh, do sit down, girl. You're beginning to get on my nerves, and take that petulant look off your face. There, that's better," as Lily slowly sat down again and picked up her spoon. "The sooner you learn who is ruler here and that my orders are to be obeyed, the happier we will all be, particularly you."

"I don't think so, Mr Crowther," she answered him icily. "Not unless you lock me in my room."

"That can be arranged, my dear." His voice was silky and

against the wall Maggie felt the bitter taste of fear in her mouth, for she remembered another locked room.

Joshua Crowther sipped his coffee, lounging indolently in his chair as he regarded Lily with narrowed eyes. His daughter was breathless with delight. "So, shall we begin with where you intended going today?"

Intended! That seemed to say it all, but Lily Elliott was far from routed on this particular battlefield. She almost smiled in her self-confidence. If he thought he could chain her to the house, bind her and bend her to his will, then he was in for a big surprise. She was no child to be told what she should do and where she should go. She had done as she pleased for a long time now and this bastard was not going to stop her. She had four months to get through and if she spent the whole time fighting him, then she would do so.

"I mean to ride Precious over to Small Ends," which was a lie, of course, since she intended walking along the river's edge and the seafront beyond Pottery Shore to the parades that fronted each dock until she reached Canning Dock where Liam had told her the *Lily-Jane* was berthed. She had no money for a hansom, since she had spent what little she had the other day when she went to see *Breeze* sail away on her long journey. Small Ends was on the bend of the river beyond Hale where the waters turned towards Runcorn Gap, a five-mile ride with the river always in sight on her right, a favourite ride of hers and one she had taken many times, but it seemed Joshua Crowther had other ideas.

"I think not, my dear, at least not alone. Arnold is to accompany Eloise and it might be best if you go with them. It would be more fitting."

Lily cast about desperately in her mind for some way out that would satisfy Mr Crowther, but she knew there really wasn't one. Blind defiance was the only weapon she had and it was not one Mr Crowther would bow down to. Still, she could but try.

"I don't think so, Mr Crowther. I'm used to riding alone and I certainly don't care for Eloise's company." By the serving table Maggie felt a great urge to turn her face to the wall. Don't do this, lass, she was begging silently. Don't antagonise him, for it'll do you no good, but, of course, she could do or say no such thing, at least not here. Just wait until they got her in the kitchen though. She and Mrs Quinn'd have something to say to her then.

"Do you know, Lily," Mr Crowther answered her in a casual tone, "what you do or do not care for is a matter of supreme indifference to me. You will ride with Eloise and Arnold or you will remain in your room. The choice is yours."

"Very well." She stood up and moved towards the door. "My room it is."

His smiling face did not alter. "Then I'll be up to see you shortly," he told her. "I like to think I might be able to change your mind."

With his words echoing menacingly round her head Lily walked up the stairs and as there was no one to see her she let her shoulders slump dispiritedly for a moment. She could feel the oppression move in her but she would not be beaten, far from it, she told herself, straightening her back courageously. The next few months in which she had hoped to spend some time on the *Lily-Jane*, for there was surely something she could do towards restoring her to her former glory even if it were only in the living quarters, were going to be tricky. She could always escape from *him*, of course. Already she had ideas teeming in her head, one of which she meant to put into practice this very day. Oh, yes, Lily Elliott could outsmart Joshua Crowther any day of the week. Just let him try . . .

The door to her bedroom stood wide open and inside Rosie was at the fireplace just putting down a scuttle of coal that she had filled and brought up the back stairs. Maggie Two was stripping the bed beside which, on a convenient chair, was a pile of clean bedding.

When they saw her both maidservants immediately stopped what they were doing and stood like a couple of intruders caught in some criminal act, their hands restlessly smoothing and plucking at their aprons as though in mortal dread. They watched her as she hesitated on the threshold, then dropped their eyes and stared dumbly at the carpet.

"What is it?" she asked sharply, their very attitude frightening her. A wave of apprehension turned her blood to ice, for it was very evident that there was something wrong, something out of place, something missing, but it seemed they were afraid to speak. It was very quiet. Where were the usual sounds that greeted her whenever she returned to her room? The joyful prancing and whining of Villy, the purring pretence at indifference with which Beauty greeted her. Oh, dear God . . . where? What had that bastard done while she had been seated at the breakfast table arguing with him?

"Where are they?" she snarled at the housemaids, so that they cowered away from her. It was not their fault, was it, nor the groom who had been given his orders by the master. They were all sorry but what could they do?

It was Maggie Two who spoke up bravely. "Jimmy . . . came an' took 'em."

"Took them where?"

"Nay, I dunno, Miss Lily. "'E'd 'ad 'is orders, 'e said, from't master."

"The devil, the evil devil. How dare he do this to my animals. Honest to God I swear I'll swing for him, see if I don't."

"Oh, Miss Lily, don't . . ." Maggie Two put out her hands as though to draw Lily to her, or perhaps to stop her from doing something she might regret, but she had whirled about and was running along the passage and down the stairs, two at a time, her skirts held up to her knees so that her lace-trimmed drawers were on display for anyone to see. As she leaped down from the bottom step, almost skidding on the polished floor, the breakfast-room door opened and Joshua Crowther came out into the hall. The expression that was becoming familiar to her, but which she did not understand, clouded his eyes. Behind him was his daughter and, behind her, Maggie. Maggie told them later in the kitchen it was a bloody miracle she didn't faint, she was so terrified. Not for herself but for Miss Lily.

"Aah," said the master. "I wondered how long it would be before you came roaring down here again. You really must learn that a lady should restrain herself, my dear, or be taught. A lesson I would gladly––"

"Where's Villy and Beauty?" she screeched, so that even in the kitchen they heard and upstairs Maggie Two and Rosie clutched at one another in dread. "I promise you this, you bastard, if any harm has come to them you will live to regret the day you and I met. What have you done with them?"

"*I?*" He was vastly entertained, his manner said, while

behind him his daughter smirked her approval. "I have done nothing with them. They have merely been removed by one of the men to their rightful place."

"You devil . . ."

"What a melodramatic child you are . . ." But she did not hear the rest as she whirled away from him and began to run towards the green baize door that led into the kitchen. They watched her go by, the open-mouthed, dumbstruck servants, each one stilled to silence, except Mrs Quinn who whispered her name and made a move to intercept her. As well try to catch the wind!

They saw her come pelting across the stable yard, Jimmy, Arnold and Mr Bentley, her skirt lifted yet again to show the lace on her drawers. Jimmy and Arnold were mucking out and Mr Bentley was polishing the brass on a tangle of harness. Like the indoor servants they all three stopped and stared and, though he had been expecting it, he was so startled Mr Bentley's pipe fell from between his teeth and shattered on the cobbles.

"Where are they? Where have you put them?" but there was no need of an answer. Hearing her voice, Villy began to howl piteously, springing frantically against the bottom half of the tackroom door. Henry, Wally and Alex, Mr Crowther's game dogs, who had lived in the stables ever since they left their mothers, were restlessly padding about inside, disturbed by Villy's agitation, ready to howl themselves in sympathy.

Lily opened the door and was about to lift Villy into her arms, to soothe her and tell her that it was all right now, speaking as though the animal were a child who had been unfairly treated, and at the same time looking about her for a sign of Beauty, when a hand came to rest on her shoulder. She knew at once who it was, for it seemed to fondle her flesh, to caress as well as restrain and her skin crawled with horror but she took no notice. Twitching it away she bent down and picked up the small dog, hugging her to her, kissing her passionately about the ears, overcome for a moment by the rough tongue on her face, and by memories. Villy was her dog but she could never forget that Pa had been with her, indeed had helped to rescue Villy when the big boys in Walton Lane had tied her tail to that of a cat. Pa and Villy would always be inextricably linked, just as Ma and Beauty were. They were hers, these animals and these memories and no one, least of all this loathsome stepfather of hers, was going to part her from them.

"My dear, if you will insist on keeping them in your room I shall be forced—"

"Where's Beauty? Where's my mother's cat?" Her voice was flat and deadly and even Joshua Crowther found himself stepping back, which vastly annoyed him.

"I'm sure I couldn't say and neither do I—"

"She . . . ran off, Miss Lily," Jimmy mumbled, earning a frown from his master. It was difficult to keep a cat where it didn't want to be, surely the master knew that. Put it in a cage, or fasten it in somewhere and you could bet your last farthing the animal would find some way out of it, but he knew where this one had gone though he wasn't going to say in front of the master. Likely he'd drown the poor creature and her such a favourite of the dead mistress. Followed her everywhere, it had, but as though it knew, and they said cats were intelligent, it had settled down in front of Mrs Diggle's fire where, as far as he knew, it had remained.

"I must go and look for her," Lily said distractedly, still hugging Villy to her as though afraid to let her go.

Mr Crowther tried to put a hand on her arm then decided against it. "I don't think that's a good idea, Lily. Cats have a way of surviving in the most dire circumstances, so just put the dog back in the stable and we'll go inside and have that—"

"She is not going back in there. She's always been with me."

"We all have to learn new things, my dear, and the dog is no exception. If she can't learn, or is not *allowed* to, then I shall be forced to make other arrangements."

The men didn't know where to look, for the little lass – she might be as tall as they were but she was a little lass to them – looked as though she had been punched in the stomach by a hard fist. White as the freshly painted whitewash in the tackroom, she was, ready to fall if someone didn't catch her, for it was clear she didn't know what the hell to do. She wanted to defy him, that was obvious, tell him to go to the devil but the dog's life was at stake. There was nothing surer in this world than the fact that if the master was not obeyed someone would pay for it. They wouldn't put it past him to shoot the animal, or at least order one of them to do it. He'd not soil his own hands with an unpleasant task like that, not him, the bastard. They'd seen the way he'd treated his wife and now it seemed he was to grind her daughter down beneath his expensive and well-polished boot, poor little beggar.

It was Mr Bentley who stepped forward and with gentle hands took the small, wriggling animal from her. Her incredible eyes, so big and such an unusual colour, like lavender set in a coating of grey ice, stared into his and he stared back, doing his best to tell her that as long as he was here the dog would come to no harm. But *she* must do as the master said or not only the dog but she would suffer for it.

"She'll be all right in't stable wi't other dogs, Miss Lily," he told her, braving his master's glare. "Yer can come across an' see 'er whenever yer want. Jimmy'll walk 'er when 'e walks t'other 'uns, don't yer fret."

Villy whined as Lily walked docilely back across the yard with Mr Crowther but she did not look back. He had defeated her this time. He had threatened the life of her dog, she was well aware of that, and there would be other punishments if she did not conform to the life he thought a daughter of his should lead. She was to become a second Eloise, sitting in the schoolroom with her and Miss Yates, embroidering, doing fatuous little watercolours, walking along the tediously safe paths of the garden, riding with Arnold always in attendance and never escaping down to the seashore or to any of the loved and familiar places she had made her own along the river. In one day her life had been turned upside down and she didn't know why. She didn't know why he had suddenly decided that she was his daughter. Didn't he recognise that she loathed him, in her ignorance not knowing that her feelings for him were part of her attraction.

Well, she thought, as she walked ahead of him into his study where he wanted to have a little talk with her, he said, he had won this time but what did they say about forewarned is forearmed?

23

It had turned bitterly cold and the youth who stepped out from among the trees was well wrapped up against the keen wind that blew off the river. He wore a pair of well-cut, sand-coloured cord breeches, knee-high riding boots, a tweed shooting jacket with many pockets which was a couple of sizes too big for him, and a muffler of enormous proportions which wrapped round his neck several times and covered the lower half of his face. On his head was a cloth "quartered" cap, popular several decades ago. At his heels was a small, scruffy brown dog.

The young man jumped with the supple grace and buoyancy of healthy youth from the rough grass bank that edged the seashore, followed by the dog, both of them landing lightly in the sand, then began to run northwards, weightless as the birds that rode the wind above the river. The dog ran straight for the water, jumping madly in and out of the tiny, rippling, white-edged waves, turning to look expectantly at the young man, then, when no notice was taken, shook itself vigorously, then ran after him.

The youth kept to just below the high-water mark where the sand was firm, leaping puddles of seawater in which long strands of seaweed made patterns against the wet sand. His long legs pumped, his arms flailed and his face became bright red with his exertions but he did not stop for a breather, forging ahead along Jericho Shore, cutting across the inlet known as Knotty Hole and skimming the wet sand to Dingle Point. A man busy sawing dead branches off an ancient oak tree on the edge of Dingle Bank stopped and stared at him in astonishment, letting the saw slip across a finger. He jumped and cursed and put the finger to his mouth, then turned, following the young man's mad passage round the point to Pottery Shore. The dog was ahead now, its ears flat to its head as it ran, turning every few seconds to make sure the man was still with him and it was not until they reached the Pottery Slip, down which pleasure boats were launched in the summer, that they stopped. Sitting down close together on the cold grey stone of the slip, they gasped and floundered like two fish just landed from the river.

For several minutes they sat, the man's arm about the dog's neck, his head bent, then he stood up and with a click of his fingers to the animal began to walk more sedately in the direction of Brunswick Dock. A long, steady stride with the dog so close to his heel its nose might have been fastened to it until he reached the Albert Dock Parade and the massive structure of Albert Dock. He kept in the shadows thrown by a pale wintering sun which had not yet crept up from behind the buildings on his right. At least two hundred windows looked out on to the parade, for the colonnaded warehouses each had four floors, every one crowded from wall to wall with goods that were either waiting to be loaded on to ships, or had just been discharged. It had been opened by the Prince Consort in 1845 and named after him and a handsome building it was too, a massive square built round the quays that served the sailing ships at berth there.

The youth turned the corner and the low sun shone directly into his eyes which were a silvery grey, glittering like diamonds under water. The place was teeming with waggons and horses, dockers and drays, hansom cabs delivering passengers, and those on foot taking a short cut across the iron bridge that led to the next granite island and then on to the landing stage and the ferry.

His footsteps slowed, then, noticing an old seaman studying him suspiciously, he pulled his cap further down over his brow, put his hands in his pockets and began to whistle tunelessly as he imagined a young man would do. He was sauntering now, though his heart wanted him to hurry, hurry, hurry on to where he was going and yet to slip backwards in time to where he had been.

He came to the bridge that led across the lock gates, moving as though in a dream until he stood on the quay beside Canning Dock. And there she was, what the young man had come to see, pulling gently at her moorings, leaning a little to one side like some slightly tipsy old lady who, though she has had a bit too much to drink, is not totally drunk. She dipped on a small wave created by the movement of a square rigger as it left the dock, almost curtseying in welcome as though she were glad, at last, of the sight of someone who loved her, since she had been sadly neglected.

The young man sat down on one of the iron bollards that edged the dock and to which the ship's mooring ropes were fastened. He seemed to be unware of the bustle around him, his hand moving gently in the fur of the dog sitting beside him.

"There she is, Villy," he whispered. "There she is. My pa's schooner. *Lily-Jane*, my beautiful, beautiful *Lily-Jane*. Dear God, I've waited for this day a long, long time and at last it's here. It's the *Lily-Jane*, Villy." A long, bewitched sigh drifted from his lungs and into the cold morning air.

She had found the clothing in a sandalwood chest in the attic one day when, since it was raining stair-rods, as Mrs Quinn put it, she had been unable to go out. Left to herself she would have been perfectly happy to put on her stout, high-laced boots and wrap herself in the mackintosh she had found hanging on a hook inside the cupboard beneath the stairs. She had no idea who the mackintosh belonged to, probably Nicholas Crowther since it was the kind of thing a boy might wear. It was fashioned from a sort of waterproof cloth made with India rubber and smelled absolutely horrible but it certainly kept out the rain. She often wore it when she went for a walk with the animals, but today she took notice of Mrs Quinn, knowing that the housekeeper, who was more than a housekeeper to Lily, was afraid of what Mr Crowther might do to her lamb if she disobeyed him, and stayed indoors.

She read for an hour or two, curled up with a book, a great favourite, Trollope's *Barchester Towers*, in Mr Crowther's study, knowing he was out on some business of his own and would not be back until late afternoon. But she was restless and after a turn or two about the study looking at the prints on the wall, mostly of horses, and scenes of men shooting at birds, at the fishing rods and old smoking pipes of which Mr Crowther had a great number, at the skeleton clock on the mantelpiece, at the desktop telescope and the globe of the world set in a brass meridian on a wood stand, all of which she had seen a score of times before, she wandered out into the hall. She peered from the window beside the front door at the rain which seemed to be coming down heavier than ever. She trailed upstairs, her fingers drifting along the banister, wondering whether to go and have a peep at Abby, who was probably having her afternoon nap, or brave the elements and run across the yard to the tackroom and talk to Villy. It was a week now since she had been removed from Lily's bedroom and though Lily meant to get her back, and Beauty as well, as soon as Mr Crowther had forgotten all about the furore of last week, she had thought it wise to give it a few more days before she attempted it.

It was a dark afternoon, November now and the lamps on the upstairs landing had not yet been lit. She moved on up the stairs that led to the nursery and then, instead of going into the nursery, which was quiet except for the faint sound of Dorcas having forty winks, she continued on until she was at the foot of the stairs that led up to the attics. She peered up them but it was so dark she could barely make out the top of the stairs. She stood for several moments, then, on a whim, went back to the table against the wall opposite the nursery on which a number of candles in holders stood. There were matches and, striking one, she lit a candle then crept back up the stairs in its flickering light. The door to the attic had evidently not been opened for a while, since it gave a shriek like a soul in torment and Lily held her breath, for surely it had woken Dorcas from her light snooze but there was no further sound from the nursery.

The place was filled from the high arched roof to the floor with boxes and baskets and wooden chests, with strange shapes shrouded in sheets and vague pictures in frames leaning against the wall. For a while she had poked about, studying this and that, wondering what half the objects were and what they had been used for, but the sandalwood chest, the smell of which reminded her of the docks, drew her to it as though she knew it were to have some importance for her. It had a beautifully carved design on the lid, of birds and exotic flowers and at each side a black enamelled carrying handle.

She lifted the lid with the raptness of a high priest at the altar. Though it had a lock on it, it was not locked and inside, wrapped by some careful hand in tissue paper, were jackets and trousers, shirts and caps, a pair of riding breeches, mufflers and boots and even a long, sleeved cloak made of wool. All good stuff so why had it been relegated to the attic? Then it came to her and with the thought came the plan. These were the discarded clothes of a schoolboy. Garments he had outgrown but which were too good, in somebody's opinion, probably Maggie since she was known for her thriftiness, to be thrown away or given to charity. So here they had sat, probably for years, just waiting for Lily Elliott to come along and make use of them.

Because she was tall they had fitted her perfectly in length, though across the shoulders and in the waist she had to do a bit of careful arranging to make them fit. A good belt was a help and with the jacket fastened none would be the wiser. Since it was winter the cloak would be a godsend, not only because it was warm but because it disguised her very obvious female figure. With her hair dragged up to the top of her head and fastened securely with ribbon and the cap jammed down over it, the cloak collar turned up or the muffler fastened about her neck she knew she could pass for a youth. She would have to keep her face hidden as much as she could but that was easy at this time of the year when everyone was muffled up to the eyebrows because of the cold.

So, here she was, sitting on a bollard, seeing for the first time in six years her Pa's schooner. She wanted to cry, not just because the poor old *Lily-Jane* looked such a pitiful sight, but because she was overwhelmed by the memories that flooded into her mind and heart. She and her pa at the wheel that last time they had gone up the coast to Barrow to pick up a cargo of pig-iron. Oh, yes, she could even remember the cargo it was so clearly etched in her brain. Her ma standing at the rails watching the bathers, her smile radiant as she turned to smile at Pa. Mr Porter – where was he now? – and Johnno, her pa's crew and friends, she liked to think, for who could fail to make a friend of her pa? And now they were both dead, her pa and ma and all that was left of that lovely time was this poor old schooner which looked as though she were about to sink into the waters of the dock where she had been berthed, where she had been deserted by whoever had sold her to Liam.

"Grand ole' ship, tha'," a laconic voice, thick with the tones of Liverpool, said in her ear. "Or she were once."

"She still is, or will be when I've finished with her."

She didn't even turn, for her eyes were still lovingly drifting over the wooden sailing ship, studying her two masts which swayed gracefully with the slight movement of the water. The spanker, a small mast made to carry a large fore and aft sail, moved with them, dipping and swaying, and at the pointed stern the ropes that held her to the quayside slapped impatiently against the cold grey stones.

"Oh, aye, young feller-me-lad, an' 'oo might yer be, then?" the voice said, a strong voice but with a quaver in it as though its owner were getting on a bit.

"She's my schooner, mine and Liam's," she said, carelessly she realised afterwards but at that moment of joy she had allowed her defences to drop.

"Is tha' right, an' 'oo's Liam an' . . ."

Lily swung round then and found herself looking into an ancient, seamed brown face with faded old eyes that had squinted into a thousand suns and across a thousand seas. It was the old sailor who had eyed her suspiciously. He had a neat, snowy white beard. He wore a cap which had obviously been with him since he had gone to sea as a lad, a faded gansey and drill trousers tucked into his boots. He had a pipe clamped between his stained and broken teeth but there was something enduring about him, something permanent and fixed like the very granite from which the quayside was built.

Instinctively Lily lowered her voice in the way she had practised, thanking her mother for the slight huskiness she had inherited from her. She didn't know who this old sailor was and she didn't care, but she didn't want anybody poking their nose too deeply into what she was about.

"The vessel belongs to a friend of mine. He means to renovate her when . . . well, at the moment he's at sea but when he gets home we are . . ."

The old man was studying her, still suspicious it seemed, as though already he knew there was something very strange about this rather girlish young man, this . . . well, you could only call him a *pretty* young man. Fair-skinned and rosy-lipped and if he wasn't careful he could fall into the hands of men who liked that sort of thing. Many seaman did. Not him, of course. He liked his women, or did when he was an age for such foolishness, to be women, with deep bosoms and a bum you could hang on to. He felt in his pocket, never taking his eyes off the lad, fetching out a piece of chewing tobacco. He put his pipe in the same pocket, then cut off a scrap of tobacco, shoved it in his mouth and began to chew.

Suddenly he smiled, a genial smile but one that said he might be old but he wasn't soft in the head.

"Wan' a 'and?"

"Pardon?"

"I'm doin' nowt at present," just as though his services were in great demand normally, "an' I know me way round a ship. Bin at sea fer fifty year so I bloody should."

"Indeed."

"So, what d'yer say? I'm lookin' fer a berth an' could sleep aboard. Keep me eye on 'er, like. Tommy Graham's me name an' yer can ask anyone round 'ere, even the piermaster 'imself 'oo'll tell yer I'm 'onest an' reliable."

"Oh, I'm sure you are, Mr Graham, but you see—"

"Polite young feller, aincher?" The old eyes looked into hers and Lily's heart sank. She'd only been here five minutes, five minutes into this big adventure, this wonderful escape into the new life she and Liam were going to share and already she had attracted attention, with this chap looking at her knowingly as though he were perfectly aware that beneath her men's clothing there was a woman.

She lifted her head in the familar gesture of imperious hauteur she had learned over the years but the old seaman continued to smile.

"But that don't mean owt ter me," he went on. "I don't give a bugger what folks do as long as it don't interfere wi' me. I know a good vessel when I see 'er," then he winked though the expression on his face didn't change, "an' this craft's a good 'un. I'd like ter see 'er set up proper an' I know the very place where it could be done."

Lily stared at him, mesmerised, her eyes wide and frightened but he winked again, then, with a gesture to her which seemed to ask her permission, climbed down the little ladder at the side of the quay and jumped lithely on to the deck of the *Lily-Jane*.

For half an hour he poked about, ducking his head into the cabin, the wheelhouse, the bilges, getting out his penknife and jabbing it into the wood. He stamped on the deck and ran his hands round the rail while Lily trailed round behind him, her heart beating so fast with excitement she thought she might choke. She didn't know why she felt she could trust this old seadog, probably because he *was* old and therefore – she hoped – of no danger to her, as a woman she meant. She had the feeling that he knew and if he knew perhaps others would, but she also had the feeling that this was a very astute old man, shrewd, not easily hoodwinked and if he was prepared to accept her as a male, then perhaps others on the docks would do the same.

"Sound as a bell, lad," he told her, looking her straight in the eye. "Wants a bit doin' to 'er but there's nowt a birra new plankin' an' a lick o' paint won't cure. Burrit needs doin' by someone 'oo knows wharr 'e's about."

"You, Mr Graham?"

"Nay, not me, lad, though I knows me way round more'n some. Bu' there's a boatbuildin' yard at Runcorn could fix 'er up a treat."

"She was built there, Mr Graham."

"Aye, I reckoned so. She's the look about 'er of the firm I were thinkin' on. Sturdy an' built ter last or she'd've not lasted this long. A nice little craft." He stood and looked about him, nodding his head as though agreeing with his own words, then turned to Lily.

"What's yer name, lad?" It was said quietly, with no intent to trick. He would say nothing, he was telling her, but still she hesitated. She had learned in the past weeks to trust no man, except Liam, of course, and how did she know that this old chap might not run straight to Joshua Crowther, who had an office in Water Street, and tell him that a "person" was about to take over the running of the ship that had once been his.

Tommy Graham watched the lad as he dithered over the question of his name, wondering what the bloody hell he was up to. Oh, it was well known that it had recently been sold to some chap, some young chap, but this wasn't him. The movement of every vessel, small or large, in this port was known to all the old seamen, men who had existed in dockland for all their lives and *Lily-Jane* was a familiar sight since she had been in and out of Liverpool for years. Belonged to a Richard Elliott once but he'd died and it had been taken over by Joshua Crowther and now, it seemed, this young lad was claiming ownership, so what was it all about? Not that he gave a fish's tit. All he wanted was a bit of work about the docks, about the ships, about the place he had worked in and loved all his life.

Strangely enough, though Lily thought he had seen through her disguise she was wrong. Tommy Graham was short-sighted and, like many an old man who has once been young and strong, was too proud even to think of wearing spectacles. He sensed there was something odd about this young man but though he had given the impression to Lily that he was aware of her gender, in fact he was not. There were some lads who were prettier than others, more feminine in their ways than others and this youth was one of them.

"Dick," Lily said abruptly. After all, Richard had been her pa.

"Right, Dick, wha' d'yer say? Will yer tekk me on? I'll not let yer down."

"Mr Graham, the thing is—"

"Afore we go any further, Dick, d'yer reckon yer could call me Tommy?"

She nodded her head shyly, a treacherously feminine gesture which, had he not been so eager to be taken on, Tommy Graham might have recognised as one belonging to no youth.

"Very well, Tommy, but you see, I have no money as yet. When my . . . my friend comes home – he's on the China run – we hope to have enough to put the *Lily-Jane* to rights, but until then she must—"

"Nay, lad, yer can't leave 'er 'ere in't wet basin or she'll rot inter't water. She needs ter be in dry dock, yer see."

Lily felt her heart sink but then it lightened again, for surely Liam would not have left the schooner he had just bought in a wet dock if he had thought she might be damaged by it.

She said so to Tommy, willing to trust him a little bit, for it didn't seem to her that it could do any harm.

"When'll 'e be back, this friend o' yourn?"

"February at the latest."

Tommy took off his cap and scratched his head, studying the *Lily-Jane* with a critical eye. He sighed deeply, then walked up and down her length which was exactly ninety-nine feet. He stood and pulled at his bottom lip then turned away to gaze out to the river as though looking for inspiration.

"Well, I dunno, 'appen it'd be all right fer a few weeks. She's bin in't water all this time an' p'raps . . ."

"There is simply nothing else I can do, Tommy. She must stay where she is until we have the money, but . . ."

"Aye, lad?"

"I would be grateful if you would keep an eye on her. You see, I can't get down here every day." She shifted her gaze from his steady one. "I . . . I'm . . ."

"Yer don't 'ave ter explain owt ter me, Dick. I'd be glad of a berth on 'er, even if she's only stoppin' in't dock. I've a few bob."

"Oh, no, I couldn't possibly . . ."

"I meant ter keep meself, lad, that's all. I do odd jobs about docks burr I'll sleep on board and watch out fer 'er an' when yer can yer can come down an' we'll do a birra work on 'er tergether. Will that suit?"

Would that suit? She almost fell on his neck and kissed him on his whiskery cheek but she remembered just in time that she was a young man and that young men were supposed to be controlled and unemotional, so she told him that it would and that she would probably be over next week and she did hope he would be comfortable. He said he would be and he'd just fetch his tack over from the seamen's mission where he had a bed at the moment and with much goodwill on both sides they parted company.

She was surprised at how easy it was. She slipped in at the side door without anyone apparently having even missed her and when she glided in to the dining-room that evening with that grace and style she had inherited from her mother she failed entirely to see the speculative gleam in Joshua Crowther's eye. She had been dining with him and Eloise now ever since the day he had taken Villy to the stables, where she had remained, and it seemed that things were running smoothly, effortlessly and Lily wished it to remain like that. After all, it was November and perhaps in eight or ten weeks Liam would be home so best not rock the boat, so to speak. She was polite. She did as she was told. She even took herself to the schoolroom where Miss Kaye was reading aloud to them the tale of *The Swiss Family Robinson*, which she herself had read as a child of eight, but she pretended to listen as she pretended to sew on a sampler and so far Mr Crowther seemed to be satisfied with her behaviour.

She was startled when, as they stood up at the end of the meal, he turned to her and with a courteous smile asked her if she could spare him a moment or two in his study, since there was something he thought they should discuss.

"What about?" she asked him brusquely, the colour of her eyes turning to a glinted silver, her mouth thinning to a mutinous line. Joshua Crowther saw it and was jubilant. He had been seriously disappointed by her docile acceptance of his ruling that she was his daughter and must therefore act as Eloise did. He had heard of her volte-face and consequent return to the schoolroom, her walks with Eloise and Miss Kaye about the gardens, and her acquiescence over the matter of her dog's relegation to the tackroom. He had not liked her submission, which reminded him too much of her mother. He had expected fireworks, a stormy refusal to fall in with his wishes, total defiance which he had been prepared to enjoy before he quenched it. For quench it he meant to do and, by God, he'd take great pleasure in doing it, however it came about. She was glaring at him now, quite forgetting what seemed to be a definite effort on her part during these past weeks to appear meek and accommodating. And he wondered why. It had not occurred to him before but now it did. Why had she surrendered to his dictatorship? Why was she putting on this act of being his compliant puppet when it was so far from her own nature of stubborn determination to do as she pleased, which had been so very evident for the past six years? For that was what it had been, he could see it now, an act.

Now, with just a word or two, she had reverted to her real self, truculent, self-willed, ready to tell him to go to hell in a handcart. She had let the mask of conciliation slip and he gloried in it, for he was ready to enjoy the battle to come.

"Well, shall we go into my study and see?" He smiled.

She wanted to refuse, he could see it in her clamped jawline, but she merely nodded her head and walked stiffly into his study. He followed her, shutting the door behind him. He was still smiling and Lily felt the apprehension rise to her throat, choking her, though she wouldn't let him see it.

"Well?" she said. "What do you want?"

"This," he answered, stepping forward and putting his hand on her breast. For a second, perhaps two, she was so dumbfounded she stood and allowed him to fondle her, to cup her breast and squeeze it, then with a cry of revulsion she knocked his hand away and sprang back from him. He was still smiling, not at all put out by her obvious repugnance, her rage, her loathing.

"You bastard," she hissed, her face contorted but he continued to smile, his hands busy in his pockets. "You killed my mother, oh, yes, you did, you killed her even if it did take six years for her to die, but I'm made of stronger stuff, Mr Crowther, and you won't defeat me."

"My dear, I do hope not but what a great deal of pleasure I shall have trying."

24

She didn't remember very much about the next few hours except in flashes which kept repeating themselves in her brain, distorted and filthy. Filthy, that's how she felt and as she fled from the study and ran up the stairs she wanted to scrabble at herself as though she were crawling with lice or fleas. She tripped on every stair, the hem of her wide silk skirt caught in the toe of her kid slippers so that she was forced to clutch at the banister. She remembered thinking, close to hysteria and already beginning to weep, that that was all she needed, to fall and break her leg or her neck. She tumbled into her bedroom, slamming the door fiercely behind her, desperate to lock it on the horror that seemed to creep up the stairs after her, but there was no key, nothing to keep it out, to keep *him* out should he take it into his head to follow her.

Where was Villy? She needed someone, something to cling to until she had recovered – would she ever do that? – from the shock and panic and dread which Joshua Crowther's hand on her had released in her. Now she realised fully what her mother had suffered, day after day, week after week, month after month, year after year. She had more awareness now of what men and women did together in the act of love. Liam's body next to hers had told her that, his hands on her breasts, his mouth on hers, the surge of his masculinity against her which had filled her with a rapturous joy and need, but she and Liam loved one another, not just physically but with a love that had grown from friendship over the past six years. But this, this . . . greed . . . this lust which she had finally recognised and which had glittered in Joshua Crowther's dark eyes was what had dominated Ma's life and at the end, Lily firmly believed, killed her. She had not fought to live when her child was born and her life's blood had poured from her. She had drifted away with a tranquil smile on her ash white face, Mrs Quinn had told her, glad to leave the man who had treated her like a whore, going to the husband she had never ceased to love.

Now, it seemed, Joshua Crowther had transferred his nasty intentions to her daughter. He had made her uneasy for weeks but she had not attached much importance to it, believing that he did it to frighten her into being the young woman he thought she should be now that she was his daughter. But she had been wrong, woefully, terrifyingly wrong and what was she to do? Liam would be home in February and then she would be safe, but until then who could she turn to to protect her from Joshua's evil? She was alone. She had not even Villy to comfort her. Mrs Quinn was there, of course, where she had always been in Lily's life, willing to do all she could to support Jane Elliott's daughter, but Mrs Quinn was six years older, a grandmother now since her Victoria had married Arnold, the Oakwood groom, and had in four years given birth to three little girls whom Mrs Quinn doted on. There was a whisper that her Victoria wanted her to go and live with her and Arnold and the children in the cottage at the edge of the Oakwood estate, which would mean Victoria could go back to work, but so far Mrs Quinn had resisted as though she knew her lamb's daughter still needed her, the only "family" she had.

Lily huddled on the window seat, staring out into the bitter winter's night. There was a wind keening through the trees; she could hear it even though the windows were firmly shut. The bare branches of the tree that stood beyond the window tapped against the glass and in a small way she felt a tiny shred of comfort, for the tree had always been a symbol of escape for her. A way of winning freedom, a secret way that *he* knew nothing of should he lock her in her bedroom. She had never used it, not yet, but if this man's attentions continued, became worse, if she became trapped she might have to.

Lord, she wished Villy was here. She felt the need to put her arms about some warm creature who would make no demands on her, who would sense her despair and offer comfort, give love and devotion without stint, asking nothing in return. Beauty seemed to have settled quite comfortably with Mrs Diggle, her loyalty to her former mistress a frail thing, but then that was what Ma would have wanted. But Villy. She fretted in the confines of the tackroom. She had Henry and Wally and Alex for company but she pined to be with Lily and had grown thin in the last few weeks. She was only a small dog but her heart and courage were big and she would die in an attempt to defend her beloved mistress. It would give Lily some small measure of comfort, a small feeling of security to have her here in this room, the key to which was in Joshua Crowther's possession. It was little enough to ask, to have Villy with her but he, in his spiteful determination to bend her to his will, would not allow it and the thought that he was winning put a stiffener in her spine and dried her tears which she knew were self-pitying. She was alone. She had been alone since Pa died and alone she would stand up to Joshua Crowther. The first act of defiance would be to bring Villy back.

Without even stopping to put on her warm cloak she was across the room and at the door. Opening it a crack she listened intently but there was no sound bar the slight hiss and splutter of the lamps beyond it. Tiptoeing along the carpeted hallway, past closed bedroom doors and shadowy cupboards, she came to the top of the back stairs leading to the narrow passage which in turn led to the side door and into the small herb garden her mother had revived. Silently as a wisp of fog she eased herself down the stairs and out of the door. As she stole through the garden she could smell the pungent aroma of tansy leaves and for a moment her strength faltered as her mother's sad ghost walked beside her, but then Ma was sad no longer and surely she and Pa, wherever they were, would be watching over her?

She slipped quietly through the well-oiled wrought-iron gate and eased herself left round the dark bulk of the house, the many windows of which threw oblongs of golden light across the dark path. She stepped away from the house to avoid passing through them, moving stealthily round another corner and into the yard at the back of the kitchen. Someone had drawn the window blinds and though she could hear a murmur of voices she knew she could not be seen as she passed through the arched gateway and into the stable yard where again there was no sound except a soft whining which she recognised as Villy in the tackroom.

The blast of icy air whipped round her, lifting her skirts and petticoats and tearing her hair from its neat arrangement of curls, done for her earlier that evening by Mary. Mary was the lady's maid who had looked after her mother and her wardrobe for the past six years and who was now in charge of herself and Eloise. She was a pleasant girl who had been kind to Ma and had the added virtue of being able to keep her mouth shut. She was quiet and self-effacing and could turn the wildest tangle of curls into a most pleasing hairstyle, which she had done this evening, first with Eloise, then with Lily, before going down to the kitchen to join the other servants in their evening meal.

The tackroom door was tightly closed but inside Villy began to make strange noises as though she sensed Lily's presence outside in the yard. She was snuffling at the bottom of the door, scratching a little in her effort to get out and Lily felt a small lift in her spirits at the thought of having the animal with her. She could hear men's voices now, soft and murmuring, coming from the sleeping quarters above the stables and tackroom and one of them laughed. At the end of the row of buildings was Mr Diggle's cottage with a neat little garden in front and a path leading to the orchards, the vegetable gardens, the hothouses which were his domain. A light shone across the garden, warm and golden in the darkness of the night and Lily felt her heart constrict, for she would have given anything to be knocking at Mr Diggle's door and entering its safe haven.

She opened the tackroom door, expecting Villy's warm, rough little body to come hurtling out, dancing on her rear legs in her attempt to jump up into Lily's arms in her joy, but though she could still hear her and the sound of the other dogs as they rustled in the straw at the back of the room, none of them moved and it was perhaps then, in the strange atmosphere that enveloped her, that she knew something was not right. Villy was whining piteously in the back of her throat but Lily couldn't see her, for it was as black as pitch, just as though she had fallen into a deep hole, the earth sliding over her and cutting off any light.

The terror held her for a moment in a frozen block of ice, unable to move, unable to speak to the dogs, to breathe or even think and in that moment, as she became aware that she was not alone, when his voice whispered to her from the blackness she was not surprised.

"I wondered how long it would take you to come for the dog, my dear," it said. It had a hint of amusement in it, a feeling that its owner was pleased and not only pleased but excited. From behind a hard arm wound round her waist, dragging her further inside. A hand gripped her viciously about her breasts and his face pressed itself into the nape of her neck beneath her hair. She could smell brandy – or was it whisky? – on his breath, hot and nasty and his mouth was wet against her shrinking flesh. A second hand came to cover her mouth and the scream that might have saved her was cut off before it had time to reach the men above them. The dogs were silent and she had time to wonder why, even Villy's voice dwindling into what seemed to be a strangled snore, but she had no time for conjecture since she was fighting now, fighting not for her life since he did not want that, but for the sum and substance of Lily Elliott, for the intrinsic quality and core that was peculiar to Lily Elliott. She was fighting for her spirit which would be broken if she lost the battle, for her future with Liam, for her sanity which her ma had clung to somehow in the grip of the vile creature who had now transferred his beastliness to her. If she lost *she* would be lost for ever. It would all be in ashes, what she and Liam had planned, their future together, the *Lily-Jane* and what they were to do with her, so she lifted her feet, going with his weight as he dragged her to the rear of the room. His back hit the wall and he grunted with the force of it, expecting resistance, then she kicked him, backwards and upwards, feeling her soft slippers strike him just above his knees. Dear sweet Christ, if only she had taken the time to change into her boots she could have done him some serious damage, she had time to think, then, turning her towards him, he hit her savagely across her face and she felt the consciousness spin about in her head, looking for a way to escape.

She could feel the prickle of it on her back as he laid her down in the straw next to the snoring dogs. Her arms were flung wide on either side of her like a soul on a cross and his hands began to tear at her skirts, lifting them above her waist, his fingers tugging at the ribbons in her drawers. Her head was thudding on the straw-covered setts as he lifted her this way and that and her hand caught on something that was leaning against the wall. She had no thought in her head about what it might be, no thoughts about anything really, for she was almost senseless as she felt the cold air creep across her naked belly and thighs.

Her hand gripped whatever it was and with the powerful and primitive instinct that is bred in the defenceless female, and with an action that was without coherent thought, she lifted it and brought it down across his back. It was heavy and afterwards she was to dwell on how desperation makes giants of us all, gives strength where none should really be. He made a sound in the back of his throat, not loud, as if even now he wished to keep this loathsome act secret.

Joshua Crowther, inflamed by his lust beyond reasonable thought, beyond rational objectivity, beyond his need to consider his own reputation as a man of shrewdness and cunning, believing only in his own arrogant invincibility, had meant to overpower her and when she was senseless carry her to his room by the same route she, and he, had come by. But the feel of her in his arms, the struggling female fear, the squirming, bewitching movement of her young body, the smell of her in his nostrils, had sent a message to his brain, and to that other mindless but potent part of his body telling it that he could not wait. Not another minute. He must take this lovely, defiant child, dominate and violate her and turn her into his creature, as her mother had been his creature.

He collapsed on top of her, his face pressed into her shoulder. She was almost senseless herself, her mind reeling with horror, her body shuddering with repugnance, but slowly she began to regain awareness of what was happening and though he was heavy she slid out from beneath him and struggled to her feet, dragging at her clothing and returning it to some semblance of decency. He was beginning to moan and now that she had become accustomed to the dark she could see his hands scratching in the straw. She was doing a bit of moaning herself though she was not aware of it. Her body was trembling not only with fear but with disgust, humiliation and a need to be sick.

But she must get away before he completely regained his senses. Get to where there were people, bright lights, safety, wondering as she felt about in the straw for Villy what it was she had hit him with. She didn't care. If her hand had come on a knife she would have stuck it in him without the slightest compunction and gloried in it, but for now she must get Villy and run.

She had meant to make for the kitchen, for in her mind was the thought that she must let them know, his servants, his family and indeed all of Liverpool what sort of man this was. In fact she did not know why she was not screaming her bloody head off right this minute. It would bring them all out, the grooms and gardener's lads who lived above the stables, the maidservants in the kitchen, even Miss prim and proper Eloise to see what kind of a man her father was. She would have him arrested for attempted rape. She would see him in gaol, shown up for what he was. Tell the world what a devil her mother had married. That hidden in the respectable, respected man of business was a lecher, a . . . a pervert – yes, that was what he was and by God she'd have his name all over the town before the week was out. She'd see him dragged through the filth with which he had tried to coat her. She'd finish him in Liverpool and when she'd . . .

"Don't even think about it, girl." His voice came at her from the dark corner where he was attempting to stand up. He was creeping up the wall, hand over hand, his voice shaking, but whether it was with pain or malevolence she could not tell. It slithered about her, menacing and dangerous but in it was the absolute certainty that she would denounce him at her peril!

"It would be your word against mine," he went on, his voice harsh and flat, "and who would believe that an upright, *influential* man such as myself would treat a defenceless girl as you might be considering telling them I did. Oh, yes, I know what you are about to do but think twice before you take on Joshua Crowther, girl. I have a great deal of power in this town. Those with wealth do, you know. I would sue you for slander and, believe me, there is not a court in the country that would believe the word of a hysterical sixteen-year-old over that of a man such as myself. Now, I'd advise you to get back to your room and keep your mouth shut and I'll do the same. We'll keep this between you and I, do you understand, girl, or I promise you you'll regret it."

He was completely upright by now, his back to the wall but it was evident he was in some pain for he made no move towards her.

Without taking her eyes off his shadowy figure she leaned down and picked up the twitching form of Villy, holding her to her like a shield between his voice and herself. She wanted to scream her defiance, tell him to go to hell and rot there but though she had known terror during the last minutes when she had believed with despair that she was to be overpowered and defiled by this man, it was nothing to the dread that crept through her now at his words. She could tell her story to the servants and she believed they would recognise that she was telling the truth, for did they not know what had been done to her own mother. They had seen him dominate her, Lily, over the matter of the dog, and she was sure Maggie and Betsy could not be unaware of the nasty overtones of his conversation at the dinner table, the sordid insinuations which in her naïvety she had ignored.

But that was what they were, servants, ignorant of the ways of the law, most of them unable to read and write, the possessers of good jobs with a man who had been a good master. None of them had been threatened by his peculiar sexual proclivities, indeed they probably were unaware of them. He paid them no attention, for in reality they were no more to him than hands that put his meals – on time – in front of him, well cooked and served, laundered his shirts and polished his boots, groomed his horses and looked after his house and garden. They were satisfied with what they had in a town that was heaving with the homeless, the jobless, the deprived, the underprivileged and would they risk that for the sake of a young girl who would not be believed anyway? *He* would see to that.

She backed away from him though he still leaned awkwardly against the wall. He was no threat to her at the moment, for she had hurt him with whatever it was she had hit him with. She could make out the paleness of his face and his shirt front but that was all and though every nerve in her wanted to scream and run wild and shout to the world that she had been badly wronged, some instinct kept her quiet. She didn't know what, at this moment, she meant to do, but it was not run to the servants and blurt out her horror and pain.

Without a sound she turned and, holding Villy awkwardly in her arms, she began to run back the way she had come. He must have drugged the dogs, she remembered thinking, all four of them, while she was dithering in her bedroom, then waited for her to come to the tackroom. How did he know? He was a devil, Satan himself, with some power, some way of divining in which direction people were going to go and something had told him that she would need comfort, warm flesh-and-blood comfort and since he had not as yet done anything beyond touch her, she would hardly run to the servants with that, would she? He knew her too well. He knew of her attachment for her dog and so . . . Oh, God . . . Oh, God, what was she to do? Liam, Liam, where are you? I need you, I need someone . . . somewhere to hide, for there was nothing surer in her mind than the belief that this was far from over. It was no good appealing to Mrs Quinn or Mr Diggle who, though they would be horrified, would not be able to help her, not with real help that would keep her safe until Liam came for her.

She reached her bedroom and just as though the cry to Liam had brought sanity, a calm reason to soothe her inflamed mind, she knew exactly what she should do. Liam's voice came back to her over the years from when she had been a child, an innocent, confident child who had believed that with the death of her father the worst that could happen to her had happened. He had told her then what to do if she was in trouble though she had scarcely listened but he was telling her again now and this time she did. Though she could not believe that Mr Crowther would come for her again, not tonight, she wished she had a key to lock her door, but she hadn't so in the calmness that had come with Liam's voice she propped a chair beneath the handle of the door and began to make her preparations.

Her mind was clear as it considered the future but her heart was already grieving for what she must leave behind. But what could she do? She had made a vow that she would love and cherish her mother's baby daughter, her own half-sister, but the reality that she now confronted was that it had been a childish vow, impossible to fulfil. Should she go up to the nursery and smuggle Abby out, which would be difficult with Dorcas sleeping beside her, how was she to get the child out of the house and to the destination she had chosen for herself? There would be no room for an infant in that future and besides, Mr Crowther, even if he didn't want her for himself, would not allow his daughter to be taken from him. He would move heaven and earth to get her back and where Lily meant to hide until Liam returned would soon be discovered. Oh, Ma, I'm sorry . . . I'm sorry but what else can I do? I must defend myself and this is the only way. Perhaps . . . perhaps later when . . . when . . . She didn't know how to finish the thought, for she could see no answer to it nor to the future, so with her face wet with tears she turned her mind determinedly to what she would need to go forward into it. Her newest gown of silk, the colour of heather. There was a puff bonnet to match with her pale grey kid boots and her plush patelot trimmed with pale grey fur, for who knew when she might need to look the part of a lady. Petticoats and underwear and all crammed hastily into a carpet bag which was strong, light and roomy. It needed to be light, for she had a long way to carry it.

Dragging out the lady's basket trunk that had belonged to her ma, she dug about underneath the pile of her own clothes which she had long outgrown and which had been kept for some reason, though she didn't know why. It seemed that some habit of thriftiness was ingrained in the servants and it had shown itself in an inability to throw things away. She had not questioned it but had merely burrowed under them to hide her other clothing which she had found similarly packed away in the attic. She took them out now and with that same sense of calm that had come upon her at the thought of Liam began to turn herself from a young girl into a young man. She thought that at some moment in the future she would have to cut her hair, for it was very difficult to get such a mass of it under her cap. It drifted and wisped in the most irritating curls about her face and neck, but she certainly hadn't the time now.

At the last moment she was overcome by the memories invoked by her ma's basket trunk. It was with this piece of luggage that she and Ma had accompanied Pa on coastal voyages aboard the *Lily-Jane*. Happy, it was almost more than she could bear to remember how happy, and unthinking they had been, the three of them. It would last for ever, they had thought, that's if they had thought at all, which she didn't think they did. This was their life, Pa and Ma and her with Mrs Quinn waiting at home for their return, but a twist of cruel fate had decreed otherwise and Pa had gone, and though she had still been alive, so had Ma. There was only Mrs Quinn and Villy left and she was to leave Mrs Quinn behind. Mrs Quinn would probably go and live with Victoria and Arnold and there was nothing Mr Crowther could do to her, unless he sacked Arnold which was unlikely. She doubted if Mr Crowther even knew that his groom was married to his housekeeper's daughter. She must leave a little note for Mrs Quinn before she left, she told herself as she patted her ma's trunk for the last time. She smoothed the rough basketwork and ran her hands round the velvet lining, remembering Ma, and it was then that she came across a small bulge in one of the pockets that ran along the inside at the front.

Her hands trembled, she didn't know why, for it had not yet occurred to her that Jane Elliott might have left some message for her, some message she could not pass on while she herself lived.

She drew it out, a little velvet pouch and inside, beside a scrap of paper, was a necklace, one she had never seen before. Mr Crowther had hung her mother with many fine jewels, all of which must have been worth a small fortune, but this one was simple, a fine network of gold chains like a spider's web no thicker than a thread of cotton among which a dozen green stones hung. That was all it was, nothing ostentatious which was probably why Ma had liked it.

She held it against her breast as she read what was on the note.

Dearest, there is nothing I can give you, or do for you now. You will understand why but there may come a day when you need my help and this is all I have for you. It might buy your freedom, Lily. Forgive me. I love you. I always have and I always will.
   Your loving Ma

She wept in earnest then, burying her face into Villy's rough fur. Villy, though still inclined to totter a bit, had come round and was in raptures to be back with her mistress. She licked Lily's face dry of tears and whined but, knowing she must be away, Lily got to her feet and put the dog on her lead, sniffing and wiping her nose on the back of her hand as she did so. She placed the pouch carefully in her jacket pocket, her heart swelling with love, for Ma had given her and Liam the means to restore the *Lily-Jane* which had meant so much to Jane Elliott's beloved husband but she had no time to sit and marvel at it.

Shoving her arms into the sleeves of the mackintosh which she wore over the overcoat and jacket and pulling her cap down over her forehead, she propped the note she had left for Mrs Quinn on the mantelpiece where it would be found first thing in the morning. It said little, bar she was going away and would be quite safe and that as soon as she could she would be in touch.

Looking round her for the last time she moved bravely to the door on the first of her steps to freedom, to Liam and their new life. Villy kept close to her heels as though she too knew this was a decisive moment in their lives and when the door refused to open they were both somewhat taken aback. Lily gave it a slight shake, turning the knob quietly, slowly, then with more vigour but it was no good. It was locked. Somehow, without being heard, someone, and there were no prizes for guessing who, had crept upstairs and locked it!

But it didn't matter. She had meant to slip out of the side door which would have been much easier with Villy but if that devil thought he had her prisoner, then he was wrong. It would be difficult but she and Villy would get down the tree and be off into the night as she had planned. The devil take him, she hissed viciously, her young face hard and bitter, but there was no time for recriminations. She turned to the dog.

"Come on, Villy. Now you must be a good girl and lie still against me and not make a noise, for it will be the devil's own job to get you down the tree. I'll take the bag first and then come back for you. Not a sound, there's a good girl. I'll have to tie you to me. It's a good job you aren't a labrador."

The house was in total darkness as the two shadows slipped across the lawn.

25

Eva Earnshaw was sleeping the light, restive sleep of the elderly, not achieving the dreamless depths the young know and take for granted, and yet not awake. Somewhere between the two, and when the light tapping impinged on her semi-dreaming state it brought her at once to full wakefulness. Ginger, her marmalade-coloured tabby who slept on the bed beside her, raised her head in the dark, light from somewhere catching her eyes and turning them to a silver translucency. She stretched and yawned and Eva put out a hand to her as though seeking some support, for Eva lived alone and did not care for unexplained happenings, particularly in the dead of night. She listened, her hand still smoothing the cat's fur and when the sound repeated itself she felt the rhythm of her heart pick up in alarm.

"What's tha', d'yer think, Puss?" she whispered to the cat who, despite being named Ginger as a kitten she always addressed as Puss. "It . . . it sounds like someone knocking on t'door but 'oo on earth could it be at this time o' night?"

Like most people who live alone she talked out loud, particularly to the cat, and though she received no answer she always felt that Ginger knew exactly what was going on in her mind. Picking up the cat and cradling her to her flannelette-covered breast, she cautiously threw back the covers, lifted her old, heavily veined legs, and edged her way out of her warm bed, stepping first on to the rag rug which she herself had made and then on to the icy cold expanse of the oilcloth. Her flesh cringed from the contact as she moved hesitantly across the bedroom to the window which overlooked the front of her cottage and the stretch of Lower Breck Road on which it stood. Pulling back the curtains with an unsteady hand, for callers at this time of night surely meant bad news, she peeped through the misted glass to the square of garden that fronted her home. She had not stopped to put on her spectacles but in the hazy light from a million stars she could just make out what looked like a man and beside him a dog. The man was looking over his shoulder as though in dread of something and the dog huddled close to his leg. Their breath wreathed about their heads, for it was a cold night with a touch of the first of winter's frosts coating the grass and spiking the shrubs in Eva's garden to an ivory stillness.

Well, whoever it was out there, she didn't know him and if he thought she was going to open her door to a perfect stranger then he was a fool. Her cottage stood in a row of others, separated from one another by a bit of garden and a hawthorn hedge but if she was to open her window and scream blue murder one of her neighbours would be over here before you could say "knife". But before she raised the alarm it might be a good idea to find out who the chap was and what he wanted.

Cradling the cat closer to her for comfort, she opened the window and put her head out into the cold night.

"Yes?" she asked sternly as though to tell whoever was there that she would stand no nonsense. At once the man looked up, his face a white mask in the starlight. The dog looked up too and gave a warning yip. The animal was not happy, anyone could see that, its glance everywhere at once as though fully expecting every night creature for miles around to be making for this particular cottage.

"Good evening," a voice quavered from below. "I've been given your address . . ."

"Good evening!" exclaimed Eva, her voice amazed, no longer alarmed though she could not have said why. "Good evening! It's middle o't night, my lad, an' wharr I wanter know is wha' yer doin' knockin' at my door this late. 'Oo are yer an' yer'd best 'ave a proper answer or I'll shout fer Charlie Ainsworth 'oo lives next door. Now, speak up," she added tartly.

"I'm that sorry, ma'am, to disturb you at this time of night but, you see, I had no choice. I simply have nowhere else to go."

A refined voice, not of the working classes, curiously light for a man, and not in the least threatening. A tired voice and yet it seemed to be making an effort to be courteous. Not a voice to be afraid of but then would a man with wickedness in his heart sound as though he had?

"An' why is tha', pray? 'Ave yer no 'ome o' yer own tha' yer must be knockin' on decent folks' door at this ungodly hour?" Though in truth she had no idea what time of night it was.

"No, ma'am. And I'm so sorry but I seem to have forgotten your name. I remembered the address when Liam told—"

"Liam!" Eva Earnshaw's voice was sharp. "What's our Liam ter do wi' you?"

"It was Liam who told me I was to come to you if I was in trouble. And I'm in trouble, ma'am. He said . . ."

Eva Earnshaw's heart was doing more than picking up its rhythm now, it was thumping and thudding in her chest, for the word trouble had set it moving far faster than was safe in a woman of her age. Trouble, and yet her Liam was on the far side of the world and what connection was there between him and this thin lad who was hunched on her doorstep? It was weeks since he had left her, kissing her lovingly and holding her against his broad chest and promising to bring her back some magical thing from China, so why, after all this time was . . .

Heavens above, would you listen to her picking over in her mind what the lad wanted and why Liam had told him to come here. She really must pull herself together if she was to get to the bottom of the mystery. There was only one way to find out, of course, and that was to ask the lad in, though she knew that Liam would give her what for if he knew she was inviting a complete stranger into her home in the dark of a winter's night. Still, she couldn't carry on a conversation with her head hanging out of the window and the bitter frost already freezing the flesh off her, could she?

"Wait there," she ordered the lad, just as though he were going to run off the minute she closed the window.

Lily Elliott waited. She had walked mile after mile in the starlit dark, her heart in her mouth a dozen times as unfamiliar night sounds whispered about her, always going north, keeping the lights of the town on her left but avoiding any streets that might have some life in them. She knew roughly where West Derby was, east of Liverpool, but she had no idea how many miles she must walk to get there. She had the sovereign Liam had given her all those years ago but though she had been tempted she had decided against taking a hansom, for it would be easy to find and she was pretty certain Mr Crowther would try to trace her.

And so she had set off, the carpet bag in one hand and Villy's lead in the other, moving along Aigburth Road making towards Princes Park and Lodge Lane which ran in a direct line due north. She had studied maps in Mr Crowther's library, at the time having the vague thought that it might be a good idea to know how to get from Oakwood Place to Liam's granny's, for who knew what emergency might arise, but that had been years ago, while Ma was still alive and she herself had been no more than a child.

She had crossed the shining tracks of the London and North Western Railway, stepping carefully in the pitch dark, murmuring encouragingly to Villy whose ears were back and whose tail was down and between her legs in her alarm. Like Lily she had never been out at night before, except in the familiar surroundings of the garden and she snarled and twitched at every sound. Once some creature ran across their path, making Lily let out a stifled scream and Villy began to bark furiously, more in terror than defiance. The worst part was as they passed the Zoological Gardens where, catching the scent of the animals there, Villy began to bark madly, setting off what sounded like a lion which roared its displeasure. The noise woke several dogs in the vicinity and they all howled frantically and Villy did the same. Lily had to crouch down beside her and hold her head which she kept trying to jerk away but gradually she quietened, shivering against Lily's breast.

Lily knew she was on West Derby Road by this time, for that was where the zoo was situated but she was so tired she wanted to sink down, anywhere would do, and sleep until it was light but she knew that would be fatal. She must find Lower Breck Road which she knew was off West Derby Road but the trouble was she didn't know in which direction. She was pretty sure it must be away from the town and so she turned in that direction, blundering on in the dark, ready to fall into the frozen ditch and even when she found a turn to the left she was not certain in the dark that this was it.

She took a chance. Already she could sense a sort of lightening in the starlit blackness of the night and her instinct told her she must be off the road, it didn't matter if it was in a barn, if she couldn't find Liam's granny's house before the dawn broke. A tall, well-dressed young man with a dog in tow and carrying a carpet bag would be a sight not many would forget on these country lanes and her terror that Mr Crowther might cast his net even as far as this gave her the strength to go on.

She walked on and on, passing the dark bulk of a house now and then. She could feel the rutted lane beneath her boots and smell the aromas of the countryside, for there were farms in the vicinity, but at last she came to the four cottages on her right and on the end one was a small sign that she could just make out. It said "Ronald Biddle, Carpenter" and underneath in small letters, "Ivy Cottage, Lower Breck Road". She was here.

For a moment she felt the tiredness slip away from her in her elation but then came the perplexity of how she was to know which cottage belonged to Liam's granny. She could knock on any door, except Mr Biddle's, and find some disgruntled stranger staring out at her which wouldn't matter if that stranger turned out to be Liam's granny, but she had three cottages to choose from and two were not the right ones. She had no desire to wake them up, one after the other, and ask for . . . for . . . Lord, she didn't even remember her name, she only knew it wasn't O'Connor, or it would have struck in her mind, but then she couldn't just stand dithering here at the gate, could she? She must just take a chance and if the first one was wrong she would keep her head down, apologise, ask for Liam's granny – Dear God, she wished she could remember her name – and make her escape.

For some reason she chose the end cottage. Well, she had to start somewhere and it seemed logical to make it the first cottage in the row. Well, the last really, for Mr Biddle was the first. It was the right one! She had found Liam's granny.

A light appeared in the bedroom, then vanished, blooming again in the far reaches of the cottage which she could just make out through the small pane of glass in the stout door. It came nearer, then wandered off into a side room where a faint orange glow still showed, where presumably a fire had been banked down for the night. Again it shone through the pane of door glass and at last the door opened a crack and a suspicious face appeared. The candle in the old lady's hand revealed a stern and wrinkled face, a face that was highly coloured as though it were accustomed to being out of doors and from that face shone Liam's eyes.

It was the first thing Lily said and if she had thought carefully and chosen wisely she could not have spoken words more likely to please Eva Earnshaw. Not only to please but to reassure.

"You have Liam's eyes," she said impulsively.

"Who told you that, lad?"

"No one, ma'am. I can see them, even in this light."

Lily stood patiently while Villy wagged her tail eagerly and the cat at Eva's back shot straight in the air and began to hiss angrily. It was clear that Eva was confused, not knowing whether to put the candlestick down on the table that stood to one side of the door, reach for the cat and heave it out of harm's way, or open the door wider to allow her visitor to enter.

She tut-tutted irritably. "Be quiet, Puss, yer've sin a dog before now so stop actin' like a fool. Is that dog house-trained, lad? Yer'd best come in an' get door shut an' wipe yer feet an' all . . . I dunno, knockin' on folks' door at this time o' night, it's not proper that's wharr I say burr if yer say our Liam sent yer then I can't refuse yer. Come in, come in outer't cold, an' see, set yerself by't fire. Yer look 'alf clemmed an' yer'd best tie that there dog to't chair afore it goes for our Ginger."

"She won't do that, ma'am." Lily sank gratefully into the armchair by the fire, a visible look of relief on her face. "She's used to cats. My ma had a cat. She had it from being a kitten and Beauty, that was the cat's name, and Villy," placing a restraining hand on Villy's neck, "got on very well together."

"Tha's as mebbe but our Ginger's not used ter dogs so I'd best purrer in't kitchen fer now. She'll not like it," which Ginger didn't, struggling to get through the rapidly closing crack in the door.

"Poor Ginger," the lad said, surprising Eva. "it doesn't seem fair to banish her in her own home but . . ."

Lily's voice trailed away uncertainly as she realised that Liam's granny was looking at her with a very strange expression on her face. It was clear that something was bothering her, something that filled her with suspicion, a wavering look of doubt narrowing her eyes and firming her lips into a distrustful line.

"Never mind our Ginger," she said, lifting her head and folding her arms across her bosom. She had taken time to throw a colourful shawl about her shoulders, one that looked as though it might have come from some far-flung corner of the globe and she held it defensively about her. There was something strange here, her expression said, not just in this lad's sudden appearance on her doorstep in the middle of the night but in his *appearance*, the way he looked and spoke, for in her bone-weary exhaustion Lily had quite lost control of the deeper, more masculine way she spoke and the masculine manner she had adopted.

But Eva was the sort of woman who could not let a visitor into her cosy parlour without offering that visitor a nice cup of tea, as she always phrased it. She was hospitable and warm-hearted and this . . . this person looked as though a breath of wind might blow . . . well, she would say *him* for the moment . . . might blow him clean away. His face was quite grey and there were deep mushroom-coloured smudges beneath his eyes. He was a handsome lad, she decided. In fact he was not merely handsome, but beautiful if such a word could be used to describe a young man. She studied him from beneath her lowered lids as her hands busied themselves with sturdy mugs, with the teapot and caddy, with a pretty sugar bowl and milk jug to match, placing them on a round table across which a snow white, embroidered cloth was flung. She had carefully placed some nuggets of coal on the fire and it was blazing nicely and the lad, his head on the back of the chair was already beginning to doze.

Moving lightly, for, despite her years, Eva Earnshaw was agile, she stepped across another of her rag rugs and before the lad knew what she was about she had whipped off his cap. Even she, who had had suspicions about it, was taken aback at the waterfall of silvery, silken hair which fell over the back of her chair, reaching almost to the floor in its lively tumble of curls. Lily cowered away as though expecting a blow, perhaps not from Eva but from someone of whom she was afraid and Eva put out her hand and smoothed that glorious fall of hair back from the grey face.

"Nay, lass, tha's nowt' ter fear in this 'ouse. I know 'oo yer are now. Our Liam's told me all about yer. An' me name's Mrs Earnshaw. Liam's mam was my daughter."

That night, with the help of Mrs Earnshaw's old hands,

which were steadier than hers, her boyish clothes were removed and she was put in a clean, lavender-scented night-dress which Mrs Earnshaw said had once belonged to her lass who had died when Liam was born. It was said without asking for pity, just a simple remark to let Lily know why she had such a pretty thing, obviously belonging to a young woman, in her chest of drawers. A clean bed, also scented with lavender, a touch of Mrs Earnshaw's hand on her brow, a reassuring lick of the tongue from Villy who crouched on the rug beside the bed and would not be moved, and that was the last Lily knew.

She remembered, with her last thought, begging Mrs Earnshaw not to tell a soul that she was here, for even yet, in the aching depths of exhaustion and shock she was in, she could still feel Mr Crowther's hard hands on her body.

"Nay, lass, I'll tell no one. Sleep tight." And so she did, safe, she knew, at last.

It was dark again when she awoke, dark and quiet except for what she thought might be the tweet and twitter of a bird. No other sound but homely, comfortable sounds. The sighing of the wind in the trees and the patter of rain against the window which helped to make her feel even more cosy. There was a small fire in the grate which sang merrily and before it, stretched out as though she were totally at home, was Villy, her nose on her paws and almost touching the flickering coals. Lily smiled and stretched and yawned, knowing exactly where she was with no sense of the disorientation that afflicts someone who awakes in a strange bedroom. She was warm and rested and ravenously hungry. And no wonder, for it must be twenty-four hours since she had last eaten anything.

There was a chair beside the bed on which was thrown a warm woollen robe which she put on. Villy raised her head and then sauntered over, herself yawning and stretching first one back leg then the other. She pushed her nose into Lily's hand and seemed to grin in that almost human way dogs have, as though to say she was well satisfied with this place they had fetched up in.

Mrs Earnshaw was sitting comfortably before her fire in what seemed to be the only sitting-room in the house. The stairs from the tiny landing led directly down into it and behind it was a kitchen and beyond that a scullery. For the first time Lily looked about her, conscious of warmth and homely comfort, of shining copper and brass, of polish and deep plush curtains, of the fire's glow winking on gleaming surfaces, of peace and, best of all, safety. The bird she had heard was in a cage, a bright yellow thing with beautiful plumage that trilled its heart out in ecstasy. Mrs Earnshaw had fallen asleep, her head resting on the back of the chair, her mouth partially open and from it tiny bubbling snores emerged. Ginger was curled on her lap but at the sight of Villy she affected to be not only furious but terrified, spitting and clinging with open claws to Mrs Earnshaw's bibbed apron. Mrs Earnshaw awoke with a start and a mutter of irritation.

"Yer daft beast," she scolded the cat. "'Tis only Lily an' 'er dog. Anyone'd think it were a pack o' wolves, way yer carry on. Now 'old yer tongue or I'll shut yer in't kitchen again."

All the while she spoke she was smoothing the cat's pretended alarm and Lily was reminded of Beauty who was just such a consummate actress as Ginger.

She thought she would never stop eating and felt quite guilty that as fast as Mrs Earnshaw put the food in front of her she wolfed it down, as did Villy.

"That there animal o' yourn wouldn't 'ave a bite, lass, not so much as a sip o' water whilst yer were sleepin'. She stood guard over yer like a good 'un."

There was hot broth to start with, thick with barley and vegetables and tasty shin of beef, followed by home-made bread and freshly churned butter come from Newsham Farm which was just the other side of West Derby Road, and a couple of soft-boiled eggs. There was a rich fruit cake, only just come out of the oven, Mrs Earnshaw told her, accompanied by a mug of strong sweet tea and she'd a bit of cheese if she fancied it. Or perhaps an apple come from her own bit of an orchard at the back of the cottage and stored away for the winter.

She talked all the time Lily ate, glad, it seemed, of an interested audience, not aware as yet that anything anybody said to Lily Elliott about Liam O'Connor was fascinating to the young woman who loved him. About his mam's death when he was born and his no-good pa who had run off soon after, not wanting the responsibility of a child, and had never been seen since. About his childhood with Eva, his brightness and longing to make something of himself other than a farm labourer which was the usual employment in these parts.

About his goodness to her who, since he had begun to earn, had never had to work in a dairy again. That was her trade, dairymaid, and a hard trade it was, too, but it had kept her and Liam out of the poorhouse until he left his childhood behind. She did not mention the hours she had spent on her knees scrubbing other women's sculleries and kitchens after her long day in the dairy was ended, the evenings potato picking, or fruit picking to earn a couple of extra shillings a week to get Liam through his schooling and on the road to his Master's Certificate. Her pride and love shone out of her rosy face as she related his slow but steady rise to success, his small triumphs as a boy, his escapades, for he was no angel, his cheerfulness in the face of hardship, his gentleness with those smaller and weaker than himself, which was everyone really since he had always been a big lad, like his feckless Irish father before him.

And now he was off to China to make his fortune, he had laughingly told her, for he meant to be his own master. In fact – here she leaned forward confidentially, glancing round as though to make sure that no one could overhear what she was about to divulge – he had already bought a boat. When he had the wherewithal to restore her he meant to trade across the oceans of the world, or at least, smiling at her own foolishness, to the ports about the Irish Sea. He would be a sea captain who owned his own ship and there was no prouder man in the world of shipping and no prouder woman than his grandmother would be when he achieved it.

There was silence for a long moment as both the women who loved Liam O'Connor contemplated his wonderful future. They gazed into the fire, mesmerised, both of them, by the sheer joy of it, then Lily broke the silence.

"The *Lily-Jane*. She was my pa's ship."

Eva turned to her in surprise. "Yer pa 'ad a ship called *Lily-Jane* an' all?"

"There is only one *Lily-Jane*, Mrs Earnshaw. She was named after my ma and me, and when Pa died she was taken from us. I swore I would get her back one day but it was Liam who did it. Liam found me – I was only ten years old – and we became friends. He . . . was good to me . . ."

"Aye, that'd be our Liam," Eva said solemnly.

"When the *Lily-Jane* was put up for sale Liam bought her."

"Aye, my lass, 'e told me."

"He bought her for me, Mrs Earnshaw. You see . . ."

Eva Earnshaw's face became stern and her mouth firmed. Her eyes grew flinty, the lovely blue turning to grey just like Liam's did when he was disturbed.

"What're yer sayin', my girl? If yer tellin' me our Liam 'as done summat shameful then yer can gerrout o' my 'ouse right this minnit fer I'll not believe it."

"No, no, Mrs Earnshaw. You must know that Liam would never shame anybody, you or me. He knew how I felt about my pa and about *Lily-Jane* and . . . well, I say he bought her for me but she belongs to him." Just as I do, she thought, but she did not say this last. Some intuition, a woman's intuition told her this was not the right time to tell Liam's granny that Lily and he were to be married on his return, but she could tell her of their plans to restore the schooner to her former glory and to become partners in her endeavours.

But first she must recount to Liam's granny what had happened to her over the last six years, to her and to her ma. She must go over it all again, painful as it was, shameful as it was, particularly the events of the last few days, for Mrs Earnshaw must be made to realise how important it was for Lily to go about as a young man. There was so much to do before Liam came home and she could only do it under the guise of a male. Any female moving about the docks would be sure to excite interest and it would soon get back to Mr Crowther that a well-dressed young lady was concerning herself with an old schooner, once owned by him, that had just been purchased by a seaman. He might even now know about Liam, for she was certain that he would already have put his spies about looking for her and there were men, labourers and dockers who worked with the ships who had seen her and Liam together.

"Mrs Earnshaw . . ."

"Yes, lass? 'Ave yer summat ter tell me?"

"Yes, I have . . ." and already, before she had begun her tale tears were slipping across her cheeks. Not tears of self-pity but of relief that at last she could tend to the wounds that had been inflicted on her by the cruelty of the man her mother had married. Apply to them the ointment that the telling to another woman would heal and feel them soothed and begin to fade.

She sat on the rug before the fire. She laid her cheek against Mrs Earnshaw's knee and, with Mrs Earnshaw's hand smoothing the tangle of her hair and Villy's muzzle resting in her lap, she began.

26

The young and elegant salesman behind the counter felt his breath quicken and for a moment he forgot the ritual that one employed with the rich and well bred and simply stared, mouth agape.

The beautiful and beautifully dressed young lady, accompanied by a respectable elderly woman in sober grey, stood just inside the door looking about her enquiringly, the expression on her face revealing nothing of her inner feelings which, if the salesman had been aware of them, might have surprised him. She turned and smiled coolly in his direction in that way the gentry have when faced with an inferior, then gracefully crossed the vast expanse of luxurious carpet towards him, her wide skirts swaying, and it was then that he remembered who and where he was.

He hurried out from behind his counter and bowed. This was no tuppeny-halfpenny establishment catering to the lower middle classes but a well-known jeweller's and silversmith's where the grand and wealthy families of Liverpool were wont to spend an hour or so choosing something that was invariably connected with precious stones. Nevertheless he felt he was in the presence of someone special, perhaps even a member of the aristocracy. He had never seen her before but the patrician lift to her head and her slightly condescending air impressed him immeasurably.

"Good morning, miss," he declared, his manner somewhat obsequious, for though he was sure of his establishment's worth as a superior jeweller's among the high-class shops of Liverpool, he felt the need to be more than polite. He allowed his admiration to show in his eyes for a moment, for it did no harm to flatter a lady a little as long as it was respectful, and his admiration was not only respectful but genuine. "May I be of help to you?"

He bowed again and pulled out a chair, a little gilt and velvet thing with legs so frail it seemed incapable of supporting even the slender weight of the young lady, fussing about her until she was seated, then did the same with the elderly woman though not quite so tenderly.

"I'm not sure. We were admiring one or two pieces in your window, weren't we, Mrs Earnshaw, and decided to come in and have a closer look. By the way, I have left my carriage just beyond the corner. Will it be safe there? My coachman is somewhat nervous of the traffic where his horses are concerned but I assured him that it would be all right."

"Oh, I'm sure it will, miss. There is always a constable on duty along Bold Street keeping an eye on the carriages of the ladies who shop here."

"Well, that is a relief. Now, if we might . . ."

"Of course. If you would just point out the piece of jewellery you wish to look at I will get it for you."

Another gentleman appeared from some back recess of the shop, bowing and smiling and wishing them good morning. It was plain from his manner that he had appraised the quality of the young lady who was sitting as straight-backed as a duchess in the velvet chair, noting the cut of her gown of heather blue silk and the handsome three-quarter-length sleeved cloak she wore over it. It was slightly shaped to her waist, spreading widely over the fashionable, crinoline-supported skirt of her gown and had wide, pagoda-like sleeves. It was made from plush in the same blue as her gown and was much trimmed about its edges with a pale grey fur. Her bonnet, which he knew to be called a puff bonnet, since he made it his business to know the world of fashion, was the very latest, worn with a forward tilt to accommodate her full and shining, silver pale chignon. She was *very* fashionable; expensive, he would have called her. His expert's eye also noticed that though she wore no other jewellery she had a very fine pair of pearls in her ears. She was very evidently come from a good family which did not let its daughters out alone, for she had her chaperone with her.

"Aah, Mr Dismore." The young salesman addressed him deferentially. "This young lady . . ."

"Yes, yes, thank you, Mr Andrews." Mr Dismore was quite

resplendent in his black frock-coat and waistcoat to match. He wore well-fitting dark grey striped trousers with a strap beneath his highly polished black boots. His collar stood up stiffly under his chin, keeping it in a somewhat supercilious position. His large neckcloth was also in black. Mr Andrews was similarly attired but it seemed to Eva Earnshaw, who spoke little but saw all, that the quality was not so good as his employer's. They both wore a neat buttonhole, a white carnation, specially supplied each day from the florist's on the market. It was a touch Mr Dismore thought in keeping with his reputation as one of Liverpool's finest jewellers.

He waved away the young gentleman, who was obviously his underling, with a disdainful gesture. "I will attend to Miss . . . ?" He waited urbanely, enquiringly, for "Miss" to reveal her name but she merely smiled and said nothing.

"I am Thomas Dismore." He had no choice but to go on, since she seemed unwilling to do so. "The proprietor of this establishment. I happened to overhear you telling Mr Andrews that you were interested in something in my window. Now if you would be good enough to point out . . ."

"Having seen the display you have inside your shop, Mr Dismore, I must admit to being spoiled for choice but if it is no trouble to you might I have a look at that beautiful silverwork set with . . . well, I'm not sure what the stones are but, really, I don't think I have ever seen anything quite so exquisite. Have you, Mrs Earnshaw?" turning to her companion.

Wooden-faced, Mrs Earnshaw said she hadn't.

"It is no trouble at all. You have good taste, Miss . . . er, if I might say so. The pieces are Scandinavian and the gems are called peridot. That particular shade of palest green goes so well with the silver, don't you think? Mr Andrews" – he clicked his fingers peremptorily – "be so good as to get the Scandinavian pieces from the window."

Lily was enchanted with the jewellery and had no need to act out the part. There was a fine bracelet, delicate leaves set in links, between each link a peridot surrounded by finely wrought silver which was shaped to look exactly like diamonds. There were earrings, tiny bunches of grapes hanging from silver leaves and a brooch that was fashioned like a newly opening rosebud, in its centre a pale green gem.

"Might I . . . ?" She held the earrings to her ears.

Mr Dismore clicked his fingers for a mirror and at once Mr

Andrews produced one, watching, both of them, with evident pleasure, as the young lady tried them on, turning her head this way and that. Mr Dismore managed to sneak a quick look at the pearls she had removed from her ears, noting their fineness and even the hallmark on the setting of gold.

"Mmm," she said, glancing about her. "I really love them don't you, Mrs Earnshaw, and I'm sure Papa would approve but . . ."

"Perhaps you might care to glance at some other pieces, miss?" Mr Andrews said boldly.

"What a good idea." She stood up. "Might I . . . ?"

"Of course, please look around."

The shop was tastefully appointed as befitted a jeweller's and silversmith's of Mr Thomas Dismore's standing. There were discreet, glass-fronted cases in which, on velvet cushions, were arranged perhaps one small piece, a delicate gold-framed pendant set with diamonds or a white jade necklace comprising five square pendants set with rubies and emeralds in gold. In one case was what was known as a *grande parure*, a complete set of matching jewellery including a tiara, earrings, a necklace, bracelet and a ring glowing with rubies and sparkling with diamonds.

"It belonged to a celebrated European princess," Mr Dismore breathed into her ear. "The stones are of the finest quality so naturally that is reflected in the price."

"Exquisite," Lily murmured, drifting gracefully across the deep pile of the royal blue carpet to study a necklace of dark purple amethysts, each gem surrounded by natural pearls and set in gold.

"Look, Mrs Earnshaw." She turned to smile at her chaperone. "Oh, do look, is this not exactly like the one Aunt Julia has?"

Mrs Earnshaw obediently got to her feet and moved to stand next to her, regal as a queen, looking down into the glass case with her charge.

"Aye, I believe it is, lass," she said, pressing her shoulder against Lily's and Lily began to think Mrs Earnshaw was enjoying this charade as much as she was. The two gentlemen hovered behind them, eager to show her this and that, watching her as she studied a tray of rings, exclaiming over one that held a rose diamond set in leaf-shaped silver on a triple silver shank.

"Oh, look at this, Mrs Earnshaw. I love this one. Perhaps

I could persuade Papa to buy it for me for Christmas. Is it not beautiful?" She slipped it on her finger and the two gentlemen sighed, mesmerised that it not only fitted her, but that she should do them the honour of admiring it. They watched her every movement, their eyes dwelling on her lovely, expressive face, on the exquisite shape of her rosy mouth which curled at the corners as she smiled, at the soft swell of her breasts which peaked delightfully above her tiny waist, at the widening of her incredible eyes as she caught sight of some further wonder. There was a tiara of diamonds and pearls, a necklace of mother of pearl so fine it was transparent, a gold chased locket studded with emeralds, pearl chokers and exquisite hatpins of gold and silver, of ivory and amber.

"Mr Dismore, I really have not seen such lovely things, even in London. Don't you agree, Mrs Earnshaw?" Mr Dismore swelled visibly with pride and Lily was to wonder, in the part of her mind not involved in this play-acting, how easy it was to dupe a man. Smile and simper and flatter and the fool was eating out of your hand, even a businessman like Mr Dismore, but then they had not yet got to the important part, the tricky part and of course that would be the test. If he did not oblige her in that then her plan would fall apart about her ears.

"You are most kind, Miss . . . er . . . most kind." Still she did not supply her name.

Suddenly she whirled about, her skirts dipping to reveal a tantalising froth of lace, her face rosy and smiling.

"Mr Dismore, would it be too much to ask that I bring Papa to . . . well, it is almost Christmas." She dimpled enchantingly, wondering as she did so how she knew how. "There are so many lovely things here and I'm sure my sisters – I have three, Mr Dismore, not to mention two sisters-in-law – would be thrilled to . . . Oh, Mrs Earnshaw, shall we take the carriage back at once? Papa will be back from hunting, I'm sure . . . We are staying at Knowsley, Mr Dismore. Do you know it?"

Did he know it? Was there any man in Liverpool in the world of business and trading who did not wish he could be connected in some way with the greatest estate in the north-west? His elation was such that he was ready to kiss the young lady's hand, for already his head was juggling with figures which, if his calculations were correct, might run into thousands. Three sisters and two sisters-in-law, if you please, and, of course, the added benefit of becoming known to the family who resided at Knowsley. What a feather in his cap that would be.

"I would be honoured to meet your father, Miss . . . I am here at his disposal—"

"Oh, Mr Dismore, there is just one more thing," she interrupted him, putting her small white hand on his sleeve. He resisted the temptation to pat it, in an avuncular manner, naturally.

"Yes?" he enquired, his expression almost fond.

"Papa did ask me if I might do an errand for him."

"Yes."

"It is this . . . this . . ." She reached for her reticule and rummaged about in it, bringing out a velvet pouch. "It belonged to my . . . mama." Her voice broke quite genuinely and Mr Dismore, sensing tragedy, allowed himself this time to pat her hand. "She . . . she died early this year and . . . well, in the aftermath, this necklace was never insured. Papa asked me to have it valued for that purpose. Could I prevail upon you . . . ?"

"My dear young lady. Nothing could be simpler. It is a lovely piece, certainly." Taking an eyeglass from his pocket he scrutinised the stones which, he noted to himself, were particularly fine emeralds. "Might I have a few moments?"

"Of course, but if I may I must just send Mrs Earnshaw to let Thomas – he is the coachman – know we shall be no more than . . . than . . . ?" She raised her eyebrows and smiled enquiringly at Mr Dismore.

"Five minutes, my dear." Mr Dismore felt he might be allowed to call this bewitching young lady that.

"Five minutes, Mrs Earnshaw. Oh, and you may as well wait for me in the carriage. It is not our carriage, you understand, Mr Dismore. Our host insisted on lending it to me this morning. He is kindness itself."

Mr Dismore was so gratified to be allied to the owner of the great estate of Knowsley, even in such a tenuous way, he was ready to do a jig and when he told Lily the value of Ma's necklace, so was she. He bowed her out of the shop, stepping on to the pavement so that for a horrid moment she was afraid he was going to escort her to the non-existent carriage, but she shook his hand and smiled in that way the pedigreed class have when they are dismissing an underling, then sauntered off with the velvet pouch in which was her and Liam's future tucked safely inside her glove.

There were several good-class jewellers along Bold Street, Lord Street, Upper Arcade and Church Street and in each one she and Mrs Earnshaw repeated the performance they had put on for Mr Dismore and in each one it succeeded. By the time they had reached the last one in Upper Arcade Lily knew exactly how much the necklace was worth, having had it confirmed, with a guinea or two difference here and there, by five experts and therefore knew how much she was going to ask for it. Perhaps she might have to come down, ask less than it was worth if only to get rid of it but at least she was aware of its true value and could state a price.

And that is exactly what she did. The last jeweller they called on was somewhat taken aback when she bluntly told him that she wished to sell the necklace and even more taken aback when she told him how much she wanted for it.

"Now then, young lady," he began, smiling. "I cannot possibly give you that much for a piece of jewellery which, for all I know, will be hard to resell," believing that a lady, for that was what she was, surely, would have no idea of the quality of the emeralds and even less what to ask for them. He was nonplussed when she began to gather up her reticule, the velvet pouch and the necklace, standing up with her companion and preparing to leave his shop which was not quite so sumptuous as Mr Dismore's.

"I'll waste no more of your time then, Mr Jenkinson. I might have been prepared to come down a fraction but . . ."

"How much is a fraction?" he asked her bluntly.

From there, over a period of twenty minutes in which Mrs Earnshaw had to sit down she felt so faint and Lily could feel the sweat break out and cool under her clothes, they haggled, but at last, knowing she could do no more, Lily agreed on a price, her only condition being that he paid her in cash and at once.

The jeweller, who knew he had got the best of the deal, sent his man to the bank, since he did not keep such a large sum in his shop, she must understand that, and for a further twenty minutes she and Mrs Earnshaw sat and waited, doing their best to look unconcerned and wondered whether, instead of the cash, the assistant might fetch a constable.

That night, in the safety and warmth of Mrs Earnshaw's

little cottage they sat, one on either side of the fire, their knees up to the blaze and went over every minute, their eyes, even the old lady's, alive with glee. They relived every perilous instant, reminding one another of this moment and that when they had been certain the game was up, laughing now that it was over but telling one another that they would not have missed it for the world. Mrs Earnshaw, who had not known such a vast amount of money existed, was to a certain degree concerned to have it casually left lying about in her cottage, saying that her Joseph had never earned as much in the whole of his life.

"Mrs Earnshaw, dear. No one but you and me know the money exists, except the man who gave it to us and he hasn't the faintest idea where we live. He is hardly likely to go knocking on the door of his lordship's house to find out, is he? He knew he had made a good deal. Besides, it is safely hidden under the floorboards in Liam's room with a chest of drawers over it. How did you know that that hidey-hole was there, by the way?" she asked curiously.

"Oh, when t' lad were a nipper 'e liked to 'ide 'is bits o' treasures, conkers an' such, thinkin' I knew nowt about 'em so I never lerron. I never dreamed it would come in so 'andy one day."

Lily gazed into the fire, absorbing this new picture of Liam as a young boy, a young boy growing up before she was even born. A boy with conkers and old coins and a catapult, and all the other things dear to the heart of a growing lad, things he had kept secret, or so he thought, from his granny. She knew she was sleeping in his room, in the very bed he had slept in then, and all about the room were signs of his occupancy. Books like *Masterman Ready* by Captain Marryat, *The Last of the Mohicans* and *The Three Musketeers*. Pictures framed by himself, his granny told her, of lovely sailing ships on stormy seas, small jade carvings he had brought back from India and China, and his boyhood clothes, which she was to wear on her next trip down to the docks, hanging in his wardrobe and smelling of the lavender his grandmother dried herself.

Eva smiled into the fire then turned to Lily, bringing her from her reverie.

"Lass, I 'aven't 'ad such a good time since our Liam an' me threw a party fer't neighbours when 'e went away. By gum, I'll not forget that chap's face in a 'urry when yer sed that about

Knowsley. 'E nearly curtseyed to yer. Eeh, it were a stroke o'
genius an' I'll say this, yer a clever lass an' if anyone can get
that there boat back on't watter 'tis you. An' thing is, we did
nutten wrong. It might've felt like it but yer never done owt
wrong. I wouldn't've 'elped if yer 'ad, yer know that, don't
yer? That were yer ma's necklace what she give yer" – for
Mrs Earnshaw had been shown Ma's last note to Lily – "an'
yer was entitled ter sell it if yer wanted."

"Yes, I know that, Mrs Earnshaw, but if I could have kept
it I would have done. It belonged to Ma and I believe Pa must
have bought it for her. She would not have left it for me if
. . . if *he* had given it to her, but there's just one more thing
I want you to do for me. I know you won't like it and I'm
sorry myself, but I have no choice. I . . . I must be safe, you
see, until Liam comes home when . . . well . . ."

"Wharris it, lass?"

"Will you cut my hair for me?"

Tommy Graham was delighted to see his young friend again
and said so a dozen times as they studied what needed to
be done to the *Lily-Jane* to get her ready for her sail up to
Runcorn. Dick was dressed more suitably today in an old
pair of breeches of dun grey and a navy blue knitted gansey
which had seen better days, with a pair of rough woollen
trousers and sturdy boots. Over it he wore a pea jacket of
warm pilot cloth which was too wide in the shoulders but
apart from that fitted well enough, and a battered peaked cap
of tweed pulled well down over his pale hair. He also had
on a pair of wire-rimmed spectacles and smelled strongly of
lavender. Tommy made no comment, however, at least about
the lavender.

"I'd about give yer up, Dick, 'onest ter God. It's four weeks
since yer was 'ere burr I've kept me eye on 'er. Slept on board
an' all an' wait 'till yer see wharr I done in't cabin. Well, I
thought as 'ow I might as well mekk meself useful an' be
gerrin on wi' summat 'til yer come back. I didn't know yer was
short-sighted, lad," he added as he led Lily along the deck.

The spectacles belonged to Mrs Earnshaw's dead husband
who could not read but liked to pretend he could. He used
to study any old newspaper he found lying about in the
ale-house he frequented on a Friday night after he had been
paid, sitting outside his cottage of a summer evening with it in

his hands. He would shake it out and peer at the print through his spectacles just as though he were reading the news but the spectacles were made of plain glass and were for effect only. It was his one weakness and his widow told Lily she believed that if a man had one weakness only, a good man who was a good husband, then where was the harm in it? The spectacles, more than anything else, helped Lily with her disguise. They drew the eye away from her lovely face, making her seem not exactly plain, for that she could never be, but, as Mrs Earnshaw said, it was a well-known fact that anyone, man or woman, who wore spectacles was considered homely.

"Oh, yes, just a little bit," she said in answer to Tommy's remark. "I can manage without them most days but sometimes when I'm tired . . ." Her voice trailed away indecisively but Tommy, who was a man who could keep his own counsel, said nothing more.

The cabin was quite splendid. Tommy had relined the walls with a lovely polished walnut, so pale it was almost the colour of honey. The floor he had relaid with a darker wood, and set against the wall were two new bunks, one above the other and carved most intricately with a pattern of leaves and flowers. The ones her parents had slept in when Ma was aboard and which had been rotten with worm and damp had gone. It smelled of the fresh aroma of new wood and polish and though there was nothing else in the cabin in the way of furniture it seemed to breathe of life and hope and the future.

"Oh, Tommy, how lovely," she whispered. "How on earth . . . ?"

"There were a brig bein' done up in dry dock up yonder so I scouted about a bit ter see what were bein' chucked out an' got this lot cheap."

"You must let me reimburse you."

"Yer wha'?"

"I . . . I have some money now, Tommy, enough to get *Lily-Jane* back to what she was before . . . before" – she had almost said before Pa died but caught herself in time – "she fell into disrepair and whatever you spent I shall pay you, and a wage as well. I want you to be part of the crew, if you are willing, because . . . well, though I love the sea and *Lily-Jane* I'm sadly lacking in seamanship. I need someone to teach me and I was hoping . . ."

She could swear there were tears in the old man's eyes as he gazed in wonder, first from his efforts in the cabin, to her face and then back again. He stumped over to the small porthole and rubbed the glass vigorously as though it were that and not his eyes that were blurred, then, with a hurried wipe with the back of his hand across his face, he turned.

"I don't know 'oo yer are, Dick, or even if that's yer name but I'll tell yer summat. Yer've found a shipmate in old Tommy Graham an' that's a bloody fact. D'yer know, lad, I'd sail wi' yer fer nowt just ter ge' watter under me feet again. An' I'll tell yer this an' all, yer'll be t'finest seaman ter sail from't port o' Liverpool when I've done wi' yer. Shake on it, will yer?"

It caused quite a commotion in the vicinity of Canning Dock when the *Lily-Jane* edged her way from the quayside towards the lock gates where the piermaster supervised her leaving, along with a dozen others, when the tide was right. She had mouldered for months, falling more and more into a state of disrepair and the men who worked the docks had known that if someone didn't take her in hand before long she would be beyond repair. They hated to see it, even those who did not go to sea, for they loved ships and the sea did these Liverpool men. When old Tommy Graham began to take an interest, lovingly doing this and that they could scarcely believe what he told them about her resurrection which was to take place in the near future. But here she was, floundering like some wounded animal but under the guidance of old Tommy, helped by the slender youth who looked as though the first stiff breeze in the river would have him over the side. Nevertheless, under Tommy's shouted commands he was making a fair job of deck-hand and good luck to the pair of them. Off to Runcorn to have her seen to, old Tommy had told them proudly, and as she turned into the river with Tommy at her wheel there was a great cheer and waving of caps just as if a new ship were being launched. Even the piermaster was fired with enthusiasm, wondering as he watched her sail slowly out into the middle of the river why the lad who was working under Tommy Graham's guidance seemed so familiar!

27

Joshua Crowther studied the tall, lounging figure of his son, envying him his youth and vitality, the smart uniform he wore which made him immediately attractive to every woman in the room, and the dashing nonchalance he seemed to have acquired since he left home. He had always been a mother's boy – when his mother was alive, of course – and by the time she was dead it was apparent to Joshua that it was too late to make him into the son he would have liked. A copy of himself, in fact. Nicholas was gentle, kind to those who served him, considerate of ladies, soft-spoken, meticulously polite, and nervous with his father! Of his own father. He seemed to be perfectly at ease with others, with guests who came to the house, with his friends, those he brought home from school, with the young ladies and gentlemen with whom he went riding, shooting, hunting, in the company of others of his own class, but he appeared to shrink within himself the moment he was alone with his father. Personable, popular, but weak, that was how Joshua would have described him, taking after his mother and what man wants a son who takes after his mother?

But he was exactly what all young girls dream of, as the circle about him testified. He was tall and lean, his years in the army slimming him down to the strength and fineness of the sword he carried. He had a narrow waist and the tight soldier's trousers he wore clung to his hips and the contours of his slim buttocks. His legs were long and shapely in exact proportion to his body. His eyes were a deep chocolate brown framed by long, girlish lashes and his well-shaped mouth was inclined to smile, providing he was not in the vicinity of his father. His hair was thick, dark, curling in a most delightful way about his ears and neck and falling over his forehead in an untidy tumble that was the despair of his commanding officer.

He was wearing the uniform of the Liverpool Regiment in which he was an officer: a scarlet tunic with a high, stiff collar and a silk net sash over his left shoulder. His sword belt was of white enamelled leather and his trousers were a dark blue with a narrow red welt down the outside of each leg. Since he was only a second lieutenant he bore no badge of rank. He was laughing at something one of the young ladies had said to him but the moment he became aware that his father was watching him he flushed, like a young girl, Joshua thought contemptuously. He was not the man his father wanted him to be and, therefore, Joshua had not been totally disappointed when Nicholas had stated, boldly for him, that he did not wish to follow a career in Joshua's business but was intent on taking a commission in the army. Joshua realised that it would have been very irksome to work beside this hesitant, irresolute son of his who flinched when his father raised his voice, so he had made no objection, particularly as it cost him nothing. Nicky had money of his own, for his mother had been a wealthy woman in her own right and had left her son well provided for. He was the catch of the county and surely would be irresistible to any young woman, the still, small voice in Joshua Crowther's warped mind whispered.

Nicholas Crowther had joined the 1st Battalion of the King's Regiment (Liverpool) when he was eighteen and now he was almost twenty-two. It seemed army life suited him. He had served in the second Chinese war in Peking and on the North-West Frontier, honourably it was said, though the picture of his son with a sword in his hand was one that did not come easily to his father, and was due another tour of Ireland when his leave was finished. But before that his father wished to discuss a little matter with him which he intended doing the moment the party was over.

He turned to look at his daughter, his eldest daughter that is, for his youngest was a mere babe in arms and was asleep in her nursery.

He was proud of Eloise. She had done well for him, since this evening was an engagement party for her and the young man she was to marry in the spring, John Patrick, the son of

Sir William Patrick who held a hereditary baronetcy and had a vast estate in Derbyshire. His girl would be *Lady* Patrick one day when the old man had gone and though there was little money, which was probably why Eloise's somewhat meagre claim to breeding had been overlooked, what did it matter? He was prepared to part with some of his cash since it could do no harm in business to mention casually his landed son-in-law. He was a complete nincompoop, of course, with a laugh like a horse and a face to match but Eloise was, like himself, a realist, and was well satisfied with the bargain that had been struck for her. She stood beside him now, already practising her gracious role as a baronet's wife, her arm through that of her future husband, looking quite glorious in a dress of cream satin with an enormous skirt. It had a tiny bodice covered in crystal drops with short puff sleeves. Her bosom was quite magnificent, as every man in the room was aware, even her future father-in-law, though her future mother-in-law was none too pleased about it, believing it was not suitable for so young a girl to have on display the charms that should be seen only by her husband in the privacy of their bedroom. Not even then sometimes! Eloise sported a great, old-fashioned sapphire ring which had been in the Patrick family for generations and was well suited as the half-smile she directed at her father informed him. He smiled back. They understood one another, did he and Eloise.

"There's a man to see you, sir," the quiet voice of Maggie, his head parlourmaid whispered in his ear, and he swung round sharply, for surely the stupid woman could see this was no time for callers. He said so, his mouth twisting in the snarl that was becoming more and more familiar to his servants.

"Get rid of him, Maggie."

"Sir, he was most insistent. He said I was to tell you it was about the little matter of . . . of the young lady."

Joshua Crowther's face did not change expression but a gleam lit his eye, a strange gleam which Maggie did not care for and she stepped back hastily.

"Show him into my study, Maggie, and tell him I'll be along directly."

"Yes, sir." Maggie dropped a curtsey and slid from the room. She had been serving drinks at the buffet supper

314

which Mr Crowther had asked Mrs Kelly to arrange to celebrate Miss Eloise's betrothal. Rosie, Betsy and Maggie Two were still in the drawing-room, circulating among the guests with trays filled with glasses of the most expensive champagne money could buy and later would help to serve the buffet laid out in the dining-room. Mrs Kelly had made a wonderful feast and even Mrs Quinn had been roped in to help. Mrs Quinn, ever since the disappearance of Miss Lily, had lived over at her daughter's cottage which stood on Holmes Lane, right on the edge of Mr Crowther's property. She had been devastated, they all had, wondering what had happened to drive the child away like that, though most of them, including herself, had had a fair idea. But Mrs Quinn had whispered in her ear that she had word that Miss Lily was safe and staying with a friend, probably to do with that big chap who used to come along the shore to meet the child.

She didn't like the look of the man who waited for her in the hall. A ferrety-faced sort of chap with small eyes and a big nose and a mass of face hair hiding his mouth. He was polite enough though, thanking her profusely as she led him into the master's study and asked him please to be seated.

She was on her way across the hall in the direction of the kitchen when the master hurried out of the noise-filled drawing-room, in so much of a hurry he almost knocked her down.

"Sorry, sir," she apologised though it was not her fault, but he took no notice, hurrying towards his study door with the strangest look of anticipation on his face, just like a child on its way to a much-looked-for treat.

The guests had all gone. His daughter had retired and those guests who were staying over – her future husband and in-laws included – were safely tucked up in the comfort his money provided. They pretended they were indifferent to it, being used to a draughty old mansion two hundred years old between Buxton and the Peak Forest and he supposed he would be expected to restore it to some sort of habitable state, the kind his daughter was used to. In the meanwhile they wallowed, there was no other word for it, in the warmth and luxury of Oakwood Place. He'd be glad to see the back of them all, though he thought he might miss Eloise, but if his plans came to fruition and by God, he meant to see they did, then he would not be lonely.

The knock on the door interrupted his pleasant reverie.

"Come in," he called, turning to smile at the tall and honourable figure of his son who already looked distinctly uneasy.

"You wanted to see me, sir?"

"Come in, boy, come in. What d'you say to a nightcap?"

"Well, I have had—"

"Nonsense, one more won't hurt," overruling his son as he always did and his son allowed it, as he always did.

"Now, sit down and let's you and I have a little talk, shall we?"

When they were comfortably seated he raised his glass, smiling in his son's direction. "A toast, I think, to your future, my boy, which is what I wished to discuss with you."

He took a deep swallow of his whisky, indicating that Nicky must do the same and though his heartbeat had quickened at his father's words about his future, Nicky obediently took a sip. He shuddered slightly, for he did not care for the taste of whisky. His father noticed it and his lip curled but he said nothing. The last thing he wanted at the moment was to antagonise his son, for he was the linchpin of his plan, a tortuous plan which, if he had divulged it to anyone, would have been considered the work of a madman. And he supposed he was slightly mad on the subject of Lily Elliott but that did not worry him. He had gone through life bulldozing aside anyone or any obstacle that had stood in the way of his achieving whatever it was he wanted. In business and in his private and social life. One way or the other he got his way and he meant to have it in this. He was prepared to wait. He didn't care how long it took but he meant to succeed. He had brooded over it for weeks now and it was as clear and sharp in his mind as any strategy he had ever devised. But first he must persuade – *force* – his son to come round to his way of thinking. Well, that was not exactly it, for, naturally, he would not tell him the way of it all but he meant to make him see, and would not the girl herself do that, what a splendid idea it was.

He had known almost from the start that there was a man involved. He had questioned every one of the servants, indoor and out, and it had not taken long for him to force it out of the half-witted gardener's lad that Miss Lily met a "big chap" down on the seashore. A big chap! Sweet Christ, the thought that some other man might have taken what he himself lusted after was at first enough to turn his mind, which is probably what it had done, he supposed, not at all concerned. The images of some other man tasting that youthfulness, that freshness, that ripe innocence, that sexual attraction of which she was unaware nearly undid him and the gardener's lad had backed away from him, terrified of the blood that suffused his face and eyes, the harshness of his breathing, and when the boy had bolted from the room it had taken Joshua an hour to compose himself to a semblance of his normal self. And tonight the man he had hired had brought him the news he wanted!

He stared into his glass of whisky and said idly, "Have you ever considered marriage, my boy?"

Nicky gaped. He almost dropped his whisky glass, the question was so unexpected. He had thought his father was about to do his best to persuade him to leave the army, which he loved, and join him in the business or . . . or . . . well, he couldn't think of anything else that might be to his father's advantage, for that was what everything in this house was concerned with. His father's advantage. No one else mattered, not even Eloise who had been sold to the highest bidder, the son of a baronet, which would bring prestige to the Crowther family. It was not that Eloise minded, far from it, she loved the idea of becoming *Lady* Patrick but if she hadn't, if she had fallen in love with a man her father did not approve of, it would have been just too bad!

He couldn't answer he was so confounded.

"I see you are surprised, my boy, and I suppose it is because Eloise is to be comfortably settled that it entered my mind. I would like you to be the same."

"But I'm not yet twenty-two, sir," Nicky managed to gasp, "and my career has not yet really begun. I love the army and—"

"I am not asking you to leave the army, Nicholas. Far from it but . . . well, it is the fact that you are in a somewhat dangerous job that makes me think that if anything were to happen to you our name would die out. Oh, I know we are not what is called an old family, but we are an honourable one and I would like to see it continue. If you were to marry some suitable young lady, with you commanding officer's permission, of course, she could remain here while you continue to soldier wherever you were sent. She would bear your children and eventually become mistress of this house. In fact, she *would* be mistress of this house, here waiting for you when you have had enough of soldiering. I know that many wives of soldiers accompany their husbands when they go abroad but it is a custom of which I do not approve. The climate ages them and kills their children, or so I have heard. In my opinion it is far better they remain at home and—"

He stopped speaking abruptly, aware that he was becoming too intense and that his son was staring at him with something like horror on his face. He had gone too far, too quickly, talking as though Nicky were already betrothed, as though the girl in question were already a fact – as she was to him – as though it were more or less settled and only the matter of where the bride was to live while her husband was abroad was all that needed to be decided.

"I'm sorry, my boy." He grinned in that particularly engaging way he could summon at will and was relieved to see his son relax and even smile a little. "I'm carried away, you see, at the idea of grandchildren to continue our name and . . . our business. I know you have no interest in it, which was a sore disappointment to me – no . . . no, say nothing, it is too late now – but the thought of all that I and my father built up crumbling away for the want of a firm hand on the tiller is sometimes . . ." He even managed a break in his voice as he bowed his head and he was jubilant to see his son edge forward in his seat in sympathy. But he had not yet finished!

"I had not told you this, Nicky, but some months ago I saw a . . . a chap in Harley Street; you know, the place in London." He sighed dramatically. "Well, it seems I've been overdoing it a bit and must . . . take it easy, or at least *easier*. Oh, don't fret, lad, I'm far from done for yet and I have some good men working for me, but it would give me no end of a lift to know that one day there would be someone to carry on. Perhaps even yourself when you have had your fill of adventuring."

"Father, I had no idea." Nicky's voice was soft with compassion and his father felt the contempt work in him, wondering how a grown man could be so taken in by a few sad words. But what the hell, if it worked with this boy, for that was what he still was, then that was all to the good. Now, all he had to do was introduce Lily Elliott into the conversation, but he had no need to fret since his son did that for him. Well, not exactly her name, but the subject that they were discussing.

"It need be of no concern to you, my boy. These things happen but you see now why I'm so keen for you to . . . to be settled."

"I do, sir, but I cannot marry without a bride and how can I find such a person when I'm away so much? She would have to be . . . I would have to be . . . attached to her. You understand? I could not marry without . . . love."

Dear sweet God, did you ever hear such balderdash, but wasn't it typical of this soft-headed son of his. Love! As if that mattered when the woman in question was Lily Elliott. He remembered the day he had seen her mother and the way he had been bowled over by her frail beauty. That had been the closest he had ever come to loving a woman. It had come on him like a thunderclap, changing him from one man to another in the fraction of a second but it had not lasted. He had wanted her, her body and her soul, and when he had them both he had lost interest. He had been obsessed by her for months but it had taken the act of physical possession to cure him, for she had been as passive as a dove in their marriage bed. But her daughter would be different, he was convinced of that. What he had wanted from Jane Elliott was multiplied a hundredfold to what he wanted from Lily. If his obsession for Jane had spurred him on until he had her, this with her daughter was different in every way, as different as Lily was to Jane. Jane had bowed her head to him but Lily had defied him, sneered at him, shown her contempt and total lack of fear for him, her hate and loathing and she would fight him to the end. This was far, far more than an obsession. It was driving him to madness, a goad, a spur in his side that would not let him be. He knew he could never, ever get her back in his house, never, but his son could. If Nicholas could be persuaded to take her to wife and she could be persuaded to accept him, be convinced that he, Joshua Crowther, as Nicky's father and her father-in-law, was no threat to her, then he had won. He would win!

"Nicholas, dear boy, I have the very girl for you and since you already know her and, I think, are fond of her, then I can see no need for looking about us any further. Ah, I see you are bewildered."

"Bewildered is hardly the word for it, sir. I am totally amazed and can only say that I think you must be—" He almost said "mad" but something in his father's face stopped him. "I am to sail for Ireland at the end of January and can hardly conduct a courtship in that time. Then there is the girl's family, whoever they are . . ."

"There will be no difficulty there, my boy, since she has none."

"Has none? What do you mean? Who is she? And how do we know she will be willing and how do you know *I* will be willing, sir?" Nicky Crowther's face was set hard in the first defiance he had ever shown his father and Joshua took a deep breath, for this might be tricky. But then when had he ever shirked a challenge? In fact he loved one. It was the stuff of life to him and if this callow youth thought he was going to put a stop to his, Joshua Crowther's carefully conceived plans then he was in for a rude awakening.

"Son, will you do something for me . . ."

"I must warn you I cannot marry unless my heart is in it, sir." Nicky's voice was stern.

"I know that, my boy. You have told me so quite forcibly but will you listen to me for a moment, then decide. You must, of course, visit Lily before—"

"Lily?" Nicky's mouth fell open.

"Yes, our own Lily who has been so ill I have had to . . . well, you must remember her mother who suffered with a nervous complaint but who fully regained her health and even, at the end, gave me another child."

A child he had not seen in the six months since she was born, though Nicky was meant to believe by the way he said it that he cherished her.

"Of course . . ."

"Lily was devastated by her mother's death, as I was, and I'm afraid . . . well, I was forced to put her in the care of a woman in West Derby. Country air and total peace and quiet and I'm happy to say it is doing her the world of good. I could not leave her here with the child since she was unstable. You understand . . ."

"Dear God!"

"Indeed."

"Then . . . ?"

"I propose you go and visit her. Nothing would be more suitable but there is one thing I must add before you do."

"Yes, sir?"

"She . . . it . . . the illness left her with some strange fancies in her head which the doctor assures me will fade in time. She imagines things, poor girl, though in every other respect she is quite normal. I have decided to leave her with Mrs O'Connor for the time being since she is making such a wonderful recovery but I can only impress on you, that's if you take to each other, how happy I would be to know she is . . . safe. Safe with you."

Nicky shook his head in wonderment, not only at the sad tale his father had told him, but at his father's goodness and compassion, two characteristics he would not have believed could thrive in his father's heart. It seemed he was mistaken and he didn't quite know how to answer. He had been home on several occasions when he had had leave, just for a day or two now and again, and had been conscious of his father's wife and her pretty daughter on the periphery of his own life. But that was all. He had never really known either of them. He had been at school and then in the army, spending most of his holidays and leave with relatives or friends, since he was well aware what his father thought of him, and, more to the point, what he thought of his father. But it seemed he had misjudged him, and, besides, he would like to see the delightfully pretty little girl who had lived in this house for the past six years.

"There is just one more thing, Nicky, if you would oblige me."

"Of course, sir." Nicky found he quite enjoyed this comradeship, this warmth, this feeling of being in his father's confidence which he had never known before.

"The servants know nothing about Lily. They believe she has gone to stay with friends and I would like them to remain in the dark. You know what these women are like. They'd be visiting her on their days off, since I know she was a favourite of theirs so . . ."

"Of course, sir, you can rely on me."

"And Nicky . . ."

"Yes, sir?"

"If you don't find Lily to your liking you have only to say so, but if she is anything like her mother she will be a blessing to you, as her mother was to me."

For a second a picture flashed through Nicholas Crowther's mind and he grasped it uneasily. It was of a woman on the seashore, a woman of delicate beauty and yet at the same time of desperate sadness. A woman who carried tragedy about her in an almost tangible aura, like a mist which blurred that same beauty. She had been afraid of him, he had sensed that even though he had been no more than a boy, and he had wondered why. Why should he be a threat to his father's new wife who clung to her young daughter's hand as though to let go would heap all the horrors of hell on her?

He shook his head to clear the vision and at once it had gone, though it seemed to leave an unpleasant taste in his mouth.

"So, Nicky, will you go and see Lily? Will you call on her and tell her . . . well, perhaps it might be better if you took no messages from me."

"Oh, and why is that, sir?"

"She . . . in her illness she took against me, my boy, and I don't wish her to be reminded. Just visit her as though it were the most natural thing in the world for you to do, which it is since you are in a way related. If she asks how you knew where she was, tell her . . . tell her Mrs Quinn gave you her address. You remember Mrs Quinn, don't you? She was housekeeper when your stepmother was alive but she has retired now and gone to live with her daughter. I believe Lily kept in touch with her."

There was nothing Joshua Crowther did not know about his household and all those who lived in it. And all those who had once lived in it. For the past eight weeks he had been gathering information, unbeknown to them, using the clever, ferrety-faced man who had called on him this evening. He had gathered it all in, like a farmer harvesting his crop or a squirrel hoarding nuts against a harsh winter, collecting every whisper and rumour no matter how trivial it might seem. He even had the name of the "big chap". He knew of the *Lily-Jane* which had once been his in lieu of a debt owed him by Richard Elliott, and the identity of the man who had worked on her recently.

And he knew that he and Lily Elliott had sailed on her to Runcorn only a few days ago, delivering her to a shipbuilder to be restored and had returned via the steam ferry which plied between there and Liverpool.

She would be at the cottage in West Derby now.

28

The old lady who answered the door blinked at the sight of him. Her eyes had the vague and unfocused look of the dim-sighted and yet despite their vagueness they were the most vivid blue. With the arrogant ignorance of the young he thought she must be near a hundred, she was so wrinkled and grey-haired, and yet behind her stare of feeble-mindedness he had the feeling her brain was as alert as his own. Her eyes wandered from him to his bay which he had tethered to the gatepost and which was settling down to a good feed of hawthorn hedge.

"Aye?" That was all. Polite enough but letting him know she had neither the time nor the inclination to stand gossiping on the doorstep, even if he was the smartest thing she had ever seen in his soldier's uniform. He was not to know that her heart was thumping so hard she was sure he could see the beat of it under the bib of her apron. Her expression remained impassive.

"Am I speaking to Mrs O'Connor?" he asked her, removing his forage cap gallantly, ready to salute her, she thought, and had she not been so alarmed she might have preened a little. And really, *alarmed* was not the right word, for she was terrified out of her wits since she knew exactly who he was. Had not the child described to her in the minutest detail every single member of the household at Oakwood Place, just to be on the safe side, she had said, and this could only be that devil's sons. A soldier, Lily had said, and this was a soldier and though he was smiling the nicest smile and looked as though he hadn't a mean bone in his body Eva felt the thrill of dread creep along her old veins. How had he found them? How, after such a few short weeks, had Joshua Crowther's son found the secret haven Lily had secured for herself? She had felt safe, or as safe as she could be until Liam came home, she had said earnestly to Liam's grandmother, unaware that her innocent little face gave her away. Liam was her hero, it seemed, her support and comfort and when he came home she would be truly safe, but until then only Liam's grandmother, herself, in fact, stood between her and the family from whom she had fled.

"Mrs O'Connor?" the soldier repeated, his smile deepening, although he was beginning to believe that perhaps the old lady was a bit simple. The old lady thought it might be advisable to let him continue to think so.

"There's no Mrs O'Connor 'ere, lad, an' I'd be right obliged if yer'd tekk that animal away from me front gate. It's eatin' me 'edge," she snapped at him, ready to shut the door in his face, for hiding behind it was the girl who, presumably, he was looking for. Lily had just come back from her trip to Runcorn and they had been about to sit down and drink a cup of tea while she told Mrs Earnshaw all about the marvels and wonders she had seen and the marvels and wonders that were to take place on her pa's schooner. And not only that, for on the journey Tommy had told her she had the makings of a first-class seaman! It had only been a short trip from Liverpool to Runcorn but she had obeyed all his orders regarding the sails, knowing which one was which and standing ready to adjust one should it be needed. *Lily-Jane* needed a crew of four but somehow they had managed it between them, sailing into the dock at Runcorn quite unscathed. Of course, they had chosen a calm day. Enough wind to drive them smartly along but the river as flat as a pewter plate.

She had been that excited, hopping about from foot to foot like some overgrown child, her face flushed, her eyes ablaze with exhilaration, her sadly shorn hair standing in a silvery halo about her head. It was a mass of tangled curls, blown about by the breeze on the river, for she had taken off her cap on the outward journey and already it was beginning to grow again, falling about her ears and neck in the most endearing way. That was what she was, endearing, this child who loved Liam; oh, yes, she could not hide it from Eva Earnshaw, and whom, she suspected, Liam loved in return. How could he help it? She had a way with her, a warmth and liveliness which had worked itself into Eva's heart and if this soldier thought he was about to come in here and wreck all their lives he was sadly mistaken. They had been so careful, too. Lily never left nor returned by the front door, slipping out from the scullery into the secluded bit of back garden, making sure there was no one about before moving like a breath of wind through the back hedge, the bit of orchard, across the field at the back of Elm House and on to Breck Road which led to Everton Brow, Richmond Row, across Scotland Road and on to the dock area.

It was fortunate that it was winter, they were to tell each other every time she went out, and cold, for it meant she could wrap up well in her layers of young man's clothing, Liam's boyhood clothing which Eva had altered for her, and which totally diguised her femaleness. With her cap pulled well down and her scarf pulled well up, it was hard to see even her lovely eyes which were almost invisible behind her Bert's spectacles.

It might have been easy to hide Lily when one of her neighbours called on her, which they had a habit of doing, for she was a sociable woman and had always welcomed them in the past, but it had been a bit tricky to explain away the dog. Villy barked, as dogs do, at every sound that was not familiar, and when Sadie Ainsworth had called, Eva could hardly shut the door in her face, could she? Sadie and she had been good neighbours for years, a comfort, not only to Eva but to Liam who liked to think someone was keeping an eye on his granny while he was away.

"I'm just mindin' 'er fer a friend." It was all she could think of to say when Sadie stood on the doorstop and stared in surprise at the small furry animal who leaped up to greet her like she had springs in her back legs. She was a friendly little thing who welcomed company and, like her mistress, you couldn't help but take to her, which made Puss very jealous.

"Wha' friends tha', then, Mrs Earnshaw?" Sadie asked, stepping over the threshold as she always did in expectation of a cup of tea and Eva had no choice but to let her, hoping to God Lily was well hidden behind the bedroom door. It had to be faced sometimes, the neighbours' questions, for they must have heard Villy bark. Dear God in heaven, it was hard to remember where she was up to sometimes, but she'd lie her head off for the poor lass who had been so badly treated and who, it seemed, their Liam loved, and so she did, hoping the good Lord would forgive her.

"Oh, 'tis one o' my Bert's old drinkin' pals from't Grimshaw Arms. 'E . . . 'e died, yer see, an' . . . well, 'is lad come up an' said would I see to 'is dog fer a week o' two, so I said I would. She's a grand little thing, though our Ginger don't like 'er."

"No, I don't suppose she would."

If Sadie was surprised, since Mrs Earnshaw's Bert had been dead these twenty years, she said nothing. Not daft was Sadie, and if Mrs Earnshaw had some secret, which Sadie had begun to think was the case, it was nowt to do with her.

The soldier stood his ground though his face showed his surprise. He was a good-looking lad, dark as the night with eyes like chocolate and skin the colour of old amber just as though he'd been in the sun for too long. She remembered Lily telling her that he was in some God-forsaken place on the other side of the world so she supposed that was where he'd got his dark skin.

"Well, I was given this address by a Mrs Quinn," he said, flushing – she could see it even through his amber colour – as though he were lying and for some reason she became even more afraid. He couldn't get past her without becoming aggressive and if he tried she'd scream her bloody head off until Ronny Biddle, who lived at the end and had a small carpentry business in the shed at the back of his cottage, and was always about, came running.

"I don't know anyone o' that name," she lied politely, her face inscrutable. At the back of the door she sensed Lily's sudden start but her hand, which the soldier could not see, made a gesture that told Lily to keep quiet and to keep still. The lad had been given the wrong name, a name that was not hers but was Liam's and it would be wise to keep that fact from him until she and Lily had a chance to talk. He'd said Mrs Quinn, who was about Lily's only friend, had given him this address but, knowing Mrs Quinn by reputation, Eva was convinced she would not give it to the son of the man who Lily feared above any other. She was tempted to ask him, right here and now, if he knew what his father had attempted with a sixteen-year-old girl, the daughter of his own wife, but if she did it would give it away that she knew Lily. And besides, her instinct told her that not only was Lily in danger but that menace might be directed at Eva's grandson.

"Will that be all?" she asked the soldier, preparing to shut the door but at that moment, as though she caught the scent of something familiar, the blasted dog ran to the door and wagged her tail. She put her head on one side, considering the man at the door, her ears pricked, then, losing interest, she turned away and began to nose at Lily's hand where she stood hidden.

"Why . . . I know that dog," the soldier said. "I can't remember her name but she belonged to my . . . my step-sister. I've seen them together on several occasions. What is she doing here, Mrs . . . ?"

"Wha' she's doin' 'ere is nowt ter do wi' you, young man. That's if she's t' same dog which she's not. She's my dog, give me by . . . anyroad, I'd be glad if yer'd gerrof me doorstep."

"Villy, that was her name. Villy." The soldier looked inordinately pleased with himself, his young face breaking into a smile and at the sound of her name the dog, struggling in Lily's arms and not caring for the restraint on her, gave a heave and ran out from behind the door. She sat down abruptly and scratched her ear, then stood up again and looked at him, waiting to see what he would do.

"I've come to see Lily, madam. I mean her no harm, really I don't. I'm sorry that I told you a lie about Mrs Quinn but I thought . . ."

"There's no Lily 'ere neither, young man," Eva said despairingly. "I dunno, first Mrs . . . whatsername . . . then Lily. Yer'd do well ter get yer facts right afore yer go botherin' decent folks wi' yer nonsense. Me name's . . . well, what me name is is nowt ter do wi' you so you'd best be off. If yer don't I'll shout fer me neighbour an' then yer'll cop it."

She was doing her best to shut the door, dragging at Villy's collar as she did so when Lily stepped quietly out from behind it. Her face was like paper, her eyes enormous, haunted as though by some nightmare, but she squared her shoulders bravely and lifted her shorn head.

He did not recognise her. It was January, mid-winter and though it was not quite three o'clock, already a misty dusk was falling. The candles had not yet been lit and the only light was from the briskly crackling fire.

He was turning away, he was actually turning away, ready to apologise, returning his forage cap to his head, drawing his soldier's grey frock-coat about him when the flames of the fire caught on a fresh piece of wood that Eva had thrown to the back of the fire before the knock came to the door. As it flared up it lit the left side of Lily's face and he gasped, for though this was a young man standing before him he was the reincarnation of his father's second wife.

"Who . . . ?" His voice could barely be heard.

"You'd better come in," the apparition said, then turned away, shoulders that had been so courageously held slumping in what looked like despair.

"She wasn't there, Father. Whoever gave you the information made a mistake. There is no Mrs O'Connor. There is no one living at that address but an old lady whose name I forget and her young grandson who, I suppose, is about twelve years old. They did their best to be helpful, even calling in the woman next door to see if she knew of anyone answering the description of Lily but I'm afraid a blank was drawn."

Joshua Crowther looked into the bland face of his son and knew he was lying. True, the man he had hired to find Lily had not actually seen her at the address in Lower Breck Road but he was a man who had a reputation for reliability and tenacity and if he said Lily Elliott was living there, then she was. So he had got the name of the old woman wrong. Well, that didn't matter, but what did matter was that this son of his, who had gone cantering off on his bay this noon to call on the girl who was his step-sister, to befriend her, and then, if Joshua's plan worked, to court her, was lying to him, which meant that whatever tale Lily had told him he had believed.

And yet his face was as innocent as an infant's. His eyes were steady and clear of all deception and his father wondered what it was that had put backbone in his son at long last. He was not to know that Nicky had fallen, like Lily's father before him when he saw her mother, instantly and enduringly in love. He had followed the old lady, who had shut the door firmly behind him, in a daze of bewilderment into the tiny, firelit parlour. He had been ordered to sit down in an armchair by the side of the fire and he had obeyed silently, all the while staring at the back of the slim youth with the silver-gold curls, thick and swirling in a short cap about his head. The young man had stood with his hand on the frame of the doorway leading into some back recess of the cottage, clinging to it as though for support. The old lady lowered herself into the chair opposite him, folded her hands in her apron and waited.

The boy turned then and was not a boy but Lily Elliott!

"I don't understand," Nicky stammered. "Why are you dressed like that . . . like a boy? I don't understand. My father said . . ."

"So you are here on behalf of your father, are you, Nicholas Crowther? What has he told you to say to me? Are you to coax me to come back to Oakwood and . . . and . . ." She bowed her head, unable to go on, then she raised it again and her eyes were fierce with hatred.

"He killed my mother, did you know?" Her voice had taken on a light, conversational tone as though she were relating some misfortune that had happened to someone else. "My mother was not to have any more children, so I was told by . . . a friend. When I was born the doctor . . . but *he* didn't care. He wanted another son, so it was said, and so he never left her alone. They say that rape cannot take place between husband and wife but he raped her for six long years. But the death of my mother bearing the child he forced on her was not the only thing he did to her, for she was his . . . Once he locked her in their bedroom for a week and Mrs Quinn said he . . . Dear God . . . he did many dreadful things that I knew nothing of then since I was a child but I know now. So, now that my mother is dead it seems he has taken a fancy . . . to me. I am to be his next victim, did you know that, Nicky? He . . . laid hands on me." Her voice became ragged but she forced herself to go on. "He . . . he tried to rape me."

"Please, Lily . . ."

"He didn't say 'please, Lily'. He just threw me down and tore at my clothes and he would have succeeded had I not . . . I hit him with something but even then, when I had freed myself, he threatened me so I had no choice but to run away. He was right, you see. It would have been his word against mine, though I dare say Mrs Quinn might have backed me up. She knew what had been done to my mother, you see. So, there you have it. Your father is an evil man and, it seems, has even persuaded his son to do his filthy work for him. I don't know how you found me but it certainly wasn't Mrs Quinn who told you where I am for she doesn't know."

"He said you had been ill and that he—"

"I could have been ill. It quite makes you feel ill to be mauled by . . ."

The old lady stood up and moved towards the girl who stood, head bowed, by the kitchen door. She put her arm round her shoulders, clucking soothingly as a mother would with a child, but Lily inched away from her comfort as though she would stand on her own, as she had vowed to do when she left Oakwood Place.

"I shall have to find another hiding place now, for I know he will hound me, as he hounded my mother, until he has what he wants."

"No, Lily, believe me, I won't tell him, I promise." As he was speaking he wondered why it was he had been so naïve as to believe his father's tale of compassion and pity for his devasted step-daughter on the death of her mother, for there was no man in Liverpool who had a harder heart than Joshua Crowther. He had heard tales of his ruthlessness in business, his lack of any sort of feeling for those weaker than himself whom he watched go under without a qualm then took what little they had. He had despised his own son because he was not cut from the same cloth as himself. He had sent him away to school as soon as his mother had died and had not encouraged him to come home, even in the holidays. Nicholas had known no affection since the death of his mother and not until he had become an officer in the army had he found what could be called a family. So why had he believed what his father had told him? He didn't know but he knew this, he would not be taken in again. He had lived a carefree life since joining the army, enjoying the freedom and easy camaraderie, the social life to which, as an officer in a smart Liverpool Regiment, he was entitled. He had given little thought to anything much beyond enjoying himself, but his sudden deep flowering love, he could call it nothing else, seemed to turn him, he could feel it in himself, from an easy-going boy with nothing on his mind but pleasure to a man, a man with a great responsibility to this young woman whom his father had done his best to damage.

He would do anything in his power to keep her safe. He

would not let him get his hands on Lily Elliott again. Oh, if he could persuade her to it he would marry her as his father wanted him to do but he would never take her back to Oakwood Place. What a bastard he was, what a clever, conniving bastard he was, using his own son to get his filthy hands on this lovely girl, for Nicholas Crowther believed her story implicitly and if it had not involved a great deal of dreadful publicity for Lily, would have persuaded her to go to the police.

But that wouldn't do so he must protect her.

Joshua Crowther was still dressed in the black of mourning into which the whole country had fallen at the death of the Prince Consort just before Christmas and Nicky wore a black armband on his sleeve. The sad event had irritated Joshua inordinately, for it had been expected that all businesses would put up their shutters until after the funeral and he had lost one or two good deals because of it.

"So," he said disarmingly, drawing on his expensive cigar and reaching for the glass of brandy that stood at his elbow, "you are telling me that Lily no longer resides with the woman who was looking after her."

"That's if she was ever there, sir, which seems unlikely."

"You could be right, my boy. I never actually took her there myself so it seems we have both been made a fool of. Well, she must be somewhere and as I am concerned for her safety I shall make it my business to find out where."

"Oh, is that necessary, sir?" Nicholas said smoothly. "She is probably with relatives. Surely her mother's family would take her in."

"As far as I know she has no family. Her mother was an only child and I know nothing about her father. He died before I met Jane."

"I see, sir, then . . ."

"Then it seems she has . . . run away, my boy, and God only knows where she could be. But can I just say how much I appreciate your trouble. As to marriage, well" – he smiled his engaging smile, his dark eyes twinkling almost roguishly – "we must look elsewhere for a bride, mustn't we? A well-set-up chap like yourself will have no trouble in that quarter, I'm sure. Now, I'm for bed so I'll say goodnight and see you in the morning. Would you care to come hunting with me, perhaps? It starts from old Anstruther's place so . . ."

He noticed the hesitation in his son's voice and he smiled inwardly, for if the boy thought he could get the better of Joshua Crowther he was a worse fool than even he had believed.

"I'm sorry, sir, I have other plans."

"Of course, then perhaps we will meet at dinner. The Patricks are to go tomorrow, thank God, and it will be pleasant to be alone again."

"Are you telling me that there is absolutely no recourse open to me to get my ward back home again, Barker? That a sixteen-year-old child, a young girl, is to be allowed to wander about unprotected, living God knows where."

"You don't know where she is living, Mr Crowther? But I thought—"

Joshua made a sound of extreme irritation. "Of course I know, you fool, but I can hardly go barging in without some legal paper to say I am entitled to bring her home, can I? If she were my daughter . . ."

"But she is not your daughter, Mr Crowther." Mr Barker, of Barker, Barker and Jenkins, Solicitors, did not like to be called a fool, even by such an influential man as Joshua Crowther. "She is not even your ward from what you tell me, since you did not make the necessary legal arrangements. Is that correct?"

"Yes." Joshua shifted in his chair and pushed to the back of his mind the lie he had told Lily to the contrary.

"When her mother died you made no arrangements to become her guardian?"

"No."

"Why not, sir?"

"Because I did not think it would be necessary. I was not to know the silly child would take it into her head to run away, was I? And if—"

"Why *did* she run away, Mr Crowther? Have you any idea? She had a good home, luxury, affection, one presumes, and—"

"Dear God, man, are you implying she was mistreated?"

Joshua's brow was drawn down menacingly over his eyes and they glared into those of the solicitor. He had come to the conclusion after the sorry affair with Nicky had failed so miserably – and he supposed now it had been a daft idea, for could you expect such a fool to do anything right – he had better do what he should have done in the first place and that was to get the law on his side. It would be easy enough. Lily was a minor with no known living relatives. He himself was a family man with an impeccable reputation, so surely all he had to do was tell this blithering idiot to get on with it. To draw up the documents needed and then he could ride over to the cottage in Lower Breck Road and, with the help of the man he had hired, remove her from the protection of that woman, whoever she was, and return her to her rightful place which was in his home.

Albert Barker watched the shift and play of expressions that crossed his client's face and felt the first stirring of alarm. There was something . . . furtive about Joshua Crowther, something that was not quite right. He supposed the man was at liberty to be concerned about his dead wife's daughter but he had the strangest feeling that there was more to it than that. And he didn't really know why. Crowther had always been an arrogant man, even boorish at times, powerful in the town and therefore feared by many of the men with whom he did business. If he was crossed Albert had heard he could be quite terrifying and looking at him now he could quite believe it.

"So, what do you wish me to do, Mr Crowther?" he asked him patiently.

"My dear man, you have just told me there is nothing you can do. If there is no legal document you can draw up to . . . to insist that Lily, as a minor, must return to her home, to her family, then I am wasting my time."

"You could always have her made a ward of court, sir, if you believe she is in moral or physical danger."

Joshua sat forward eagerly. "That sounds just the ticket, Barker. What does it entail?" ·

"You would have to take your step-daughter to a magistrate's court where it must be proved that—"

"Would *she* have to be there?"

"Oh, yes, indeed."

"Allowed to speak to . . . to the judge or the magistrate or whoever presides over such matters."

"Oh, yes." Mr Barker sat back in his chair and wondered again why it was he felt so damned uneasy. Crowther was biting his thumbnail, frowning, his eyes staring at something only he could see and when, suddenly, he stood up and made for the door, Mr Barker also wondered why he felt no surprise.

"I'll think it over, Barker, and let you know. Who knows, the minx might come home of her own accord."

"I do hope so, Mr Crowther, I really do."

29

They had been in Upper Duke Street for two weeks when Tommy sent word that *Breeze* had been sighted in the mouth of the river. It was the second week in February and the vessel was a fortnight late.

For a moment she and Mrs Earnshaw just stared at one another in stunned, open-mouthed wonder, for though they had been waiting for this day since the beginning of the month, expecting the moment daily, now that it was here they were speechless. Then, as though prodded by the same goad, they were galvanised into action, beginning to rush about in high excitement, even Eva Earnshaw who, though fifty years older, became infected by Lily's intoxication.

"I want to look my best so I must wear my gown, Mrs Earnshaw, even if it will be a shock for Tommy and the other men to realise that I'm a girl and not a boy." Mrs Earnshaw smiled inwardly, for she had the feeling that the old seaman, who had been to their rooms a time or two in the last weeks to report on the progress of the *Lily-Jane*, had already guessed.

"I must be as presentable as possible, you see." Presentable, what a word to use to describe the girl who was as lovely as a spring morning, as exquisite and sweet-smelling as newly bloomed jasmine and yet as unconscious of it as a new-born infant.

"Now that Liam will be home there is no more danger," she chattered on. "Not with him to protect me. I won't have to wear boy's clothing any more, except when we sail on *Lily-Jane* which we will be doing soon. Oh, Lord, what d' you think he'll make of my hair?" with a quick, almost despairing look in the mirror. "He'll be shocked, I know, but I'm sure he'll understand, won't he, Mrs Earnshaw, though truth to tell I think it might be as well not to let on about . . . about what happened to me . . . or *almost* happened to me," shuddering. "Not yet anyway. Of course we'll have to explain why you are here and not in West Derby and why I'm not at Oakwood but . . . well, I'll think of that when the time comes. We can go straight back to the cottage now. You'll like that, won't you, Mrs Earnshaw? Oh, won't he be thrilled when he hears about the *Lily-Jane*. I think I'll take him at once to Runcorn to see how the work's getting on."

"Lerrim gerris legs under t'table, lass, afore yer go rattlin' off ter Runcorn. An' yes, it'll be nice ter gerrome," as it had been a great wrench for Eva to leave the cottage to which she had gone as a bride fifty years ago. Naturally she couldn't let the child go to stay in Upper Duke Street on her own, especially with that lad hanging about night and day, but now, with her grandson home, they could all go back.

"Of course, but I'm so excited I don't know what I'm doing or saying."

"I can see tha', queen. Now settle yerself down a minnit while I get me breath."

"Oh, please, Mrs Earnshaw, please don't ask me to calm down, I just can't. I've waited for so long. Nearly four months and now, in a few hours I'm going to see him."

"I know, lass." Mrs Earnshaw's face was calm and understanding. They had not spoken of it, she and Lily, but Lily gave it away in a hundred ways, the love, the strong, unbreakable bond that existed between her and Eva's grandson. Eva believed that as yet there had been nothing much of a physical nature between them, for in many ways Lily was still a child and her Liam was a full-grown man with a man's appetites. And he was too decent to take advantage of this sweet young girl who loved him. Lily Elliott was strong, brave, loyal and would make Liam a steadfast partner in life. She was seventeen in May and maturity would come.

Not that you'd think so to see her now, whirling about the three small rooms that Second Lieutenant Crowther had rented for them, her face as rosy as an apple, her eyes brilliant, her mouth stretched wide, either in high laughter or in the babble of words she could not seem to control. Villy raced round with her, sure that this was some wondrous new game and Ginger squirmed gracefully round a table leg begging for attention. The two animals were somewhat confused by this new place they lived in and, in a strange way, just as though they felt a trifle insecure, they now seemed prepared to lie down together in a comfortable tangle, friends in adversity.

They had come here in the dead of night, whispering from the cottage and into the hansom cab Nicholas Crowther had hired for them, their scant wardrobe hastily packed in Lily's carpet bag and an old lidded basket of Eva's. Eva had left a note pinned to Sadie's door to say she was going away for a week or two and Sadie was not to worry and she'd be in touch. Lily had written it for her, since Eva could neither read nor write, and neither could Sadie but she knew someone would read it to her.

So when the ferrety-faced man knocked on Sadie's door asking if she knew the whereabouts of the lady next door Sadie could say in all truthfulness that she'd no idea. Not that she'd have told him if she had, she said to Mary Jarvis who lived on her other side. Nasty eyes he had, the man who'd enquired, set close together and you couldn't see his mouth for the wealth of hair on his face. He'd looked none too pleased and had wanted to press her but Charlie had come to the door and he'd soon buggered off.

Lily and Eva had been quite amazed at Nicky Crowther's ingenuity, for the hansom cab had taken them no further than the stand in West Derby – going *away* from town – where they had changed to another cab which took them to the Zoological Gardens. They had walked from there, Nicky, not wearing his uniform, naturally, carrying their bags, Villy trotting on her lead and Ginger telling them all in no uncertain terms exactly what she thought of the adventure, even if she was tucked up snugly in a basket!

When they reached London Road and the cab stand at the end of Falkland Street, they had taken another hansom which this time went all the way to the furnished rooms in Upper Duke Street. If the cab driver was astonished, and he was, to be picking up a respectable elderly lady, a young lad with a dog and a well-dressed toff carrying a carpet bag and a straw basket in the middle of the night he made no mention of it, no doubt satisfied with the large tip the toff gave him.

They had been exhausted and though Mrs Earnshaw would have liked to inspect the beds before they got into them, even she was too tired to bother. Neither of them had heard Nicky let himself out and had slept until the middle of the next morning, causing Mrs Earnshaw to feel quite wicked. She had never before been up later than six thirty in her life!

Nicky Crowther had never enjoyed anything in his life as much as he did those eight days he spent calling at Upper Duke Street. He left Oakwood Place as soon as it was light, cantering off on Jasper, telling no one where he was going, startling the stable lads with his impatience to be away. He dressed in his oldest clothes, a pair of riding breeches he had discarded years ago, a warm tweed jacket and high-buttoned vest and shirt, with a sleeved cloak sporting slits up the back which was draped over his bay's rump. He wore no hat.

On the third day he did not notice a man on an ancient nag, a man who looked as though he were not accustomed to riding, follow discreetly behind him as he took the road to town. He was in love but only Mrs Earnshaw knew it and she said nothing. His love was as beautiful as her mother had been, even with her hair cut into a cap of short curls. It was streaked with gold and silver and swirled, shining in the sunlight or the candlelight, whenever she moved her head and he longed for nothing more, at that moment, than to run his hands through it. Her eyes reminded him of silvered ice in a winter's sunlight, silver and yet with a touch of lavender – or was it violet? – in them that was quite incredible. He would watch the slow rise and fall of her long, fine lashes, quite mesmerised by the unconsciously seductive movement. When she spoke, or even when she didn't, his eyes would drop to her full, poppy mouth, studying the way her tongue would moisten her lips. Her skin was like satin, smooth and fine with a bloom on it like a peach and he wondered what it would feel like to touch. Eva often marvelled that Lily never seemed to notice his close attention.

When they went out he wished that Lily would discard her boy's clothing and dress as a female, since she was safe enough with him, but when he asked her she refused, saying she wished to take no chances at this last moment. He was not even sure what she meant, though he supposed it was something to do with Mrs Earnshaw's grandson who was due home soon and who would take over Nicholas's self-imposed duty of guard while he was in Ireland. He meant to give up his commission in the army as soon as he and Lily were married, which he hoped would be in the very near future. She seemed to like him, to enjoy being with him which gave him great encouragement, laughing at his jokes, showing great interest when he spoke of his life abroad, listening most attentively to whatever he had to say, which he found quite exhilarating. As soon as his regiment had done its service in Ireland he meant to ask her but until then he would go slowly, for who knew how her brush, if one could call such a horrifying experience a "brush", with his father had affected her feelings for the male sex. She needed time to recover and as she was so young time was what he meant to give her. He was finding it very difficult living with his father, knowing what he had attempted with Lily but he knew he must keep up the charade, for Lily's safety was at stake. They met only at the dinner table and his father and Eloise kept up a light chatter, his father going out of his way to be amusing. His sister seemed to think that her forthcoming wedding was as fascinating to everyone as it was to her, so conversation flowed smoothly with little effort on his part. It was only for a few more days then he would be off, he told himself, and when he came back it would not be to Oakwood Place. He would buy a small house somewhere and settle down, hopefully with Lily as his wife. He had no need to work, thanks to his mother. Life stretched out before him in all its perfection and in the meantime he saw his love every day. They would take walks along the Marine Parade, to the casual observer two young men on their morning constitutional, and stroll beside the docks to study the ships and watch the cargoes being discharged, which was her favourite pastime. They would lean on the railings of the parade and watch the ships running before the wind up the river, the graceful vigour of the schooner, *My Lady of Plymouth*, a dozen small, iron, full-rigged ships, brigs and three-masted barques, flying clipper ships barely seeming to touch the water, clumsy foreign coasters come from Holland and France and Spain, or just watching the tally man checking off the cargo as it came ashore.

Sometimes she would consent to go up to St James's Walk at the top of Duke Street. There was a long gravelled terrace with a seat on it from where you could see across the river to the hills of Flintshire and Denbighshire. To the right of the lighthouse there was a break in the hills which gave a splendid prospect of the sea and the ships in the distance as they came in on the tide and made for the harbour. Further right the eye reached the most northern extremity of the Cheshire shore, called the Rock and it was round this that every vessel passed going in and out of the river mouth.

It was to this that Lily's eyes constantly turned though Nicky did not notice it.

When he left for the steamship that was to take him and his regiment to Ireland she kissed his cheek warmly and told him they didn't know what they would have done without him and the minute he was home he was to come and see them. They would be back in West Derby by then, of course, she told him and her eyes had shone with tears that he thought were for him. Would she write, he begged her, longing to pull her into his arms and if Mrs Earnshaw had not been standing beside them he might have attempted at least a brotherly hug.

So, yesterday he had gone and now, at last, the day had come for which she had waited since last October.

They took a hansom from the bottom end of Upper Duke Street to the cab stand in Castle Street, alighting behind the Custom House and walking down Canning Street to Canning Dock which was where Tommy had told them that *Breeze* would berth. They meant to proceed alongside the Canning Half Tide Basin to the lock gates and see her come in, perhaps with Liam at the wheel, Lily breathed ecstatically to Mrs Earnshaw, and then, when she was inside the basin, run back to the place where she would berth. Well, Lily could run, Mrs Earnshaw told her, while she followed on behind at her own pace, making that the excuse for letting Lily and her grandson have a minute or two to greet each other without her hanging at their backs. Her turn would come, but she had seen the glow in Lily's eyes and the hectic flush on her cheek and she was aware, for had she not once been in love, that she could not wait to run into Liam's arms.

Lily stood, as silently and as still as she had been almost four months ago when she had watched the lovely ship sail away, taking her heart, her strength, her love with it, her whole being concentrating on the quiet approach of the graceful vessel, quite unaware of the bustle around her. The deck and rigging swarmed with seamen all intent on the important task of getting *Breeze* through the gates and into safe harbourage. After the long and often dangerous journey they had just undertaken they did not want any accidents at this last moment.

Tommy was there and the piermaster, who had time to give her a surprised nod as he supervised the opening of the lock gates to allow the ship inside. The thrusting bow of the tall-masted clipper was very close to brushing the lock gate as she entered but it was not at her bow that Lily looked but at the wheelhouse, for it was there that she would catch her first sight of Liam. She felt as though she could not breathe, for her heart was beating so violently it seemed as if it were determined to leap up into her throat and she could feel herself shivering though she was not cold. Her eyes appeared to be misting over, for the figures in the wheelhouse would not sharpen and become clear and she tried to steady herself. Liam, my love . . . my love . . . where are you? I shall die if I don't see your smiling brown face in a moment, your hand raised to let me know you've seen me. Where are you?

The clipper passed beyond the lock gates and began to move slowly between the other sailing ships berthed there, through Canning Half Dock to Canning Dock where a dozen men were waiting with lines and all the paraphernalia needed in the docking of a ship. There was a gentle bump as whoever was at the helm in the wheelhouse guided *Breeze* to her berth and on the dock Lily felt the first thrill of terror grip at her guts, for it had not been Liam. Behind her Tommy exchanged an anxious glance with the man beside him whom Lily had not noticed and might not have recognised as her pa's old shipmate, Johnno, if she had. The glance said that there was something wrong here, for the first mate always stood either at the helm, or beside the captain at the helm when moving in or out of a port. It was a tricky business. There were tides and currents in the river that needed watching and often a pilot boat was used to give a hand. So where was the man whose job it was to be the right-hand man, second-in-command, if you like, of the master of the clipper?

The gangway was thrown out and several seamen moved down it while other men went up, making for the captain, stepping across a deck littered with ropes and lashed barrels.

A hand on Lily's arm made her jump, for she had been

frozen in a world she could not escape. Though her face was impassive and her figure as still as a statue, inside her mind was a writhing, seething coil of fear, none of it making any particular sense except the words, like a litany repeated again and again: Where is Liam? Where is Liam? Where is Liam?

"Come, lass," a stern voice said in her ears. "Let's gerr aboard. See, 'old me 'and an' 'elp me up that there gangway," which was as good a way as any, Eva Earnshaw thought, of fetching the petrified figure of Lily out of her trance.

The men on the gangway moved respectfully aside as the two women approached and the man who watched from behind a stack of barrels was not surprised, for the girl he had been following for weeks now was the sort of woman men could only stand and stare at in sheer disbelief. He had done so himself the first time he had seen her and he could understand the obsession of the man who had hired him. Now that the soldier had gone they were to make some sort of a move, his employer had intimated, but of what sort he had not yet said.

Lily was incapable of speech her mouth was so dry, but Mrs Earnshaw put out a hand to a seaman, telling him she'd be glad of a word with the captain.

"Well, 'e's right busy at moment, missus," looking at her askance and then relenting she was so upset and, anyroad, what did women know about the difficulties entailed in berthing a ship.

"Then . . . 'appen yer could tell me where I can find Liam O'Connor? 'E's first mate."

At once the man's eyes slid away, looking round for someone to take these women off his hands, for he was only a deck-hand and this was nothing to do with him.

"Well . . . I dunno as . . . yer'd best speak ter't captain, missus . . ." His voice trailed away and again so did his eyes, frantically searching for help.

"What's going on down there," a voice bellowed from the wheelhouse, "and what are those two doing on my ship? Don't they know no women are allowed on board? They must wait with the rest on the quayside."

There were indeed several women and some children, evidently waiting for their men, whom they had not seen for four months. Some, who had spotted husbands or fathers, were waving joyously and there was a feeling of great relief and happiness in the air which contrasted sharply with the dread despair that enfolded Eva and Lily. They stood numbly on the deck, waiting for God to tell them that their reason for living was gone for ever. Or perhaps for Liam to appear suddenly and swing them both into his strong arms. For someone to explain why he was not here among the men who, each and every one of them, was busy at some task. For the captain to . . . to . . .

The man they had accosted was seen to move hastily to the wheelhouse and say a word or two in the captain's ear and the captain, who had been red-faced with anger at the temerity of the two women, became quiet. He studied them uneasily then spoke over his shoulder to another seaman and with a heavy and obviously reluctant step, walked towards them.

They huddled together, Liam's grandmother and the girl who loved him and in those few seconds it took for him to reach them they both felt the life wither away and die inside them. His face was grave and yet his eyes were kind. He had the sort of pitying look assumed when bad news is about to be imparted.

"You were asking for Liam O'Connor, madam?" he asked Eva, since she looked the more composed of the two. The girl, who had been beautiful when she came on his ship but was now as haggard-faced as an old crone, stared into his face with terrible eyes.

"Yes." Eva spoke through clenched teeth.

"And you are?"

"Eva Earnshaw. Liam O'Connor's grandmother. We were told . . ."

"Will you come to my cabin, ma'am, you and the young lady. It is not suitable for you to stand here under the gaze of . . . Please, come this way."

They went obediently, following the captain down some steps so narrow it was hard to accommodate Lily's full crinoline, along a slip of a passage and into a tiny but neat cabin with a bunk tucked into one corner. In the bunk lay the figure of a man, a man so tall he was forced to bend his knees to lie in it. He was shivering violently, his wasted frame twisting and turning as though to escape something, his head thudding from side to side on the pillow. His eyes were closed. He was moaning softly. His lips were cracked and peeling and from him came a heat and a smell so dreadful both Lily and Eva recoiled away from him.

"I'm so sorry, Mrs Earnshaw," the captain said helplessly and it was only then that they knew that the mumbling, moaning body in the bunk was Liam O'Connor.

Eva put her hand to her mouth and swayed slightly, looking as though she might be about to fall, her small reserve of strength gone and the captain put out a solicitous hand to steady her. With a small agonised cry Lily flung herself at the bunk, kneeling down at the side and with a gesture that almost brought tears to the eyes of the watching man, drew his first mate's head to her breast, folding her arms about it and pressing her lips to his bony face.

"Liam ... Liam, oh, my love ... what has been done to you?" she cried softly, looking down at the emaciated caricature of the man she had last seen as an attractive, smiling giant before whom all other men were mere puppets.

"He had a ... well, I don't know what it was, Mrs Earnshaw," the captain was explaining to Eva. "A fever of some sort when we were in Foochow but he insisted he was all right and I could not leave him in such a place. It must be something he picked up there ... a pestilential hole if ever I saw one. None of the rest of the crew was affected but as the journey went on he became worse and ... well, this is my cabin," which, though it was not meant to, revealed what a kind and Christian man Captain Fletcher was. Not many captains would give up their own cabins for a sick seaman.

"The men have been taking it in turns to watch over him, but there was little we could do. He has eaten nothing for days now and cannot keep even a sip of water down. I did not know what else to do, Mrs Earnshaw, having no doctor on board, except try to get him home. I'm surprised he has lasted as long as this."

He faltered to a halt, turning away from Mrs Earnshaw to look at the woman by the bunk who was smoothing the limp hair away from the face of the man who, in his opinion, was dying.

"He's a strong man, Captain, that is why, and because he knew I was waiting for him," she said without turning. "He has lasted this long ... coming home to me ... to us and we'll mend him, won't we, Mrs Earnshaw? I can only thank

God. I believed he was dead, you see. I know it's . . . Well, I would rather he was like this than dead." She kissed him passionately, this time on his cracked lips and as she did so his lids rolled back, revealing glazed and unfocused eyes. With a painfulness that was agony to watch he turned them towards the girl and into them came a glint of life.

"Lovebud?" he whispered wonderingly. The captain was amazed, for he had known no one for days.

"Yes, my darling, it's me. Your grandmother and I have come to take you home. Now, we shall need a . . . a . . . something to carry him home in, Captain, if you would see to it," the young lady told him crisply, "so if you would be so good as to get one of your men to fetch a cab and then accompany us to West Derby."

"West Derby? But I have a cargo to discharge, miss. I cannot spare—"

"Then see if there are a couple of men on the quayside who would be willing to help us. They would, of course, be paid, and quickly, please," for the man on the bed had lapsed once more into unconsciousness. "In fact there is an old chap, Tommy Graham, who was there when you docked. Ask him to come to me. Now, I shall want warm blankets, probably hot-water bottles, if you have such a thing. No? Well, warm bricks and . . . and . . ."

Suddenly her control went and she began to weep, but the man on the bunk did not feel her tears on his face, nor the strong arms that lifted him on to a makeshift stretcher. She held his hand for a moment, kissing it with such love the men who held the ends of it shifted uneasily as though they were prying into someone else's grief.

"Please be careful with him," she begged them, which they were, though if she could have seen the way he was tossed about coming round the Horn she wouldn't have bothered.

The man on the quayside watched in some surprise as the stretcher was carried awkwardly down the narrow gangway, the figure lying in it wrapped about like a parcel, the girl, *his* girl, the one he was following, anxiously hovering at his side, giving orders, snapping at the men when the stretcher slipped for a moment. It was quite a little group, what with the captain and his men, two chaps brought from the quayside, one of them as old as Methuselah with a white beard, the girl and the old

346

woman, who seemed not to know what day it was, she was so bemused.

"Come along, dearest," he heard the girl say to her, taking her hand. "You won't mind sitting in the second cab, will you, then Liam will be more comfortable. I know you'd like to be with him but it's only for another half-hour then we'll have him home and in his own bed. We'll nurse him together, you and I. Tommy has the key and will collect Villy and Ginger and our things. Dearest, he's home, Liam's home and between us we'll make him well again."

As the two hansom cabs moved slowly off the man hurried back to his tiny slit of an office in Water Street to write his report to the man who employed him, eager to let him know about this surprising turn of events.

30

It took the cab driver, Tommy Graham's mate Johnno, Ronny Biddle and Lou Jarvis, who lived on the other side of the Ainsworths and happened to be at home, to get him out of the hansom, through the door of the cottage, across the parlour and – the most difficult part of the whole operation – up the stairs to the bedroom where he had been born and where he had slept, on and off, for twenty-seven years.

"Lay 'im 'on't floor, lads," Eva said briskly, herself again now she had recovered from the shock of his appearance and was busy with a task she understood. "Bed'll 'ave ter be aired and fires lit so keep 'im well wrapped up in them blankets. Aye, you stay wi' 'im, Lily," for Lily could not seem able to convince herself that she should let him out of her arms. She knelt on the floor with his head in her lap, his face turned towards her, her arms about his shoulders, never taking her eyes from his ravaged face. As long as she could hold on to him, see and hear his breathing, dreadful as it was, she knew he was still alive and until she'd got him well again she meant never to let him out of her sight. She'd sleep in this room beside him, she didn't care what anyone thought, and when he was recovered she'd sleep in the *bed* beside him, wedding or no, and if anyone objected, meaning, she supposed, Liam's grandmother, then she was sorry but it would make no difference. She was to spend the rest of her life with this man in her arms, the man she had loved as a child and as a woman for six, almost seven long years and she wasn't going to waste another precious minute!

They were all there, the men hanging about with their hands in their pockets, longing to help, for, as they muttered to one another, they'd not have believed it was Liam if they'd not seen him with their own eyes. That giant of a chap who looked as though he'd knock you for six no trouble at all, and was in reality as gentle as a lamb. It had been most unnerving, heaving him about like that even though he must be about six stone lighter than when he left, and that moaning, had Ronny noticed it? Lou muttered. Enough to really put the wind up you, and if you asked him, which nobody had, he'd not last the night.

The women came to see what Mrs Earnshaw wanted them to do, bustling round with kindling for the fires, the first to be lit in Liam's bedroom, the second in the kitchen range, for the oven would be needed for heating the bricks for his bed, and the third in the parlour where they meant to get Mrs Earnshaw to sit down and have a nice cup of tea. It was a waste of time, of course, for was it likely that Eva Earnshaw would sit on her bum drinking tea when her grandson was in urgent need of her attention, she asked them, rude with them, but they understood. Liam was her pride and joy. She had brought him up, got him to where he was today, and it could only be expected that she would be worried out of her mind about him, but what they wanted to know was, their exchanged glances said, who the hell was the young woman who was holding on to Eva's Liam like a limpet? A beautiful, anguished face, she had, and all the while they were moving about the bedroom, stepping over Liam to make up his bed and get out the clean nightshirt Mrs Earnshaw had ordered for him, they were thunderstruck when they observed her showering kisses on his face. Her bonnet, a pretty little thing of heather blue silk and decorated with fragile white silk rosebuds, had fallen off and they could hardly believe it when they saw how short her hair was. A tangled cap of silver pale curls shot through with gold. The loveliest colour they had ever seen and she, when she was herself, must be just as lovely.

It was like Lime Street Station, Sadie Ainsworth was heard to say, for no sooner had the men begun to drift away, leaving the women to their work, when, lo and behold, a splendid carriage drew up at the door with a groom in livery just as splendid at the reins. A respectable, grey-haired lady was helped down and the men drifted back, for it looked as though their day was going to become even more entertaining.

"Ta, Arnold, yer can gerron 'ome now," she said. "I'll find me own way back." She swept into the cottage without so much as a by your leave, pushing past them all, demanding to know where "her lamb" was, and if the women, who were trying to restrain her, didn't get out of her way she'd knock their blocks off.

They had begun to explain to her what was going on, as best they could, for they didn't know what was wrong with Liam O'Connor, when Tommy arrived in a second cab with Villy barking her head off at the commotion and Ginger spitting and scratching at everyone who came near her. A carpet bag and a straw basket were dumped on the parlour floor, then Tommy paid the driver and joined the men in the front garden, ready to run for the doctor, for surely he would be needed. It seemed to Molly that all that needed to be done, was being done. Her lamb was safe and so she sat down by the fire, her bags about her, and waited.

They had Liam warmly tucked up in his clean and aired bed when the doctor arrived and still the men shuffled about outside. The women were busy with kettles and pans of broth, eyeing the stranger and wondering who she was and, more importantly, who "her lamb" might be, shooing out the children who didn't see why they should be excluded from all the excitement.

It was only Lily and Eva who stood by the bed as the doctor examined Liam. Well, Eva moved respectfully away from the bed, standing back like a wooden image, her face carved and expressionless, but Lily hung over Liam, holding his hand, murmuring his name and kissing his cheek and Eva had time to wonder for a moment how strange it was that they were to take turns, she and Lily, in being calm. She had gone to pieces on the ship and Lily had taken over. Now, when they had him safely home Lily didn't seem to know what she was doing.

"Would you stand aside, young lady," the doctor told her irritably.

"Oh, no, please, let me stay here where he can see me when he opens his eyes," she begged him.

"I cannot examine him properly if you remain there. And . . . well" – he turned to Eva – "I shall need to strip him, Mrs Earnshaw and as this young lady is, presumably, not his wife, it would not be proper . . ."

"I'm not leaving the room, Mrs Earnshaw, tell him, will you and if he tries to make me I shall hit him."

"Well!" The doctor was clearly shocked, sensing hysteria which must be nipped in the bud before it spread, for there was nothing worse for a patient than a woman weeping and wailing all over the place. Not that she was doing either of these things but her face was a peculiar colour and her eyes wide and glittering which usually heralded a commotion. He knew Mrs Earnshaw only slightly, her grandson not at all, for the man had been at sea and, as far as he knew, had the constitution of an ox. The young man on the bed did not look as healthy as an ox now and, like the men outside, he privately thought they had called him too late.

"Explain to me the circumstances, madam, if you please. How has this man got into this . . . sad condition?"

"'E's me grandson, Doctor. 'E's just got back from a sea voyage. China . . . where were it, Lily?"

"Foochow." Lily didn't even lift her head.

"Aah," the doctor said, as though that explained everything. "It seems your grandson might have picked up some eastern disease, a fever of some sort, for I believe they are rife in those parts. They are not as concerned as some of us are about hygiene and . . . well, cholera, typhoid, though I don't think this is either of those."

"Then what the devil is it?" the young woman at the bed hissed, turning a livid face to him. "Tell us what it is and how it is to be cured and we will cure him. He shall have the best of care."

"First I will examine him." The room was warm now and the doctor threw back the covers and draped them over the end of the bed.

"Help me with his nightgown," he said brusquely to no one in particular but expecting to be obeyed. At once, with something positive to do in the nursing of her love, Lily held Liam's head against her breast while Eva and the doctor removed his nightshirt and laid him naked on the bed. Eva was heard to moan, no more than a whisper in her throat, for she had seen her grandson when he was in his prime, a hard, muscular body, broad shoulders, firm flesh on him, his body shaped with that male beauty which is not often seen. Now the flesh was gone, leaving loose skin that lay in folds like that of a very old man over the skeleton of his frame. His closed eyes lay deep in their sockets, the cheekbones protruding, his lips loose and flat against the high ridge of his teeth, his nose arched above them. He had a thick golden stubble on the bony structure of his chin, like the plush of the cloth on Eva's parlour table. Every bone in his body stood proud, from the deep hollows of his collar bone, to his chest and below to where his ribcage stood out like the jutting of a sail. His belly was completely concave so that it seemed that at any moment what was beneath might break through. The bony ring of his pelvis formed a circle from which his stick-like legs appeared to dangle, like those of a puppet without the strength to move for themselves, even while lying down. Between them was the golden brush of thick hair that hid his genitals and though Lily had never before seen a man naked she seemed unsurprised that there was no apparent difference between male and female. Apart from the fine mat golden of hair that ran from his throat to the base of his belly and the absence of breasts, he looked scarcely dissimilar to herself. His feet were long, the fine bones in them vulnerable, fragile-looking, the nails long, horny and curved over the end of his toes.

The heat coming off him was fierce and so was the stink.

The doctor prodded and poked and did what Lily thought to be all manner of strange things. He pressed what he called a stethoscope to his chest, listening to his heart, he said, which had a good strong beat, which was encouraging. He peered into his eyes, rolling back the lids, lifting his arms and pressing in the armpits, then the groin, turning his ankles and wrists, twisting his head on his neck, studying every inch of him, even his back but there were no marks, no rash, nothing to tell him, it seemed, what was causing Liam O'Connor to lie like a dead man, or one soon to be dead.

"I don't know, Mrs Earnshaw, really I don't. Apart from the high fever I can find nothing to indicate what is wrong with your grandson."

"What shall we do, then?" the young woman at the side of his patient rasped. "Tell us what to do."

"There is nothing you can do, young lady, except pray."

"Pray! You call yourself a doctor and all you can tell us to do is pray. Well, I shan't pray so you can go to hell with your advice. Mrs Earnshaw and I will ... will make him better, won't we, Mrs Earnshaw? He needs warmth and care ... good food and between us we'll see that he has it, won't we, Mrs Earnshaw? I think a bath first, don't you?"

"Young lady, I know you are upset about your ... your ..."

"We are to be married, Doctor," she told him defiantly. "I love him and I intend to walk up the bloody aisle to him when he's better. I'll make him well. I'll make him well and without your damn prayers. When has God ever listened to my prayers, tell me that? What about my mother? Well, that is another story. Now, give him his fee, Mrs Earnshaw, and let us get down to the business of getting Liam back on his feet."

The doctor's voice was suddenly gentle, recognising what was in this young woman. "Get rid of his fever, Miss ... Miss ... and you might have a chance."

"How do I do that?"

"Cool him down. This room is far too warm. Cool his body. It is fighting the fever and he is almost dried out. Make him drink or his organs will be irreparably damaged. His body must maintain its normal functions. How long is it since he passed water?"

"Water?"

"Urine," the doctor said irritably.

"We don't know. We have only just brought him from the ship. The captain told us he couldn't keep even a sip of water down."

"He must be made to. Send someone to find some ice and pack it round him. Now, I'll leave you but I'll call again this evening."

Lily bowed her head, resting her cheek in what seemed to the doctor to be an indecent gesture on the man's bare chest but when she turned to him he could see the desolation and yet determination in her young face.

"I'm sorry if I was rude, Doctor," she said simply. "But you see I love him so much my own life will be ended if he does not recover. He is really all I have or care about."

There were enough of them, they told one another, to run the infirmary, let alone take turns in looking after one sick man. They'd form a sort of – what was the word? – a sort of programme so that one of them was always on call to give Mrs Earnshaw and the incredible young woman a break, but it seemed the young woman did not want a break. She would stay here, she said firmly, until Liam was well again, fixed to his side like a leech. If someone would bring her some water she would have a wash and change into . . . Into what? they asked her. And when she produced her shirt and breeches they were dumbfounded.

And so, not caring what she wore providing it was suitable for nursing Liam, she had changed from her lovely silk gown into a plain grey serge skirt and bodice loaned her by Elsie Biddle who was about the same height though much plumper. A belt was found from somewhere which she fastened round her tiny waist and even in the midst of so much drama Elsie was heard to remark that the dress had never looked like that on *her*.

It was not until an hour or so later that the woman who had arrived in the carriage and who had sat waiting patiently by the fire in the parlour stood up forcefully and said she must speak at once with Lily Elliott. Her face was pale and drawn and though she had drunk innumerable cups of the hot, sweet tea they had pressed absentmindedly on her, she was obviously at the end of her tether.

"Eeh, I don't think there's anyone o' that name round about 'ere, queen," Sadie answered her doubtfully. "'Appen yer've got the wrong 'ouse, or even t'street."

"Mrs Earnshaw's place in Lower Breck Road I were told," the woman answered firmly, "an' I believe this is it."

"Aye, but Mrs Earnshaw's norrin a fit state fer visitors . . . well, with 'er grandson poorly she's—"

"It's Lily I've come ter see an' I'm not movin' until I've seen 'er so yer'd best fetch 'er."

"'Ere, don't you go givin' me orders."

"Look, I've bin outer me mind fer weeks now wonderin' where she was."

"Well, she's norrere."

Sadie folded her arms dangerously over her broad bosom but when Elsie tapped her on the arm and whispered in her ear, she turned back uncertainly.

"Well, there's a lass upstairs wi' . . ."

"Fair lass wi' a lovely face?"

"Aye, that's 'er. She's wi' Liam."

"She would be. They've bin courtin' . . ."

"Yer what?"

"You 'eard. Now, if yer'd oblige me by runnin' an' tellin' 'er that Mrs Quinn's 'ere I'd be grateful."

It took but a moment, then Sadie came spinning downstairs again, the doctor behind her.

"She ses yer ter go up,' she hissed in great excitement as she handed the doctor his coat and led him outside, since he had professed a wish to speak to one of the men. Which one? Any would do as long as he was capable of obeying an order. And they were not to forget he wanted ice delivered at once. Where from? He didn't know, he said, but surely one of the inns had an ice house. He'd leave it to them, he told them, expecting to be obeyed.

Lily allowed Mrs Quinn no more than ten seconds of her time. Ten seconds in which they embraced silently, tearfully, then she was back at Liam's side prepared to sponge him down with cool water until the ice was brought.

"Eeh, lamb." Mrs Quinn was clearly horrified, for the lad hadn't a stitch on him and her lamb was as unworldly as the baby in the nursery at Oakwood. "Can someone else not do tha'?" She turned to the quiet figure on the other side of the bed. "You'll be Mrs Earnshaw, I reckon. Me name's Mrs Quinn," she explained. "I 'ope yer'll forgive this . . . this intrusion burr I've known our Lily since she were born, yer see, and 'er bein' a lass . . . if yer know wharr I mean, it's not right she should be . . . well, not wi't lad nekkid like that."

"I thought it were you, Mrs Quinn." Eva Earnshaw bowed her head politely in Mrs Quinn's direction, then rested it on the chair back in a gesture of total exhaustion. "Lily's spoke of yer times, but you try tellin' 'er to let someone else see to 'im. Yer might as well save yer breath ter cool yer porridge."

"Aye." Mrs Quinn sighed gustily. "She were allus like that from being a bairn. Like 'er pa, she were. Liked 'er own way burra a sweeter child yer'd never find. Give yer't shirt off 'er back, she would, so yer see, when she run off like that . . . well, she left me a note, like, burr I didn't know where she were, norr until Master Nicky told me. 'Don't breathe a word to me pa, Mrs Quinn,' 'e said, so I knew exactly what 'ad gone on an' why she'd run off. I . . . I looked after 'er ma, yer see." There was no need to elaborate. Mrs Earnshaw knew exactly what Mrs Quinn was getting at.

"Anyroad, soon as I knew where she were I were up 'ere like a shot. Me son-in-law's groom at Oakwood an' a chap ter be trusted so 'e fetched me up 'ere but yer were gone. No one knew where, or wouldn't say, more like. Yer've some good neighbours there, lass."

"I know."

"An' if yer need any 'elp yer've only ter ask. I've nowt ter do all day now 'cept look after me grandchildren an' I reckon our Victoria can cope on 'er own fer a bit."

"That's kind o' yer, Mrs Quinn, an' yer welcome ter come whenever yer want burrit seems lass won't give 'im up to anyone an' if she does I've plenty o' folk what'll tekk over."

"Can I . . . can I stop fer a while then, Mrs Earnshaw? Not that child's gonner tekk any notice o' me at moment burr I . . . well, I've missed 'er an' just ter sit an' watch 'er'd do me a power o' good. 'Ave yer tried borage?" she asked abruptly.

"Pardon?" Mrs Earnshaw was clearly startled and even Lily looked up from her frantic effort to get a sip of water between Liam's cracked lips. She had devised the simple method of holding his nose and when he opened his mouth involuntarily, she poured a teaspoon of the liquid into his mouth. He would retch a little and the water would come back but each time it happened she patiently repeated the process, hoping some of it would stay down.

"Borage. It fetches down a fever. That's if yer can gerrim ter keep it down. Or hawkweed which yer can pick on't roadside. Then there's marigold." She stopped apologetically. "Me granny were a country woman, yer see. From up north somewhere an' she wouldn't 'ave a doctor in th'ouse. She allus said what God sent were good enough fer 'er. 'God always puts cure alongside ill.' I've 'eard 'er say that times. She lived ter be eighty-four," she finished simply.

A deep silence followed as the two women who loved Liam O'Connor digested this astonishing fact, then: "Borage?"

"Aye. It's what's known as a febrifuge. That's what Granny called it. It'd do 'is waterworks good an' all. Funny 'ow yer remember things. Granny used ter send us out ter gather it when we was nippers, then dry it so I suppose—"

"Where would we get it?" Lily interrupted.

"Well, anywhere in't th'edges. It must grow along this lane an' if yer can't find it—"

"What does it look like, Mrs Quinn? If you went with Tommy or one of the other men could you point it out to them?"

Mrs Quinn looked thoughtful. "Well, it's bin a long time burr I reckon I'd know it. Aye, then all I 'ave ter do is remember 'ow Granny did it. An infusion . . . an' if I can't find it I reckon apothecary in't village'd 'ave it in stock. Dried. Now hawkweed, yer 'ave ter infuse it in white wine an' . . . Dear 'eaven, it's bin so long . . ." She wrinkled her brow and Eva and Lily held their breath. "Three or four cupfuls a day."

Lily felt the despair catch her in its iron grip. Three or four cupfuls a day and it was all she could do to get a teaspoonful of water past his lips. He lay like a man laid out for his coffin, his skin stretched, parched, fiery with heat and with no trace of relieving sweat. He was dying before her eyes, she knew he was and there was nothing she could do to stop him. Nothing even the doctor could do to stop him except advise her to pray but she'd be damned if she'd give in. She had known Liam for six years. She had met him on the seashore every few months during those six years, reinforcing their friendship, a child's friendship with a grown man which had not seemed extraordinary to her who was the child. She had loved him with the simple, trusting love of a child but she had not really known him, she realised that. He had had another life running parallel to the one in which she was a part and it was only his kind heart, his sweet nature, his compassion for a lonely child that had kept him coming back to her.

But the child had grown into a woman and the child's love had become a woman's love. Liam had told her before he went to China that he loved her. She had clung to him, a woman's body clinging to a man's and she knew enough now to realise that a man's body is easily aroused. He had kissed her and held her in his arms but how much of that was due to his good heart, his sympathy, indeed to her own firmness of purpose which had always led her to believe that she had only to fight for something long enough and hard enough and she would have it. Like the *Lily-Jane*! Like Liam O'Connor. She was that same woman who had said goodbye to him that day on the quayside but she wasn't that woman any more, which sounded very muddled but it was true. She knew with every instinct in her that she loved Liam, that she would never love another man, ever. It was deep inside her and she knew, as a woman knows, that it was right. And, when he was recovered, for recovered he would be, she thought savagely, if it turned out that what Liam felt was no more than strong affection for the child he had rescued, a sense of responsibility that had grown with the years, then she would fight for him, turn his feelings of affection to desire, to love, to need. She had loved two men in her life, her pa and Liam, and now, if Liam was to survive and she was to survive she must measure her strength, wrestle with the forces that had turned Liam into this twitching, mumbling, stinking hulk on the bed. She had to bring him back if only to find out if Liam, the man, loved Lily the woman, as a woman and not as the child he had been kind to.

While she continued to ease the water, teaspoon by slow teaspoon into his mouth, forcing it open by pinching his nostrils, first Eva, then, when she was ready to faint with exhaustion, Sadie or Mary or Elsie, sponged him down with cool water. They turned his poor, emaciated body with ease, the indignity of it no one's concern, for if they stopped for a moment to consider the poor bugger who they manhandled, young Lily Elliott, as they knew her now, was at them, cutting as a whip. Four of them in turns, all through that day and then the night, not even stopping when the doctor came, and at the head of the bed Lily went on hour after hour, dripping water into Liam's dried-up body, allowing no one to take a turn, for she did not trust anyone but herself not to drift into sleep or generally fall by the wayside. Her face was a ghastly mask and her eyes sunken and haunted.

"Well, he's holding on," the doctor said after he had poked at him again, listened to his heart and asked if he had passed any water, shaking his head when he was told that he hadn't.

He sighed then, pulling at his lip and Lily knew that though he was not totally dissatisfied, he did not believe Liam would make it.

"And you'd best take a rest, young lady," he told her, "or we'll have two patients on our hands." She ignored him, of course, that's if she even heard him.

Tommy and Mrs Quinn had found the hawkweed and

infused the leaves in some white wine which Ronny Biddle had run to fetch from the Rose and Crown on West Derby Road and in between the water Lily forced a teaspoon of the febrifuge between his lips.

He began to hallucinate the next day, shouting for someone called Frank to "get that sail sorted out", throwing himself about so that in the end they had to tie him to the bed with soft rags to stop himself from flinging himself out of bed. It was difficult, almost impossible, in fact, for Lily to get any sort of liquid inside him. They had to hold him down, the women, forcibly restraining his head while in desperation she poured a half-cupful of the infusion down his throat, waiting hopelessly for it to come back. Which it did and in it was the first spotting of blood.

"Mrs Quinn . . . oh God, Mrs Quinn," she moaned to the woman whose turn it was to sit with her. "I'm losing him . . . I'm losing him."

"No, lamb, no . . . don't give up. Never give up. See, let me 'ave a turn while yer rest in the chair for 'alf an 'our. Mrs Biddle'll be 'ere in a minute to 'elp me."

"No, I can't leave him. I'm so afraid that he might . . . go without me here to hold him back. I . . . I feel that's what I'm doing, Mrs Quinn. Though he doesn't know me, or anyone, I have this strange feeling that . . . that it's only because I'm here that he doesn't slip away."

Tears poured unchecked down her face which was a travesty of her lovely one of a few days ago. Her hair was in a snarl of sweat about her head and she smelled almost as bad as the man on the bed. Apart from the necessary few moments when she left the room to relieve herself, she had not left Liam's side since they had brought him home.

Suddenly, without warning, her eyes rolled up and she slid into a boneless, graceful heap beside the bed.

31

She was in Mrs Earnshaw's bed when she came to and for a moment, though she was surprised to find herself where she was, it was just like any other morning. She sighed and stretched and yawned, turning to gaze out of the window at the silky strand of blue sky she could see beyond it. There was a horse chestnut tree, bare now of leaves, and usually found in and around fields to provide shade for farm animals, which had somehow rooted itself in the corner of the small garden where it had been even before Mrs Earnshaw and her new husband had come to live there. A blackbird fluttered from branch to branch, its song a melodious trill rising and falling, its tail raised and fanned and she watched it from the bed. The cottage windows were small, but low, the sills almost on the floor and she could see the tree, the hedge on the other side of the lane, and the fields beyond the hedge where a man was ploughing, plodding along in the straight furrows behind the steady, rhythmic pull of the horse.

She turned and stretched again and beside her Villy raised her head and pricked her ears. Lily smiled, reaching out her hand to her then suddenly remembrance hit her and with a frantic leap she was out of bed and across the tiny landing to the bedroom where Liam lay. Her heart was pounding so fiercely she thought she might faint in sheer terror. She had no idea how long it was since she had . . . well, she supposed she must have fainted, for you don't just fall asleep standing up, do you? She had no idea of time, barely of place, for everywhere was quiet except for the pitter patter of Villy's paws following her across the polished wooden floor.

He was there, just where she had last seen him, lying neatly in the bed and sitting beside him, one on either side of the bed, were Mrs Earnshaw and Mrs Quinn. Mrs Quinn was holding his nose while Mrs Earnshaw dribbled something into his obediently opening mouth. They had established a pattern, it seemed, working in perfect harmony, smiling at one another, exchanging the occasional word as they gazed down at the gaunt, stubbled face on the pillow.

She tiptoed to the door of the room, almost tripping on the hem of the voluminous nightgown which she recognised as Mrs Earnshaw's, wondering why they had not put her in one of her own. She had been bathed, she could sense that, for her skin felt clean for the first time since they had brought Liam from the ship, and she felt refreshed, she realised, but still the anger began to grow in her. They had washed her and put her to bed while she was not herself, just as though she were a child to be bundled off to bed when the grown-ups had something important to do. How dare they! How bloody well dare they, and here they both were, smiling and nodding at one another as though there was absolutely nothing wrong.

"What in hell's name d'you think you're doing?" she hissed venomously from the doorway and they both turned in surprise. Mrs Earnshaw's expression at once became disapproving, but Mrs Quinn's fell into that familiar, long-suffering look which said what else could you expect from a self-willed young woman like her lamb. They'd got her to bed only because she was unconscious and she'd slept the night through and looked much better for it, but Molly knew they were going to get it in the neck for daring to nurse the young man without her being there to watch over it all. She said the only thing that she knew would distract her.

"'E's keepin' it down, lamb. 'E's still unconscious, though I reckon it'll not be long afore he ses summat. Me an' Mrs Earnshaw 'ave tekken it in turns ter see to 'im while yer 'ad a rest burr 'e's—"

"Has the fever broken?" She flung herself at the bed, crouching down beside it, putting her hands on his face and forehead, brushing back his lank hair in an agony of love and remorse for leaving him, almost tipping over the small bowl Mrs Earnshaw was holding and from which she was spooning the infusion.

"No, not yet, lamb, but doctor's 'opeful it'll be terday and then 'e'll be on't mend."

"I'll get dressed then and take over. Where are the things Mrs Biddle lent me?"

"I sponged an' pressed 'em while yer were asleep. They're on't chair. Mrs Earnshaw's gonner mekk over summat of 'ers for yer, then . . . Eeh, Lily Elliott, yer can't do that 'ere. Not wi't lad lyin' in't bed. Wharrif 'e opens 'is eyes?" for Lily had dragged the nightgown over her head, revealing her slim and lovely body in all its nakedness. Both the women stared in horror at the perky lift of her breasts, the nipples pink and bud-like, her waist no more than a handspan, her buttocks tight, her legs long and shapely. It was the figure of a young girl, only just matured but the strangest sight was the thick bush of *dark* hair between the confluence of her legs. They didn't know where to look, really they didn't, for neither woman had seen another female naked and even their husbands' bodies had been a secret thing in the night. Naturally, Mrs Earnshaw had been privy to Liam's body as a child and, though she would never have told him, had caught a glimpse of him in his full manhood when he took a stripped wash in his bedroom. That was why she had been so dreadfully shocked at his present state.

"If he opened his eyes then I should get down on my knees and pray as the good doctor advised; in the meanwhile I shall put on my drawers and shift; see, I'm decent already," she went on, tugging Elsie Biddle's sensible garments over her tangled curls. "I'm ready now so I'll take over, Mrs Earnshaw."

Mrs Earnshaw was elbowed aside and her mouth thinned dangerously. She and Lily had got on well during the weeks they had been alone together, waiting in harmony for Liam's homecoming. She had been appalled at the reason for the child's escape and flight from Oakwood Place and was happy to take her in, but this was her grandson and she didn't like being pushed aside as though she counted for nothing. She was well aware of the child's devotion to Liam and her terrible need to be nursing him back to health, if that was possible, but she resented this total disregard for her own commitment to Liam.

"Wharrabout summat ter eat, lamb?" Mrs Quinn was saying diplomatically. "Yer've 'ad nowt much fer days an' if yer not careful yer'll fade away ter skin an' bone."

"I'm not hungry, Mrs Quinn, really I'm not. Please, hold

his nose for me so that I can get this spoon in his mouth," for in her distress Mrs Quinn had forgotten to continue with her task.

"Then let me bring yer a bite up 'ere. Wharrabout a bacon sandwich wi' porridge ter start with and a nice cuppa tea?"

"I think Lily should go downstairs an' 'ave a proper breakfast," Mrs Earnshaw interrupted brusquely. "Sadie's in't kitchen an' she'll cook it for 'er an' then there's that dog ter be walked. It'd do yer good, lass, ter gerrout a bit."

"I can't leave Liam, Mrs Earnshaw, not for another minute. I've spent enough time away from him as it is. What if he should come to and not find me here?"

"I'll be here, child."

"I know," Lily said patiently, as though speaking to a half-witted child, "but I would rather . . ."

The old lady drew herself up and, leaning over Lily, took the spoon from her hand. "I think it might be as well if summat were established right 'ere an' now, lass. This is my 'ome an' this is my grandson an' I'd be obliged if yer'd give over ordering me about as if I were a housemaid. Now, go an' 'ave summat to eat and then when yer come back yer can tekk over for me. D'yer understand?"

It looked as though Lily were going to argue. Her face, which had been pale and drawn despite the night's sleep she had had, turned turkey red. She looked from Mrs Earnshaw's face to Liam's where it lay so appallingly still on the spotlessly white pillow and she could feel her heart wrench as she was pulled into a whirlpool of terror. He looked just as he had for the past few days and now and again a faint moan escaped him. Even the strongest body cannot endure the ravages of a consumingly high fever for long and it seemed to her that Liam had very little reserve to see him through. She could not bear to leave him but her innate sense of fair-mindedness told her that Mrs Earnshaw was right. Though she wanted to send them all away, take Liam in her arms and hold him, force the breath of life and living into him, her *own* life, her absolute will that would bring him back to her, she knew that she couldn't do it on her own. She had to keep strong. She had to keep her health in order to give Liam's back to him and she couldn't do it if she didn't eat.

With that surprising sweetness that was part of her she bent impulsively and kissed Mrs Earnshaw's cheek.

"I'm sorry," she told her. "I'll go and get something to eat and take Villy up to the orchard but . . . but I won't be long."

"I know that, child," and the two women smiled at one another and began patiently to spoon the infusion once more between Liam's cracked lips.

She was by herself, both Mrs Quinn and Mrs Earnshaw having creaked downstairs to drink a cup of tea with a promise to send up whoever was on duty in the kitchen to help her, when she sensed the difference in him.

She was leaning over him, her elbows on the bed, her chin resting in her cupped hands, her eyes studying every hollow and protruding peak of bone in his face when something ran, like a tear, from just below his hairline. It was slow-moving, thick and viscous. She watched it in fascination, then there was another and another until his whole face was bathed in it. It popped out in greater and greater gobs from his neck and the backs of his skeletal hands which rested on the covers and even as she watched the light sheets were wet with it. She put her hand wonderingly to his face and it came away with a slick film on it. She was puzzled, confused, but as her eyes looked down at him his eyes opened. His face was blank in the thin shaft of sunlight that peeped through the partly opened windows, then his eyes focused and turned, looking straight at her.

"Lovebud . . . ?" he asked questioningly, just as he had on the ship, his voice no more than a breath and the hairs stood up on the back of her neck.

"Liam . . . oh, Liam, my love," she whispered.

"Lovebud . . . is it . . ."

"Yes, yes, it's me," and the bed shook with the force of her weeping.

"I dreamed . . ."

"Dearest, don't talk . . ."

"Put . . . your . . . arms . . . round me, lovebud. Don't let me go . . . again . . ."

She scrubbed at her face with the palms of her hands, then got to her feet and lay down beside him. With infinite care and tenderness she slipped one arm beneath his neck and drew his head to her breast where he settled with a sigh, too weak to do more than let her cling to him. She kissed him, lifting his chin a little with trembling fingers so that her lips could rest on his, all the while the healing sweat pouring from him in such a torrent she knew she must call the others to change the bed, to sponge him down, to send for the doctor and do all the things that would begin the process of healing, but just for this moment she must have him to herself. To savour the feel of him in her arms even if he was scarcely aware of it. To allow herself for a few precious minutes the joy of having and holding this dear man to herself. She was so completely his. She had been for many years, living only for him to come home to her, even as a child. Now he was completely hers and she held him in gentle but strong arms, putting off the moment for a little while when she must share him again with others. His sweat was soaking into her bodice and it was turning cold but for that moment Liam O'Connor belonged absolutely to Lily Elliott.

They all wanted to come in and have a look at him, even the men, believing that this miracle must surely have returned him at once to the giant of a man they had all known. His face was still shadowed with his illness and of course Lily would not hear of it, for she guarded him now like some ferocious little terrier, taking no notice of his grandmother's pleas to see to her grandson, for he was hers, *hers*, Lily Elliott's and she was going to nurse him back to full health. They could help her if they wanted, she told them loftily, take turns while she rested in the chair by the fire in his bedroom but she would not leave his side, no, not if the Queen up in London demanded it.

The doctor had been and gone, quietly optimistic that his patient had turned the corner, praising the nursing he had received, saying his pulse was slow and strong and his heartbeat good, telling them to keep him warm now, build up the fire, but leave the windows open, for clean air was efficacious to a man who has been ill. Light food, milk, eggs, broth, sleep and more sleep.

Liam slept for two days, a deep, natural, healing sleep, waking only to take the nourishment Lily spooned into him. He had begun to recover in the normal fashion of a healthy young male, beginning to look more like himself though still painfully thin. He watched Lily whenever he was awake, his eyes following her round the room and when she came back after a necessary trip to the privy, they would be waiting for her return. She would kneel at once by the bed, leaning over to kiss his healing lips as though they had been parted for days, gently at first, then with growing urgency, for it seemed both their bodies were in the grip of some sort of growing need. His flesh was weak, feeble, laughing ruefully about it, but his mind wasn't, his eyes told her.

When she was not there, even for half an hour while she took a bath in front of the fire in Mrs Earnshaw's room, he became restive, testy, irritable, fractious, demanding to get up, pushing aside the restraining arms of Mrs Quinn or his grandmother and saying he thought he might take a turn round the bedroom at least. He quietened the moment Lily came back, sinking into his pillows, overcome with his exertions but sighing contentedly when he saw her.

It was this that exploded the vast battle of wills between not only Mrs Earnshaw and herself but with Mrs Quinn. They found her on the third day of his recovery sorting out a pile of clean sheets and blankets, and several pillows, folding them and tucking them neatly into the corner of the room. She was wearing the pale grey woollen skirt and bodice that Mrs Quinn and Mrs Earnshaw had contrived between them for her to wear in the sickroom. Well, Mrs Biddle's reeked of Liam's sweat and needed to be scrubbed before being given back to her. She had washed her hair and it stood about her head in a cloud of soft silver, curls tumbling about her neck and ears and drifting across her forehead. Her eyes were clear and shining with happiness and in her cheek had crept a tinge of carnation. She was thin, like a scarecrow, she said, though Liam, on the mend now, denied it, his eyes straying to the soft swell of her breast.

"What's them for, queen?" Mrs Earnshaw queried, her eyes narrowing suspiciously as she placed a glass of milk, in which a tot of whisky and two eggs had been beaten, on the table beside Liam's bed.

"They're for me," Lily answered airily, hoping even now that there would be no argument. She looked at Mrs Earnshaw from the corner of her eye, then sighed, for she knew it was a vain hope. There had been fierce disagreements, carried on in whispers, over the return of Liam's normal bodily functions.

Mrs Earnshaw had said, and Mrs Quinn had agreed with her, that it was not right and proper for a young, unmarried female to be involved in the embarrassing fetching and carrying, not to mention the cleaning of his body, of a young, unmarried male. She had been overruled only because Liam had turned awkward, and could you blame him, Mrs Quinn said, at the idea of Lily performing such an intimate task for him. She had given in over that but she wasn't going to give in over this.

"For you?"

"Yes, I intend to sleep in here next to Liam's bed until he is well enough to get up himself."

"Over my dead body, lady."

"Mrs Earnshaw, I have been sleeping in that chair by the fire ever since Liam came home so what difference—"

"Aye, so yer 'ave, burr 'e were unconscious then, an' me and Mrs Quinn" – who had been sleeping on the sofa in the parlour – "were close at 'and."

"You'll still be close at hand but I can't leave him alone."

"'E'll not be alone, lass."

"Mrs Earnshaw, will you stop interfering in what is mine and Liam's business. We are to be married, for God's sake."

"Liam 'asn't said so an' until 'e does . . ."

He hadn't said it to her either, not recently, but his eyes had told her what was in his mind and hers had responded, but how could she explain that to his grandmother. They had discussed nothing yet, for he was still too weak to do much at all beyond a nod of his head, a quiet yes or no to a question, but she knew and so did he. The doubts and uncertainties that had plagued her while he was ill had been swept away the moment he had turned his head into her breast when the fever broke, but it was all so recent she was afraid, terrified, to let him out of her sight, even while she slept, even while he slept. He was still so frail, so helpless and until he was strong again, himself again, she meant to sleep beside his bed.

They couldn't move her, saying it was not proper, that it was not suitable, that it was not decent.

"D'you think I gave a damn about that?" she snarled. "I love him, don't you understand, and I need to be with him," which was true. Her need was greater than his in reality and at last they understood and though they were in unison in their disapproval of it, they let it be.

At the beginning of March he could sit up with a heap of pillows behind him. Whenever anyone came to see how he was, which Lily allowed now as long as they did not tire him, and they asked him how he was he always answered "hungry", his grin stretched wide across his gaunt face. They had begun to make plans. Tommy Graham had been to tell them of the progress of *Lily-Jane*, asking hesitantly had "the captain" sorted out a crew yet, believing implicitly what the "lad", now, amazingly, the "lass", had told him about the future enterprise that was to begin as soon as the captain was up and about again.

"Well, I think I have one crew member here, Tommy," Liam told him, taking Lily's hand in his and putting the back of it to his lips, which so embarrassed the old man he nearly fell off his chair. "But I shall need a mate and a deck-hand so . . ."

"Well, sir, there's Johnno, which is why I asked. Miss Lily'll remember 'im. 'E sailed on't *Lily-Jane* wi' 'er pa, 'e ses, so 'e knows the craft like back of 'is 'and."

"Well, there we are then. A full ship's complement before she has her first cargo."

"An' what'll that be, Captain?" Tommy wanted to know, his seamed face showing his eagerness to be on the deck of a ship once more. Old he might be, but he was experienced and as lively as a man twenty years his junior.

"I don't know yet. But Lily and I will come down to the docks as soon as I'm on my feet, won't we, lovebud," and the questions that bubbled in Tommy Graham's practical mind froze on his lips at the strange promise, not of cargoes, he was sure, that lay behind the words.

He had been home three weeks. Mrs Quinn had finally gone back to Victoria's cottage, quite reluctant to leave, for she and Mrs Earnshaw had taken a great fancy to one another. Mrs Earnshaw was in her own bed and across the small landing her gentle snores could be heard. It was midnight and the house was quiet with the peace that comes when great content has entered it. The fire was aglow in the fireplace and the clock ticked sweetly above it. Lily was sprawled in the chair, her feet bare, her nightgown riding slightly up her calf. She was half asleep already. Beside her was the little bed she had made for herself and when she was sure Liam was asleep she would get into it. She slept lightly, waking at the slightest sound, lifting her head to look at Liam, ready to call Mrs Earnshaw if he needed the special "slipper" bedpan made from brown glazed earthenware, or the glass urinal the doctor had provided.

She sighed and turned to look at him, smiling when she saw that he was watching her. There was a spark of something in his eye which suddenly excited her and she sat up slowly.

He held out his hand and she rose and went to him, putting her hand in his. He drew her down to sit bedside him on the bed, then reached up a hand to the back of her head, drawing her mouth down to his. His kiss was gentle but she sensed a compulsion in it, something urgent that he was making a decent effort to control.

"I love you, lovebud," he murmured, smoothing his hand over the tumbled cap of her curls, smiling a little at the absurdity of it. His lips moved to her jaw then dipped to the faint, childish hollow of her collar bone and without conscious thought she wrapped her arms about his head and pressed his face close to her. He murmured something, his hands at her shoulders now and when they pushed aside the neckline of her nightgown, drawing it down to reveal the satin smoothness of her breasts, she did not object. His hand moved to cup one tight, hard-nippled bud, then his mouth followed and she arched her neck and back to accommodate him, moaning softly in the back of her throat.

"You're beautiful . . . so lovely," he told her, his eyes filled with wondering delight. The child was no longer a child but a woman who was ready to flaunt her love and her desire for him with no thought of false modesty or even the shyness that a woman displays when she is beneath a man's ardent gaze for the first time. His hands began a slow, enchanted wandering, exploring the fine bones beneath of her shoulders, her ribs and finally, as the nightgown was disposed of by one of them – did it matter who? – the curving column of her spine, the soft curve of her waist and hips and down to the vibrant centre of her woman's body.

She was breathing hard now and so was he but he knew she must be the dominant one, for though his masculinity was urging him on and on, his slowly recovering body was lagging behind.

"My love . . . lovebud . . . you'll have to help me . . ."

"Tell me . . . tell me what to do," she gasped, ready to fling herself down beside him, or should she sit up; she didn't know, she only knew she wanted something this man could give her and she wanted it at once. Her body, *inside* her body there was a rippling like overlapping flames, hot and ready to burn her and yet her skin was so tender, so sensitive, she thought a touch could . . . could bruise her. Dear Lord, she was so . . . so . . . she didn't know . . . she didn't know.

"Lie here, beside me, face to face. Dear God, I've watched you, wanted this, but . . ."

"Liam, dearest . . . let me . . ."

"Yes," guiding her hand, "but please . . ." He was gasping a little with what seemed to be laughter.

"What?"

"Be gentle with me."

"Oh, Liam, I love you . . . love you."

Some instinct, some intuition that had come to her woman's body told her what she must do. Slow, delicate, her movements fitting to his, hers the stronger but the building pleasure of his body giving him strength. When he entered her it was as it should be, hard and thrusting and she gasped as she bore down to meet him, then she knew no more as a flood of something she had never before experienced carried her up and up and into a world of colour and light and darkness and shadowed wonder, and when she came down from it he held her in trembling arms, his face pressed to hers, his breath harsh.

"Liam . . ." Her voice was high, almost like a child's, and yet with something in it that was not at all child-ish.

"Yes, my lovebud?"

"Did you . . . did you experience what . . . ?"

"Oh, yes, my darling, but you were so . . . overcome you didn't notice." He was smiling in great satisfaction.

"I'm sorry."

"Don't be sorry, my love. What you had was what every man wants to give to the woman he loves."

"Will it always be . . . like this?"

"I've no doubt of it, lovebud. Now, put your head on my shoulder and go to sleep."

32

"As soon as I can get out of this bed, Gran, Lily and I will be married," he told his grandmother the next morning, just as though he were informing her of an appointment he had made and forgotten to tell her about. He and Lily studiously avoided each other's glance, both of them aware that the flush of remembrance was warming their faces. Lily could actually feel it flood from her hairline right down to her toes. Not that she was ashamed nor even embarrassed, but it had been so startling, so wonderful, so passionately tender, so ... so private, belonging only to herself and Liam she was reluctant even to share a hint of it with Mrs Earnshaw. She wanted to turn away and busy herself at some task, like the folding of the blankets which, last night, had not been used, but she could hardly show indifference when Liam was announcing their intention to marry, could she? She was still floating in some separate space that was not vouchsafed to other women, and until Mrs Earnshaw had entered the bedroom, carrying Liam's breakfast tray, had been kneeling at his bedside, fully dressed by now, naturally, and engaged in the pleasant pastime of telling him of her love and wonder, of kissing him at the back of his ear which he seemed to like and of arching her back as his fingers traced the nipples of her breasts. If Mrs Earnshaw had not been somewhat heavy-footed she might have caught them at it. As it was Lily had only time to leap up and hastily rearrange her clothing before she came into the bedroom.

"Is that so?" Mrs Earnshaw said grimly, as though Lily were the last girl she would have chosen for her Liam.

"Yes, it is so, Gran. Have you any objection?"

"I'm not sayin' I've any objection; wharr I am sayin' is

it's not before time. All these weeks sharin' a bedroom an' what the neighbours must be sayin' I shudder ter think, fer that Sadie, though a more good – 'earted woman I've yet ter meet, she's a sharp one an' misses nowt. Mrs Quinn agrees wi' me, an' all, an' as she's the only one 'oo can claim a kinship o' some sort wi' Lily, then she's entitled to 'er say."

She banged the tray down on the table with great force, slopping the creamy porridge that she insisted on spooning into Liam at least once a day over the side of the bowl, appearing to be deeply offended; then with a gesture that showed her true feelings she turned and dragged Lily into her arms and kissed her soundly.

"Eeh, lady," she said, apropos of nothing, it seemed, but it was as though she were telling her she was completely aware of everything that went on under her own roof. She wasn't born yesterday, nor even the day before!

She turned back to her grandson, a glint of tears in her eyes, holding his head to her breast for a moment of deep emotion. Then, with a sniff, she picked up the tray and set it before him.

"Yer'd best get that down yer then, fer yer'll need all 't strength yer can get. It'll be a few weeks afore yer can gerrout o' that bed so . . ."

"I intend to try this very day, Gran." With his free hand he reached for Lily's, confirming Eva Earnshaw's suspicions, for the child blushed the rosiest red. In her eyes was that look she had seen in her own when she and her Bert had first been wed and it came from something more then being young and healthy.

"Well, lad, yer can fergerrabout that, can't he, Lily? Now, lass, yer must back me up on this," she added anxiously. "'E's not fit enough ter swing 'is legs over 't side o't bed, lerralone walk."

"We'll see, Gran. With Lily helping me . . ."

"Lily! Look at 'er. She couldn't carry our Ginger, she's that thin."

Lily trusted her voice for the first time since Mrs Earnshaw had come into the bedroom. Just the touch of Liam's hand on hers had the power to spin her into this delicious sensation of melting, particularly at her knees, a melting pleasure so strong she wanted to sit down before she fell down. She could feel her insides beginning to flutter, as though a bird were trapped there, and she could sense a gasp of something that might have been a moan similar to the ones she had uttered last night, rising to her throat as she spoke.

She had to clear her throat before the words would come out. "I think he should try, Mrs Earnshaw. Look how much better he is now. Even if it's only across the bedroom. He's . . . he's quite strong."

"Aye, I shouldn't wonder," Mrs Earnshaw said drily. "Now, go and 'ave yer breakfast. There's bacon an' egg in th'oven. Anyroad, I want ter talk ter me grandson, so off yer go."

There was a letter propped up against a jar of primroses set in the middle of the white-clothed table. It had come by the first of the nine daily postal deliveries and was addressed to her. It was from Nicky Crowther, asking her why she had not answered his letters, for this was not the first he had sent. Almost from the first day they had arrived, sometimes two a week, and in each one he begged her to be careful, to be wary of his father, to stay beside Mrs Earnshaw and never go out alone. He missed her so much, he said, and though he had not wanted to say anything just yet, her silence was worrying him and he felt the need to tell her that the feelings he had for her were very strong. Please, please would she write and let him know she was safe, otherwise he would simply desert and come back to England to find her.

The bacon and egg were left to congeal on the plate as she sat back slowly in the chair. During the past weeks she had been vaguely aware of the letters coming from Nicky. She had even read them, though their contents had gone by her, as insubstantial as smoke from a chimney. She had been too concerned with Liam, too preoccupied with wresting him back from the snapping jaws of death to bother about Nicky Crowther's anxiety for her. She would be eternally grateful to him for what he had done for her and Mrs Earnshaw and she would write and tell him so, but she would also tell him she was to marry Liam O'Connor, Mrs Earnshaw's grandson, as soon as possible, and he must not write to her again. Liam wouldn't care to have his wife corresponding with another man, would he, particularly an officer in the army. Besides, she wanted to forget that part of her life now that she was to embark on a new one. Not forget Ma, of course. She could never do that, but forget the family who had wreaked such havoc on hers. She had heard that Eloise was to marry in a week or two. Mrs Quinn had said the servants were all going to watch the ceremony at St Anne's Church on Holmes Lane but that didn't concern her. Nothing the Crowther family did concerned her. She would marry Liam, that was all that mattered to her, and they would take *Lily-Jane* and sail away just like Pa and Ma used to do. The dream she had dreamed as a small girl was about to be fulfilled. She would never be a seaman, not like her pa and Liam were seaman, with a Master's Certificate to prove it, but she would have the next best thing which was Liam teaching her what *he* had learned. She would be part of the schooner's life, she would be part of Liam's life, not just as his wife but as his partner in a business they would build up together.

It was enough. It was all she had ever wanted. Except for one small thing, and as the picture of the baby her mother had given birth to last year came into her mind she leaned forward and, crossing her arms on the table, put her forehead on them. Abby. She would be nine months old now, living with her nursemaid in the nursery, and though Mrs Quinn had told her that the servants made a big fuss of her, spoiled her when they could, for all children need a bit of spoiling, she was a child without family, without a father's or a mother's love and the thought distressed Lily immeasurably. There was nothing to be done about it, but sometimes she felt the pain and guilt of it pierce her heart. She knew about loneliness, for since Pa died, though Ma had done her best, Lily had missed that absolute security, those loving arms to hold her and she felt guilty that she could not provide them for her half-sister.

Mrs Earnshaw bustled into the kitchen, putting the tray down on the table and moving to the oven where Liam's bacon and eggs were keeping warm.

She tutted when she saw Lily's plate. "I told yer ter get that lot down yer, child, unless yer want ter be ill an' all. There's not a pick on yer. An' what's that lad in Ireland said ter upset yer? Oh, aye, I knew t' letter were from 'im, that's why I never mentioned it in front of our Liam." The look on her face implied she'd skin Nicky Crowther alive if he hurt her, or indeed anyone in her family.

Lily sighed and pushed the heavy fringe of her hair off her forehead. "Oh, it's not him, Mrs Earnshaw."

"Granny!"

Lily blinked. "Pardon?"

"Yer'll 'ave ter call me Granny, now that yer ter be me granddaughter-in-law." She smiled complacently, as though the whole affair had been personally contrived by her.

Lily stood up and put her arms about her. She was taller by half a head but somehow she managed to put her forehead on Eva's shoulder.

"It will be lovely to have a family again," she said softly. "So . . . Granny." They stood for a moment smiling at one another in affectionate understanding, then she drew away, beginning to frown again.

"It's . . . I was thinking about my sister. My half-sister. The thought that she is to be brought up by that monster gives me nightmares, but there's nothing I can do about it. This letter from Nicky reminded me and then there are other things that must be spoken of. You understand?"

"Aye, lass, I do."

She would have to tell Liam. So far, he had not even questioned why she was here at his grandmother's cottage, presuming, she supposed, that she had come as soon as Mrs Earnshaw had got word of his arrival in port. That day when *Breeze* had berthed was not in his memory at the moment but it must all be explained to him before they married. The thought terrified her. Not for herself who had been an innocent victim but for Liam who, when he heard what he had attempted and when he was able, would simply tear Joshua Crowther limb from limb. She knew it without a shadow of a doubt. Easy-going, good-hearted, gentle as big men often are, a man who abhorred violence, his rage would be an explosion of such proportions it could scarcely be imagined. He was a man with a man's need to protect his woman, and his woman's reputation, his *wife's* reputation. She was to be his wife, take his name, and the man who had been her mother's husband would be made to pay for what he had done. Liam had walked through the years beside her, seven years now, and had seen, perhaps even known what sort of a man Joshua Crowther was, but it had not been his business then. Now it was!

Eva took her hand in hers. "Let's get lad on 'is feet, child, afore we start worryin' about what's ter come. When 'e's ready we'll tell 'im together." Though she sounded cheerful, optimistic even, Eva shook her head at the thought of it.

Liam continued to improve, eating enormous amounts of his granny's home-made bread thick with fresh butter, piled high with slabs of cheese. Broths thick with meat and vegetables, beefsteak puddings with mashed potatoes and freshly picked cabbage, home-cured ham with eggs, roast chicken with the skin crisp and brown, apple pies and cream, rice pudding and lemon creams and the flesh crept back on his bones almost overnight. He drank the milk that was brought over from the farm and when, at last, he got out of bed and tottered down the stairs, to the accompanied cheers of every inhabitant of the four cottages, including five dogs, six cats and an assortment of kittens who capered about the garden like butterflies on the wing, it was like a party. Villy and Ginger, who were devoted to one another now, watched in astonishment before curling up companionably together in the warm sunshine.

Mrs Earnshaw had whispered in Sadie's ear that Liam was to come downstairs that day and though there was not enough room in the house for everyone, they were all there. The men drank the ale Mrs Earnshaw had had fetched up from the ale-house and the women had a glass, or even two, of her cowslip wine and the merriment was loud and boisterous. It was a Sunday. It was April and winter had finally let go of its hold and allowed spring to take its place and the improvement in Liam's health was a joy to them all. They sat in the deliciously warm sunshine, crowding about the bit of grass, the children spilling out into the road, watching slyly as Liam held Lily's hand, for they all knew by now that they were to be married at the end of the month. The banns had been called at St Mary's Church in West Derby and a dress was being made by Miss Jenny Hardcastle, a clever young seamstress who had just started up a business in the area and was eager to please. There was a rumour that a double bed had been ordered for the young newly weds who were to stay with Liam's granny until the ship, that one he and Lily had bought, was ready, when, presumably, they would sail away together, or so Lily said, though the women smiled, for if Liam was any sort of a man, and he was, his bride would be pregnant before the may was in bloom. They had all been invited to the wedding, every last one of them, and though Lily was, in their opinion, a lady, a lady with a way of talking that was nothing like theirs, they forgave her for it, accepting her into their midst if only for the fact that her love for their Liam, whom they had known since he was a nipper, had saved his life and shone even now like a candle in her eyes.

There had been, to both Liam's and Lily's regret, no resumption of that one night of love they had shared several weeks back in Liam's bed, for Granny had declared that as he was so much better, Lily's bed could now be brought into *her* room. They were to be decently married, she told them tartly, as though she were well aware of what had happened, fixing them with a stern look that made them both blush. Of course, now that he was on his feet again and the weather fine enough for a walk across the stretch of back garden and into the orchard, which was an enchantment of budding apple blossom, they had the opportunity for many a stolen moment and in the days that followed they would both return in a breathless state, flushed and glowing, and Eva was thankful it was only two weeks to the wedding.

Liam's chests containing the artefacts he had bought while he was in China had been stored at a small warehouse at the back of Canning Dock, Tommy told them on one of his visits. Tommy seemed to have taken up the duty of first mate on the *Lily-Jane* before she had even put to sea, trudging up from the docks with messages on the progress of the schooner, which was expected to be ready by the middle of May, expressions of goodwill from the piermaster and from the captain of *Breeze* who had been delighted that Liam had made such a wonderful recovery. As he had said to Tommy, in confidence, of course, and he was not to repeat it, he had not expected to see him reach Liverpool. No, a funeral at sea had been his forecast, he had said, shaking his head gloomily. There was a message from Johnno who was made up at the thought of sailing on the *Lily-Jane* again and, as word got round, and perhaps remembering Richard Elliott's reputation for fair dealing, expert seamanship and trustworthiness, there had been one or two enquiries on the possibility of cargo. A Mr Atkinson, a merchant in a small way of business in Water Street, but growing, wished to have a consignment of salt taken across the Irish Sea, bringing back cattle and would be glad if Captain O'Connor would call when convenient. There were men who needed someone to carry their iron and steel, their machinery, their cotton goods, their woollen goods, their bricks, cement, their timber, stone, manure, china clay and pitwood. There was no shortage of cargoes to be carried to small ports around the Irish Sea and Lily and Liam clasped hands, their heads together, their kisses scarcely interrupted as they planned for their vivid future. Liam had several buyers for his exotic imports from China – fine porcelain, silks, fans, silver dishes and ornate ivory and lacquerware – which were to be sold to help to pay for the renovations to *Lily-Jane*. Several days before the wedding Sadie Ainsworth's lad ran down to the hackney stand at the corner by the Zoological Gardens to fetch a cab to take Liam and Lily to the docks.

Lily was dressed in her heather blue gown and puff bonnet, a parasol of white lace lined with blue silk that Liam had brought back for her held above her just like the lady she was, the neighbours told one another as they watched her and Liam climb into the hackney. Liam, though still somewhat lean, not quite fitting into his good suit as yet but becoming bronzed by the sun that had shone for the past month, was as tender with her as if she were made of spun sugar, which made the women smile. They had seen her perform gargantuan tasks when Liam was at his worst, almost physically lifting him single-handed, going on hour after hour in the wearying task of nursing him back to health. She was beautiful again now, with that ethereal radiance that she had lost when it seemed Liam was not to recover. Her hair, which Liam had insisted she grow again, was beginning to fall about her shoulders and her slenderness, in that strange way of women in love, women who are loved, had begun to fill out. Man feedeth woman, the saying went, and if Lily Elliott was anything to go by, it was true. Not that the plumpness of her own hips and breast was anything to do with her Charlie, Sadie was heard to remark. Mind you, he never left her alone which probably accounted for the seven children she still had at home, *and* her comfortable frame!

They took the excursion steamboat to Runcorn, disembarking there while the remainder of the passengers were to go on to Manchester by the Canal Packet via the Mersey and Irwell Navigation. They would do it one day, they promised one another, for it should be very interesting, but at that precise moment their whole attention was focused on the walk down to the docks and the schooner that awaited them there.

Lily was ready to weep, clinging to Liam's arm, so filled with joy was her heart. It was the happiest day of her life and yet, she sniffed to Liam, the saddest. If only Pa could have seen her as she is now, she said, looking at the sleek lines of her newly painted timber, the polished wood of her deck, the elegant lift of her two new masts, the gleam of her new white sails, furled up neatly to the cross-spar. He had done his best, she knew that now, but *Lily-Jane* had been allowed to slip away into disrepair and now she and Liam had brought her back to life and she did her best to imagine that somewhere, wherever seamen go when they die, he was watching and gloating over his schooner's resurrection. She'd be ready in two weeks, the shipwright told them and did they want him to fetch her up to Liverpool? an eager expression on his face, since she was a lovely ship.

"No," they said in unison, then looked at one another, smiling, their minds attuned so that they each knew that what they wanted was to bring her home themselves. "Let us know when she'll be ready and we'll be over to pick her up."

"What, both of yer?" The man was clearly surprised.

"Yes, my future wife is as keen a seaman as I am."

They were married on a day of pale pearly blue skies and glowing golden sunshine, the last day in April when the swallows went mad with joy as though in celebration of the day, swooping and swirling about the trees surrounding the churchyard and a carpet of newly blooming harebells hazed the grass with azure. They were trampled on by a hundred pairs of feet, for the crowd come to watch the serious bridegroom and his exquisite young bride as they passed out of the church into the sunshine was extensive. Mrs Earnshaw had lived in these parts for fifty years and was well known, and, of course, the recent illness of her handsome grandson, who had not been expected to survive it, had been a miracle. Mind you, they had heard that his bride, a lady, no less, had fought tooth and nail to keep him alive, though to look at her you wouldn't think she could nurse a kitten. All in white and looking as though she were treading on moonbeams with a face on her that would charm the gods. Smile, she was in heaven with it all, you could tell that, and he looked as though he'd been given the moon and the stars all rolled into one. They told one another they had never seen a happier-looking couple, though it was a well-known fact that a girl's wedding day was the happiest day of her life.

Mrs Quinn cried sharply, telling anyone who would listen that the child was the spit of her mother who Mrs Quinn had known at almost the same age. All those from Oakwood Place who could sneak time off had come, even if it was only a quick dash in Mr Crowther's carriage – he didn't know, naturally – driven by Arnold who was Mrs Quinn's son-in-law and would get the sack if he was found out. Jenny, who once Lily had read to while she peeled the spuds, Dorcas, Rosie, Betsy and both Maggies. They waved and threw flower petals and told one another that she deserved it, the dear little thing, and even Mr Diggle, with Will hanging bashfully at his back, had thrown down his spade and come across to see her wed.

They watched her climb into the hired carriage, the big chap, as they had always called him, fussing tenderly about his bride, their erstwhile little mistress, though she had never really been that, and blessed the gods who had sent someone, at last, to protect her. It was the happiest day and well worth the chance they had taken of slipping across to see her.

The rest, neighbours and friends, guests, even Tommy and Johnno and the piermaster, who had been invited to bring his wife, crammed themselves into Granny Earnshaw's small cottage, or sat on the grass in the garden beneath the shade of the massive and beautiful horse chestnut tree which was in full bloom. They toasted the bride and groom, not only with ale and cowslip wine but with, of all things, a sip of champagne purchased for the occasion by the groom. Mrs Earnshaw, with the help of Mrs Quinn, who came over regularly now, had made the bridecake, rich in fruit and brandy and decorated with the most intricate white icing and, at the end of the day, as darkness fell, though some of them, the men particularly, wanted to carry out the old tradition of seeing the new husband and wife to their bed, they left reluctantly, telling one another it had been a wonderful day and wasn't it splendid that after all the drama of the last few months it had all ended so happily.

They slept at last in their new bed, Mr and Mrs Liam O'Connor, the door firmly and legitimately closed against all comers, conscious of Granny across the landing but not minding, for she was slightly deaf after all.

He had made love to her, not with the uncertain frailty of the last time when he had been only just recovering from his illness, but with the full and lusty passion of a healthy young man. Strong, forceful, claiming what was his, with no concern for gallantry or gentleness, hasty in his need to make her his *wife*, his woman, *his*. He took her with a force that nailed them together, his heavy body crushing hers and she answered him fiercely, for there had been weeks in which his hands and his lips had driven her mad with a desire that they could not satisfy. His invasion, when it came, almost split her asunder and again, as it had the last time, waves poured over her, flames devoured her, leaving her drained, docile, submissive, possessed. His!

He sighed with great satisfaction when she lay against him, her sweated body plastered to his, her face in the hollow beneath his chin, his arms possessively about her.

"I love you, you know that, don't you," he told her almost angrily as though still contesting any man's right to take what was his.

"Dear God, I should hope so," she murmured drowsily, her lips against his throat, "after all that."

"You liked it?" He sounded a trifle smug.

"Mmm. I was just wondering when we were going to do it again."

33

They were to sail the day after tomorrow, taking Mr Atkinson's cargo of salt to Londonderry in Northern Ireland, bringing back Irish cattle, a round trip of ten days, allowing for the discharge of the cargo and the loading of another. They had brought back *Lily-Jane* three days ago, the short journey from Runcorn to Liverpool nothing short of a triumphal journey of hopes fulfilled. It had culminated in the schooner's entry into her berth at Canning Dock where men who knew her, and of her new owners, Captain and Mrs Liam O'Connor, cheered her progress. The piermaster was there in person to open the lock gates, serious-faced, for it was a serious business, but winking at the lovely girl who leaned against her new husband as he steered the sailing ship expertly to her berth. They made a handsome couple, she and her new husband, and their happiness and joy, not only in the vessel but in each other shone out like the Rock Ferry Lighthouse on a dark night.

The crew were smart in their new ganseys and drill trousers, Johnno smirking and red-faced with satisfaction, for it was nearly seven years since he had sailed with Mrs O'Connor's pa in this very ship. It seemed strange to call her Mrs O'Connor, for he could still see that small girl, her own face rosy with excitement, standing before her pa with her hands on the wheel, believing that she was steering *Lily-Jane* up the channel towards the mouth of the river. He could remember Mr Porter's face, his expression of deep disapproval, but the new captain did not look disapproving, in fact his eyes shone with something so deep and loving Johnno felt compelled to look away in guilt as though he were prying into something private.

Tommy shouted orders, first to Johnno and then to the men on the dock, bobbing and weaving about the deck as though he were sixteen instead of sixty, everywhere at once in his efforts to bring the vessel in to his captain's satisfaction. He thought he had died and gone to heaven, he told his mates in the ale-house later, for until the child, meaning Mrs O'Connor, had come into his life he had thought he was beached.

Granny Earnshaw said she was going to miss them, since she had had Lily and then Liam with her for almost six months, but her friend Mrs Quinn was going to come over and stay with her for a few days so that would be very pleasant. Mrs Quinn was not at all settled in her daughter's house, for she was used to her own ways, and Victoria, though a good girl and a splendid housekeeper, was not prepared to take advice from her mother. There it was, that was the younger generation for you and, no doubt, when the time came, meaning when the babies came, for come they surely would, Lily would want her own place too. A bride likes to have supreme domestic authority in her own kitchen, not play second fiddle to some other woman no matter how fond.

Lily had given it no thought, looking no further than the day after tomorrow when she would set sail in *Lily-Jane* for the first time, the first of many journeys she and Liam were to take beyond the shining water of the River Mersey, and talk of houses and housekeeping and domestic doings were of no interest to her. She was to be a seaman, not a housewife. She was to be a friend, a lover, a partner to the man she loved. She had a new gansey and pea jacket, just like Tommy and Johnno, and a pair of navy blue woollen trousers made for her by the clever Miss Jenny Hardcastle, who, though astounded by the order, buckled to and designed, fitted and made it up to her customer's needs. They were all packed neatly in her old carpet bag, the one with which she had arrived on Granny's doorstep last year, along with a change of undergarments and a certain gauzy bit of nonsense trimmed with satin ribbons which Liam liked her to wear.

She wandered to the window of the bedroom she shared with Liam, her face serene and dreaming, pulling back the snowy nets and looking out over the garden, beyond the horse chestnut tree, beyond the splash of red and white where Granny's peonies, planted in a sheltered corner, blazed like a fire, where the lavender-mauve of phlox and the yellow of evening primrose rioted, to the barley field splashed by crimson poppies on the other side of the hawthorn hedge. It was all so beautiful, which was a poor word, really, to describe what was inside her, what she looked at and felt, and the day after tomorrow when—

Her dreaming thoughts were interrupted by the sound of Granny's voice coming up the stairs and when she poked her head round the doorway she was standing at the bottom with Ginger in her arms, her face somewhat flushed and querulous.

"That there 'usband o' yours 'as drunk all't milk. I know I said 'e were ter gerras much down 'him as 'e could burr I wish 'e'd tell me. I were just goin' ter give Puss a drink an' then mekk a custard tart an' now . . ."

"Granny, don't worry. Goodness me, what a to-do. I can easily slip down the lane to Newsham Farm and get some. I'll only be a minute. Liam's at Ronny Biddle's on some great and secretive errand which I am not supposed to know about, but as he's been telling me for days that there is no need for me to pack my clothes just yet I have a feeling it might be something to do with our travels."

As she spoke she was running lightly down the stairs. Granny Earnshaw had begun to smile, turning away to hide it, for she knew all about the sea chest Liam was having made for his new wife. Ronny had found a beautiful piece of mahogany which, he had told Liam, would have a finish like satin when he had done with it. There would be a lid, intricately carved with Lily's initials, L.O'C., intertwined with sailing ships and seabirds, and it would be fitted with drawers, each one lined with strong cambric. A lovely and yet eminently practical piece of luggage for any traveller.

"Yer a sharp one, Lily O'Connor, but when yer gerrit pretend ter be surprised, won't yer. 'E's that pleased wi' 'imself."

"I know, Granny, and I shall be the most surprised wife in Liverpool."

They both smiled, highly delighted, the sound of her new name on Granny's lips and the word "wife" giving them both inordinate pleasure.

"I think I'll take Villy. She hasn't had a walk today."

"She's 'ad a good run, though. She were chasin' a rabbit through th' orchard last time I seen 'er."

"Thank goodness she never catches one."

"Aye. I'm right fond of a birra rabbit but not one mangled up by that there dog."

So Villy was left behind.

As Lily passed Ronny Biddle's cottage she stopped for a moment to see if Liam was in sight but it was evident that he and Ronny were deep in consultation in Ronny's workshed. It would have been pleasant to stroll hand in hand down Upper Breck Road in the soft morning sunshine to the farm which was just across the main West Derby Road and along the rough track, but she hated to disturb him, especially as she might surprise and intrude on a moment Liam did not want her to share.

She had not stopped to put on a bonnet, nor a shawl, since it was May now and the air was warm and pleasant. She drew great breaths of it deep into her lungs, catching the fragrance of sorrel and cranesbill, of sweet Cecily and hedge parsley, which was rising in a tide as summer approached, ready to submerge the banks and hedges on the sides of the lane. Chaffinches were rattling in the hedges, searching for food and one flew up, its pinkish underside flashing for a moment in the sunshine.

She sauntered on, the milk pail in her hand, her silver pale hair glinting and gleaming, lighting to streaks of silvery gold as she moved her head from side to side. She had on the plain country dress Granny and Mrs Quinn had made for her, but round her waist she had knotted a broad scarlet ribbon with a bow at the back, the ends of which hung almost to the hem of her skirt.

She met one of the Ainsworths' boys almost at the end of the road, just where it entered West Derby Road, smiling at him with such brilliance he was quite bowled over. Well, he was almost thirteen and all females were a mystery to him, but Liam's wife was the most beautiful woman he had ever seen.

"Mornin," Mrs O'Connor," he said to her shyly, scarcely daring to raise his eyes.

"Morning . . . Sam, isn't it?"

"Aye," he managed to gasp before dashing off towards the cottages as though the devil were at his heels.

There was a small dog-leg at the junction, turning to the right and then to the left up the farm track and the hansom cab was standing at the corner. The cab driver, perched on the seat behind the enclosed cab looked as though he had dropped off to sleep and so did the horse. It was all so still and when the woman, grey-haired and respectable-looking, opened the door and popped her head out, Lily walked towards her, smiling. It was obvious she was going to ask for directions and though Lily was not particularly conversant with the area or those who lived in it she could only be polite, couldn't she?

He watched her walk innocently towards him. He had been watching for days, patient as a beast of prey waiting for its quarry. He was crouched as far back in the hansom cab as he could get, the woman who leaned out screening him from the approaching girl, but he could still see her, her rosy, smiling face, the long stalk of her slender white neck, the lift and thrust of her young breasts, the swing of her hips, the way she placed her feet as she moved. She walked differently now, her head high and proud as she had always done, but with that sensual, graceful movement of a woman who was no longer a girl. No longer a maiden, a virgin. His heart was doing the most peculiar things, pounding and roaring in his ears, for he had waited for this moment for six long months and now it was here. Now, at last, she was almost in his grasp and though it was not quite the same as it might have been a few weeks ago, before she married that oaf, nevertheless it was a moment of triumph. He was not to be the first, which, initially, had nearly tipped him over the top in his vitriolic anger, but he had got over that since it made no difference to what he meant to do to her. She would probably put up more of a struggle since it appeared her marriage had been a love match and it quite titillated his senses to think he was to take what was another man's, and to take it against her will. He wanted her to fight him, and she would, at least in the beginning, and when she had stopped fighting he would no longer want her. For weeks, months he had watched and waited, receiving reports from the man he had hired, but the trouble was she never went out alone. In the beginning she had completely outwitted them for weeks by wearing boy's clothing and when, finally, the man he hired to follow her had cottoned on, the big chap had returned and been ill, so his man had told him, and for weeks she'd never gone over the doorstep. He was aware that the pair of them were to sail on that schooner they had somehow found the money to purchase and that if he didn't get her before then, he never would. Before long she would be pregnant, there was no doubt of that, for that was what the working classes did. Produce children like rabbits and then it would be over for him. He wanted her, but not when she was the mother of a child. Some lout's child.

No, this was his last chance and he held his breath as she smiled up into the woman's face.

"Can I help?" she asked, something in her voice, something soft and lilting that he had never heard before and it sickened him for *he* had put it there.

"Pardon?" the woman beside him said. "I'm a little hard of hearing, dear."

"I asked if I could help." Lily raised her voice.

"Ah, yes, I'm looking for someone called Huggett. Now I know they live somewhere on West Derby Road but this driver doesn't seem to have an ounce of sense in his head. Now, dear, have you heard of them?"

"Well, unfortunately, I don't know the—"

"Speak up, dear, I can't hear you. See, put your foot up on the step so that you can get a bit closer."

Lily did as she was told. "I said," she began patiently, then, like a devil from the pits of hell, *he* was there, the nightmare figure she had prayed never to see again, leering over the old woman's shoulder, his eyes wide with what she knew was madness. Hands pulled her in over the woman's lap, his hands and the woman's hands, and before she could scream her fear and loathing he had yelled to the cabbie to move on at once. The man urged the horse forward, the cab began to rock and though she fought like a demon, terror lending her strength, a pad was pressed over her face, blinding her, choking her, filling her head with mist. She struggled for a second or two, doing her best to defend herself but the pad was heavily impregnated with ether and she fell, swiftly and with a roaring in her ears that filled her with despair, into an empty, echoing black hole.

* * *

She had been gone for an hour when Granny began to worry. Puss had been twining round her legs, begging for her milk, and in the end Eva had gone next door to beg a saucerful off Sadie, for the dratted animal was a nuisance. Villy came back, a dejected look on her face, for her nose had been on the rabbit's white scut when it disappeared down its hole. She flopped down by the hearth after first looking about her for Lily, morosely staring into the flames of the fire.

"She's norrere so there's no use lookin' for 'er," Eva told her sharply, "an' if she's not back wi' that there milk soon it'll be too late fer't custard. An' after I've told our Liam 'e were to 'ave one, an' all. God knows wharr 'e'll get ter eat on that there boat an' 'e still needs feedin' up. I'll not be 'appy till I see another couple o' stone on 'im, an' that's the truth."

Her face brightened. "I bet she's stopped off at Ronny's, the little minx, an' after I told 'er I needed milk special. I'll box 'er ears fer 'er, see if I don't, worryin' me like this."

Leaving the front door open, she trudged off down the lane until she reached the last, or first, depending on which way you were approaching, cottage in the row. Pushing open the lopsided gate, wondering why it was that whatever his trade might be a man never seemed to be troubled with what needed doing in his own home. Ronny was a carpenter and yet there were loose window frames, doors hanging skew-whiff, this gate which was ready to come off its hinges, so it seemed, and many other jobs that he was just going to get round to, or so he told his Elsie.

The two men had their heads together over the chest lid which was on the bench. They were agreeing amiably that Ronny had never done a finer bit of work and as soon as the lid was on Liam would come and fetch it and bring Ronny's money.

"Look at this, Gran," he said, taking her arm and guiding her towards the bench, but it seemed Gran wasn't interested, not one little bit, and for a moment Ronny looked offended.

"Never mind chest. 'Ave yer seen our Lily?" she asked abruptly, pulling away from Liam and both men gawped.

"Lily?' Liam asked, as though he didn't know who she meant and Granny wondered again on the daftness of the male sex.

"Yes, Lily. Yer wife, yer big lug. 'Ave yer seen 'er?" She did her best to keep the fear out of her voice, and really, should she be surprised by Liam's confusion? He knew nothing of what had happened to his wife before Christmas for the simple reason Lily had been afraid to tell him. She had confided to Eva that when they reached Ireland, putting the Irish Sea between them and Joshua Crowther, she would tell him, for it would mean that it would be a week before Liam could get at him and perhaps in that time he might have calmed down and she would perhaps be able to persuade him to let it go. She was safe and unharmed and it was unlikely the law would look kindly on a man who killed, or at the very least, maimed another because he had made an improper advance, or so she would imply it had been, to the woman who was now his wife. Six months and they would want to know why he had waited until now. Well, Granny knew what she meant, didn't she, and Granny did.

But where was she now? Ten minutes, or perhaps fifteen for the round trip to the farm and here it was an hour later and her not back. She may have stopped to talk to the dairymaid but dairymaids were hard worked and had not the time to stop and gossip with customers, had they? She should have been back here at least half an hour ago.

She said so, her voice high and beginning to crack with terror and Liam rose slowly from where he was leaning on the bench.

"Gran?" he asked her, her fear beginning to reach out to him. He gripped her forearms so tightly she winced, trying to pull away from him and Ronny Biddle was heard to remonstrate, for the old lady was clearly in great distress.

"'E's gorrer. Dear sweet Jesus, that bugger's gorrer an' it were me what sent 'er for't milk."

"Milk? Who's gorrer? Whar yer talkin' about?" he began to stammer, lapsing into his old way of speaking in his alarm. He started to shake her, his face as white as the milk Granny had sent Lily for. Her head flopped about on her neck and she began to weep.

"'Ere, lad, give over," Ronny told him, doing his best to rescue the old lady from her grandson's frantic grasp, but Liam clipped him under the chin with his elbow and he fell back against the bench, biting his tongue.

"Tell me . . . tell me or I'll kill you," he was saying to his own grandmother, spittle spraying her, his face so close to hers their noses were touching.

"Liam, lad . . . I'm sorry . . . I'll never forgive meself if owt . . . Oh, please, dear Lord, keep 'er safe . . . don't lerrim 'urt 'er."

"*Where is she, you stupid old woman?*" Liam was so far gone in his frantic fear – he didn't know what of – that he was saying dreadful things, doing dreadful things, and to an old woman who loved him and whom he loved and who could not defend herself against him. "'Oo is it? 'Oo's gorrer? What's bin goin' on? Wharr 'appened while I was away? Tell me or I'll break yer bloody neck."

He was shouting so loudly that a crowd had begun to gather at Ronny's gate, women mostly, for the men were at work, but a passing carter had stopped, and the postman, who was just making his third delivery of the day, peered over his shoulder.

"Fer Christ's sake, gerrin 'ere," Ronny yelled at them and after a moment's hesitation they came, appalled to see Liam O'Connor apparently trying to strangle his own grandmother.

"Gerrold of 'im," Ronny screeched at the two men, hanging on for dear life to Liam's arm while the woman managed to snatch Eva from her grandson's stranglehold. He fought the three men to get to her again, just as though she were the one who had done something dreadful to the woman he loved, but he was weakening, sense coming back, his mind beginning to shape itself into thought and reason.

"Fer God's sake, Gran . . ." He was almost sobbing. "What the hell is it that's got yer so terrified? Who are yer talking about? What yer sayin? Where's Lily gone? Fer pity's sake . . ."

Eva trembled against Sadie's shoulder, but she was beginning to get a control of the terrible fear that had consumed her, a fear that had communicated itself to Liam. She knew Liam must get over to Oakwood Place – if that was where he'd taken her. How where they to know? Sweet Jesus . . . so she must tell him the story at once, for there was no time to be lost.

"Joshua Crowther." Her voice was like ice and those crowded about them in Ronny Biddle's workshed gasped. "She 'ad ter run away . . . that's why she were 'ere wi' me.

You told 'er if she were in trouble she were ter come ter me, so she did. 'E'd tried ter . . . interfere wi' 'er after 'er mam died."

Liam tossed his head from side to side like an animal tormented beyond endurance and a roar of violent rage echoed about the shed. The postman and the carter, who really should be getting about their business, could not bear to tear themselves away.

"She dressed as a lad ter ge' down ter't docks ter see ter't *Lily-Jane*; there were a chap lookin' for 'er, Crowther's chap, I were told by someone I know but Crowther's lad, 'is son what were a soldier, 'elped 'er, gorrus somewhere safe ter stay until . . . then when you come 'ome she never left th'ouse so . . ."

"Why didn't yer tell me then I could 'ave protected 'er?" he asked her, his voice totally without expression. He had his head in his hands as though he had just been hit by a brick and couldn't, somehow, get coherent thoughts together, and never would, but there was something to be done and only he could do it and if it was too late he would kill him, the man who had tried to violate his little love, perhaps had even succeeded by now. He could not bear it and when he got hold of him, even if . . . oh, please, God . . . please, God, even if she was unhurt he would knock him to the ground and kick him until the blood ran, then pick him up and start all over again.

He looked up and the suffering and anguish on his face had Sadie Ainsworth in tears and even Ronny felt a prickle at the back of his eyes. He'd always been fond of his Elsie and she of him but what this man felt and suffered for his new wife was beyond his comprehension and he was glad, for the pain of it was surely too much for one man to bear.

Liam stood up and without another word strode out of the shed. When he reached the gate, pushing past the curious onlookers, he crossed the road and with no effort leaped the hedge, then began to run across the field, moving in a straight line from Upper Breck Road to Oakwood Place.

"Go wi' 'im, Ronny," Elsie said to her husband. Ronny was a big man, not as big as Liam, nor as fit, but surely a helping hand; even a bit of moral support would not go amiss.

"I'll borrow Ernie Jenkin's mare," he told them, as though it needed explaining. "I can't run all't way ter – where was it?

– Oakwood Place or I'd be no use ter anyone by't time I got there. Tell me 'ow ter get there, Mrs Earnshaw, will yer?"

The hansom cab turned into the gateway between the two stone posts and drove up the gravelled driveway, stopping at the steps that led up to the front door. Ted Diggle, who was by the front flowerbed on his knees, shaded his eyes, for the sun was in them, then sat back. He and Will were putting in the summer bedding plants, a slow, pleasant task in the midday sunshine, and they both wondered who was calling in a hansom cab. Carriages were the order of the day in the society Mr Crowther moved in.

The front door opened, for Maggie was trained to be on hand at once to see to callers, of which this must be one. She nodded pleasantly at Mr Diggle then stood smiling on the top step, waiting to receive the visitor.

She was totally bemused when the master climbed down, for he had his own carriage in the stable yard so what on earth was he doing in a hired conveyance? She watched him in astonishment as he paid the cab driver then reached back inside the cab and with little effort dragged out a limp figure, a tall young woman, arranging her to his liking across his arms. Her own arms dangled lifelessly and her head hung back, her throat arched and Maggie noticed she wore only one boot. She stood, frozen in horror as she recognised the recently married bride whom she herself had seen wed to the big, handsome sailor only a few weeks ago. Lily, their Lily, Lily Elliott who was now Lily O'Connor.

Putting her hand to her mouth she began to back away, her eyes wide with terror, watching as Mr Crowther turned to the cab driver again, baring his teeth in what was meant to be a smile.

"My daughter," he said. "She's been taken ill so I've brought her home to be nursed."

A small moan escaped from between Maggie's lips and both Mr Diggle and Will stood up uncertainly, sensing something was wrong but not quite knowing what it was, or if they did, how to deal with it.

The cab driver watched his passenger climb the steps, the figure of the girl in his arms. She'd not looked ill to him when she'd walked towards his cab. Far from it, for a handsomer young woman he had yet to see. The old woman had been dropped off at the end of West Derby Road and he himself had been paid and given a good tip so this was nowt to do with him. Besides, there was a respectable housemaid at the door so it must be all right. He clucked to his horse and the cab moved off slowly.

Joshua Crowther strode past his maidservant with that arrogant indifference of his class to those beneath it. He held Lily close to his chest, cuddling her, Maggie wildly thought, and if she was not mistaken her clothing was already disarranged so ... Jesus ... Oh, sweet God in heaven ...

She watched him climb the stairs, his face close to Lily's, then, with a soft cry, she leaped down the steps, almost falling in her haste, and across the lawn to where Mr Diggle and Will stood.

Grabbing Will by the shirt she began to shake him. "Run for Mrs Quinn, Will. Run, lad, fetch Mrs Quinn and a couple of the men from the yard. Run like you've never run before ... run ..."

Will ran.

34

Unlike his wife who had kept to roads and lanes as she moved through the dark towards his grandmother's cottage six months ago, he ran in as straight a line as he could manage towards the river where Oakwood Place stood. Like a greyhound just left the slips he went past Newsham Farm where the dairymaid, who was carrying churns across the yard, stopped and stared as he flashed by her. Fields of growing hay and corn and oats and barley were churned through, leaving a track where his flight had taken him and where men, mouths open, gaped at him in amazement, for didn't he know he could damage crops flinging himself about like that. One shouted after him and shook his fist but Liam O'Connor saw none of them, for he had one picture in his mind's eye and it was consuming him with terror. His wife, his lovely bride who came to him every night with such passion and tenderness, the love and treasure of his life, the heart and soul of him, beneath the ravaging hands and body of another man, a perverted man, a madman, surely? The image of it was ready to destroy him and he wanted to stop and scream his rage and fear, shaking his fists at whoever it was up there who had allowed this to happen, but he must go on, and on, and on though his heart was bursting in his chest and his breath rasping in his throat so that it was rubbed raw.

Across Edge Lane, almost careering into a slow plodding waggon loaded with barrels. The horses pulling it shied with terror and the driver hauled on the reins and the whole lot of them nearly ended up in the ditch at the side of the lane but it is doubtful Liam even saw them. He was aware that there were obstacles in his path but he couldn't go round them so he would leap them or knock them down to get to his love who was in the worst danger any woman can be.

He fell down time and again, catching his feet in rabbit holes, on rocks and branches from trees rotting at the edge of fields since winter, picking himself up and flinging himself on without a break in the rhythm of his running.

He ran across the lines of the London and North Western Railway almost under the engine of an oncoming train, unaware of the repeated hoot of the whistle the angry engine driver directed at him.

Through a stretch of woodland that edged Wavertree Road, blundering into trees and catching his bare arms on brambles, the blood beginning to flow, for he had gashed his forehead on a sharp branch. It dripped down his face and on to his shirt but he was not concerned, crossing the road and plunging across more fields in which cows grazed. They backed away as he flew past them, turning their anxious gaze after him as he prepared to leap a hedge as high as himself and when it proved impossible, simply tearing through it and into an orchard which was an enchanting haze of apple blossom. His head and shoulders caught branches and the blossom showered down on him and at the far end the farmer's wife, who was hanging out her washing, let out a shriek piercing enough to wake the dead.

He raced passed her and the neat farmhouse like the wind, his legs pumping, his chest labouring, his face on fire, his eyes blank and unfocused and at last he reached Holmes Lane.

Even here he did not continue along it to Beech Lane, at the end of which was Oakwood Place, but ran in a straight line through the extensive and immaculate gardens of Silverdale and Ladymeadow, both houses belonging to prominent men of business in Liverpool. Gardeners shouted after him, one of them threatening to fetch his gun, but like an arrow from a bow, direct and true, he came to the gates of Oakwood Place.

He began to shout her name as he pounded up the drive and Mr Diggle, who, with Will, and, surprisingly, two small children, was hanging about by the front door, caring nothing for niceties, waiting for word, watched him helplessly as he ran straight at the closed door, going through it like a bull charging a gate.

"Lily . . . Lily . . . Dear God . . . dear God, where is she? Where is she? Lily," he was screaming, twisting and turning in the hall like a cornered beast. He was too late, he knew he was. It was so quiet. He had not run fast enough. His strength had not been up to it. His illness had weakened him and Mrs Quinn, coming down the stairs towards him, her face wrenched by some dreadful thing, watched as he looked up at her, then sank hopelessly to his knees.

Mrs Quinn had been just about to rebuke her eldest grandson, a little beggar if ever she saw one and far too cheeky for his own good, when the gardener's lad burst into Victoria's kitchen without even the pretence of a knock, flinging back the door so violently she, young Jimmy and his brother Eddy all cowered back, thinking the hordes of China were at the gates.

He couldn't speak. For several wasted moments he remained bent over with his hands on his knees, his head hanging down as the breath laboured in his lungs and the words tried to get out. He was wet through with sweat, even under his thatch of hair and when at last he managed to lift his head and look at her, the expression in his eyes terrified her.

"Wha'? Wha'? Dear God, lad, wharrisit?" She thrust the two small boys, who had begun to cry, behind her as though it might be Will who was the threat but he gasped and floundered, clutching at the tiny mouthful of breath he had managed to retrieve from somewhere.

"Miss . . . Lily . . ."

"Lily . . . *Our* Lily . . . wha' . . . ?"

"Maggie ses . . . ter come . . ."

"Why . . . why, what's 'appened?"

In her terror she gripped his shirt collar and forced his head up, her face up close to his, shaking him, and he was a big lad, shaking him until she got the truth from him which she could see was going to be horrific.

"Lad, for God's sake, wharrisit . . . please?"

"The master's gorrer . . . Maggie ses ter come an' fetch a couple o' men."

For a moment she couldn't take it in. The master had got her. What sort of nonsense was that? Lily was married now and as safe as houses with her new husband up at his grandmother's cottage and if there was anything dafter than the idea that Liam O'Connor would allow any harm to come to his lovely and adored young wife, then Molly Quinn had yet to hear it. She had been there only yesterday to say goodbye to them and wish them well on their trip, promising to keep an eye on Eva; in fact she and Eva had decided that she should stay there while they were away. But this . . . this . . . what . . . ?

"Will, talk sense, lad."

Will had got his breath back now. "'E come in a cab, Mrs Quinn, an' 'e 'ad Miss Lily in 'is arms. All of a drift, she were."

"Adrift?"

"Aye, senseless wi' 'er 'ead all over 't place an' 'er lovely arms just 'angin' down." He gulped, clearly agonised by what he had witnessed. "Me an' Mr Diggle saw it wi' our own eyes. Oh, please come, Mrs Quinn. T'others're frightened of 'im, burrif yer fetch Arnold an'—"

"Watch them bairns," she shrieked as she lifted her skirts and began to run across the rough grass that stretched between Victoria and Arnold's cottage and the woodland surrounding the house. Beyond were the orchards, the paddocks in which fine horses grazed, the vegetable gardens, the stable, the stable yard, the kitchen yard and the entrance to the kitchen. Her face was mottled quite dangerously with white and red streaks, for Molly Quinn was no longer a young woman, and besides which the rage boiling up inside her threatened to break out of every pore.

She crashed through the kitchen door like some avenging warrior woman, her shield before her, her spear ready to thrust itself into the enemy's wicked heart. Her hair had come loose in her frantic dash and it streamed about her face and down her back, grey and yet writhing with life.

"Where is 'e?" she snarled, so that even the women, who were all weeping, their aprons to their faces, recoiled away from her. She was a terrifying sight and Mrs Kelly had a moment to think the master had better watch out, for he'd met his match in Molly Quinn. Jenny was hiccuping softly in the chimney corner and Rosie was patting her shoulder, telling her it would be all right and she wasn't to upset herself, just as though Jenny were the only one in tears. The rest were grouped together as though there might be safety in numbers. They could none of them speak, it seemed, they were so terrified, even Maggie, who had had the presence of mind to send for the one person who was not afraid of their master. They were not even sure what was to happen. Perhaps the master had found their Miss Lily ill by the roadside and had brought her home for her own good and if that was the truth of it they dare not interfere, for this was his house and they were his servants and what would he do to them if they tried to intervene? They didn't know, but then neither did they really believe that was the case, but Mrs Quinn would be needed either way, wouldn't she and besides, she no longer worked for him. He was a powerful man in Liverpool, with friends in high places and they, his servants, were the underclasses with no powers to speak of, taught to look up to their betters, to wait on them and keep their traps shut.

Maggie pointed towards the door that led to the front of the house with a trembling finger. As Molly turned, ready to race towards it and up the stairs, ready to knock the bloody door down with her own female and elderly strength, Arnold came through the kitchen door behind her with Will at his back. Under each arm Will carried a small, struggling child, the older one shouting that his dad would fight Will if he didn't put him down at once.

"Where?" Arnold asked, his face like a mask, an iron mask, but underneath it was the horror of a decent man who abhors violence against a defenceless woman and from what he'd been told by Will Miss Lily was in great danger. Behind them were Jimmy and Mr Bentley, both of them ready to batter and bruise any man who would harm the child of the mistress they had all loved.

Molly did not speak but flew out of the kitchen door, along the passage to the foot of the stairs and was up them like a whippet after a rabbit, Arnold close on her heels and, behind him, Jimmy and Mr Bentley.

Straight to the closed door of Joshua Crowther's room she led them since, being outdoor men who had no reason to come inside, they did not know the way.

"Knock it down," she hissed, giving Jimmy a clip across his ear when he would have hesitated, for this was his master's bedroom door, or so he presumed, and the habit of obedience to his master's will was strong in him.

He had laid her on the bed and was just pulling her

pretty lace chemise over her head, the one she wore to please her husband whom she loved. Her dress with the glowing red ribbon lay on the floor and so did her three full white cotton petticoats. Her drawers, again edged with lace, had been drawn down to her knees and the centre of her, the full sweet bush that hid the centre of her womanhood, was dark against the whiteness of her belly.

He turned as they all four crashed through the door, jammed for a moment in the opening, then, as Mrs Quinn launched herself at him, he stood up straight, his face twisting in a grimace of amazement.

"What the devil d'you think you're doing?" he snarled, catching her wrists and flinging her back against the three men. "How dare you break in here, and you three, get out, d'you hear? You'll lose your jobs over this," spitting his venom at the three men, who, with the habit of a life's bowing to authority ingrained in them, began to hesitate, despite the almost naked figure of the woman on the bed. His class's supremacy over them and every man in the land like them was so absolute that almost automatically they fell back before him.

"Get out of this room before I send for the law." His arrogance, his absolute belief in his own authority and power to do as he pleased in his own home, his total unconcern for anything beyond his own gratification, made him a formidable figure. He came from generations of privilege and his rage that these servants of his had had the temerity to break into his bedroom was supreme, but Mrs Quinn cared nothing for that. She was beyond the point where reason or thought or fear for her own future or even life might matter and she launched herself at him again, aiming for his eyes, lifting her knee as she had seen women do in Brooke Alley when defending themselves against predatory males.

"Yer filthy beast," she screamed and down in the kitchen the maids cowered against one another and her two grand-children, recognising her voice, began to cry.

"You'll pay for this, woman," Joshua Crowther screeched, his face flooded with bright red blood, clutching at the spot between his legs where her knee had connected. "You'll be in Walton Gaol by nightfall and I shall personally see that you spend the rest of your life there."

"Yer mad . . . insane. D'yer think yer can . . . can do this

to that girl on't 'ed, like yer did to 'er ma, an' gerraway wi'
it? See, Arnold, gerrold of 'im. Don't just 'ang about, yer daft
lummox, gerrold of 'im."

They came to their senses then, avoiding the pitiful sight
of the girl on the bed, advancing on him with the slitted eyes
and knotted fists of men who have seen enough and do not
like it, and even before they had touched him something
exploded like a live shell inside him, blowing the safety
valves, rushing like a swollen maddened river to his brain
and as they watched in astonishment he dropped to the
floor as if poleaxed.

Mrs Quinn, beside herself, no longer in control of anything
that might be called sense, let alone herself, began to kick at
his lifeless figure where it sprawled by the bed, obscenities
that she had learned in Brooke Alley pouring from her mouth.
In her mindless fury her lamb was, for the moment, forgotten
and it was Mr Bentley who hastily threw a blanket over the
senseless figure of their Lily. After that first appalled look,
unable to believe the evidence of their own eyes, they had
shifted their gaze away, for they were, though not gentlemen,
decent men and the sight of the child – no longer a child,
of course – unconscious and almost naked on the master's
bed was more then they could handle.

"Mrs Quinn, see to the child," Mr Bentley told her sternly.
The words reached her maddened brain and though she
was still breathing heavily, at once she turned away from
Joshua Crowther, herself again and ready to take charge if
anything of a . . . a . . . nasty nature had taken place. He had
been up here with Lily for almost fifteen minutes in which
the worst could have happened, but then she was not to
know of Joshua Crowther's strange proclivities, his dreaming
contemplation of what he had hungered for for nearly a year,
and even before his wife died, if he was honest. She did not
know of the festering plans he had harboured in his mind
for Lily and it did not entail a quick rape but a lingering,
bestial ravaging, lasting hours, days, in fact for as long as it
suited him. As he had done with her mother. He was out of
his mind, of course, quite, quite mad, for how did he think
he could get away with kidnapping another man's wife and
keeping her in his house? A house filled with servants who
knew exactly what was happening and, eventually, when
they regained their courage, would send for the husband

not to mention the police. He was mad. Out of his mind and she'd see him in a lunatic asylum where he belonged, Mrs Quinn was telling herself as she pulled up Lily's drawers – discreetly beneath the blanket, of course – then tucked the blanket about her neck with careful, comforting hands. She loved this girl, just as she had loved her mother and, by God, he'd be made to pay for this.

The strange silence behind her at last caught her attention. She was on her knees beside the bed, smoothing back Lily's hair, thanking God that the child had known nothing about it. She was heavily drugged and one of the men must ride for the doctor at once but there was something wrong, something unusual going on – or not going on – at her back, and when she turned enquiringly, expecting to see Mr Crowther glowering at her as the men pulled him to his feet she was surprised to see him still in exactly the same position into which he had fallen. She didn't know why. No one had laid a finger on him but despite that he was still lolling on the floor, his arms and legs all over the place, his face in the light from the window drawn up into what looked like a mask of agony. The three men were grouped about him, staring down in growing fear and when Mr Bentley turned away and walked slowly to the door she knew at once that Joshua Crowther was dead.

"Ride for't doctor, Arnold, there's a good lad, while I get Lily decent."

The men left the room, Arnold patting her shoulder reassuringly for a moment as though to tell her there were nothing to fear. As if she cared. She'd gladly swing for him if it meant her Lily was safe. In fact for two pins she'd spit on him, on his dead body for all the pain and misery he had brought to both her lambs.

She settled herself in a low chair by the bed to watch over Lily, for the child would be afraid when she woke. She was very pale but her heartbeat was steady. Mrs Quinn had put her ear to her chest to listen to it and she watched the slow rise and fall of her breast, never taking her eyes from the girl who had become more precious to her than her own daughters.

When she heard the crash of the front door, and the loud, harsh voice, though she couldn't think why he was making such a commotion, she moved to the head of the stairs to meet the doctor, beginning to walk down them. She was just in time to see Liam O'Connor sink to his knees.

She came to just as dusk was falling, wondering why her head was thumping like a steam engine and her mouth was so dry but she was not concerned, for she was in her husband's arms and what could be safer and more comforting than that. They were lying on a bed, a strange bed in a strange room and not their comfortable brass-ended bed at home, she knew that, although she had not yet opened her eyes. It didn't matter. As long as Liam was with her, whether in the depths of darkest Africa, the wilds of the tropical jungles, the vast dry wastes of the Sahara, if Liam was with her it was all right.

She must have moved and made a small noise, for at once Liam's arms tightened about her, so tight, in fact, he was hurting her.

"Lovebud," he said. His voice was hoarse as though he had a sore throat and at once she sat up in his arms, for always in the back of her mind was the terror that his illness would return. She peered at him in the gloom, for the room was lit only by a cheerfully crackling fire in the grate.

She put a hand on his forehead. "Are you coming down with a cold?" she asked him accusingly and was seriously frightened when he began to weep. Now that she had got a good look at him she could see blood on his face and shirt and his arms were a mass of bruises and scratches as though he had crawled through a wilderness.

"Liam . . . Liam, dearest, what is it?" she begged him in an agony of love, pulling him to her so that his wet face was pressed into the curve of her neck.

"Jesus . . . Jesus, if I had lost you I would have run mad," he said, amazingly. She stared at him in wonder then looked about her and was further amazed to find that she and Liam were lying on her bed in what had been her room when she had lived at Oakwood Place. A pleasant room, warm, airy, comfortable, elegantly furnished but a room where she had known nothing but worry and dread and fear, first for her mother and then for herself. A room she had left six months ago and had hoped never to see again and now here she was, she and Liam, lying in one another's arms as though it were quite the most normal thing to do.

Suddenly the face of the madman sprang out at her in all

its terror, looming over the shoulder of a woman . . . hands
. . . hands pulling at her, holding her and something pressed
over her face. She began to twist and turn in an effort to
escape it, and him.

"Liam," she began to scream in a high voice, the voice of
a child lost with the bogeyman on her heels, but at once
Liam's arms closed round her and at once she was safe.

"He's gone, lovebud," he murmured into her hair. "He's
finally gone . . . for ever."

She sat up in renewed terror, her hair falling in a tangle
about her pale face, her eyes huge and terrified.

"You've . . . not you, Liam. You've not . . . ?"

"No, not me, my darling, though I would have done if . . .
It seems he has had some sort of apoplexy. The men were
here . . ."

"The men?"

"Aye, Mrs Quinn's Arnold and two others come to help
you but not one of them laid a hand on him. The doctor's
been and gone."

"And . . ." She could not seem to get the words out, the
dreadful words that would reveal what had happened to her
while she had been unconscious.

"And . . . me?" She hung her head as though in shame,
but he lifted her chin, cupping her face and kissing her,
smoothing her cheek with his thumbs as his eyes told her
what she wanted to know.

"Not you, lovebud. You . . . you are totally mine."

They left soon after, driven in the carriage by Arnold, her
and Liam and Mrs Quinn, who seemed unable to let her
lamb out of her sight again. The servants in the kitchen had
embraced Lily quite tearfully when she went down, looking,
Jenny said, just as she always did, as though attempted rape
must surely change a woman for ever. Of course, she had
been unconscious, Maggie had told them all, and of them
all, had been the least aware of what was happening, which
was just as well, for the master was a frightening man. *Had
been* a frightening man, for his body was laid out on the
bed in his room where he had tried to . . . well, the least
said about that the better, Maggie told them firmly, looking
at Jenny's big eyes and trembling mouth. None of them
knew what was to happen to them now but with Captain
Crowther coming home, summoned by the telegram telling

him his father was dead, perhaps their positions were safe. They did hope so, for good jobs were hard to come by.

And wasn't it lovely the way the bairn had been with Miss Lily? It was as if she knew who she was, which was a bit fanciful but she'd put her plump little arms round Miss Lily's neck and pressed her rosy mouth to her cheek, just as Dorcas had taught her. An affectionate little thing and though they were not sure what was to become of her she would be all right now. Either with Miss Lily who was her sister or Captain Crowther who was her brother, and as different to his father as chalk to cheese.

Miss Lily and that handsome husband of hers were off to Ireland themselves the day after tomorrow, so she had told them over a cup of tea while he sat beside her holding her hand as though he must touch her and watch over her even in the safety of the kitchen. Lovely chap, he was and he had told them himself that Miss Abby would never want for a ... well, he had been going to say father, you could tell, and then Miss Lily had turned and kissed him, right in front of them all, before saying goodbye and climbing into the carriage, telling them she'd see them in ten days' time, promise.

The lovely ship, her sails filled with a hatful of wind, raced towards the mouth of the river, taking advantage of the tide, her captain steering her expertly through the dozens of others who were doing the same. There was a clipper ship off to the far east for the exotic things available nowhere else, whose sails had her flying faster than any of them; several schooners like their own, sailing to Furness or North Wales, small, full-bodied merchant sailing ships with complex rigging, paddle-steamers, four-masted barques and all making for the broad mouth of the River Mersey. Frigates and brigantines and for a moment Lily was taken back to that day nearly seven years ago when she had leaned against her pa on this very same ship. Then she had gazed back at the hazed morning skyline of Liverpool, a small child caught up in the excitement of entering an adult's world, dreaming about the day when she would sail this ship, be a seaman like Pa had been.

Now she was a woman and understood that the dream was no more than that, a dream. Today she would sail through the wide estuary at the mouth of the river towards Liverpool Bay, her back against the broad, safe chest of her husband, his left arm about her while the right guided his ship. For as long as she was allowed she would accompany him but she had other responsibilities now and must give up her dream when the time came. She was not sure how long it would last, this freedom of the sea but when it ended this man would always come back to her, wherever she was.

She would always be waiting.

AUDREY HOWARD

THE WOMAN FROM BROWHEAD

Annie Abbott returns to Browhead, the beautiful lonely hill farm above Bassenthwaite Lake, with only her pride and her baby daughter to sustain her. Her parents are dead, her old friends dare not be seen with an unmarried mother and the other farmers will not help a woman who presumes to buy sheep and raise crops without a husband at her side.

Except for one man. Reed Macaulay, son of the district's most prosperous landowner, knows that Annie is the only woman he will ever love. Secretly, he helps her any way he can. Secretly, because Reed has married another woman ...

HODDER AND STOUGHTON PAPERBACKS

AUDREY HOWARD

WHEN MORNING COMES

Lucy Dean is a young woman of eighteen with no money, no job and four young brothers and sisters to support. James Buchanan is a young man of thirty-four with a great fortune, who thinks that Lucy Dean is the most remarkable girl he has ever met.

What could be more natural than their marriage? James – whom everyone had thought was all but engaged to the wilful beauty Charlotte Gibson – proposes, and a grateful Lucy accepts.

But the surprising marriage that by turns charms and scandalizes Ambleside does not bring them happiness. And all too soon, they are separated by the brutal Great War. When Lucy finally realizes where her heart truly lies, it may be too late to undo the misunderstandings that have dogged them since their first encounter.

HODDER AND STOUGHTON PAPERBACKS

AUDREY HOWARD

NOT A BIRD WILL SING

Though Poppy Appleton has grown up in ignorance and poverty, she grabs her chance of a better life with the kindly Goodall family.

At Long Reach Farm, Eliza Goodall teaches Poppy all the skills she would have passed on to her own daugher: the skills that would enable a young lady to become the mistress of a farm like Long Reach. And when the time comes for Eliza's son Richard to choose a wife, it seems only natural that he should choose Poppy.

But though Poppy feels nothing but affection for her new family, the only man for whom she has ever felt love is Conn MacConnell. And when he returns unexpectedly, Poppy has to choose between loyalty and love.

HODDER AND STOUGHTON PAPERBACKS

AUDREY HOWARD

THE SILENCE OF STRANGERS

Nella Fielden marries Jonas Townley believing he is the one man who deserves her hand and her fortune. The Lancashire colliery heiress, as proud and ambitious as any man, cannot believe the truth: that Jonas has married her for her money.

He tries to be true to her. But soon, his heart belongs to another woman: Nella's protégée Leah Wood, the girl from Colliers Row.

Torn between her loyalty to her protector and her love for Jonas Townley, Leah tries to be true to both. But she cannot cure Nella's broken heart – or avoid the tragedy that lies in wait for them all.

HODDER AND STOUGHTON PAPERBACKS

AUDREY HOWARD

A WORLD OF DIFFERENCE

Cosseted heiress Jenna Townley is used to getting her own way. And when she meets ambitious young Conal MacRae, she soon knows that this is the man she must marry, despite her father's disapproval.

Their courtship is fiery and their marriage passionate. But their happiness is threatened by tragic and sinister family secrets which refuse to be buried. Is Jenna destined to repeat her mother's tragedy or can she triumph over the past and keep both the Townley legacy and the man she was meant to love?

HODDER AND STOUGHTON PAPERBACKS

A selection of bestsellers from Hodder and Stoughton

AUDREY HOWARD

All Hodder & Stoughton books are available at your local bookshop or newsagent, or can be ordered direct from the publisher. Just tick the titles you want and fill in the form below. Prices and availability subject to change without notice.

Hodder & Stoughton Books, Cash Sales Department, Bookpoint, 39 Milton Park, Abingdon, OXON, OX14 4TD, UK. E-mail address: order@bookpoint.co.uk. If you have a credit card you may order by telephone – (01235) 400414.

Please enclose a cheque or postal order made payable to Bookpoint Ltd to the value of the cover price and allow the following for postage and packing:
UK & BFPO – £1.00 for the first book, 50p for the second book, and 30p for each additional book ordered up to a maximum charge of £3.00.
OVERSEAS & EIRE – £2.00 for the first book, £1.00 for the second book, and 50p for each additional book.

Name ....

Address ....

....

....

If you would prefer to pay by credit card, please complete:
Please debit my Visa/Access/Diner's Card/American Express (delete as applicable) card no:

☐☐☐☐ ☐☐☐☐ ☐☐☐☐ ☐☐☐☐

Signature ....

Expiry Date ....

If you would NOT like to receive further information on our products please tick the box. ☐